RILEY

NEW YORK TIMES BESTSELLING AUTHOR
LORI FOSTER

Recycling programs
for this product may
not exist in your area.

ISBN-13: 978-1-335-40664-4

Riley
First published in 2003. This edition published in 2022
Copyright © 2003 by Lori Foster

Lone Star Lovers
First published in 2018. This edition published in 2022.
Copyright © 2018 by Jessica Lemmon

For questions and comments about the quality of this book,
please contact us at CustomerService@Harlequin.com.

Harlequin Enterprises ULC
22 Adelaide St. West, 41st Floor
Toronto, Ontario M5H 4E3, Canada
www.Harlequin.com

Printed in U.S.A.

CONTENTS

Lori Foster is a *New York Times* and *USA TODAY* bestselling author of more than one hundred titles. Lori has been a recipient of the prestigious *RT Book Reviews* Career Achievement Award for Series Romantic Fantasy and for Contemporary Romance. For more about Lori, visit her website at lorifoster.com.

Books by Lori Foster

HQN

Road to Love

Driven to Distraction
Slow Ride
All Fired Up

Body Armor

Under Pressure
Hard Justice
Close Contact
Fast Burn

The Ultimate series

Hard Knocks (prequel ebook novella)
No Limits
Holding Strong
Tough Love
Fighting Dirty

Visit the Author Profile page at
Harlequin.com for more titles.

RILEY

Lori Foster

Chapter 1

"Raise your knees."

Wide-eyed, breathless and straining, she said, *"No,"* in such a scandalized voice that Riley Moore grinned. That was the thing about Red—she made him laugh, made him feel lighthearted when he hadn't thought such a thing would be possible ever again. Not a bad start.

But he had other things to accomplish here besides smiling.

"I'm not letting you up till you do." Hell, he'd be happy to stay put for hours. Not only did she amuse him, she also aroused him more than any woman he'd ever known. Her body was slight but very soft, a nice cushion under his larger, harder frame. And the warmth he felt in the cradle of her thighs could drive him over the edge.

Her big green eyes darted left and right. "Riley, people are *watching*."

"I know." He decided to taunt her. After all, this was important. She needed to learn how to handle him. No sense in wasting all his instruction. "They're waiting to see if you've learned anything through all these lessons. Most of them think not. Others are pretty damn doubtful."

New determination drew her slim auburn brows down into a frown and turned her green eyes stormy. Suddenly her knees were along his sides, catching him off guard with the carnality of it. While his mind wandered down a salacious path, she bucked, rolled—and onto his back he went.

Proud as a peahen, she bounced on his abdomen and cheered herself. *Wrong move, sweetheart,* he thought, and deftly flipped her straight back and into the same position that she'd just escaped, except that this time her legs were trapped around his waist. With the wind temporarily knocked out of her, she gasped.

Half frustrated, half amused, Riley straightened. Because he knew his own ability, even if most others didn't, he always utilized strict control and caution. Especially with women, and most especially with Red. He'd sooner break his own leg than ever bruise her.

He pulled her upright, forced her arms straight up high to help her breathe, and shook his head. "When you get the upper hand on an attacker, honey, you do not stop to congratulate yourself."

Seeing that the display was over, the crowd dispersed, going back to their own training. Riley stood and gently pulled Regina Foxworth to her feet. She wasn't necessarily a short woman, but next to his height, she seemed almost puny. The top of her head reached his shoulder. Her wrists were like chicken bones. Narrow shoulders, a delicate frame…and yet, she wanted him to teach her self-defense.

Riley snorted. Hell, whenever he got this close to her he had things other than fighting on his mind. And the fact that, regardless of what he'd tried to teach her, she still ended up on her back with him in the mounted position put all kinds of considerations in his mind.

Like what it'd be like to have her situated that way, with no clothes between them and without her attempting to escape.

Soon, he promised himself. Very soon.

In a huff, Regina promptly jerked away and began straightening her glorious red hair. If the woman thought half as much about applying herself as she did about her appearance, they'd make more progress.

For her lessons today she'd restrained her hair in a braid as thick as his wrist that hung to the middle of her back. Already silky tendrils had worked loose, giving her a softened, just-laid look. Riley shook his head in awe. He worked with other women and they just got sweaty and rumpled. Not Regina. Somehow, no matter what, the woman always managed to look more appealing.

Watching her tidy her braid sent tension rippling through his muscles. A man could conjure quite a few fantasies over that hair, not to mention the delicate, ultrafeminine body that came with it. Hell, he even found the sprinkling of freckles over her nose adorable.

Riley snatched up a towel. "Quit pouting, Red."

"I'm not." But her bottom lip stuck out in a most becoming way. Normally a princess like her wouldn't have appealed to him. But Red had guts beneath the fussy exterior. And in the time he'd known her, he'd also realized she was gentle, compassionate, under-standing, and damn it, he wanted her, had from the very start.

If that had been his only problem, he'd have coaxed her into bed by now. But it was more than that. He hadn't thought to ever want involvement with another woman, but he wanted it with Red.

Riley slung his arm around her shoulders and headed her toward the shower. Not that she needed to shower. The natural fragrance of her skin and hair was warm and womanly. His body tensed a bit more in masculine awareness, on the verge of cramping. "We're wasting our time with these lessons."

"I need to be able to defend myself."

True enough. Three weeks ago, Regina had been caught in a burning building while on assignment for the *Chester Daily Press*. As a reporter, she liked to stick her cute little freckled nose into places where it didn't belong, and that particular building had been in a disreputable part of town. That should have been her first clue not to be there. The fact that the fireworks dealer had already had trouble in the past should have been her second.

She'd forged on anyway and had come damn close to dying for her efforts. Most were inclined to call the fire an accident due to the shoddy management of the owner, who left opened pyrotechnics scattered around. But there was more to it. Long before Red got caught up in that fire, she'd been afraid. Riley first met her while she attempted to interview his friend, Ethan, for commendable work as a firefighter. Even then, she'd been as jumpy as a turkey on Thanksgiving morning.

She'd seemed so strained, Riley had expected her to scream at any minute.

The day after the interview, she'd come into his gym and asked for lessons to protect herself. Unlike most of the women who approached him with the same request, Red had seemed more desperate, as if she needed the lessons for an imminent threat, not for general assurances.

Before the fire, he'd discarded her claims of endangerment, as had the county police where he worked as an evidence tech. *They* still didn't believe her, but at thirty-two, through life and some hard lessons, Riley had learned to read people, to sift real from feigned. Red was afraid, and he'd bet she had reason.

Someone was after her. She didn't know why. He didn't care why.

The day she'd almost died in that fire, he'd staked a claim. Little Red just hadn't figured that out yet. But no way in hell would he let anyone hurt her.

"Why don't you shower up and we'll talk about it?"

"Again?" She gave her long-suffering look. "There's nothing more to say. The police don't believe me, nothing else major has happened—"

Riley jumped on her choice of words. "What do you mean, nothing major? Has something minor happened?"

She shrugged, which did interesting things to her petite breasts. Dressed in snug biker shorts and a matching sports tank, there wasn't much of her body left to his imagination. But then, he'd wrestled with her enough and studied her in such detail that Riley already knew she had a discreet rack. Her breasts were small, firm and a definite draw to his eyes.

He could span her waist easily in his big hands, but from there she flared out. Her bottom was fuller, nicely rounded, as he liked. Not that it mattered. He already knew you couldn't judge the woman by the package. A facade of innocence, of kindness, or honor, meant nothing, less than nothing.

Regina could have looked a dozen different ways and he'd still want her because her draw on him went deeper than appearances. He felt an affinity to her, a vague basis he could trust in and that, more than anything, appealed to him. It seemed the moment he'd met her something had sparked.

So far, she'd shut him out.

"My apartment door was vandalized the other day."

Riley stopped dead in his tracks, right in front of the entrance to the women's shower. In a voice low with annoyance and disbelief, he growled, "Why the hell didn't you tell me?"

"I'm telling you now."

"Now is too damn late." He felt like shaking her, but she was so dainty a good shake would rattle her teeth.

"There were three other doors that got egged, so I figured it was random, not personal. And really, there's no threat in an egging, just an aggravation."

"Unless someone is trying to bug you enough to make you move." The fact that she lived in a nice apartment building with good security and lots of neighbors around reassured Riley many a night. It was the only thing that had kept him from forcing his pursuit of her. Because he felt she was safe at night, he intended to let her get used to him at her own pace. Little by little, he'd make his intentions known.

Still, he felt compelled to point out the facts. "I don't

care what *you* figured, Red. From now on, tell me everything. I'm the expert here."

Her gaze dipped over his chest, now damp with sweat so that his T-shirt stuck to him. Wrestling with her hadn't caused any exertion, but he'd been in the private studio all morning giving lessons. Besides, just being near Red fired his blood. Having her open and vulnerable beneath him brought out a possessive sweat. He'd conquer her—in his own time.

"Yes, you're an expert, Riley." Staring up at him, her big eyes full of serious regard, she added, "At a lot of things."

"At a..." His voice trailed off. Was she coming on to him? 'Bout damn time. He crowded closer to her, letting her feel the heat of his body, instinctively overpowering her with his size and masculinity and interest. "Just what does that mean, Regina?" He sounded gruff, half-aroused, but then she had that effect on him.

Head tipped way back to meet his gaze, she sighed. "You're an amazing guy, Riley Moore. That's all I meant. I don't know any other man who used to be part of a SWAT team, now serves as a crime scene evidence technician, *and* owns his own gym."

Deflated, mouth flat, Riley said, "No."

With a ludicrous show of innocence, she blinked. "No, what?"

"No, I won't do the damn interview." He should have seen right through her. He was good at deciphering motives, but his perspective was blown around her, clouded by lust. She'd been after an interview for over a week now, but his past was just that: the past. He wouldn't dredge it up for anyone, not even Little Red.

"But—"

At that moment, Rosie Winters shoved her way out of the showers, forcing them both to back up. Now Rosie, bless her, knew how to work out. She got sweaty, red-faced and hot. *Not* more appealing. She cursed, grunted, struggled, and she gave it her all, showing constant improvement without a single thought to her hair or audience.

Like Riley, Rosie fought to win and she was now good enough that she just might stand a chance against a man without Riley's special training. But as ex-SWAT, Riley could be lethal when necessary. His job had taught him how to come out the victor in any scenario. But long before that, when he'd still been a kid, nature had taught him that he didn't like to lose.

At anything.

As one of his best friends, Rosie had been coming to his gym a lot, much to Ethan's dismay. She and Ethan had married last week, but that hadn't slowed down Rosie. Nothing slowed her down. The newlyweds supplied endless hours of entertainment with the way they clashed wills, and the way they loved.

"Hey, Riley." Rosie gave him a resounding smooch on the cheek before turning to Regina. Her brown hair, still wet, hung down her back. "I lingered in the shower so I could talk to you."

Regina lifted her brows. "Really? What about?"

"Prepare yourself," Rosie warned with a lot of suspenseful anticipation. "Your loan went through. You're all set to close on the house!"

That announcement seemed to set off both women. Regina squealed as females are wont to do, and Rosie, who never squealed, laughed heartily. But around Regina, Rosie often got pulled into the more feminine mannerisms. Like now, with Regina holding her hands and dancing in circles and bouncing around.

Watching them, Riley crossed his arms and leaned back against the wall. He just adored women, the way they reacted, their expressions, their unique mindset that was so different from men's. Rosie and Regina couldn't be more dissimilar in most ways, yet they had similarities, too, just by virtue of being female.

It gave him pleasure to listen in—until it dawned on him what Rosie had said. He shoved away from the wall. "A house? You bought a house?"

They quieted, but both still grinned hugely. "It's adorable," Regina confided. "Just the right size for me."

"And such a great bargain," Rosie added. "Because it's empty, she can have immediate occupancy."

"Immediate occupancy?" The words emerged a dark whisper. "As in alone in a house, unprotected, immediately?"

Rosie paused. "Oh. I hadn't thought of that. I mean, it's in a nice quiet neighborhood with half-acre yards—"

"Great. Just great."

Regina gave him a level look. "Really, Riley. You act like I'll be camping in the open with wild bears all around me. I can lock my doors and windows." When he only narrowed his eyes, she added, "I'll even buy an alarm system, okay?"

"It's a lousy idea. Have you two forgotten that someone recently tried to burn you alive?"

Rosie shuddered. "I'll never forget." She'd gone with Regina that day, and damn near died because of it. "But the police seem to think that it was either vandalism that got out of hand, negligence on the part of the owner, or at the very worst, vengeance aimed at the owner, not at us."

Regina watched Riley closely. "They think we were innocent bystanders."

"Right. And that's why your camera was taken and the owner has disappeared?"

Looking guilty, Rosie turned to Regina. "Maybe he's right."

"No, he is not right. I have to live somewhere, so it might as well be my own house." She patted Riley on the chest. Though she did it negligently, without a single sign of awareness on her part, he felt the damn pat clear through to his masculine being. "I'll get an alarm system *and* a dog. How's that?"

Seeing that he wouldn't win, Riley gave up that particular argument. At least she wanted to take steps in the right direction. A big, well-trained German shepherd or Doberman would certainly be a deterrent to anyone thinking to harm her. In the meantime, he'd just have to see about advancing his courtship. Once she gave in, he'd have the right to keep her close, to watch over her.

And all her spare time would be spent in bed, giving her less time to get into trouble.

With Ethan and Rosie's rushed wedding plans, they'd been forced together more frequently than otherwise. Adding to that her lessons at the gym, he'd seen her almost daily for the past three weeks. Their time together had been platonic because he couldn't possibly wrestle with her and have romantic thoughts without embarrassing them both, and possibly breaking a few sexual harassment laws. He felt certain a boner would have been out of line.

But he knew how he felt. Maybe it was time she knew, too.

It wouldn't be a bad idea to live with her until he felt secure that she'd be safe alone. The benefits to that scenario were more than obvious. To both of them.

"When's the closing on the house?"

Rosie winced.

Resigned, Riley asked again, "How soon, Rosie?"

"Weeeelll…" Rosie cast a quick look at Regina, but she was too busy smiling over her good news to share Rosie's uncertainty. "Because the house was empty and her credit impeccable, I sort of rushed it through. We have a date set for the middle of next week."

Regina squealed again, but with Riley so subdued, she quickly quieted. "You're being such a stick in the mud, Riley. Can't you be just a little happy for me?"

If it weren't such bad timing, he would be. But he worried about her enough already without her being off on her own, away from the safety of the apartment complex. In his mind, she was already his. He wanted to protect her, not leave her safety dependent on a dog and alarm.

He studied her for a long moment, deciding how best to proceed without making her more skittish. Then he realized his stare alone had her squirming uncomfortably. He tried a smile, but it felt more predatory than anything else. "I'll take you to dinner to celebrate." He made it a statement rather than an invitation, on the off chance she thought to refuse.

Her hesitation fell heavy between them. "I don't know…"

Riley took a step closer. "Say yes, Regina."

Rosie's gaze bounced back and forth, watching them with great interest.

A blush tinged Regina's cheeks. "The thing is, I wanted to get my dog today. I figure I might as well potty train him at my apartment so he won't mess up my house."

Riley didn't let her off the hook. He waited, still watching her intently until her unease was palpable.

Finally, she sighed. "If you can come over around six, I can cook dinner at my place."

Now that sounded promising. Much better suited to his purpose than being in a crowded restaurant. "I'm on vacation for the next two weeks, so I'm at your disposal." He realized suddenly that Rosie had a vacuous grin on her face. She knew him better than Regina did, so she'd probably already realized how territorial he felt.

Glancing over his shoulder at the workout area of the gym, he said, "I have to get back on the floor. I have three more hours of personal instruction before I'm free." He touched Regina's cheek. "Promise me you'll be careful, Red."

She blinked, then stepped out of reach. Her laugh sounded forced. "It's the middle of the day. I swear, Riley, you're more fretful than I am."

That's because he knew firsthand the danger that could befall a woman alone. He shook off that dark thought and raised her chin. "Promise?"

"Cross my heart." With a last platonic pat on his chest, she said, "Don't be late."

Riley watched her disappear into the shower room, spellbound until Rosie started snickering. When he gave her his attention, she clutched her heart and pretended to swoon.

"Brat." Riley put her in a chokehold and knuckled the top of her head. Though she was gorgeous and sexy, Rosie was like a pal, permanently safe from any lecherous intentions, especially since she'd married Ethan.

"Hey," she gasped out, "no fair. I don't want to get messy again. I have a showing this afternoon."

Riley released her and got a sharp elbow to his middle. He grunted while Rosie quickly backed away. "Sucker," she said with a grin, then she turned and jogged toward the door.

Riley laughed. He did love Rosie, but he didn't want her. He didn't burn for her.

Not the way he did for Ms. Regina Foxworth.

Regina knew it wasn't the wisest decision she'd ever made. And for a woman who prided herself on only making wise decisions, she should have been appalled at herself. She only had so much money for decorating her new house and putting in the alarm system that she'd promised Riley.

She tried to talk herself out of it, she really did. But as she stared at those big brown eyes, she fell madly in love. He was so cute with the way he laid his enormous ears back on his little round head, how he stared at her with bulging eyes, shivering with uncertainty. He probably wasn't the type of dog Riley had in mind, but the man said they were loyal pets, dedicated to their owners.

"I'll take him." Sometimes things just felt right. Like being a journalist. Like buying the house.

Like being near Riley.

This felt right, too. Now that she'd met this dog, no other would do, so she shelled out the six hundred dollars that she really couldn't spare. Love was love and it should never be denied. Not that she knew a lot about love. But she did know that she wanted it more than anything. And to get it, you had to give it, she reasoned. She could really love this dog.

While she carried him outside, he continued to shake and stare at her with those big, watchful eyes. She'd never seen such a pathetic look in her life. She wanted to crush him close, but he was so puny, she didn't dare. Gently, she stroked his skinny back and rubbed his soft neck.

She'd never felt a dog so soft. He had bunny fur, so cuddly and silky. And he didn't smell like a dog either. She rubbed her nose against his neck and got a tiny lick on the ear in return.

Once in the car, secured in the carrier, his teeny tiny mouth formed an O and he began to howl.

It was both hilarious, the way he looked, and heart-wrenching the way he sounded. The mournful baying continued until Regina was in a near panic. "Shh. What's wrong?" Did he want her to hold him? "I have to drive, sweetie," she explained. "It wouldn't be safe. Soon as we get home, I'll cuddle you again, I promise."

At the sound of her voice, the dog quieted and inched to the edge of the small cage to sniff the air near her. His spindly little hind legs quivered and he continued to look sad, but trusting.

"Awww…" He was just so adorable. Big tears filled her eyes. She *had* made the right decision. Sticking one finger through the carrier, Regina rubbed behind his ear. "You're as soft as a baby bunny, did you know that?"

He cocked his head, listening to her, his ears still down in a woebegone display but he made no sounds of dismay.

"What should I name you?"

The ears came up. Regina marveled at his many expressions.

"How about... Elvis?" His ears pricked, then flattened again and he gave her a sideways look. "No? Then maybe Doe? You do look like a little deer, you know. Hmm. That doesn't appeal to you either? Something more manly then. I know. Butch. Or Butchie when you're being so adorable."

Soothed by her banter, he gave an excited yap of agreement and Regina nodded. "Butch it is."

For the rest of the ride home, Regina alternated her attention between her driving and the dog. She constantly scanned the road and surrounding area, still spooked from the time someone tried to run her off the berm. To calm herself and the dog, she spoke to him, being sure to use his name as the breeder suggested, so he could get used to it.

By the time they pulled into her apartment complex, he was looking around with interest, animated anytime she spoke to him. He continued to shake though.

People were coming and going, keeping the parking lot alive with a safe, surrounding crowd. Feeling secure again, she carried Butch, along with his paraphernalia, into her apartment. She'd bought bowls, food, chew sticks, a toothbrush, leash, collar and a cozy fleece-lined bed. She set Butch down first, watched him cower there on the floor, and decided he needed some encouragement.

Her apartment was small, only one bedroom, a bath, kitchenette and living area. "I'll be right back, Butch." She went to the kitchen to unload all the items, then came back for him. She found him sprinkling her couch.

"Oh, now that's just not right, Butch."

He slunk toward her, his head down in apology.

Regina's heart melted. "Honey, it's okay." She cuddled him close, got a tentative lick on her cheek. He was the most precious perfect dog, she decided, and carried him into the kitchen since that was where he'd spend most of his time. With a kiss to the top of his round head, she put him in his bed, then went back to clean her couch. When she returned to the kitchen, she found three more wet spots. Butch looked so very contrite, she couldn't hold it against him. She understood that he was nervous and needed reassurance. Instead of chastising him, she hugged and petted him some more, trying to let him know he was safe and secure and well loved.

By the time she had dinner going and Riley was due to arrive, Butch had relaxed enough to play a little. He followed Regina everywhere she went, sometimes bounding here or there, sometimes turning excited circles. Charmed, Regina had to keep stopping to pick him up, kiss him and hug him.

Because she was on the second floor, she put a litter box on her small balcony for him to use and in no time he got the hang of going to the glass patio door to scratch. She used a short leash that kept him from reaching the edge of the balcony so he couldn't accidentally fall off and get hurt. He did his business like a trooper and came back in.

Of course, he marked his territory everywhere inside the apartment, too. Regina wasn't yet sure if he was uncertain of his boundaries, stubborn or just not very bright. She hoped the first, because the second and third didn't bode well for her peace of mind.

The chicken was done, the potatoes already mashed, when the knock sounded on her door. She recognized Riley's knock right off. Decisive, firm, just like the man himself.

Though she hated to admit it, she felt that familiar leap of her heart whenever he was near. They'd known each other three weeks now, and so far Riley had been attentive, courteous and understanding.

More important than that, he believed her somewhat wild stories about stalkers and threats when no one else would. Of course, Regina thought his belief just might be attributed to boredom. Riley used to be SWAT, for heaven's sake. He was used to excitement and danger.

In Chester, the most excitement he got was photographing old man Tilburn's house because the neighborhood rascals had toilet-papered it once again. For a man like Riley, a man of his skills and background, that had to add up to a lot of frustration. Even chasing Regina's ghosts had to be better than that.

But she wouldn't complain. Regardless of what motivated him, she needed his help, so she'd take what she could get.

She expected the thrill that skated through her when she started to open the door.

What she didn't anticipate was Butch going into a

complete hostile frenzy. He transformed from tiny shivering dog into Tasmanian devil right before her eyes.

Riley called out, "Regina? It's me. Open up."

"Just a second." She picked up Butch, but holding the snarling, rigid, four-pound mass of meanness was nearly impossible. Outrage stiffened every muscle in his lean little body and he fought her to be free—so he could attack her visitor.

What a courageous dog!

Using one hand, Regina turned the locks on the door and then struggled to maintain her hold on Butch while Riley stepped inside. The dog broke free. Regina almost dropped him but managed to get him to the floor, head first.

He rolled, landed on his feet and like a shot, went after Riley.

Riley stood there, brows high, expression arrested, while Butch tried to tear his pant leg off. "What the hell? Is that a rabid squirrel?"

Indignant, Regina closed the door and crossed her arms. "Of course not. It's my dog, Butch."

"*That's* a dog?" Incredulity rang in his voice. "Are you sure?" His head tilted down at the wriggling fury hanging from his leg. "How can you tell?"

Offended on Butch's behalf, Regina huffed. She pulled the dog free and went about soothing him. "Shh. Butchie, it's okay. He's allowed in. Such a good dog. So brave."

Riley looked like he might puke. "That *is* a dog. What the hell is wrong with it?"

Regina sat on the couch. "Nothing. He's perfect."

"He can't weigh more than four pounds."

"He's four exactly." She rubbed Butch's belly and

he rolled to his back, his skinny legs falling open, his eyes half-closed.

Riley pulled back. "Good God."

Regina didn't take him to task for that comment. After all, Butch was showing his equipment with no evidence of modesty whatsoever. She cleared her throat. "The breeder said I should have him neutered."

"He'll only weigh three pounds if you do." Grinning at his own joke, Riley took the seat beside her and reached out to pet the dog. Butch went berserk again, his doggy lips pulled back tight, rippling with menace, the whites of his eyes showing. One second he looked so innocent and sweet and the next he appeared like a vicious gnat.

"He needs time to get used to you," Regina explained in a rush, and hoped that was true. If Butch continued to act so contrary, what would she do?

In his usual calm manner, Riley surveyed Butch. "What kind of dog is it?"

"He's a pure bred Chihuahua. His beautiful coloring is very unique." She certainly thought him beautiful. "Red with black brindling."

Riley only nodded. "How much bigger will he get?"

"Oh, he's full-grown." She rubbed Butch's ears and watched his bulgy eyes narrow in bliss. "Isn't he just precious?"

"No." Riley frowned at her. "Please tell me this isn't your idea of a guard dog."

"But he's perfect," she said by way of answer. "You saw how he attacked you."

"And you saw how I held real still so I wouldn't accidentally hurt him."

She had noticed that. Riley was always so cautious

with people, so careful. She knew a lot of that had to do with his training and his ability. It would be so easy for him to hurt someone, that he naturally tempered himself in almost all situations. Others might not be aware of his restraint, but Regina had seen it in his intense blue eyes, and she'd felt it during her lessons.

She'd also noticed that he hadn't been startled by Butch's attack. Most people would have jumped, maybe even screeched.

Not Riley. She couldn't imagine anything unsettling Riley enough to wring a screech out of him. With unparalleled calm, he'd taken in the situation and then reacted, without haste, careful not to hurt Butch.

Such an incredible guy.

Nodding, she said, "I did notice. Thank you."

Lounging back in his seat, Riley put one arm along the couch back, almost touching her shoulder. Without leaving Regina's lap, Butch slanted a mean gaze his way, his rumbling growls a warning. Riley continued to watch the dog while speaking to Regina. "When do we eat? It smells good."

Flustered by the compliment, she came to her feet, holding Butch like an infant—which he seemed to enjoy. "It's ready now. We have to eat in the kitchen. I don't have a dining room. Once I get moved in I'll have a dining room, and we can use it then. I mean, if you're ever over for dinner at my new house…" Turning her back on Riley and rolling her eyes at her own rambling nonsense, she rushed into the kitchen. Hostesses should not ramble. They should feed their guests.

Riley followed. "Regina?"

"Hmm?" She turned after setting Butch in his bed. He came right back out of it, still watching Riley, inching closer for a sniff. Now that Regina no longer held him, he was jumpy enough to lurch back a step each time Riley moved.

"We'll be having plenty of dinners together."

The sneaky way the dog advanced distracted her. "We will?"

Butch was at Riley's foot now, his sniffing more purposeful. Knowing what Butch probably intended, Regina scrambled to find a chew stick. In no way did she want Butch to mark Riley. He was not part of the permanent territory and unlikely to become so.

Riley crouched down and held out a hand to Butch. The dog gave his fingers a thorough inspection, donned an angelic expression complete with big innocent eyes and a small doggy smile, and even allowed Riley to rub under his chin. Teasing, Riley said, "You sure he wasn't bred with a rat?"

Regina, too, bent down to hand Butch the rawhide chew. The second she got near, Butch did an about-face. He snapped at Riley in warning, squirmed up close to Regina and accepted the chew.

"Contrary dog," Riley commented while standing up straight again.

Butch retreated to his bed to work over the chew. "He's getting used to you already."

Riley caught her hand and pulled her upright in front of him. Her heart pounded when his strong, warm fingers laced with hers, palm to palm.

"What about you, Red? You getting used to me, too?"

Oh boy, there was a load of innuendo in the way Riley said that. And truthfully, she was so used to him that when he wasn't around, she missed him. Dumb.

Regina Foxworth did not allow herself fanciful infatu-
ations. She thought to tell him that yes, she was used
to him and why shouldn't she be? He was no different from any other man. But with his callused fingers
holding hers, words stuck in her throat. She barely
managed a shrug.

With his gaze holding her captive, his hand opened,
slid slowly up her arm, over her shoulder and the side of
her neck, along her jaw until his fingers curled around
the back of her neck. Where he'd touched, gooseflesh
sprang up and she trembled.

Softly, Riley whispered, "Wrong answer."

Her startled gasp emerged just as he urged her to
her tiptoes. "Riley?"

"You need to accept a few things, Red."

She felt spellbound, uncertain. Anxious. But if she
hesitated much longer, her chicken would burn and
then she'd make a bad impression. She forced herself
to say "Like?"

"Like this." He bent and kissed her.

Chapter 2

The touch of his mouth was brief, warm, firm. Regina barely had time to appreciate his taste before he lifted away the tiniest bit.

"Oh." Tentatively, thoughts of chicken obliterated, Regina laid her hands on his chest. He'd dressed in casual chinos and a polo shirt, but the domestic clothes couldn't hide the true nature of the man. The soft cotton fabric served an enticing contrast to the hard muscle, long bones and crisp hair underneath.

His eyes were more gray than blue now, glittering with heat. There was nothing even remotely domestic in the way he watched her. "More than anything," he rumbled low, "I'd like to carry you into your bedroom right now, strip you naked and make love all night." He closed his eyes a moment, drew a breath. When he looked at her again, some of that intense heat had been tempered. "But we've got a lot to get cleared up first."

Regina faltered. Make love all night? *Strip her naked?* They hadn't known each other *that* long. Regardless of her strong attraction to Riley, she wasn't the type of woman to leap into an affair. Responsible people utilized caution and thought before making that type of commitment.

Stepping back from him, she gestured to her tiny two-seater table. Her hand shook and she had to clear her throat twice before she could speak. "Sounds like we have a long talk ahead." Thankfully, her voice was only a little shaky. "Sit down while I serve dinner."

Riley watched her with indecision before silently agreeing. Regina could feel his gaze on her rump when she bent to pull the perfectly browned chicken out of the oven. Martha Stewart would be proud. Ms. Manners would applaud her.

As the delicious scents of stuffing and chicken wafted through the air, Butch perked up, his little nose raised and quivering with interest. Regina looked at him, but Riley said, "I wouldn't. Once you feed him table food, you'll never be able to stop. And it's not good for him anyway."

"Right." She knew that, and since she always tried to do the right thing, she hoped her dog would do the right thing as well. Giving Butch an apologetic shake of her head, she filled his bowl with dog food. Appeased, he began to eat while Regina carried the food to the table. The chicken was placed perfectly on a platter, the potatoes looked fluffy in a decorative bowl, and steam rose from the broccoli with melting butter atop it. She lit a scented candle in the middle of the table and everything was complete. Beautiful.

"What can I do to help?"

Regina stared at Riley, and he stared back, studying her. She'd expected him to sit and admire her dinner preparation skills, not watch her every move. But if he wanted to help...wasn't it a man's job to carve? She'd never had a man around long enough to know, and her father certainly hadn't been the type to worry about how food was cut. He was more a grab-and-stuff-it-in-your-mouth kind of guy.

Regina handed Riley the butcher knife and fork with a flourish. "Iced tea, milk?"

"Tea is fine." He stood to begin slicing apart the chicken. Regina noticed that he did an admirable job. He glanced up at her. "Why are you so nervous, Red?"

"I'm not."

"You are."

She sighed, unable to deny the obvious. "No more so than usual. That is, I'm always nervous." It was a complaint she often got from men. But now, with the man being Riley, she felt doubly unsettled. Add to that some unknown assailant who had tried to hurt her several times and might just try again, and to her way of thinking she had plenty of reason to be nervous.

"Because you're worried?"

"Yes." She poured the iced tea, sat, remembered she wanted music and popped back up. "I'll be right back." Seconds later, the stereo in her bedroom played low, adding soft sounds to the clink of china and silver.

Riley waited for her to return. He held her chair, but when she sat, he didn't retreat. Instead he bent down and kissed the side of her neck. Oh Lord, she'd never get used to this spontaneous kissing of his. At Mach speed, he'd taken them from acquaintances, maybe friends, to something much more intimate.

Fighting the urge to gasp again, she stiffened. Where he'd pressed his mouth, her neck tingled and felt damp. A strange but pleasant warmth rippled through her.

Riley spoke softly into her ear, adding to her awareness. "You need to be comfortable being alone with me, Red."

The way he said that, all seductive and low, made her stomach flip-flop. "I do?" At this rate, she'd never be able to eat. It'd look like she didn't appreciate her own culinary skills.

"Yeah." He brushed her nape with the back of one finger, then circled the table and sat in his chair, facing her, casual as you please, as if he hadn't just been teasing her, turning her on.

"Um…why?"

He picked up his fork. "Starting today, we're going to be alone together." His gaze caught and held hers. "A lot."

The food was delicious. He'd had no idea that Regina was such a fine cook. For long moments, they ate in silence. He waited to see what Regina would say to his statement, but she just sat there, watching him cautiously, occasionally nibbling on her food.

He didn't want to spoil her dinner, so he sat back and studied her. "I guess you want me to explain?"

She cleared her throat. "That'd be nice, yes."

A starched linen napkin had been placed beside his plate. Since it was there, Riley used it to pat his mouth. "All right. You're not showing much improvement at the gym."

Her shoulders sank the tiniest bit. Riley wasn't sure

if it was disappointment or relief. "I know. I'm not a very physical person."

He intended to hold all judgments on that until he had her in bed. Then he'd see just how physical he could coax her into being. "You don't need physical strength, Regina. But you do have to stop worrying about other people watching you."

She winced. "I know. It's just that I hate looking like a fool."

"Once you know what you're doing, you'll look like a pro."

"Yes, of course," she quickly agreed. "I'll try harder, I promise."

He didn't believe that for a minute. "Regina?"

She glanced up at him, her brows raised quizzically.

"I'm going to give you very private lessons from now on. Just the two of us." He looked at her mouth. "All alone. No spectators."

She stared at him for three seconds. "You are?"

Riley nodded, a little put out that she questioned every damn thing he said, like she couldn't believe it or doubted it to be true. He wasn't a liar, damn it.

Stunned by that mental statement, he shook his head and made a quick amendment: he wouldn't lie to *her,* and not about this. Other lies, lies from his past, were well buried.

Holding on to his patience, Riley continued his explanation. "There's not much room here at your place, so we can't really get going tonight."

Her mouth opened. In anticipation, shock or horror? Riley couldn't quite tell. "You can either come to my place, or the gym after hours."

She held perfectly still. Tonight she had her thick

hair twisted at the back of her head and held in place with a fancy gold clip. It had been somewhat loosened by the kiss he'd given her earlier. The florescent overhead lights brought out the deeper reds and lighter golds, mixed in with the auburn. It also reflected the wariness in her green eyes.

She wore a freshly pressed sleeveless green V-neck shirt and low-riding cotton slacks. Her sandals showed off her meticulous pedicure.

From the top of her head to the tips of her toes, she was polished to a shine. She'd even managed to do dinner with no additional mess, putting things away as she used them so that no empty pans sat on the stove and no seasonings were out.

Riley wanted to see her mussed.

He wanted to see her sweat.

He wanted to hear Ms. Suzy Homemaker crying out in raw sexual excitement without a single thought as to how she looked, concerned only with the deep, driving pleasure.

Damn, he had to stop that train of thought or he'd be seducing her right now.

Finally, she nodded. "Thank you." Her voice sounded a little raspy. "It does embarrass me. I think it'll be easier without others watching. But, Riley, mostly it's you that I worry about."

"Me?" Sipping his iced tea, he watched her, thinking it wasn't such a bad thing if he unsettled her. It meant she held at least a small amount of awareness for him as a man.

She pleated her napkin. She straightened her fork. Suddenly she blurted, "Are you attracted to me?"

"Yes."

She seemed surprised by his immediate answer. Then she chewed on her lips. "I'm attracted to you, too."

She made that admission with the same regret she might have given a murder confession.

"I know." He hadn't known. He'd hoped. He was pretty sure. But he'd wanted confirmation.

Now he had it.

"It...bothers me, the idea of you seeing me all messy and sweaty."

Hearing her say it sharpened his desire. "Eventually, I'll see you every way there is." He toyed with his iced tea glass, his gaze never wavering from hers. "When we have sex, you'll definitely be sweaty. Messy, too. That's the way it is with good sex. But I'm willing to bet you'll look hot as hell."

Her breathing deepened and her brows puckered in thought. After a long hesitation, she said, "You, um, you treat Rosie like a pal."

"Rosie is a pal."

"But she's also a very attractive woman."

Leaning back in his seat, Riley nodded. "Agreed."

"And yet you never have romantic thoughts about her because she's become your pal."

Riley had no idea where she was going with this. Women could be so confusing, even to a man who prided himself on getting past the surface stuff. Oh, he could detect some of her thoughts. She was uncertain, interested, wary. But he wanted to know *why* she felt so uncertain.

He eyed her, then decided a little truth couldn't hurt the situation. "Who says?"

Confusion left her face blank. "Who says… Well, Rosie said. She assured me that she loved Ethan and—"

"She does." It had recently become very clear that Rosie had always loved Ethan—she'd just been waiting around for him to come to his senses and realize that he loved her, too.

"—and that Ethan was a good friend of yours."

"He is." With Harris and Buck, they made a regular foursome, but he and Ethan had more in common. They were all friends, but if Riley ever had his back to the wall, he'd trust Ethan more than any other man.

"Then—"

"You think because we're friends, I shouldn't have sexual thoughts about her?" He stretched out his long legs beneath the table and bumped into her small feet. "You and I are friends, and I have plenty of sexual thoughts about you."

Her eyes widened comically. "Plenty?"

It was his turn to smile. "All day, every day, as a matter of fact."

She stewed on that for a bit before speaking again. "But see, that's just it. I thought you felt about me the way you feel about Rosie, except you're closer with her."

"Not a chance."

"You're not close to her?"

"Very close. But the way I feel about you is on the other end of the scale. I don't intend to ever sleep with Rosie." He let his gaze drop to her breasts. "You, however, I intend to get naked with just as soon as it can be arranged."

Her eyes dilated in shock, but he also saw reciprocal interest in the way her breathing deepened and how her skin warmed. Despite all that, she shook her head. "You should probably know, Riley, I don't sleep around."

"You're a virgin?"

More color stained her cheeks and she frowned. "No, I didn't say that." Then she added in a mumble, "For heaven's sake, I'm twenty-eight years old."

"So you're saying you don't want to sleep with me?" He knew damn good and well that wasn't true. But would she be honest?

"Of course I do."

He grinned.

"I mean, I do, but I'm not going to. Not anytime soon, that is. We barely know each other."

He'd known her long enough to understand exactly how he felt. "We've known each other better than three weeks now. That's not exactly a sneeze. And because of the lessons, we've been physically close."

"You're keeping count?"

She was clearly astonished by that. Hell, it still stunned Riley a little, the depth of what he felt. But he didn't want her panicking on him, so he backed off. "Let's finish eating, then we'll talk about it more. By the way, you're a hell of a cook. I'm impressed."

Relieved by the change of topic, she nodded. "I wanted you to be. Impressed, I mean." She caught herself and her gaze jerked up to his. "That is, I try to impress everyone."

"Yeah? Why is that, Red? You don't think just being yourself is good enough?" There was so much he still had to learn about her. Funny how appearances meant nothing to him because they weren't something you could trust. Yet, they meant the world to her.

The contrast in their views might have discouraged him, but he figured he was at least making headway now.

"Maybe." She propped her head on her hand, realized that wasn't the proper way to sit and jerked upright again. "Actually I've thought about this a lot, about why I'm the way I am. Every so often, I wish I could be different because sometimes it has the opposite effect and just drives people nuts."

"What people?"

"Co-workers, friends. Men."

He didn't give a damn what other men thought of her. If they steered clear, hell, he was glad. "Rosie and Ethan and Buck and Harris like you fine." He smiled. "I like you more than fine. But I am curious why you're so worried about what other people think. That is, if you care to talk about it."

She pleated and fussed with her napkin. "It's silly really. Maybe something of a habit left over from when I was young."

"You were a fussy child?"

His teasing put a self-conscious half smile on her face. "Yes. Very fussy, I guess. See, I came from a…a dirty farmhouse." She wrinkled her nose with that confession. "And when I say dirty, I'm not exaggerating. It's awful to admit, but we lived like pigs."

Not sure that he understood, Riley asked, "You were poor?"

"Poor and slovenly are not the same thing, but yes, we were poor, too. I've never been certain if it was necessary, if they just couldn't make enough money or if they simply mismanaged what they made." She shrugged. "My parents sustained us from paycheck to paycheck. If we ran out in the middle of the week, or something came up—as things always do—they'd borrow or beg."

The expression on her face twisted his heart. Softly, he said, "That had to be rough."

"I hated it and it embarrassed me."

The emotional plethora took Riley off guard. Being a private man, he couldn't imagine discussing so much of his personal background. "So you've worked to change your life. There's nothing wrong with that."

"It was never my life." She sipped her tea, scooted her broccoli around on her plate with the edge of her fork. "It was my mother's, my father's and my younger brother's. But not mine."

No, Riley couldn't quite imagine her ever being comfortable in those circumstances. She was so prim, proper and precise now, that it must have been almost painful for her.

"You didn't accept the circumstances of your youth."

"For as far back as I can remember, even as a young kid, I tried to make it different. Everything I owned was old and stained, but I did my best to always keep it clean and pressed." She glanced up at him and gave a low laugh. "My brother used to make fun of me for being so meticulous. The other kids we knew.... They liked to call us names and poke fun at us."

Riley hated that anyone had hurt her feelings, even though it had happened long ago. And her brother... It was ridiculous to be angry at him when he'd been no more than a boy, too. But that didn't change how Riley felt. "Kids can be pretty cruel when no one is teaching them better."

"Maybe. But if you'd ever seen our farm or car or

how my parents behaved in public, you'd understand why the kids treated us the way they did. I understood it. And I knew my family would never change. After I graduated high school, I moved away, got a job as an errand girl with a small paper and worked my way up to reporter."

Riley smiled. Reporter was a bit of a stretch considering the small pieces she wrote. Then again, her human-interest stories for the local paper were always entertaining. She'd done a stellar article on Ethan that had made the fire department, as well as the whole town, proud.

Riley thought about it and decided selective sharing was good. It forged a bond that would bring them closer together, and that was his ultimate goal. There were parts of himself he could discuss, parts that weren't buried deep and that wouldn't reveal anything beyond the surface.

He mentally skimmed a variety of topics and settled on his safest bet—family. "My mother isn't immaculate or anything."

Her interest obvious, she glanced up at him with a smile. "No?"

"She keeps the place tidy, but it's always well lived in. I have two younger brothers, one older."

"Four boys? My goodness."

"Yeah, Mom felt the same way." He laughed. "The others still live near to home and they drop in a lot with their broods. Between the three of them, I have ten nieces and nephews."

"Wow. A big family."

He acknowledged that with a shrug. "Mom is old-fashioned, the type who wants to feed you the minute you show up and fusses around you the whole time you're there. I haven't been home to see her in a while." That was something he should remedy, Riley decided. Funny that he hadn't much considered how long it had been until Regina started discussing her family.

Wondering how Regina would react to the casual mess around his mother's house, he pushed his plate away. "Maybe next time I go, you could come along with me."

Her eyes shot wide. "You want me to meet your mother?"

She sounded as if he'd asked her to swim with sharks. "And Dad, too. You'd like them."

She had nothing to say to that so Riley pressed her. "What about your folks? Do you visit with them at all?" He wouldn't really be surprised if she'd broken all ties, but it'd be a shame. When all was said and done, family should be there for you, and vice versa.

"They're gone now." There was a wistful, sad note to her voice. "Mom died years ago from cancer and Dad passed away from a stroke two years after. The farm was sold and my brother and I split the profits. That's how I bought my house. I've been sitting on that money for a while."

Riley had wondered about that. He didn't imagine a small-town reporter earned much income. "I'm sorry."

"It was a long time ago. I loved them, but I was never very close with them. We had a…strained relationship." She hesitated, and Riley wondered if she'd pull back now, if she'd return to being evasive. Instead, she shrugged. "They thought I was snooty."

With almost no prodding at all, she continued to open up to him. In his experience, reporters pried into anyone and everyone's life, but clammed up when it came to their own personal issues. He couldn't help wondering if her openness was a compliment reserved for special people. Did she feel safer with him? Did she trust him?

"Snooty, huh?" He pretended to study her head to toe, then nodded. "Circumspect, yes. Meticulous, maybe. But not snooty."

"Thank you." She tucked in her chin to hide her smile. "My brother still accuses me of thinking I'm better than them."

"Do you?"

"Think I'm better? No. But I'm certainly wiser about how I handle my life." Her long look seemed like a warning, one he fully intended to ignore. He would have her, and soon. "My parents had a great farm that they let go to ruin because they refused to do any real work. It should have been worth five times as much, but they'd never taken care of it. The house was so run-down it had to be demolished. There wasn't a piece of furniture or a dish to be salvaged."

"No mementos at all?"

"A few photographs that my brother and I split. My folks didn't believe in cherishing the past or planning for the future. They had the barest medical coverage and of course, it wasn't enough. Now my brother seems just like them. He flits from one job to the next, one woman to another."

Sounded like a lot of guys Riley knew, men who wouldn't grow up and so, at least in his opinion, weren't really men.

"He's already spent his inheritance and doesn't have a thing to show for it. I asked what he intended to do when he retired, but he just laughs and says he has a lifetime to worry about it. He hasn't learned at all."

"But you have?"

"Absolutely." She met his gaze squarely. "The house is an investment in my future, but I have others as well. If I get sick, I'll be able to take care of myself, not rely on others or end up in the care of the state. I'm careful about everything I do and I don't give in to impulses."

Impulses like sexual desire? Did she hope to deny the chemistry between them? Riley didn't correct her but he knew different. He could be persuasive and he never gave up easily.

At his long silence, her chin lifted. "What about you?"

"What about me?"

She looked self-conscious but forged on. "Do you have a retirement plan? And you mentioned your place. Do you have your own house or are you renting?"

The inquisition so surprised him, Riley laughed. "Tell me, Red, are you curious for personal reasons, sizing me up as husband material, or are you mentally working on that damn article?"

She stiffened, but she didn't lie. "A little of each maybe, though it's certainly too early to be thinking about anything serious between us."

"You really think so?"

Her face went blank, then pink with confusion. She forged on. "And I wouldn't write the article without your permission. It's just that the whole community hero angle worked so well with Ethan, I know people would eat up a life story on you."

He ignored that because his life wasn't anybody's business. "But you're personally interested, right?"

She chewed on her lips again. "We're not involved, Riley, so it's more curiosity than anything."

"I want to be involved."

She pressed back in her chair. She blinked, studied his face, then looked down at her hands. "You know, Riley, it occurs to me that this could get pretty muddled."

"How so?" Riley felt strangely sated. He'd had a delicious meal, cozy conversation and the sight of Regina seated across from him. It was the kind of setting he could get used to—the kind of setting he hadn't wanted again until he'd met her.

He knew exactly how he'd like to end the day, but after everything she'd confessed, he had his doubts about her cooperation. He could be patient, especially since all indications led him to believe he'd eventually win.

"You say you believe me about the attacks."

"I do."

"Then don't you think we should keep the personal and the professional separate? Won't it be hard for you to be objective if we're…well, sleeping with each other?"

Objectivity had flown out the window within hours of meeting her. He drank the last of his iced tea and nodded at her plate. "What I think is that you should eat some of this great dinner you fixed."

"I am eating." She took two more bites, then went on in a rush. "Why would you believe me when no one else does?"

"It's easy enough to understand. You finish eating and I'll tell you a story, okay?"

"All right."

She still only picked at her food, but he felt better knowing he hadn't completely ruined her meal. "Back when I was a new evidence tech, before I became SWAT, I got called to the scene where a guy had broken into his seventeen-year-old girlfriend's house. The mother had forbid the girl to see him anymore, but when she left to go shopping, he snuck over. When the girl tried to send him away, he got unreasonably furious, choking her and banging her head on the wall a few times."

Regina's head came up, a broccoli floret dangling from her fork. "Dear God."

"The mom got home in time to pull him off her," Riley assured her, but as usual, the bitter memories filled him with anger. Too many times, he hadn't been able to make a difference. "The detectives got there just before me, but the boyfriend had already fled. They were speaking with the mom and daughter, and the dad who had just arrived home. Patrol tells me that the mom wants to prosecute the guy, but the daughter doesn't. When I explain that her boyfriend committed a Felony One—aggravated burglary—which carries the same sentence as murder, the mom starts backing up, too."

"But her daughter…"

"Has purpling choke marks on her neck and bruises on her cheek and temple. Still, she just kept saying, 'But I love him. He didn't mean to hurt me.'"

Regina threw down her fork. "Well, what in the world did he think would happen when he manhandled her that way?"

"Men like that don't concern themselves with the victim. And with the daughter spouting all the classic I-have-no-self-esteem phrases that you get from abused women, there wasn't much we could do. The dad was noticeably silent, only occasionally saying, 'I think I just need to have a talk with the boy.'"

"Unbelievable."

"No, honey, unfortunately it's all too believable and cops run into that crap every day. We had to leave with no charges filed because the victims wouldn't prosecute. I was pissed, the other detective was scratching his head and then the female officer says, "I can tell you what's going on in there. Dad's beaten Mom up a few times and the daughter knows it. Mom doesn't want to say anything because she might get another beating and the poor girl thinks this is normal behavior because she's lived with it for years.'"

Riley's hands fisted on the tabletop. He wouldn't tell Regina that eventually the girl had run off with the jerk—and died because of it.

Subdued, Regina left her seat and came around to Riley's side. Immediately, Butch did the same. He ran from his bed, stretched up with his paws on her thigh and begged to be held. Regina scooped him up close, rubbing her nose against his soft fur but speaking to Riley. "I'm sorry."

Riley gave her a one-arm hug, pulling her into his side. Because he was still sitting, his face was level with the subtle swell of her breasts. Well, her breasts and a fuzzed-up, irritable Butch who didn't want Riley to touch her.

The dog was too territorial, but Riley understood how he felt. "Yeah, me, too." He forced his gaze to her face. "But you know what, Red? It taught me something. There are all kinds of perspectives and things we never see. And women, God bless them, are pretty damned intuitive. If you say someone is after you, I'd be an idiot not to take you seriously. And, believe me, I'm not an idiot."

She gave a small, tremulous smile. "Thank you. It… Well, it feels better, safer, just knowing someone isn't writing me off as a nut."

Riley pushed back his chair and came to his feet. Oh yeah, he knew exactly how Butch felt because the urge to hold her was nearly overwhelming. "Tell you what, Red. Let's put the dishes away, then go to the living room and you can tell me everything that's been going on."

"Everything?"

"From the beginning. Maybe we'll be able to sort things out." He put his hand at the small of her back and urged her away from the table. "Do you think Killer can entertain himself a few minutes?"

The dog managed a sideways glare and a roll of his lip, but when Regina put him in his bed, this time he circled, dug at the bedding for a few seconds, then plopped down to sleep with his nose noticeably close to his rump.

Her kitchen was so immaculate, it didn't take any time at all to put things away. The leftovers went into matching containers in the fridge. The dishes were rinsed and put in uniform order in the dishwasher. Regina was so orderly, so clean, it unnerved Riley a bit.

Would she expect everyone to be that tidy? Curious as to how judgmental she might be, Riley said, "You've been to Rosie's place before, right?"

"Yes, why?"

"How'd you like it?" Rosie was tidy, but nowhere near as big a neat freak as Regina.

She thought about it for a moment, then smiled. "From the first time I stepped into Rosie's house, it felt cozy, like a home." She gave a soft laugh that sank into him. "But Rosie's that way. Very warm and open and friendly. I like her a lot."

Satisfied by her answer, Riley smiled. "Yeah, me, too."

Together they washed the pans, Regina cleaning and Riley drying. Damn, but he had a good time doing it. Just being with her calmed something turbulent inside him, making him feel more at peace with himself and his life. But slowly the serenity of the moment expanded into heightened awareness. He wanted her, and not having her was torture.

When her hands were completely submersed in soapy water, Riley moved behind her. Holding her waist so she couldn't slip away, he deliberately pressed in, relishing the feel of her full bottom against his groin. A short groan rumbled in his chest.

One day soon, after she'd accepted him, he'd take her this way, from behind, sinking deep, feeling her buttocks on his abdomen and thighs. He'd be able to cover her breasts with his hands, toy with her stiffened nipples, slip his fingers down her belly to her...

"Riley?"

He ignored the hardening of his body, the surge of lust, to nibble carefully on her ear. Without intentional thought, he further aroused her, letting his breath tickle her ear, using the edge of his tongue to tantalize the sensitive nerve endings along the tendons in her neck. "You don't want to sleep with me yet, Red, but you will soon. In the meantime, a little kissing won't hurt anything, right?" Before she could answer, he dipped his tongue into her ear, then gently sucked her earlobe. His accelerated breaths fanned the delicate, baby-fine hairs at her temple.

"No." Her hands went still, just dangling over the edge of the sink, not quite in the water, not quite out. She tipped her head back to his shoulder and closed her eyes.

Riley leaned around her to see her face. "No what, honey?" He pressed one hand from her waist to her belly, spreading his fingers wide in masculine possession. His thumb dipped into her navel through her clothes, pressing gently, symbolic of so much more. Few people understood the erogenous zones of a woman's body, how small touches, when combined just right, could elicit carnal reactions.

In his training, he'd learned a lot about pressure points that could cripple, but the reverse was also true. He knew the places where exquisite, almost unbearable pleasure existed.

He could make her come, right here, right now, without undue effort, and that knowledge had his entire body straining in need. But he didn't want to push her. The constraint cost him, making him tremble and turning his voice hoarse. "No, you don't want me to do this, or no, there's nothing wrong with it?"

"There's nothing wrong with it."

A shudder rippled through him; she'd seemed so wary of sexual involvement with him that any capitulation now felt like a major triumph.

Suddenly she turned and plastered herself up against him, breasts to abdomen, belly to groin. "I want to kiss you, Riley. I just don't want you to expect it to lead to bed."

"All right."

Her green eyes narrowed with mingled surprise and uncertainty. "All right, what?"

He settled his hands on her hips, urging her closer still, so he could feel the rounded, feminine contours of her body. "All right, you can kiss me. Go ahead."

"Oh." She looked at his mouth, licked her own, and Riley nearly lost it.

"Hurry up, Red."

"Okay then." With her soapy hands sliding around his neck, she went on tiptoe and her mouth touched his.

Riley waited, his heart thundering, his erection straining, his testicles tight. With ruthless determination, he gathered his control around him and kept his stance relaxed, his expression calm, when in reality his emotions bordered on savage. He'd never wanted any woman the way he wanted Regina.

Her warm velvet tongue licked out again, this time over his lips. "Riley?"

"Yeah?"

"Open your mouth for me."

That did it. As carefully as he could manage considering the tumultuous raging of his libido, Riley gathered her fully against him. With her heartbeat echoing his, he opened his mouth but didn't let her take the lead. His tongue slid in, deep and slow, mating with hers, teasing, showing her with his mouth how he wanted to take her with his body. Their hot breaths mingled, their hands clutched. Her body relaxed and sighed into his, so soft and fluid and feminine; his grew more taut with pounding lust.

He'd promised himself only a few kisses when he started this, but then he hadn't counted on the effect of her full and enthusiastic involvement. Before he'd even had time to think it through, he had a small breast in one hand, a firm, lush cheek in the other.

Their groans sounded at the same time.

Her nipple stiffened against his palm, a plea that he couldn't ignore. Using only his open palm, Riley brushed his hand over her again and again, abrading her nipples, giving her only so much. Her fingers tightened in his hair. She pulled her mouth away to gulp for air. "Riley?"

She said his name as an invitation, an appeal for more. "Regina…"

The sudden furious yapping of the dog startled them both. As if he'd only just then realized their physical closeness, Butch ran wild circles around them, snapping at Riley's leg without actually touching, making his discontent with the situation well known.

It hit Riley that his control had definitely slipped. For that brief moment, he'd lost all sense of himself, acting solely on need. It was an awesome, almost frightening admission. No one, not even his wife, and not even the worst imaginable scene, had so much as caused a flicker of loss in his innate control. He'd considered it an unchangeable part of him, like his height and bone structure.

One glance at Regina's hot face and he wanted to curse. "I'm sorry."

She shook her head. "No. No reason to apologize." She smoothed her hands down the front of her blouse, realized they were wet and tucked them behind her. Her smile was entirely false and self-conscious. "Would you like coffee?"

Strangely insulted, Riley stared at her. They'd shared

a killer kiss, he'd had his hands all over her, and she wanted to continue playing proper hostess. "What I'd like," he muttered under his breath, "is to finish what we started."

"Excuse me?"

"Nothing." He needed a distraction and fast. The obvious distraction was now chewing on his heel while growling like a banshee. Riley reached down for Butch, but with his expression so dark the dog tucked in his tail and scurried away with due haste. Issuing a grievous sigh, Riley caught Butch with one hand and held him up close. Regina stood next to him like a fretful mother while the dog tried to brazen it out, grumbling, snarling and looking to Regina for rescue.

"Shh," Riley soothed while stroking the narrow back with one finger. The dog was smaller than his foot, his legs no thicker than Riley's baby finger and he fit fully into one hand. Butch quieted just a bit, giving Riley a suspicious look reminiscent of Regina's. "Good boy. See, I'm not so evil, huh? I saw that you weren't actually biting me, just trying to scare me off. You don't trust me with Regina. But you're going to have to get used to me touching her, buddy, because I intend to touch her a lot."

Regina said, "You do?"

Riley slanted her a look. "Since we're done here, let's go into the living room. The sooner I can figure out what the hell's going on with your attacker, the sooner we can get beyond it."

Regina dried her hands, neatly folded the dish towel to hang over the bar and hurried after him. "And then what?"

"And then I can concentrate on just you." He smiled

at her over his shoulder, a deliberate smile, hot and sug-gestive. She stopped dead in her tracks, blinked twice, then followed him into the room.

And damned if she didn't wear a coy little smile of her own.

Chapter 3

"It started after my assignment in the park."

The second Regina sat beside him, Butch snapped at Riley again and jumped over into her lap. Traitorous dog. "What park? Around here?"

"No, where I used to work before moving to Chester." While she spoke, she absently petted the dog and within minutes Butch was sound asleep again. "It was a new park opening. There'd been a lot of problems with it because some of the bigger businesses wanted to use the area for a parking lot. The arguments were pretty good on both sides: beautify the land with a park to draw visitors to the area, or use it to provide adequate parking so people would come to the stores to shop, thereby actually spending money."

"So I guess the park won?"

She nodded. "It was in the news every day. City hall

got more action than it'd seen in months. The mayor
had started to look pretty harried before everything
got settled. The paper I worked for ran regular articles
about it, then they sent me there to get photos and to do
a write-up a week before the park officially opened. It
was my biggest feature, a two-page spread."

Riley smiled at her enthusiasm. Sitting so close to
her, seeing her so animated, made it impossible not to
touch her. He reached toward her, and Butch came off
her lap like a whirlwind. Riley didn't duck away. He
held his hand out while Butch pretended to bite. He
came close, but never actually closed his teeth on Riley.

"Just like I thought. All bluster." He kept his tone
soft so he wouldn't upset the dog more. "You're fero-
ciously defensive, aren't you, squirt? I like that." And
then, despite Butch's complaints, he rubbed his ears.
Butch gave up and enjoyed the attention. "So what happened at the park?"

"Everything was going well at first. I took some
pictures of the elaborate fountain, the new swing sets,
the pond with ducks and geese. It really is a beautiful
spot." She glanced down at Butch and blushed. "I even
got to meet my favorite politician."

"Yeah? And who's that?"

"Senator Welling. He was there with an intern,
doing the same thing I was doing, checking out the
park. He'd supported it, you see. He always supports
the conservation of land whenever possible. I've admired him so long, I even took a few pictures of him.
He waved to the camera for me."

Riley sighed. For a reporter, she sure had a hard
time getting around to the point. "So what happened,

Red? Did someone attack you in the park? Did the good senator try to come on to you—"

"No! Senator Welling isn't like that." She looked genuinely annoyed by his teasing remarks. "The reason I admire him so much is because he's such a dedicated family man. He's a wonderful politician, too, of course, and I agree with most of his political stands, but it's his dedication to his wife and children that's his real appeal."

Personally, Riley thought the man was a schmooze, but then he wasn't about to get into a political debate with Regina. "I'll take your word for it."

Still disgruntled, she said, "He politely posed for my pictures, even did one with him and the intern standing on either side of the fountain. He walked me to my car *and* opened my car door for me."

Maybe he'd been coming on to her after all and Regina was just too naive to realize it. "So what happened at the park that made you feel threatened?"

"Oh, it was as I was leaving the park. I was almost to the main road when some jerk sideswiped me."

Riley straightened. "What do you mean, he sideswiped you?"

"I drive a little silver Escort, and this fancy SUV tried to pass me, but he didn't clear my hood before cutting back into my lane. His rear end hit my front bumper and my car went into a spin, then off the road. I plowed into a tree. The guy didn't even stop, just kept going."

"And you think that's related somehow to—"

"If you'll just let me finish," she said in exasperation.

"Sorry." Riley held up both hands. "By all means." He only hoped she got to the point before midnight.

"It wasn't easy, but I got the car out of the ditch and made it pretty close to the main road. I probably did even more harm to the car, but I didn't like the idea of sitting there alone in the park, especially since it was starting to get dark."

"Smart."

"I thought so. My cell phone had gone dead, so I thought I'd have a long walk ahead of me, but then the senator came by and he drove me to a phone. He even offered to wait with me, but I told him to go on. Wasn't that awfully nice of him?"

"He's supposed to serve the people, honey."

"Not as a taxi. Anyway, I called my boss from a diner. He called for a tow truck then came to pick me up and drive me back to my car. You won't believe what I found."

Numerous possibilities ran through his mind, but he said only, "What?"

"Someone had broken into it."

"You didn't lock it up?"

"Of course I did. But the driver's side window was smashed. I thought for sure my stereo, speakers and CDs would be gone."

"I gather they weren't?"

"No. The car had been ransacked, my glove box emptied, all my papers strewn around, but nothing was missing as far as I could tell."

Riley frowned. He had to admit that sounded odd. Had someone been looking for something specific? "What did the police say about it?"

"That I must have returned in time to scare the robbers off."

Possibly. But he wasn't one to always accept the most obvious explanation. "You have another theory?"

"Yes. Looking back, I think that SUV ran me off the road on purpose. I think he came back later to look for something in my car."

"If that's so, if he was really that determined, why not just follow you home?" Even saying it made Riley's protective instincts twitch. If someone *had* followed her, what might have happened? He didn't even want to contemplate such a scenario. From now on, he intended to keep a closer watch on her.

"I'm not a criminal so I can't know how a criminal's mind works. But maybe he knew I lived in a busy complex, so going through my car wouldn't have been easy. The thing is, I can't imagine what I'd have that anyone would want, but I am really grateful that Senator Welling was there to drive me into town. If he hadn't…"

"You might have been sitting in your car, all alone, when the burglar showed up." Riley reached out and took her hand. "Could be your presence would have deterred him."

"But maybe not. He did run me off the road without much concern, so maybe he'd have just hit me over the head or something. Maybe he'd have even—"

Riley's teeth hurt from clenching his jaw. "Don't." No way in hell did he want her to cavalierly discuss deadly possibilities. They'd already occurred to him, of course, so he didn't need embellishment of his own grisly thoughts.

"Well, after everything else that's happened…"

"Such as?"

"I left work one night after finishing up some research. Phone calls mostly. It was about eight, dark outside already. Just as I started to step off the curb, a black Porsche nearly ran me down. I had to jump back fast to keep from being hit. I landed on the ground, tore my panty hose, broke two fingernails and twisted my ankle."

Anger swelled inside him. "Jesus. You could have been killed."

"I think that was the point. But the police wrote it off as a sloppy driver, not a deliberate intent to hit me. They thought it was unrelated to the other incident and they said there was nothing they could do about it since I didn't get the license plate number."

Rationally, Riley knew they were right. Without a direct witness or a way to track down the car, the police were helpless. But at the very least, they could have taken the threat to her seriously.

Only, he didn't know if he would have either. Not with so little to go on. The first violation appeared to be a bungled burglary. The second *could* have been a drunk driver or a speeding kid…

"A week after that, some bully tried to grab my purse. I held on to it—"

Riley had gotten more and more rigid as the enormity of her dilemma sank in, and now his control nearly snapped. *"You held on?"*

The dog lunged at him for raising his voice. Riley pulled Butch up to his chest with one hand cradled under his body. He bounced him as he'd often done with his nieces and nephews when they were fussy babies. Butch had no idea what to make of it. He looked confused, but he quieted. His eyes were wide, his ear perked up. He peered at Regina, then back at Riley.

"It was *my* purse, Riley. No way was I going to just give it up."

"He could have hurt you, damn it."

"He *did* hurt me."

Through stiff lips, Riley growled, "Tell me."

His tone was so gruff, she gave him an uncertain look. "He...well, he belted me. Gave me a black eye."

"Son of a bitch."

"Riley!"

The dog howled and Riley released Regina's hand to stroke the dog's back, scratch his ears. "What did the police have to say about that?"

In a strange shift of mood, Regina scooted closer to him and stroked his shoulder. "It was weeks ago, Riley. There's no reason to get so upset now."

She attempted to soothe him much as Riley soothed the fractious dog. "I'm furious, not upset," Riley muttered, then added, "Women get upset."

"Your shoulders are all bunched and one eye is narrowed more than the other and you've got this strange tick in your jaw."

"Fury."

"All right, then don't get so furious. That won't help."

Knowing she was right, he drew a deep breath that didn't abate his anger one bit but gave him the elusion of calm. "Tell me what the cops said."

"Well, they were a little more concerned this time because after the guy hit me, my purse was dumped, only he didn't steal anything. My wallet was right there with two credit cards and about forty dollars, but he just rifled through the stuff on the ground, cursed me, and when we heard people coming, he ran off without a single thing."

Butch flopped onto his back in Riley's arms and went back to sleep. Apparently, he liked the rough rocking.

"What did the man look like?"

"I'm not sure. It was raining that day so he had on a slicker that closed up to his throat. He wore a hat and sunglasses, though there wasn't a speck of sunshine to be found. I noticed he was dark because he had five o'clock shadow and dark sideburns. His hands were tanned."

"Did the police try to follow him?"

"By the time they got there, he was long gone. They didn't know what to think until I explained about the other things that had happened. Then they wanted me to tell them about all my recent assignments." She shrugged. "But there hasn't been anything that would upset anyone. I don't write derogatory, cutting-edge pieces." She looked disgruntled with that admission. "I cover parks and new cookbooks and special-interest groups."

"So what had you written?" Riley continued rocking the dog. Butch twisted awkwardly, tucking the back of his head into Riley's neck and nuzzling closer in doggy bliss. Damn it, he was starting to like the dog.

"Let's see. I'd done the park feature…"

"No, before that. Everything started the day of the park, right? So it had to be something you'd done prior to that."

"That makes sense." She scrunched up her nose in thought. "Well, I did do an article on a professional football player arrested for a DUI, but my angle was on the time he donated to underprivileged children, something he'd been doing even before being assigned community service. And I did an interview with the author of a popular cookbook. The book was a hit, but it turned out the author had stolen some of the recipes from her mother-in-law's great-great-grandmother. But she in turn donated half her royalties to her mother-in-law's favorite charity, and they worked everything out amicably."

Riley frowned in thought. "Not exactly life-altering news, huh?"

Sounding defensive, Regina said, "I have done a few more critical pieces."

"Like?"

"About a month earlier I'd covered a dog shelter that wasn't treating the animals right. They were crowded, dirty, underfed, and naturally I was outraged."

The mistreatment of animals would have outraged him, as well, but Regina was so softhearted, so genuine, he could imagine how emotional she'd gotten over the whole thing.

"The article I did was small, but it ended up getting a lot of attention. The shelter got shut down and heavily fined. With the help of the paper, I spearheaded a campaign to find homes for all the dogs. We eventually succeeded. I would have loved to have kept a few of them myself, but I had no hopes of getting my own home then, and a small apartment is no place for a dog."

Riley looked down at Butch. The dog peeked at him, turned his head to lick Riley's hand and stretched. Riley grinned. "Unless the dog is really small."

Regina smiled, too. "Look at him. He's already fond of you."

Hearing that special soft tone in her voice gave Riley an idea. He could get closer to her by getting closer to her dog. "He knows I respect him. But I imagine if I touched you right now, he'd go right back to bristling." Riley gave her a long, intimate look. "He's going to have to learn to share. But I'll be patient—with him and you."

Regina's lips parted. She caught her breath, then looked at his mouth.

Oh, she was begging to be kissed. Unable to resist, Riley slowly leaned toward her.

He ended up kissing the dog when Butch leaped up between them. He nipped at Riley's mouth and nose, making an awful racket.

"You ungrateful mutt." Mindful of his intentions, Riley kept his tone friendly instead of irritated. Seeing that no kissing would occur, the dog resettled himself against Riley and gave him a big-eyed innocent look.

Regina smothered a laugh. "How could anyone ever hurt an animal? I can't understand it. I don't regret what happened with the shelter, but afterward the owners showed a lot of animosity toward me. Of course, that's understandable because I started the ball rolling that eventually lost them their business. The thing is, unless they just wanted to harass me, they wouldn't make likely suspects because I don't have anything they'd want to steal."

Riley tried to let the pieces come together naturally in his mind, but he knew Regina was right. He was too personally involved. All he could think of was how she might have been hurt worse. "Is there anyone else you can think of who'd dislike you?"

"Why would anyone dislike me?"

That made him grin. "Why indeed? Any problems with the people you work with? Why did you move here?"

The careful way she masked her expression told him he'd hit a nerve. "I got along with almost everyone at work."

"*Almost* everyone?"

She folded her hands in her lap. "There was one guy who was pretty persistent in trying to get me to go out with him. The more I refused, the more hostile he got."

"You left because of him?"

"Partially. He started showing up at my place at odd hours, watching me all the time. But he wasn't a threat, just a pest. Mostly I left because I thought I might be safer here. I hate to admit to being a coward, but I got spooked. I'm not used to being hit—"

"Hell, I would hope not."

"—and when that man slugged me, that was more than enough for me. I had to wear sunglasses for a week before the bruise faded enough that I could hide it with makeup. So I quit my job, relocated here in Chester and got hired on with the local paper."

Wishing he could get his hands on not only the man who'd dared to strike her, but the weasel who'd hassled her at work, too, Riley shook his head. "And you still found yourself in trouble."

"Right. Unless, as the local police say, it's just a co-incidence. Maybe the fire was an accident."

Any time Riley thought of the damn fire, his guts cramped. "I don't think so, Red."

"You don't? Why?" And then she asked with suspicion, "Riley Moore, do you know something I don't know?"

Careful not to disturb the dog, he touched her cheek and gave her a tender smile. "I probably know lots of things you don't know, especially about dangerous situations. But specifically about the fire, no."

"Then why?"

"I dunno. It's just that the day of the fire, you were so jumpy, so nervous. Call it women's intuition, gut instinct, or just caution, you seemed to instinctively know something was about to happen."

"I did feel especially edgy. It felt like people were watching me."

"Maybe they were." After she'd left Riley that day, he couldn't shake off the picture of her nervousness. And her nervousness had become his, until he knew he wouldn't be able to relax for worrying about her. "That sort of thing can be felt," he murmured, more to himself than her.

"That's why you were trailing me?"

"Yeah." He'd known she was meeting Ethan to complete her interview, so he'd gone along, hanging back so that no one would notice him, but close enough to keep an eye out for her. When she'd met up with Rosie first and the two of them had gone to the firework's dealership, his edginess had increased. With good reason.

"I'm glad you followed me," she said. "If you hadn't, who knows what might have happened."

The alarms had brought Ethan to the scene, only he'd thought Rosie was still inside the building. He would have gone in after her if Riley hadn't held him back. Regina and Rosie would have been safe, but Ethan would have died.

Riley shook off the awful memories, then touched the corner of Regina's mouth. It looked tender and ripe and he wanted to kiss her, but first they had to talk. "I was feeling territorial even then." He watched her eyes darken and smiled to himself. "I wish like hell I'd gotten my hands on the bastard who carried you out. He's probably the one who stole your camera."

"Likely, since I'd taken some good photos of the fire hazards. If only I'd realized how serious those hazards were, I could have saved poor Ethan a terrible scare."

"And me as well."

"You?"

"Damn right." The picture of her sitting on the curb, blood on her forehead, her eyes dazed, would stay with him for a lifetime. "I felt like I'd taken a kick to the stomach."

"You didn't look scared. Not like Ethan."

"I'd already found you, and though you were hurt, I knew you were going to be okay. Ethan thought Rosie was in the fire." And he'd been a madman, fighting to go inside after her even though it would have meant his own death. Once Rosie had shown up, having left the building on her own by an upstairs window in the back, Ethan had just collapsed. To this day, Ethan trembled when anyone mentioned the fire. Oh, he was still a fireman, still did his duty with fearless determination, but you didn't mention the fire that almost took Rosie from him.

Riley didn't ever want to be so afraid that he lost all reason and discipline. Which was why he was taking matters into his own hands. He didn't love Regina the way Ethan loved Rosie, but he liked her, he wanted her and for as long as he held a claim, he'd damn well keep her safe.

He dropped his hand. "Maybe I'm just buying into

your fears, but its possible you have a good reason to be afraid. I'm not willing to put it to chance."

She pressed back against the couch cushions. "You say that like it has some hidden meaning or something."

"It does." He stared at her hard, keeping her pinned in his gaze. "Regina, I don't want you by yourself until we figure out what's going on."

It took her a second to catch his meaning, then her eyes slanted his way in speculation. "You think you should stay with me?"

"If you move from the apartment, yes."

"No."

He went on as if she hadn't voiced the denial. "Here you're surrounded by people. Help is only a few feet away and anyone could hear you through the thin walls. In a house, you'd be all alone."

Her shoulders straightened. "I'm a big girl, Riley. I'll be extra careful. But I won't—"

"You can't be careful enough. Do you intend to be home before dark every day? And what does it even matter when by your own admission, you've been attacked during the day? You can't imagine how many ways an intruder can get into your house without you even knowing."

Her slim brows pulled down.

"What if someone doesn't want to steal from you at all? What if someone just wants revenge?"

She pushed to her feet to pace away. Riley noticed her hands had curled into fists at her sides, evidence that she'd had the same worry. "Stop it. You're trying to scare me."

Riley set the dog beside him and stepped up behind her. "Bullshit. I *am* scaring you. And you know why,

Red? Because you're smart enough to know I'm right."
He clasped her upper arms and pulled her back against
his chest. Her hair smelled sweet. *She* smelled sweet.
And soft and female and delicate. She demolished his
control and intentions without even trying.

Riley pressed his jaw against her temple, and in a
roughened voice, said, "Will you check every room,
every closet, under every bed and in every corner each
night when you first go in? What will you do if you
find someone, crouching in the dark, waiting for you?"

Jerking around to face him, she said again, *"Stop
it."*

His hands closed over her shoulders and he brought
her to her tiptoes. "The hell I will. You say the threat is
real. I believe you. So don't be dumb, Regina."

"What am I supposed to do?" She was so shaken,
she practically wailed, then thumped him solidly on
the chest. "Hide? Stop living? I have work and friends
and errands…"

He caressed her tense shoulders. "Let me help."

"By moving in?" She shook her head. "No, I won't
do that. It wouldn't be—"

"Proper? Screw proper. Who's going to know besides our friends?" She started to walk away from him
and Riley crushed her close. Her eyes flared. "Im-
proper beats the hell out of dead any day."

The dog started barking, anxiously looking for a
way off the couch. But he was too small to try jumping down.

"You're upsetting my dog."

"Misery loves company." He kissed her, hard at
first, but when she went immobile, then soft and sweet
against him, he gentled. Her hands curled against his

chest, telling him she liked the kiss almost as much as he did. He caught her face, held her still while he sank his tongue in. Her heartbeat pounded against his chest, her soft moan vibrated between them.

Riley carefully pulled back. Her eyes stayed closed, her lips parted. "Listen to me, Red. I'll do everything I can to figure this out before you're due to move. I swear it. But I don't want you living alone."

Her eyelashes fluttered, lifted. Slowly, comprehension dawned and she looked beyond him, then stepped away to scoop up the dog. With her back to Riley, she went about soothing Butch. "If you're that close, you know what will happen."

"We'll sleep together." He crossed his arms over his chest, anxious for it to happen, wondering if she'd admit it.

"Every time you touch me, I forget who I am."

"Meaning?"

"Meaning I'm not the type to get carried away with the moment, but when you're kissing me, it doesn't seem to matter."

She would be ready, more than ready, by the time he got her in bed. He'd see to it. "It's going to happen no matter what, Red. You know that."

She swallowed, then nodded. "I know." She looked none too pleased with that admission, making Riley frown.

A real gentleman would have told her not to worry about it, that he'd control himself, protect her. He wasn't that much of a gentleman, and he wanted her too much to start playing one now. "We'll go slow." As slow as he could manage, considering he'd held himself at bay for weeks already.

She walked over to the balcony doors and looked out. "I'm sorry. I don't mean to be…coy. It's just that I can't be cavalier about sex."

Her honesty was refreshing, something he hadn't expected. "You don't need to apologize to me for speaking your mind. But we're both adults, both uninvolved." When she didn't look at him, he said, "I don't mean to push you…"

Her laugh sounded strained. "That's all you do is push."

His smile caught him by surprise. "For your safety, yeah. But I'm not cavalier about sex, either. No one in their right mind is these days."

"Then I know a lot of men not in their right mind."

He wouldn't think about her with other men. It'd make him nuts. But he could be honest in return. "I can't promise not to touch you, Red, because I will."

Her shoulders lifted on a deep breath. She waited, anxious and still.

Seeing her response, Riley took two steps closer. "Is it worth your safety? Is avoiding me worth risking your life?" And because he knew she already loved her little dog, he pressed her, saying, "Is it worth risking Butch's life?"

He waited, and finally she turned. She looked sad, resigned. "No. I tried ignoring the threat. I tried to believe it was all coincidence like everyone said. I wanted to just go on with my life, keep doing what I always did, keep working." She shook her head and said in a nearly soundless whisper, "I almost got Rosie killed."

Riley knew she still felt guilty for allowing Rosie to be involved, even though everyone knew Rosie did just as she pleased. Ethan couldn't control her, so it was for certain that Regina would never sway Rosie from something she chose to do.

"I know the risks now, but the thing is, Riley, I can't just hide away. I love my job and I won't give it up. Yet, that's when a lot of things seem to happen. Out of control cars, purse snatchers…"

"I have an idea about that, too." A stupid idea, one he was sure to regret, but damn it, he had to be certain she was safe. "You wanted to interview me."

Sudden excitement lit her eyes. Both she and the dog stared at him, she with delighted surprise, Butch with mere curiosity.

After clearing his throat, Riley forged on. "Well, here's your chance. I'm on vacation for the next two weeks. While you finish up any current assignments, I'll accompany you—and no, there's no negotiating on that point, not if you want to interview me next."

"That's blackmail," she pointed out, but she didn't sound too upset about it.

"Take it or leave it."

For three heart-stopping seconds she hesitated. Her slow smile gave him warning. "I'll take it."

Already dreading it, Riley nodded. She sounded enthusiastic enough to make his stomach clench. "During the evening we'll work on your training. I want you to have at the very least a basic understanding of self-defense. While you're still in the apartment, I'll check into the things that've happened to you to see if I can turn up anything."

"But hasn't it been too long?"

"Maybe. But maybe not. Cops file all their reports, so I'll check through that and see if anything jumps out at me. Back when things first happened, they were looking at each incident with the thought that you were a hysterical woman. I'll look with the thought that you're in danger. Two very different perspectives."

She licked her lips. "It happened in Cincinnati, not Chester."

"Don't worry. I'll find what I need to get started."

Still she stood there.

Riley touched her cheek. "Try not to fret, okay? Everything will work out."

"And if you haven't found out anything when it's time for me to move?"

He'd have kissed her again, but Butch started a low rumbling, ears back, body poised to attack. The little dog had enough to get used to without worrying that Riley was accosting his new mistress. "Then you'll continue to stay with me."

"With you? But I thought you—"

"Intended to move in with you? No. My place is already secure. And look at it this way, you can use the time to get your new home up and running." And in the interim, he'd have her—in his home, under his protection and in his bed.

The setup worked for him.

Chapter 4

Butch didn't like sleeping alone.

Regina found that out after a long night of listening to pitiful howls that finally broke her down. At two in the morning she gave up, retrieved Butch from his pen in the warmest corner of her kitchen, and carried him to bed.

He did a reconnaissance of the perimeter, sniffing every corner of her bed, her pillow, the sheets, before crawling under the covers. She watched the lump move here and there, then finally settle close to her. He dug—*endlessly*. She had no idea what he thought he was doing, but he ignored her pleas to stop and finally curled up behind her knees. She couldn't move without making him grumble.

For a four-pound dog, he was sure bossy about his comfort.

At six, when her alarm went off, Butch scampered out, yawned hugely in her face, then wanted to play. When Regina only blinked at him, he reared back on his haunches, barked and nipped her on the nose. She groaned, which he took for a sign of life and started bouncing around the covers like a tiny rabbit. He could stop and start so fast, darting this way and that, it was comical. Even half-asleep, she grinned as he raced up to her, gripped the edge of her pillowcase in his teeth, and began tugging.

"Okay, okay." It was a sorry truth, but she wasn't a morning person. She'd tried over the years to become one, only because it seemed like the thing to do. Good, honest people went to bed at a decent hour and rose early to begin their day. They didn't lie around for hours, being lazy.

Well, she was decent and honest, but she just couldn't force herself to be alert first thing. It took her at least two hours and a pot of coffee to get her head together. Before that, she didn't want to face the world. And with the way she looked in the morning, she doubted the world wanted to face her.

Moving around in the dark, she made a quick trip to the bathroom, turned on the coffeepot, which she'd prepared the night before, and put Butch out on his lead so he could potty. Because the morning was damp that late July day, he finished in a flash.

With only a dim light on over the sink, she slumped at the table in her cozy cotton jammies, nursing her first steaming mug of caffeine. Butch curled in her lap, content just to be with her—until a knock sounded on her door.

She froze.

Butch did not.

In what she now considered typical Butch frenzy, he leaped from her lap and ran hell-bent for the door. He made so much noise, she knew any thoughts of ignoring her early-morning caller were shot. Through the peephole, she spied Riley standing impatiently in her hallway, and she ducked away as if he might see her, too. Good God. What was he doing at her door so early?

"Open up, Red. I can hear Butch, so I know you're up and about."

No. A thousand times no. Still plastered to the side of the door, her heart racing, she croaked, "What do you want?"

"You," he said with a discernable smile in his voice. "But I'll settle for conversation."

Eyes closing in mortification, she shook her head. "Not at six-thirty, Riley. Go away till eight." She could be ready by eight. It'd be rushing it since she usually didn't leave for work till eight-thirty, but under the circumstances— "Not happening, Red. Now open the door." And then he tacked on, "I have a gift for Butch."

"You do?" She chanced another peek out the peephole and saw that Riley held up a stuffed Chihuahua toy. It looked almost like Butch, but bigger and not as cute. She covered her face with her hands. The man had brought her dog a present. She groaned, undecided.

Beside her, Butch continued to encourage her with barks and jumps and circles. She pressed her forehead to the door. "If I let you in, will you not look at me till I've had a chance to get down the hall?"

Riley laughed. "Why?" And then in a throaty tone, "What are you wearing, Red?"

Regina looked down at herself. Sloppy, blue-flow-ered cotton pajamas hung on her body. Her loose, tan-gled hair fell in her face. Even without a mirror, she knew that her eyes were puffy and still heavy from sleep.

"I'm waiting."

This was ridiculous. Half her neighbors would hear him if she didn't do something quick. She flipped on the entry light, turned the locks and cracked the door open. "Riley?" she said in a harsh whisper.

"Yeah?"

"You can come in, but I mean it, don't you dare even think to look at me. I'm a mess and I don't like it when people see me a mess."

"All right, honey, calm down. I promise."

She could hear the laughter in his tone. "The door is unlocked, so just give me thirty seconds to—"

Behind her, the shattering of glass disturbed the early morning quiet.

Screeching, Regina whirled around to see the devas-tated ruins of her patio doors. Shards of glass glittered everywhere. "Oh my God." She snatched up Butch, who had tucked in his tail and darted behind her be-fore yapping hysterically.

Riley stormed in, moved her to the side and took in the mess in one sweeping glance.

"Close and lock this door, then call the cops." He tossed the stuffed toy dog on the couch, and sprinted across the floor, through the broken patio doors and, to her amazement, right over the balcony.

"Riley." They were only about eight feet up from the ground, but still… Regina slammed her door shut and started after him, but she was barefoot and there was

glass scattered everywhere, all over her floor, some atop her furniture. Her heart hammered so hard, it hurt.

Cautiously, she stepped up onto the couch, Butch clutched in her arms. "Ohmigod, ohmigod, damn you, Riley, ohmigod…" She stepped off the other end of the couch nearest to her kitchen. Being careful to avoid any sharp shards of glass, she went to the phone and dialed 9-1-1.

In less than two minutes that seemed like a lifetime, Riley was back. This time he climbed up and over the balcony railing. Regina didn't have a chance to worry about her appearance because he barely spared her a glance. "I need a flashlight. It's still too dark out there to see and I don't want to mess up any evidence."

Skin prickling with sick dread, Regina pointed to the middle of the floor. "It was a rock."

Riley nodded. "I know, honey. Where's a flashlight?"

Flashlight? She felt shocked, disoriented. She hadn't had near enough coffee.

"Regina?"

One deep breath, and she felt marginally more in control. "In my bedroom, in the nightstand drawer."

"Stay put." His booted feet crunched over the remains of her patio door. An early-morning breeze blew the curtains in. The blackness beyond the doors seemed fathomless, sending a chill down her spine.

Belatedly, Regina remembered what else was in her nightstand drawer. *Oh no.* Her heart dropped into her stomach and she started across the floor in a rush, the glass forgotten.

Riley reappeared. Not by look or deed did he acknowledge anything he might have uncovered beyond the flashlight. He crossed to her and handed her a housecoat and slippers.

"You okay?"

Maybe. "Yes."

He cupped the side of her face, his touch gentle and reassuring. "The cops should be here any second. Tell them I'm out back. I don't want to get shot by some overeager hero."

Shot! "Riley, wait." She closed her hand around his arm above his elbow. His muscles were bunched, thick with tension. To someone who didn't know him better, he might almost appear calm. But Regina noted the unfamiliar, killing rage in his blue eyes. He felt warm and strong and secure and she didn't want him to walk away from her.

As if he understood, he bent down to look her in the eyes and said with deadly calm, "It's okay, Red. I know what I'm doing. I want you and Butch to wait in the kitchen."

"No. Don't go out there."

Riley scrutinized her. "You should put on more coffee. The officers will appreciate it."

Coffee? That sort of made sense. At least, with her mind in a muddle, it did. "Oh. Right."

For one brief moment, his gaze moved over her, touching off a tidal wave of warmth. He paused at her mouth, her breasts, then shook his head in chagrin. "Be right back."

Butch squirmed to be let down, but she didn't dare, not with so much glass on the floor. A sort of strange numbness had set in. She blocked the kitchen off with his small pen, pulled on her robe and fuzzy slippers, and went about making more coffee by rote.

This time the knock on her door didn't startle her.

Holding Butch like a security blanket, his small warm body somehow comforting, she skirted the glass and made her way to the door again. Two officers in uniform greeted her. Young, fresh-faced and eager at the prospect of a crime, they looked the complete opposite of Riley. Regina wanted to groan.

Butch wanted to kill them both.

His rabid beast impersonation was especially realistic this time. Regina tried, but there was no shushing him, so she gave up.

At her invitation, the officers cautiously ventured inside, keeping their eyes on Butch. The first officer removed his hat, then nodded at the dog. "What is that?"

Here we go again, Regina thought. "My dog, Butch."

"What's wrong with him?"

"He doesn't like you." Regina closed the door behind them. "Would you like coffee?"

They looked at each other, then her. "Uh, sure." They had to speak loudly to be heard over Butch's furor. "Maybe after you tell us what happened here?"

"Oh." She looked behind her at the devastation. "A rock. Riley Moore is out back poking around with a flashlight. Don't shoot him."

"Riley?" The darker-haired officer lifted one brow. "Why's he here?"

"He was, uh…" Why had Riley dropped in? Oh yeah, a gift for the dog. "Visiting Butch."

"That right?" The two cops shared another look, this time of masculine comprehension.

Regina pulled herself together enough to fry them both with her censure. "Riley is a friend," she stated, emphasizing the last word. "He had just knocked on the door when the rock came crashing in."

At that moment, Riley opened the door behind them and stepped inside. His brows were down, his eyes glittering. "I thought I told you to lock this."

"I did, but then they arrived." She gestured at the officers and shrugged.

Riley glanced at both men. "Dermot, Lanny. Thanks for coming over."

The men looked like little boys next to Riley. Regina allowed herself a moment to appreciate the differences, then said again, "Coffee?"

Riley nodded. "Thanks, babe." He kissed her full on the mouth, annihilating her previous claims of friendship. "We'll be right there."

He wanted to dismiss her? Oh no. She squared her shoulders, but it wasn't easy with Butch putting on such a show.

Almost without thought, Riley took the dog from her. "Good dog." He stroked Butch's back, found just the right spot behind his big ears, and Butch magically quieted. He kept a narrowed gaze on the officers, but the awful racket ended.

Regina turned on her heel and stalked away, muttering under her breath about pigheaded males of both the human and animal variety. From her position in the kitchen, she could hear the men talking in muted tones.

Riley waited, giving the officers a chance to look around. The one he'd called Lanny shone a flashlight over the small balcony—the balcony Riley had jumped from—and shook his head before meandering out there. He came back in and looked around the floor at the broken glass.

"Better call someone to fix that window," Dermot said. "Damn vandals."

"The work of kids, no doubt," Lanny added. "No one supervises them anymore. In my day, my mother would have taken a broom to me for a prank like this."

By the time the officers entered the kitchen, Regina had four mugs out, silverware, a crystal sugar bowl and a matching pot of creamer. "Have a seat, please," she told them.

Lanny nodded. "Thanks." Then, apparently disappointed that he couldn't do more, he said, "I'll take a report, but whoever did this is long gone."

Riley leaned back in his seat, noticeably silent. He continued to stroke Butch who kept looking up at him adoringly, turning his head to get a new spot scratched.

Dermot doctored his coffee, took a long drink, then asked, "You didn't get hurt, did you? The rock didn't hit you?"

Regina shook her head. "No. I'm fine."

Dermot shook his head. "I'm sorry, Ms...?"

"Foxworth. Regina Foxworth."

"Right. You did the right thing calling us but unfortunately, there's not much we can do other than have a squad car drive by and keep an eye on things for the rest of the night."

Same old song, Regina thought. "I understand."

"Well, I don't." Riley blew out a sigh of disgust. "Neither of you went outside to look around the complex."

Dermot frowned at him. "For what? It was a rock."

Lanny nodded. "You know how it is, Riley. We get crap like this all the time."

"No, you don't. And even if you did, that's no excuse for not being thorough."

New tension filled the air. Tones and posture abruptly changed. Lanny was the first to speak up. "Look, Riley, I know you have more training, but—"

"But nothing. I went outside. I looked—just as you should have done. Someone was outside her window for about an hour, just watching."

Regina straightened in new alarm.

"Not a group of unruly kids, but one man. He's a patient son of a bitch, too, and I personally think he was waiting for her to be awake to throw that damn rock."

With sudden clarity, Regina said, "It was right after I turned the light on." She stared at Riley. "Before that, I'd been drinking my coffee in the dark."

"He probably thought it'd shake you up more to catch you when you first woke up." Riley glanced at Regina with an expression close to satisfaction. "Didn't rattle you too much though, did it, honey?"

He sounded teasing, which she didn't understand at all. She calmly sipped her coffee and hoped only she noticed how her hands shook. "No."

Riley smiled, a secret, intimate smile. Turning back to the two men, the smile disappeared to be replaced with a scowl. "If you'd checked, you'd know Ms. Foxworth has a recent history of threatening incidents. In light of that, I don't think anything, especially a rock through her window at dawn, should be taken lightly."

Lanny didn't like the criticism. "Sounds to me like you're personally involved here."

"I am."

Regina nearly choked on her coffee. Why didn't he

just take out an ad in the paper? He could tell more people that way.

"But that's irrelevant." Riley wasn't through lecturing. "What pisses me off the most is that neither of you did your job." He encompassed them both in a look.

Regina thought it might be a favorable time to intercede before Riley got too insulting. She pushed back her chair. "Good grief, Riley, have you had breakfast? Surely, a temper like that is wrought from hunger. Would you like some pancakes? Lanny, Dermot? I can put a batch together if you'd like."

Riley stared at her in disbelief. "You're not going to feed them."

"I am if they're hungry." Her chin lifted. "Pancakes would give you something to chew on besides two officers who are only trying to do their duty."

His expression darkened. "They're not doing it very well."

"It's my fault that I didn't mention the other incidents, not theirs."

"Victims get rattled and forget important details. An officer is supposed to know that and ask pertinent questions."

Regina sucked in a breath at the insult. "Are you saying I'm rattled?"

Dermot stood, interrupting the escalating argument. "So how'd you come to all these brilliant conclusions, Riley? That's what I want to know."

Almost in slow motion, his movements rigid and calculated, Riley came to his feet and handed a sleepy Butch to Regina. With his gaze on Dermot, he said, "I'll take pancakes. They'll be leaving—after I explain."

Seeing no hope for it, Regina stepped out of the line of fire.

Riley took a step closer to Dermot, which had the other man's eyes flaring a bit in alarm. "There's damn near a pack of cigarette butts below her window. Red doesn't smoke—"

"Red?"

Regina raised her hand. "He means me."

"Oh." Dermot cleared his throat, glanced at her hair. "Yeah, I guess that makes sense."

In a voice raised to regain attention, Riley continued. "—so they sure as hell aren't hers, but they were fresh, one still smoldering. You know what that means, Dermot?"

Again, he cleared his throat. "Uh, that someone was out there just a few moments ago?"

"There's also one set of prints in the ground. Big adult-size prints. There are no rocks in the apartment landscaping the size of the one now in her living room, so whoever threw it probably brought it with him, meaning this was premeditated, not just a last-minute bit of mischief."

Both officers looked dumbfounded and a little awed.

"Can you maybe get some prints off the rock?"

Riley shook his head. "To get prints, surfaces need to be smooth. Since the rock isn't, there's no point in checking it."

"So what have we got?"

"Speculation. When I stand outside, about twenty feet from the balcony, I can see right into her living room. I think he watched, and saw her light come on."

"I let the dog out before that."

Riley slued his gaze her way. "With a light?"

"Um, no."

Riley nodded in satisfaction. "You need a flood-light out there, Red. And you should never open your door in the dark."

Lanny put his hands on his hips and dropped his head forward. "Okay, so you're a big-shot crime scene tech." He looked up, eyes narrowed. "We're not."

"Learn." That one word fell like a ton of bricks, discomfiting both officers.

Silence throbbed in the kitchen, making Regina more edgy than ever. "I think I'll make those pancakes now."

"Make plenty. I'm starving." Riley didn't spare her a glance as he led both officers to the front door, where he gave them the information they needed to file a report. Regina could just make out the low drone of their voices.

Now wide-awake, she mixed up pancake batter with a vengeance. She thought of everything she now had on her to-do list: clean up glass, vacuum her furniture, have the glass replaced in her door… She probably needed to call into work because she'd surely be late.

Butch sat at her heels, staring up at her, just waiting for her to sit down again so he could reclaim her lap. Whenever she glanced at him, his eyes widened hopefully and he wagged his skinny tail in encouragement. Regina shook her head. "There won't be much sitting for me today, sweetie."

Riley strode back in just as she'd pulled out a skillet and set it on the stove top. He didn't stop at the table, though, or even slow down. Startled, Regina drew back as he stalked right up to her, his long legs carrying him quickly to her. He pulled her close and without hesitation, without warning, took her mouth with a surprising hunger that completely caught her off guard.

His big hands, hot and calloused, held her upper arms, straining her upward. His head was bent so that his mouth fit hers completely. His lips pressed hard, parting hers, and his tongue thrust in, deep and damp and insistent.

Regina hung in his grip, a little stunned, quickly warmed. Her heartbeat thundered in her ears. He changed position, gathering her to him with one arm tight around her waist so that his other hand could tangle in her hair, tipping her head farther back. He rubbed against her, groaned, then lifted his mouth enough for her to catch her breath.

Against her lips, he murmured, "Christ, you look good."

"Hmm?" With almost no effort, he aroused her to the point of incomprehension.

Damp, warm, openmouthed kisses were pressed to her throat, along her shoulder where the robe had opened and the loose neckline where her pajamas drooped...

Her pajamas.

"Riley!"

He held her head in his hands, brushed her cheeks with his thumbs. In a rushed voice, hoarse and low, he said, "You're beautiful."

Beautiful? Regina blinked over such an absurd comment. Her hair was a mess, more so now that he'd tunneled his fingers through it. Her eyes were sleep-heavy and she had not a single speck of makeup on. The pajamas were comfortably baggy, not in the least attractive. "I... I need to go get dressed."

Slowly, he shook his head. "No. I like you just how you are." He kissed her again before she could argue. This kiss was deeper, hotter. She was aware of so many things—the press of his strong fingers on her skull, keeping her immobile, the heat of his breath, the taste of him.

His tongue retreated, moved over her lips, then licked into her mouth again. When his hands released her head, she kept the kiss complete, unable to get enough of him. His tongue retreated, hers followed. His sank in again and she sucked at it.

She knew his hands were roving over her, not stroking her breasts as he had done before, so she didn't understand what he was doing—until her robe fell open and he pushed it aside.

Oh, but it was hard to think with Riley holding her so close, touching her in such remarkable ways. He smelled delicious this morning, like soap and the outdoors and like himself. He was so warm, the cotton of his T-shirt so soft over solid muscle. His callused fingertips slipped beneath the hem of her pajama top to trace the indentation of her waist, then higher, until he teased just beneath her breasts. He circled, glided over and under her nipples, not touching them but bringing her breasts to a tingly, almost acute sensitivity. She held her breath, wanting more, wanting everything.

In the next instant, his thumbs brushed up and over her nipples. The touch was so electric, so anticipated, she jolted against him, gasped, and her fingers bit into his upper arms, closing on rock-solid muscles.

Regina didn't want him ever to stop touching her; if anything, she wanted more and tried to tell him so by pressing closer with a soft moan. Though he hadn't touched her below the waist, her whole body sang with awareness. Her thighs trembled, her belly had filled with butterflies and a curling, undulating sensation of ripe pleasure expanded and retreated within her.

Riley removed his hands, then drew her head to his shoulder, rocking her a little, rubbing her back in a soothing, calming way.

She didn't understand. "Riley?"

"I have to stop, Red. When you agree to sleep with me, I want you to be totally clearheaded, so you won't have regrets."

Regina didn't know what he was muttering about. She pressed her nose into his throat and breathed in his warm male scent, filling herself up. She wanted to taste his skin, but knew that might not be wise.

Against her ear, Riley rumbled, "While you fix the pancakes, I'll clean up the glass and call someone to replace the door." His tongue touched her ear, traced the rim, dipped inside. Little shivers of excitement raced along her arms and nape and she almost melted. "After breakfast you can pack."

The fog thinned. "Pack?"

"Yeah." His hard hand drifted lower, all the way to the base of her spine. He pressed gently—and she felt his erection against her belly, long, hard.

Regina shoved back. "What do you mean, *pack?*"

As if she should have already understood, Riley held her face turned up to his so she couldn't miss his frown. His gaze bore into hers, insistent, unrelenting. "You can't stay here now."

When she still stared at him in confusion, his frown became a black scowl. "Red, someone is getting pretty bold. And if that doesn't alarm you, then look at Butch."

She glanced down at the dog. He had his tiny front paws crossed over Riley's big foot with his head resting on them. His big brown eyes stared up at her trustingly. He was so shaken, he hadn't even protested their intimacy.

"Do you really want to chance letting him outside to do his business again, knowing someone could be lurking there, that they might snatch him away or, worse, use him to upset you?"

She knew what he was saying, and her heart squeezed tight. *"No."* In a protective rush, Regina scooped him up and hugged him to her breasts. He twisted and rubbed against her, luxuriating in the human attention. She needed the comforting contact as much as her dog did.

"Look at him," Riley said, "he's still shaking."

Without removing her cheek from the dog's neck, she said, "He always shakes and you know it." She had a feeling Riley only used the dog as leverage, and still she had to admit he was right. She'd be heartsick if anything happened to him. He trusted her to keep him safe, to take care of him, and she intended to do just that.

"I have plenty of room." Riley watched her with a sort of cautious regard. "You'll be safer with me."

Regina looked past him, through the kitchen doorway. The sun was on the rise, a crimson ball that reflected like fire on every sharp, jagged shard of glass littering her once secure home. She chewed her lip in indecision, but no other option came to her. If she went with him, it wouldn't be just an agreement to share space, and she knew it. It'd be an agreement to start an affair.

Her heart pounding for an entirely different reason

now, she glanced at Riley, drew a breath, and said, "All right."

Riley encompassed both her and Butch in a bear hug.

Butch bit his nose.

Now that he'd gotten his way, Riley grinned like a rascal. "You really do look great in your pajamas and with your hair all loose and tangled." He fingered one long curl. "Sexy as hell."

Heat rushed up her neck to warm her face. She turned her back on Riley and set the dog down. "I didn't even realize…"

"You were rattled, just as I said."

Regina wanted to groan. She was *still* rattled. "I can't believe I sat there in front of those men…"

"They thought you looked hot, too. I wonder if they think we've been sleeping together."

She slanted him a sharp look. "You tried hard enough to give them that impression."

"No choice. With them both eyeing you, I had to stake a claim." Totally unrepentant, he kissed her ear again and squeezed her waist. "I didn't want them getting any ideas about pursuing you."

Feeling like a fool, Regina smoothed her hair and retied the belt of her robe. "I guess I ought to call work since it looks like I'll be late." She picked up the receiver.

"Go ahead." Riley's blue eyes twinkled with teasing. "While you do that, I think I'll just go put the flashlight back in your nightstand—"

Regina whipped around so fast she almost fell. She grabbed Riley by the back of the shirt. "No."

He cocked a brow. "No?"

She dropped her hands, dusting them nervously across her thighs. "That is, I'll do it." She snatched the flashlight away from him. "You should call about the door."

"Right." And then with feigned confusion, he said, "But I thought you were going to call work."

The unholy grin gave him away, and her temper ignited. "You snooped in my drawer, didn't you?"

"Snooped? Now why would I do that, Red? What are you hiding in there?"

Regina swatted at him, embarrassed, irritated. "You had no right." In a snit, she went past him, stepping over the dog's pen and marching toward her bedroom. Glass crunched beneath her slippers, but she barely noticed.

Riley was right on her heels. "The *Kama Sutra,* Red? That's a little dated, isn't it?" His teasing voice grated along her nerves. "But that other book…what was it called? Oh yeah. *Getting the Most Pleasure in Bed.* Now that's current, right?"

Stopping beside her bed, Regina pointed an imperious finger at the door. "Get out."

He didn't budge. "And no less than a dozen rubbers. Woman, what have you been planning?" He stepped closer, forcing her to back up until her legs hit the side of the mattress. "More importantly, any chance you were planning it with me?"

With sudden clarity, Regina knew he hadn't seen the photo. No, being typically male, he'd only noted the silly books and condoms. "No."

"No, what? You weren't planning anything with me?"

She shook her head, felt silly for going mute, and managed to say again, "No."

His smile turned smug. "I didn't really think so. After all, those condoms are smalls." And totally deadpan, "They'd never fit."

Regina's heart jumped into her throat. She licked suddenly dry lips. "No?"

He shook his head. "I'm just an average man, Regina."

"There's nothing average about you."

His slow smile nearly melted her heart. "Maybe you should wait until we've made love to make that judgment."

A tidal wave of awareness nearly took out her knees. They were in her bedroom, right next to her unmade bed. Her heart gave a hard thump, then tripped into double time.

Riley stepped closer, a grin playing about his mouth. "Such a pretty blush, Red." He looked at her bed, gave a small shake of his head, and all teasing evaporated. "So tell me, Red. What have you been planning, and with whom?"

No never. Not in a million years. "The books are just…curiosity."

"Curiosity about sex?"

It wasn't easy, but she gave a cavalier shrug. "About…variety." She knew about sex. She even knew about pleasure. But things didn't always go right, no matter how she tried. With an airy wave of her hand, she explained, "I bought the books and condoms months ago, when I was engaged."

"Engaged?"

His thunderous expression surprised her. "Yes."

"You were in love with someone?"

He said that like an accusation, confusing her even

more. Because he looked so red in the face, she decided to admit the truth. "No, I didn't love him. I thought I *could* love him, and I loved the idea of being married and starting a family…"

He'd grown so rigid, she rushed on to explain. "The engagement ended almost as soon as it began. I realized what a stupid move it was, and he made it plain he didn't love me and likely never would. I think he just used the engagement as a sham, a way to…"

"Get you into bed?"

It sounded so stupid, and she'd been so gullible, that she only shrugged. "The, um, condoms have never been opened. I just haven't had the nerve to throw them out. I didn't want anyone to see them in my garbage."

Slowly, Riley relaxed. His frown smoothed out, replaced by a tender expression that seemed so incongruous to the hard man he could be. "Wouldn't be proper, huh?"

"It's private, that's all."

He started to say more, but Butch gave an impatient howl from the kitchen.

Riley glanced that way, then back at her. "I'll get him." He touched her chin, lifted her face and pressed his mouth to hers for several heart-stopping moments. "You better get dressed before I forget my dubious code of honor and the fact that we have a lot to get done in the next couple of hours." He turned and went through the door.

The second he disappeared, Regina jerked the drawer open, took out the framed photograph and looked around for a good place to hide it. She'd just lifted her mattress, ready to shove it beneath, when Riley stepped back in with a wriggling Butch in his arms. He drew up short when he saw her, then his brows came down.

His gaze went from her guilty face to her hand, which she quickly stuck behind her back. "All right, Red. What are you up to now?"

Chapter 5

Riley watched as Regina jerked the framed photo behind her back. Green eyes wide and innocent, she said, "It's nothing."

"Right." He strode forward, watched her quickly back up and move around the bed to the other side, and his suspicions grew. He set the dog on the mattress. Butch ran to Regina, came up on his hind legs and begged to be held.

Without taking her gaze off Riley, she caught the dog up one-handed. "If you'll leave, I'll get dressed."

Riley crossed his arms over his chest, not about to oblige her. "I'm damn curious, Red, what's worth hiding from me when I already saw the dirty books and rubbers."

Her jaw firmed. "They're not *dirty* books, they're educational."

"Uh-huh."

"And it's none of your business."

"Someone is trying to hurt you. Everything is my business."

Her cheeks colored. "This is…personal. Nothing that anyone else would care about."

"You don't trust me."

"Of course I do."

"Then let me see."

"Riley."

She wailed his name, making him smile. Stalking her, he started around the bed. She took one step back, then planted her feet and glared. Butch licked her chin in commiseration. Absently, she patted his back.

She was such an affectionate woman, so soft and gentle. It didn't take much to make her blush—a smile from him, a touch and her cheeks turned pink. The more he was with her the more he wanted her, and the more he wanted to know all her secrets. She'd kept parts of herself away from him, her engagement, her insecurities…but no more.

He stopped right in front of her and held out his hand.

She shook her head in exasperation. "This is stupid."

Riley waited.

Finally, with no graciousness, she slapped the picture frame into his hand. His curiosity keen, Riley turned it over, and was met with the charismatic smile on Senator Welling's face. Riley decided it must be the photo she took in the park, given the fountain beside him and the large trees behind him. Regina had written at the bottom of the photo, *Senator Xavier Welling,* along with the date of the photo.

The senator was easily in his mid-fifties. He was

tall, gray-haired and aristocratic. In order to always make a good public appearance, he'd kept in shape. He had no paunch and his shoulders were still wide from his college football days.

Riley saw red. Through stiff lips, he said, "You keep a picture of the senator beside your bed?" And then with jealousy pricking his temper, he added, "Next to the goddamned *Kama Sutra?*"

Regina drew herself up. "Don't raise your voice to me."

It wasn't easy, but Riley reined in his temper. He tossed the picture onto the bed. "What the hell does it mean?"

"What does what mean?"

"Don't look so confused, Red. You've got his picture in your nightstand drawer, next to your bed, with books on sex and a load of rubbers." Hell, just saying it made him madder. "You got the hots for him?"

She gasped so hard, Butch started to howl again. She absently stroked him. "Of course not. He's a wonderful, respectable man with a wife he loves and a family he cherishes."

"Don't make me puke. He's a politician, first and foremost."

Regina went on tiptoes to poke him in the chest. "Yes, he's a politician. A wonderful senator. He's fought hard for the health and safety of children. He supports local law enforcement. He's won numerous awards and honors for leadership and—"

Riley turned his back on her. "Jesus, you're besotted."

Using her free hand, she caught the back of his shirt. "I am not," she all but shouted. "Senator Welling is an inspiration. I admire him, just as I admire his family and his aspirations and his beliefs." And then, in a smaller voice filled with vulnerability, she said, "I admire everything he stands for."

Riley turned to stare at her, something in her tone touching deep inside him. "Just what does he stand for, Regina?"

Still disgruntled, Regina chewed her lip, not looking at him. "Family. Community. Everything that's good. When you see him campaigning with his wife and kids, you just know that's how it *should* be, all of them smiling, happy, secure." She lifted her gaze to meet Riley's. "I see them together and I know it can happen, because it's right there, live, real."

Riley didn't know how real a politician's public persona might be, but he could tell Regina believed in it. When she'd talked of her family, she'd done so with very little emotion. He'd found that strange, but hadn't pondered it long, not when most of his thoughts centered on carnal activities.

Feeling like a complete bastard, Riley pulled her into his arms. Butch wiggled until he was up between their faces, making sure no kissing would occur. But Riley felt content just to hold her. At least for now.

"I'm sorry."

Against his chest, she murmured, "For what?"

"For prying. And for not understanding." Keeping one hand on Butch so he wouldn't fall, Riley stroked Regina's back. He wished he could touch her bare silky skin again, but he didn't dare. It had been a close thing in the kitchen, his control severely tested. Only the fact that he knew damn good and well she wasn't thinking straight had kept him from laying her across the kitchen table. She'd been ready, damn it, whether she wanted to admit it or not.

"I guess it's okay," she said while rubbing her cheek against him, setting him on fire again. "It's not a secret that I admire the senator and what he stands for."

"Looks can be deceiving, you know."

She shook her head. "Being a politician does not automatically make him a fraud, Riley."

"No. But the world is filled with cheats and liars, people you'd bet on in a pinch, who turn out to be more unscrupulous than you ever could have imagined."

Leaning back, she looked at him thoughtfully. "Have you known people like that?"

He skirted that question by stating the obvious. "I'm a cop, Red. I see the worst of mankind all the time."

Her hand smoothed over his chest. She couldn't know how the innocent touch inflamed him. If she did, she wouldn't now be looking at him with so much understanding. "You deal with that element of life. But Senator Welling is just the opposite. He's part of the good team, Riley."

Riley wanted to shake her for her naiveté. He knew firsthand how difficult it was to read the people you cared about. Blind trust was never a good thing, but since he wanted it from Regina, he didn't say so.

Riley tucked a long curl behind her ear. "Can I ask you something, honey?"

She laughed.

"What?" He held her away so he could better see her face.

"You're so funny, Riley. Demanding one minute, requesting the next."

"I'm glad you're amused." He smiled, too. "So is it all right?"

"Sure. At this rate, I won't have any secrets left at all."

That'd suit him just fine. He intended to make her his, but never again would he be made the fool. Knowing everything about her would be a safeguard against unhappy surprises.

He released her and she sat on the bed. Butch circled her lap, then nudged his way beneath her housecoat so he could curl up against her stomach. She tucked him in before looking at Riley in inquiry.

Riley settled himself beside her. "Who footed the bill when your parents died?" If she'd been the only one responsible, it'd help explain her need for doing things right, to always be prepared and proper.

She appeared confused by the question. "I did what I could, but I didn't have enough money to make a huge difference in their care. What I had to give wasn't enough, so instead I spent days researching ways to get them the help they needed. It's wasn't easy. That's one of the things about Senator Welling. His health benefit programs would have done my parents a world of good."

Riley did not want to talk about the damned senator. "What about your brother? Did he help out?"

"I told you, he's just like them. I had to loan him money to buy a suit so he'd have something decent to wear to the funerals."

Damn, that meant she alone had had the burden of her parents' care. "Loan—or give?"

She shrugged, which was all the answer Riley

needed. "What about your fiancé? What happened there?"

Hedging that question, she asked, "Just who is the reporter here, Riley? Me or you?"

With a straight face, Riley said, "I just wondered if he could possibly be the one bothering you now." He spoke the truth, but it wasn't the only reason he asked. Possessiveness had a lot to do with his interest, too.

"Oh. No, he didn't help with my parents. Our engagement was after their deaths. And, no, it's not him."

"How do you know for sure?"

She untangled a grouchy Butch from her lap and pushed to her feet. "Trust me. He has no reason to hold a grudge."

Riley took the dog from her. He immediately rooted underneath Riley's shirt, circled into a small ball, and sighed himself back to sleep. Riley looked down at the lump where his flat abdomen used to be, shook his head, and put one hand over the dog. "Men see things differently than women. Maybe your take on the breakup isn't the same as his."

Regina rubbed her head. "It's not. But that has nothing to do with anything."

Her reluctance to talk about the other man couldn't have been more plain. It nettled Riley. "So who did the breaking up, you or him?"

"I did, but he didn't mind."

"How could he not mind? That doesn't make any sense. If he'd asked you to marry him—"

"He didn't want me, all right?" She threw up her hands. "There. Happy? He called me a prude and said I was unappealing. He wanted me to change myself and

I can't do that, and he said that no man would want me, especially in bed, and so I *left*. End of story."

Stunned speechless, Riley watched her storm out of the room.

For long minutes after, he remained on the bed, soothing Butch who had gone a little frantic at Regina's raised voice. He'd crawled up Riley's chest, grumbling and growling, then poked his head out the neck of the shirt, just beneath Riley's chin. "Her fiancé sounds like a complete ass, doesn't he, Butch?"

Butch whined.

"I wonder, is that why she bought the books? Had she already realized that things weren't going well between them? Not that I'm sorry to hear it, because if she hadn't, she might have married him."

Butch whined a little louder.

"I agree." Riley had to take off his shirt to get Butch free. "Does she still love the guy, do you think?"

Butch had no answer.

When Riley entered the kitchen, Regina was on the phone with her editor, explaining about the glass. She didn't look at Riley, and after she hung up, she went past him to the living room.

"I won't be going in today at all. Most of the work I need to do for the rest of my assignment can be handled on the phone and typed up on my computer." She paused. "Is it okay if I bring my computer?"

Riley followed behind her, cautious of her new mood. "You can bring anything you want."

"Thank you." She pulled out a phone book from the closet and carried it back to the kitchen.

"What are you doing?"

"Looking up numbers for glass replacement. I want this fixed before the evening."

Riley followed her. "I'll take care of that."

"You said that half an hour ago."

"This time I mean it." He wrested the book out of her hands and plunked Butch into her arms. The poor dog had been passed around a lot that morning. "Go shower and pack whatever clothes you need right away. I'll call for the door replacement, take you to my place, then come back here and get your computer and any other stuff you need. All right?"

"I am not helpless."

"Far from it." He tried a smile that she didn't return. "C'mon, Red. You look stressed and tired and I want to take care of you just a little, okay?"

She stared up at him for long moments. "I'll finish up my work on this current piece today."

The swift change of topic threw him. "Great."

"That means tomorrow, or even later tonight, I can start my interview on you."

His smile slipped a little, but he managed to hang on to it. "Okay."

"I have so many questions, it might take a few... days."

His smile felt like a grimace. "I did agree."

"Yes, you did." She handed Butch back to him. "Can you keep an eye on him while I shower and dress? Thank you."

Both Riley and Butch watched her leave yet again, her walk a little more sassy this time. Oh, she wanted payback with the interrogation, he could tell. Riley wondered how many answers he could give without telling things he never wanted to reveal? It'd be tricky, but he could handle it.

If all else failed, he'd distract her with a kiss—and more. After all, he'd given her fair warning of what to expect. And still she'd agreed.

That thought brought back his smile in full force. In the end, he'd get what he wanted most: Regina. That made the rest worthwhile.

"Well, this answers one question, doesn't it?" Regina stated.

Riley had parked his truck behind her Escort in his allotted garage space, then joined her. She stood between the car and the opened door, staring at his apartment.

Unlike most women Riley knew, Regina hadn't lingered in the shower. Butch, unwilling to wait in the kitchen while Riley cleaned up the glass, had howled endlessly until Regina stuck her head out the bathroom door and asked Riley to hand him to her. Butch had curled up on a towel and slept while she quickly showered and dressed in white slacks and a sleeveless cotton sweater and sandals. With her long red hair restrained in a French braid, minimal makeup and small earrings, she looked classy and sexy combined.

A large satchel with files and notes from her current project was slung over her arm. Riley hadn't realized that she gathered so much info just for one story. And since she'd told him her current article was about the silly talent show held by a local television station in the mall, he was doubly surprised.

They'd both driven so Regina would have her car handy. Not that he wanted her out driving around alone until he figured out what was going on. But neither did he want her to feel trapped or overly dependent on him. He knew she would rebel over that and he'd lose her before he could get her used to being with him.

Butch was on a thin leash, so Riley lifted him out of the car, then took Regina's elbow to move her forward. He closed her car door. "You disappointed?"

"That you don't have your own house?" She glanced at him over her shoulder and smiled. "No, of course not." Then she asked, "But why don't you?"

Riley shook his head. Before meeting Regina, he'd thought he had enough of hearth and home to last him a lifetime. He said only, "This is easier. Less maintenance." He led her and Butch up the walkway. "I'll show you around, then unload your stuff."

All she'd brought this trip were a few changes of clothes, her bedding—because she claimed she needed her own pillow to sleep—Butch's belongings and the material for her current assignment. She'd packed up more stuff at the house and disconnected her computer, but Riley told her he'd get all of that when he returned to meet the glass repairmen. Everything else they could retrieve as needed.

Since his place was on the ground floor, it'd be more convenient for Butch. He only hoped Butch liked the big golden retriever next door, since they'd be sharing yard space. He unlocked the door and pushed it open for Regina to enter.

"Oh, Riley, this is very nice."

He watched her look around. Luckily, he was a tidy man, otherwise he couldn't imagine her reaction. She touched her hand to the arm of a brown leather sofa, glided her fingers over a marble tabletop. "Did you decorate yourself?"

"Yeah." At the time, he'd taken enjoyment in only pleasing himself, with no one else to consider. He hadn't expected ever again to want the approval of a woman. And Regina wasn't just any woman, but an immaculate one at that.

Only it looked as though Regina liked his choices. "There's only one bath, but we'll work that out." Maybe they could share the shower? He grinned, then covered that reaction by discussing the dog. "I'll hook a lead up for Butch so he can run a little more outside. Oh, and if you need me to pick up any groceries for you, just let me know. I tend to do a lot of fast food."

He tugged Butch inside and closed the door.

Butch's ears perked up with his first glimpse of the place, giving Riley warning. He leaned down to unleash the little rat. In a stern voice, his finger shaking in the dog's face, Riley said, "Now listen up, bud. No piddling on the furniture, okay?"

Rather than feeling intimidated, Butch snapped at his finger, making Riley grin. "I almost forgot, with all the excitement." He pulled the stuffed Chihuahua from his pocket and tossed it toward the middle of the room. Butch jerked about to watch the stuffed animal land, then he reared back on his haunches, did a bunny hop to where the floppy toy lay—and attacked.

Regina started laughing at his antics.

Riley had to admit it was pretty cute the way he shook the toy, threw it this way and that. For such a small dog, he made feral sounds. Then as if expecting it to follow, Butch went into flight. It was so funny to watch him run. Somehow he managed to streamline himself, laying his ears back, tucking in his tail and dashing around furniture and corners so fast he was practically a blur.

His tiny feet made a distinct patter on the wooden floor. He slid around the corner, took a second to get some traction, and was off again.

Regina watched in wonder. "He doesn't know your place yet. How can he be sure he won't run into anything?"

Riley slung his arm around her shoulders, already enjoying having her in his home. "Men have great reflexes."

She cocked a brow at him. "And women don't?"

"Some women do." He pinched her chin, tipped up her face and kissed her mouth. "We'll be working on yours, remember?"

A knock sounded on his door. Regina pulled back in surprise, but Riley just shook his head. He opened the door and there stood Ethan, Rosie, Harris and Buck.

As usual, Rosie was pinned up against Ethan's side, and she appeared most comfortable there.

Harris, a firefighter at the same station as Ethan, looked fatigued, a good indicator that he'd recently come off his shift. Though Riley knew he'd have showered, the scent of smoke still clung to him. He pushed his black hair back with a hand and lounged against the door frame, his blue eyes tired and a little red.

Riley gave him the critical once-over. "Hell, Harris, you look like you should be in bed."

Harris yawned hugely. "Just left bed, actually." His satisfied grin said he'd just left a woman, also.

Riley grunted. "Maybe you should have tried sleeping."

"Did that—*after*. But last night was a bitch so I'm still sluggish."

Ethan nodded. "Had a pileup on the expressway. Three cars caught fire. No one died, thank God, but we worked our asses off."

Buck threw a thick, muscular arm around Harris, nearly knocking him off balance. Being the owner of a lumberyard and used to daily physical labor kept Buck in prime shape and made him the bulkier one in the group. Like Harris, Buck was single and enjoyed playing the field.

Still holding Harris, Buck pulled off a ball cap and scratched his head, further messing his brown hair. Green eyes alight with laughter, he said, "Harris never minds toiling through the night, 'cuz the ladies like to fawn all over him the next day."

"Jealous?" Harris asked.

"Naw." Then with a huge grin and a feigned yawn, he said, "I just got out of bed myself."

Riley laughed and held the door wide open. They all piled in, and Rosie was about to say "hi" when Butch flew around the corner, skidded to a halt, and went into a rampage of spitting Chihuahua fury.

Ethan tucked Rosie close. "What the hell?"

Rosie said, "Oh, it's so cute!"

Harris shrank behind Buck, pretending to cower. "Cute? What is it?"

"Whatever it is," Buck added, "it's demonic."

Riley caught Regina's scowl and laughed. "You might as well get used to hearing that, Red. It seems to be the typical response to your dog."

Buck and Harris said in unison, "Dog? You're kidding, right?"

Riley lifted Butch, who seemed to take extreme dislike to Ethan holding his wife. Most of his ire was directed at him.

"What did I do?" he asked

Rosie laughed, saying, "What haven't you done?"

"Hey." Riley held the dog eye level. "They're friends. You can relax now."

But Butch wasn't having it. Rosie dared to try to pet him and Butch practically went over Riley's shoulder in his effort to escape her. As long as he thought he had everyone cornered, he was as brave as a German shepherd, but let someone reach for him and he tucked his tail quick enough.

Regina took her dog. "He's still getting used to me and Riley. He's…shy."

Buck forced Harris to turn him loose. "Yeah? Is that what you call it?"

"I'd call it rabid," Ethan said.

Now that he was close to Regina, Butch quieted and started to lick her chin. Harris curled his lip. "That's disgusting."

"I think he's adorable."

Harris nudged Buck. "Yeah, Rosie, but you think Ethan is adorable, too, so you obviously have lousy taste."

Riley attempted to get things back on track. "Now that you're here I can explain."

Regina froze. "Explain what?"

"What's going on, of course." He knew she wouldn't like it, but he thought the extra backup wouldn't hurt. "They're friends, Red. And I want Harris and Buck to help me move some of your stuff."

Ethan sent his wife a look, then stared at Riley. "She's moving in with you?"

"Temporarily," Regina rushed to clarify.

At the same time, Riley said, "She is."

Rosie just grinned. "This is great. But what about your house?"

"As soon as it's mine, I'll—"

"As soon as it's *safe,* she'll move in there." Riley didn't want to think about her being on her own like that until he knew for certain that no one would hurt her. "Rosie, why don't you help Red make up the guest bed?" Riley suggested, and saw Harris and Buck start elbowing each other again. "And I'll get these goons to lend a hand unloading."

Rosie frowned. "Why can't Harris help her make the bed? I'd rather hear the scoop."

Harris stepped forward eagerly, eyebrows bobbing. "Oh yeah, I'll help her—"

Riley hauled him back with a hand in his collar. "I need to talk to you." Then to Rosie, "Regina can tell you what's going on."

"Yeah, well, somehow I think I'd hear a different version from you. Guys always have a different version."

Regina looked pained. "Really, I can make the bed myself and there's not that much to carry in."

Ethan grabbed his wife and kissed her. It wasn't a quick kiss or a timid one. Against her mouth, he teased, "Riley's suffering here, sweetheart. Be agreeable for once, will you?"

Dreamy eyed, Rosie said, "I'm agreeable every night."

Ethan touched her cheek and grinned. "Yes, you are."

Harris rolled his eyes. "God, will the honeymoon never end?"

In a quick mood switch, Rosie reached around her husband and shoved Harris, who fell into Buck. In a huff, she turned and grabbed Regina's arm. "Come on. Let them do the grunt work. You'll probably tell it right where Riley will only beat his chest and play Neanderthal."

That observation had Regina laughing. Butch gave the men a bark of farewell as the women disappeared around the corner.

"Okay," Ethan said, now that they were alone. "What's going on?"

"Outside. I don't want Regina to hear me."

Harris said, "Why is it the second a guy starts really caring about a woman, he complicates things?"

Buck nodded. "It becomes one big soap opera, doesn't it?"

Ethan and Riley hauled them out the door. At Regina's car, Riley said, "Someone is trying to hurt her, or scare her. I'm not sure which, and I don't know why."

Harris leaned on her fender. "No shit?"

"She okay?" Buck asked.

"Yeah. She's hanging in there. Regina is tougher than she looks."

Harris snorted, and when Riley glared at him, he held up his hands in surrender. "Hey, I wasn't casting aspersions on the lady. It's just hard to imagine anything tough about her."

Buck grinned, adding fuel to the fire. "She is a rather soft-looking woman, huh?"

Ethan rolled his eyes. "Quit baiting him, you two. He's got enough on his mind as it is."

All humor vanished when Riley said, "Someone threw a rock through her patio doors this morning." Seeing that he now had their undivided attention, he added, "And that's not all." As quickly as possible, Riley explained what had been happening.

"Could be coincidence," Ethan pointed out. "But I gather by your expression, you don't think so."

"No."

"Any ideas?" Harris asked.

"I'm going to check into her old fiancé. Things ended only a few months ago."

"Regina was engaged?" Ethan looked startled by that disclosure.

"Yeah, and there's some idiot who made a pest of himself at her old job. I'll get names from her tonight." Riley also intended to talk to Senator Welling. That might be a little more difficult to accomplish, but if Welling had seen anything the day her car was run off the road, or if he'd noticed anything suspicious at the park, Riley wanted to know about it. The senator had an appearance scheduled at a ceremony for the historical society. Should be easy enough to grab a few words with him then.

"And in the meantime?" Ethan asked.

"I don't want her alone." Which was the main reason he'd gathered his friends together. He couldn't be with her 24/7, so he'd count on them to help out. "For right now, I figured Rosie could stay here with her while we go get some of her things. Plus, I don't want repairmen in her apartment without supervision. They're due in about an hour."

"If it's not safe, then I don't want Rosie involved."

Riley sent his best friend a long look. "Would I put Rosie in any danger?"

"I wouldn't think so."

"Then relax. They're safe enough here, especially since no one knows Red is staying with me."

Ethan scrutinized Riley. "She says it's temporary."

Riley drew a breath. "For now." And then as he walked back to the apartment carrying Butch's pen and bed, he added, "But I'm working on it."

Chapter 6

The second Riley opened her apartment door, he felt the tension. With a raised hand, he shushed the men behind him and stepped silently inside. There was no noise, but the silence was thick, somehow alive. Automatically, Riley's gaze searched out every nook and corner, fast but thorough. He noted the unfamiliar shadow in the bedroom doorway. As he stared, it shifted the tiniest bit and all his senses went on alert.

He flattened his hand on Ethan's chest. In a nearly soundless voice, he ordered, "Stay here."

Ethan took exception to that with a muttered, "Like hell."

Unwilling to waste any time, Riley started into the living area. A floorboard squeaked beneath his foot, and in the next instant motion exploded around him. A crash sounded and a tall, dark man dressed all in black bolted out of the bedroom. In one fluid motion, he went through the patio doors and over the railing, much as Riley had earlier.

Without a second thought, Riley went after him.

Behind him, he heard Ethan yell, "Call the police," and then he was at the railing, cursing as Riley hit the ground. He landed in a crouch on the balls of his feet, took only a single moment to get his balance, and gave pursuit.

The man was several feet in front of him, but Riley was fast and more than a little determined. This could be the man who'd been terrorizing Regina but, either way, he'd been in her apartment where he didn't belong. Riley could easily take him apart with his bare hands—but he was a cop, and so he'd go by the law. Even if the restraint killed him.

When he'd almost reached the intruder, Riley didn't grab him with his hands. Instead, he kicked out, sweeping the man's legs out from under him.

The big man went down with a loud grunt of pain. Riley hit hard, too, jarring his bones but unmindful of any pain. He rolled and was atop the other man before the goon could regain his feet. Riley immobilized him by catching his legs with his own, then twisting the man's thick right arm up and back at a very unnatural angle. The man howled in pain. It wouldn't take much pressure to snap a bone or pull the arm from the shoulder socket, and with the way Riley felt, he was more than willing.

Another loud groan issued from his captive.

"Be still," Riley commanded, then he glanced up to see Buck and Harris standing at his side.

Buck curled his lip. "I'm not a cop, Riley. Want me to break something on him?"

The offer was so ludicrous coming from Buck—a man known for laughter, but never aggression—that Riley almost grinned. "If he moves, kick him in the teeth."

"Right." Buck planted his muscular legs apart in what appeared to be anticipation. His size twelve-and-a-half feet were encased in sturdy steel-toed boots.

Wearing a grimace, the intruder twisted to see Riley. "You're a cop?" he gritted out.

"That's right. But I'm off duty. Some uniforms will be here shortly to haul your ass downtown."

"Christ, man, you're breaking my arm."

Harris nodded. "He's right, Riley." He turned his head, contemplating the strange hold Riley had on him. "Looks like you might be breaking a leg, too."

"Don't tempt me." He nudged the guy. "What's your name?" When the man hesitated, Riley growled, "Say it, damn it. Don't make up a lie."

"Earl! My name's Earl."

"Earl what?"

Rather than answer, he groaned in agony.

"Just Earl, huh?" Approaching sirens split the air. Riley said, "Well, Earl, you want to tell me what you were doing in the apartment?"

Sweat beaded on the man's forehead. "Saw it was open. Just wanted to have a look around."

"Right. Let's try again. What were you looking for?"

"Nothing." His head dropped forward to the ground and he panted. "It's the truth, damn it."

"So you're just a regular, run-of-the-mill burglar? You weren't here earlier, tossing rocks?"

"Rocks? No."

Maintaining his hold on Earl's arm, Riley came to his feet and hauled the other man upright. Earl tried to jerk away, but only managed to cause himself more pain. "Buck, check his pockets."

Earl kicked and fought, prompting Riley to add a little more pressure. The man's back bowed with a rank curse.

Ethan showed up then. He looked far more disgruntled and angry than Riley. "What the hell are you doing, Riley?"

Buck dug in the man's pockets and produced a pack of cigarettes, loose change, and a knife. "Sorry, Riley, no wallet, no I.D."

"Shake out a cigarette."

Buck sent him a look. "It's a hell of a time to start smoking." He smacked the pack until one cigarette emerged, saying to Earl, "Nasty habit, bud. Smoking can kill you."

Earl tried to kick out at Buck and with little effort, Riley forced him to his knees.

Ethan crossed his arms over his chest. "The cops are here. Should you be abusing him that way?"

"Since he keeps fighting me, he's lucky I don't tear him to pieces."

As luck would have it, Dermot and Lanny rounded the corner. They stiffened when they caught the occupants of the scene. "Christ almighty, Riley. What the hell is going on?"

Riley forced the big man flat again, put a knee between his shoulder blades and said to Dermot, "Give me some cuffs."

Dermot rolled his eyes, but did as told. After the

restraints were in place, Riley did a quick search of his captive, but found no other weapons. He released Earl into Lanny's legal hands. "Read him his rights."

"I know my job, Riley. You want to tell me what the hell we're arresting him for?"

"Sure thing. He was in Red's apartment when I showed up." Riley handed Lanny the cigarettes. "And he smokes the same brand I found on the ground below her balcony."

"Well, I'll be damned. What'd he do inside? Did he steal anything?"

Indicating the contents of his pockets, which Buck still held, Riley said, "That's all he had on him, and I don't think the blade is Red's, so it must be his own. You can add concealed weapon to illegal entry. I think we interrupted things, but I've yet to have a look around inside. You can go on. I'll be down to the station in a little while." Then Riley thought to add, "Hang on to him, okay?"

Dermot grinned. "Judge Ryder is on a fishing trip, not due back till Monday. I'd say it's a safe bet we'll have him till then."

Lanny and Dermot each took an arm while Lanny started the familiar litany on rights. They led Earl to the cruiser. Riley watched, still tensed, until the big man was folded into the backseat and the door securely closed.

Then he became aware of the silence around him. He looked at Harris, who had his brows raised, Buck who grinned and Ethan who stared at Riley so long, Riley finally said, "What?"

"You're a regular savage, Riley, you know that?"

Riley shoved his way past his friend. "Screw you, Ethan."

Ethan laughed. Buck stepped up and drew Riley to a halt so he could squeeze his biceps. "Pure steel," he crowed to his friends. "Like a real-life action hero, he is."

Harris tucked his hands beneath his chin and said in a falsetto voice, "My hero."

Grumbling under his breath, Riley jerked free and went to the balcony. Damned idiots. When he jumped up and grabbed the railing, all three of his foolish friends started joking again. Riley did his best to ignore them as he swung a leg up and pulled himself over the railing. He noticed Ethan, Harris and Buck followed suit, climbing the balcony rather than taking the long walk around the complex to the front door.

Several neighbors were out, watching the proceedings with great curiosity. Once he'd regained his feet, Riley waved down to them. "A minor break-in, folks."

They looked skeptical.

Of course, Buck was still scaling the balcony and Harris had only one leg caught awkwardly over the top rail. Riley shook his head and went inside. When Ethan started to follow, Riley warned him off. "Stay put a minute, okay? I want to have a look around. There's less chance of anything being disturbed if it's just me."

"If you need anything, give a yell."

Riley went to the bedroom first. He knew better than to tamper with evidence or disrupt a crime scene, but this wouldn't be the first time he'd ignored his conscience to do what he thought was best.

In this case, they weren't dealing with a death. More important, Red's feelings were at stake.

If anything would embarrass her, he wanted to know about it and, if possible, spare her. His intentions were altruistic—as unselfish as they'd been the first time he'd broken his own code of honor.

He saw right off that her dresser drawers had been dumped. Lacy panties and bras littered the floor in haphazard disarray, looking like a flock of fallen butterflies. Her pajamas and T-shirts had also been dumped.

Everything from her dresser top had been shoved to the floor, including hair combs, jewelry and perfume. Items from her closet had been sloppily rearranged and her bedding pulled apart.

What really caught Riley's eye, though, were the damn rubbers tossed everywhere. Dragging a hand over his face, Riley considered the situation, but he gave in before he had time to really think it through. Rushing, he gathered up the condoms and stuffed them into his pockets. He had more than one reason for doing so.

If his friends saw them, they might think they were his and the teasing would be endless, considering the size of the damn things. In fact, he intended to dispose of them posthaste so he didn't get caught with them in his pockets. It would give him a reputation he'd never live down.

But the biggest reason was that Red would be appalled if anyone knew she had them. Obviously, they had nothing to do with whatever Earl—if that was even his real name, which Riley doubted—was looking for.

Her nightstand drawers were now empty. Riley looked around the carnage, but didn't see the photo of Welling or the damn books anywhere. Earl hadn't had them on him, and what would he want with them anyway? That had to mean that Red had taken them with her.

He didn't mind the books—hell, he'd be happy to read them with her. But the last thing he wanted in his home was Xavier Welling's smiling face. Especially since he knew Red saw the man as some sort of paragon of goodness, a damned representation of what men should be. If she expected him to measure up to a precisely staged public persona, she was sure to be let down.

Ethan said, "Everything okay, Riley?"

With the condoms out of sight, Riley called back, "Yeah. You can come in."

Ethan entered the room, followed by Harris and Buck. "Damn, someone is definitely looking for something."

Harris stared toward her underwear. Using only his pinkie, he lifted a teeny tiny thong of shimmery pale pink. "I thought redheads weren't supposed to wear pink."

Riley grabbed the garment from him and stuffed it in his pocket—with the condoms. Hell, it was hard enough for him picturing Red in the sexy bottoms. He'd be damned if he wanted Harris doing the same.

Buck propped his hands on his hips. "Do we clean this up or leave it?"

Riley shook his head. "I have a camera in my truck. I'll take some photos then we'll tidy up before Regina sees it. It'd only upset her."

Ethan crossed his arms over his chest. "All things considered, I want to give Rosie a call. We're going to be a while and I want to make sure she's okay."

"Tell her to get a list of groceries from Regina. I'll stop at the store on my way home."

Harris grinned. "Why, don't you just sound so domesticated?" He started to reach for a satin demibra, and Buck grabbed his arm, but he was laughing, too.

"Leave the unmentionables to Riley before he twists your arm behind your neck."

Riley glared at them both before heading out to his truck, but his thoughts soon left his goofy friends. He had a man in custody. He had Red in his apartment.

Things were moving right along.

Regina heard the front door opening and her heart shot into her throat. Jumping to her feet, she ran to greet Riley.

With his tongue hanging out, Butch kept pace, pretending they were in a race. She knew it was idiotic, knew that Ethan said Riley was fine, but she wanted to see him for herself, to be sure.

He'd just stepped inside the door, awkwardly holding his keys in one hand while juggling grocery bags with his other. Regina halted in front of him.

Riley glanced at her in surprise. "Hey, what's wrong?"

A little embarrassed but still anxious, Regina blurted, "I was worried."

His gaze lingered on her face, his mouth curled. "About me?"

"Yes. And don't be insulted. I know you can take care of yourself."

"And you still worried?"

She nodded, which made his expression warm all the more.

Without looking away from her, Riley kicked the door shut and shifted both bags into one arm. Reaching out, he snagged her close and his mouth brushed hers. "Thanks, Red. But you don't need to fret, okay?"

She sighed. He sounded like the idea was unheard of. "You aren't invincible, Riley. And Ethan called and told Rosie what happened and—"

"And I'm fine." He gave her a squeeze. His hand started down her back toward her bottom, then he looked beyond her. His hand stopped at the base of her spine and he nodded. "Hey, Rosie. Ethan's right behind me."

"I figured as much." She sauntered forward, grinning. "So, hero, how you doing?"

Riley rolled his eyes and allowed Regina to take one of the bags. Suddenly Butch let out a demanding, yodeling howl, and when Riley looked down at him, he came up on his hind legs, dancing in excitement.

"Well, what a greeting." Riley lifted the little dog to eye level. "Met at the door by a beautiful woman and a faithful Chihuahua. What more could a man ask for?"

Regina wanted to smack him. "Riley, please tell me you didn't tackle some maniac who broke into my apartment."

He winked and, still holding Butch close, walked around her to the kitchen. She looked at Rosie, who shrugged, then she stalked after him. *"Riley."*

"Yes, dear." He was in the kitchen, Butch over his shoulder while he unloaded groceries one-handed. "Since you cooked last night, I'll do the deed tonight. Steaks on the grill or spaghetti? They're my two specialties, my only specialties really, so I bought both.

Or we can go simple and just have sandwiches. What's your pleasure?"

Regina held on to her temper by a thin thread. She was in his house, and he wanted to help her. She drew a breath. "Do you or do you not have a man in custody?"

"Yeah, we do. Thing is, the bastard isn't talking. We don't even have his name yet. But, luckily, Judge Ryder is out fishing."

Regina shook her head in confusion. "So?"

"So this is a small town, not the big city. Things are done differently here. Ryder's been around forever because no one cares to run against him. Because of that, he feels comfortable taking off for days at a time when the weather looks right to catch a big bass." He winked at her. "The weather looks right."

"What does some judge fishing have to do with the guy who broke in?"

"He can't be arraigned until the judge comes back. That gives us more time to check him out. I have a gut feeling that once we turn him loose on bail, he'll disappear."

Nervousness made her voice tremble. She clasped her hands together tightly, trying to calm herself. "What are you holding him for?"

"Illegal entry and concealed weapon for starters. He ransacked your bedroom, honey, but he didn't steal anything and nothing was really damaged."

The ramifications hit her. "So he was looking for something."

"I'd say so. Whatever it is, he hadn't found it before we interrupted." Riley gave Butch an absent pat as he moved from the cabinet to the refrigerator. "The guys helped me clean up the mess."

The guys. Aware of Rosie lounging in the doorway, Regina eased closer. Her heart slammed in her chest and her palms were damp. "He, uh, trashed my bedroom?"

Riley turned toward her. After a long look, he leaned down and whispered near her ear, "Hey, it's all right, babe. I confiscated the rubbers before anyone could see."

Her relief was overwhelming. "Thank you."

His grin gave her fair warning. "Harris gathered up your panties. Sexy stuff." His gaze dipped down her body. "Makes me wonder what you're wearing right now."

Rosie cleared her throat. "It's rude to whisper in front of guests."

Riley straightened with a sigh. "Since when are *you* a guest?" He glanced at his watch in a show of impatience. "Shouldn't Ethan be here by now?"

"Trying to get rid of me?" Rosie laughed. "And here I was ready to vote for steaks."

Riley looked pained, which mirrored how Regina felt. She wanted to be alone with him, to ask him details on what had happened.

Ethan sauntered in. "Soon as I get everything out of the truck, I'm taking you home, woman."

Rosie turned to drape her arms around his neck. "Really? What for?"

It was Ethan's turn to whisper, Rosie's turn to blush. In a rush, she said, "I'll help you unload."

It was another half hour before Regina was finally able to corner Riley and get some answers.

Not once had Butch left his side. He'd followed Riley to the truck time and again, then around the apartment, watching while Riley helped to put her things away in various places. He hooked up her computer in the room he'd given her to use as an office. It was a guest bedroom, but Regina knew Riley didn't want her using the bed.

With everything now in place, they sat on the back patio so Butch could run the length of the lead Riley had stretched between two trees. Regina stared at Riley, on the edge of her seat.

"What if he'd had a gun, Riley? What if he'd pulled that knife on you?"

Sprawled out on a chaise, his ankles crossed, Riley laid a forearm over his eyes to shield them from the late-afternoon sun. "If the dumb son of a bitch had dared to pull a knife on me, I'd have…" Belatedly, he lifted his arm to take in Regina's expression of horror. His frown smoothed out. "I'd have disarmed him, honey. Okay?"

She couldn't bear the thought of him being in danger because of her. "Are you really that good?"

He sat up and swung his legs around to face her. Treating her to a somber, very direct stare, he took her hands and said, "Yeah."

He'd answered without boasting, just matter-of-factly stating what he saw as a truth. Regina shook her head at such confidence.

"Later," he told her while giving her hands a squeeze, "I'm going to show you how good I am."

Oh, the way he said that. His low tone and sensual smile left her uncertain to his meaning. Cautiously, she asked, "You are?"

"Might as well get started on your training, don't you think?"

Well heck, so *that's* how he meant it. Disappointment warred with common sense. Still, private self-defense lessons wouldn't be at all the same as what they'd done in his gym. There, he'd been all business, politely distant, and a true gentleman given the other onlookers. Here, they'd be wrapped in privacy. The thought of being alone with Riley, feeling his body over hers, touching in all the most sexual places, made her breathless. "I suppose."

"So much enthusiasm." He pulled her off her seat and into his lap—something he never would have done in his gym. She thought he might kiss her, and truthfully, she wanted him to. In the short time he'd been at her apartment and then at the station, she'd missed him. She'd worried about him, too.

Instead he said, "Tell me the name of the guy who harassed you at work, and that ass you were engaged to."

"Why?" She tried to twist around to see him, but he hugged her closer so she could barely move. The fact that she was thinking about intimacy, and he apparently wasn't, left her flustered.

"I'm going to talk to them both. And no, don't argue, Red. I won't embarrass you. You have my promise on that."

It wasn't Riley she worried about. He'd already proven to have her best interests in mind. But her ex-fiancé… "I don't know what you think they can add to the equation."

Riley shrugged. "Maybe nothing. But it can't hurt to ask them a few pertinent questions, now can it?"

Actually, it could probably hurt her pride a lot. She bit her lip, but finally nodded. Riley was a professional who knew his business inside and out. It would be ridiculous to contradict him. "The man I worked with is Carl Edmond. He's a nice enough guy, just different. Sort of intense."

"Intense how?"

"Not in a bad way. Just overzealous about everything, his work, his life—"

"And you?"

She couldn't deny that. "For a while, maybe. He fixated on me. He told me he loved me, but I knew that wasn't true. His courtship became a bother before he wised up, but he was never threatening."

Riley didn't seem convinced. "And the other guy?"

Regina hated to talk about him. She couldn't mention his name without memories swamping her, leaving her hollowed out with humiliation.

But this time, seated on Riley's lap, held in his arms, it was easier. "His name is Luther Finley." She closed her eyes and prayed Luther wouldn't reveal anything of their private past to Riley. Not that Luther considered anything private. She'd found that out too late. "I assume Carl still works at the paper. He loves his job a lot. And Luther should be in the insurance building across the street. He's a salesman." She drew a breath. "Want me to write the names down for you?"

"Carl Edmond and Luther Finley. I won't forget." Riley rubbed his big hand up her arm, then down again. He was silent, introspective, and yet he kept touching her as if he couldn't help himself.

When his thoughts finally turned from the men, Regina felt the shift in his mood and she wanted to rejoice. She tipped up her face—and Riley accommodated her by capturing her mouth for a long, deep kiss. She felt the drumming of his heart, tasted the damp warmth of his mouth, and didn't want him ever to stop.

With his mouth still touching hers, he murmured, "Damn, you taste good."

He tasted better than good. Delicious. Regina pressed closer to slip her tongue into his mouth, deepening the kiss again and making Riley groan in response.

The warm sun beat down on them, cooled only by the gentle breeze. Riley's strength wrapped around her, giving the illusion that nothing bad could ever happen. From his wide chest and thick shoulders to his flat abdomen and strong thighs, he was all male. Being with him, alone each night, would make it nearly impossible to keep any emotional distance.

Had it been only a day ago that she thought she needed to know him better before becoming involved?

She knew the truth now. Already she was way too involved, and knowing him better only made it worse. Riley believed in her when no one else did. He put himself in danger for her. By his own admission and by the evidence of his actions, he was more than capable of handling any threatening situation. On every level, he fascinated her.

She was already half in love with him.

Riley's hand moved up alongside her face. His big thumb stroked her cheekbone as he lifted his mouth. "I want to ask you something, Red."

Regina felt herself floating. She smiled. "Hmm?"

"Why did you bring the books and photo here?"

Her sensual haze lifted. She opened her eyes to see Riley watching her, his expression probing, filled with command. Because their noses practically touched, it was a rather intimidating stare.

"C'mon, Red, tell me." She started to straighten, but he shook his head. "No, I like you like this. I enjoy holding you."

"Oh." She shifted a little to get more comfortable, felt his erection, heard his low groan and immediately stilled. No one had ever touched her as much as Riley did. Not even her fiancé had wanted to hold her this way. "I brought the books because I thought, well, we are going to be staying here together. I'm not an idiot. I realize what we'll likely do before too long."

The heat in his blue eyes darkened. "Today." His kiss was soft, gentle. "It's going to happen today."

Such a sensual promise shattered all other thought. She could only stare at him.

"But, honey, you don't need a book."

Brought back to the reality of the moment, she winced and gave an awful admission. "I think…maybe I do."

Without seeming to move, he gathered her closer to his body. He glanced out into the yard at Butch, saw he was sprawled out in the sweet grass in a spot of bright sunshine. Then he looked to make certain they were well hidden between the sections of privacy fence that lined his small patio.

His gaze came back to her, resting first on her eyes, then her mouth. "How can you need a book when everything you do makes me hot? You dress up all classy and it makes me think about stripping you naked. I catch you in worn pajamas and I want to feel how soft and warm you are under them. You cook dinner and

I obsess about the way your bottom sways while you stir the food."

She'd been listening with fascinated wonder until the last, then a startled laugh broke free. "You do not."

"I do." And in a growl he added, "Your backside has played prominently in all my most recent fantasies." He punctuated that statement by grasping her firmly in both hands, giving her behind an affectionate, caressing squeeze. "Damn. I can't wait to get you naked so I can explore it in more detail."

Her face flamed. "Riley."

"Regina." His smile touched her heart. "I especially like the charming way you blush. Hell, everything about you makes me hot. Believe me, honey, getting you into bed is the objective. Once we're there, it doesn't matter what you do. I won't be complaining."

Hearing him say it made her almost believe. Had she allowed Luther's spiteful comments to influence her too much? It had been such a difficult time, such a humiliation.

But Riley wouldn't lie to her, she knew. He was better than that. "All right, I'll forget about the books if you promise to tell me what you like."

He drew her marginally closer. "I like you."

"You know what I mean."

He pressed his face into her neck and gave a gruff laugh. "The way you keep talking about this, like it's going to happen any second now, has me close to exploding."

Regina thought it *was* going to happen at any moment. She frowned at him, but before she could tell him that she wanted him now, he said, "There're a few things I want to clear up before we get sidetracked."

Sidetracked? Is that what he called making love with her? Feeling put out by his blasted patience, she said, "Like what?"

He leaned away. Some of the teasing laughter in his eyes darkened to a more serious emotion. "The photo. And why the hell you brought it along."

Chapter 7

Bless Butch's little heart. He chose that moment to interrupt with a loud spate of barking. Regina sat up to see that a rather hefty golden retriever had come over to check him out. Regina started to jump up in alarm, but Riley stayed her with a hand on her arm.

"That's Blaze. She's a sweet dog, honey. She won't hurt him."

Regina doubted that after she saw Butch try to sprinkle the gorgeous creature's nose. Yet rather than snap at him, Blaze lunged back playfully, shook her head, and ran the length of his lead so that Butch could chase her.

He went so fast trying to keep up, he tripped over his own nose and managed a complete somersault without stopping. When he ran out of rope, he yelped, and Blaze trotted back to him.

Regina laughed. "I think Butch is in love."

Riley sat up behind her, his arms looped around her waist. "Poor bastard. I wonder if she'll keep pictures of other dogs around just to make him nuts."

Regina turned sharply to stare at him. Was he jealous over the picture? But no, that would be too absurd. Senator Welling represented strong values, not sexual allure. Surely, Riley understood that.

Riley lifted her away and came to his feet. The dogs were still playing, making a terrible racket that didn't bother Regina at all. She couldn't keep her eyes off Riley as he stretched, then looked up at the blazing sun.

In the next instant he reached for the hem of his shirt and pulled it off over his head.

Regina didn't so much as blink. His upper body was gorgeous. Dark hair liberally covered his well-defined chest. Sleek, prominent muscles in his shoulders bunched and moved as he haphazardly folded the shirt and laid it over the back of her chair. In unselfconscious masculine display, he dragged one hand through his chest hair, scratching a little, then flexed his shoulder and rotated his head.

Regina's mouth went dry. In something of a rasp, she asked, "What are you doing?"

"It's warm out here." He glanced down at her. "And I'm a little stiff from jumping off your damn balcony so many times." So saying, he turned to head inside and Regina caught sight of a bruise on his ribs.

"Riley." She was out of her chair in a flash, catching his arm and holding him still. "What happened?"

He looked down at the darkening flesh she indicated. "Nothing. That must be where I hit the ground when I tripped him. I had no idea there were so many little stones everywhere."

Wishing she could soothe him, even heal him, her fingertips grazed over his warm skin. "I'm sorry."

His gaze stayed on her face, piercing and bright. "No problem, Red." He unsnapped his slacks.

Regina stepped back in a rush.

"I'm going to go change before we have our little chat about that picture. Be back in a second."

Change? As in, change into *what?* Less clothes? It was bad enough when he was at the gym wearing shorts, T-shirt, socks and athletic shoes. But at the gym, there was always a crowd around, plenty of people to keep the situation less intimate.

Here, there was no one. And she just knew if Riley started flaunting himself, she'd end up the aggressor.

He was only gone a minute, but it was long enough for Regina to give herself a hot flash, thinking of the night to come.

"You getting hungry, Red?"

She jerked around, then took an automatic step toward him. Good Lord, the man oozed sex appeal. He wore gray low-slung drawstring shorts, and nothing else. She realized she'd never seen his feet before. They were big, sprinkled with golden-brown hair, narrow, and as sexy as the rest of him. Right now, braced apart as they were, he seemed to have planted himself firmly against opposition. Hers?

Not likely. Not when everything about him appealed to her.

Slowly, Regina allowed her attention to climb upward, taking in every inch of his body. Muscular, very hairy calves, nice knees. *Incredible* thighs.

Her heart raced. She already knew firsthand how strong his thighs were. She'd watched Riley grappling with some very big bruisers at his gym and he always dominated. Swallowing, she looked higher still and saw the hem of his shorts, hanging to midthigh.

A little higher and she saw... Oh my. Regina blew out a breath that sounded part whistle, part exclamation, and not in the least ladylike. Under normal circumstances, she would have been appalled at herself. But the soft cotton molded to his sex. He was right, small condoms would never fit him.

Breathing became more difficult. As an intelligent, educated and modern woman, and as one who had recently read some informed books on the subject, she knew size didn't matter. That hadn't been her problem with Luther at all.

So why did it feel like a volcano of heat had exploded inside her?

As she stared at him, unable to draw her gaze away, something twitched. Her brows lifted. Fascinated, she watched as Riley became semierect. She put a hand to her throat.

Riley, blast him, never moved.

Deciding it might be safer to continue on with her visual journey rather than keep staring at him *there,* Regina looked at his hard abdomen. That didn't help one iota. The hair around his navel and the silky trail below it appeared soft, tempting her to touch it. She wanted to so badly, but would that be crossing the line?

At the moment, did she care? How could any woman remain rational when faced with such provocation?

Almost from the start, she'd wanted Riley. Every day the feeling grew stronger. Other than her acute sense of caution and propriety, there were no real reasons for waiting.

She moved toward him.

Riley made a gruff sound of expectation.

Savoring the moment, she put her hands on his sides, luxuriating in the feel of hot smooth skin drawn taut over firm muscle. Experimentally, Regina caressed him, her thumbs inward to trace over the sleek muscles slanting toward his groin.

She looked at his face. He was rigid, flushed, waiting. "I want to touch you, Riley."

"Do."

One simple word that somehow sounded so provocative. When she looked again, she saw that he now had a full erection. *Very* full. Just from her touching his waist? Intrigued, she asked, "You like this?"

"Yeah." He drawled out the word, husky and deep.

Emboldened, she slid her hands around his back near the very bottom of his spine, close to his sexy muscled tush. The position brought her closer to his chest and she inhaled deeply. "You smell so good, Riley."

He leaned forward, pressed his mouth to her temple, and whispered, "Is that really where you want to touch me, Red?"

Her nose brushed his soft chest hair when she shook her head. She liked that, so she did it again. "No."

"I didn't think so."

Deciding to try pure honestly, she said, "We're outside…"

"No one can see us."

"But still…"

"I'm a man, not a schoolboy. I can control myself.

Nothing happens unless you say so. Feel free to touch all you want and to stop when you want."

Her heart expanded. Such an incredibly generous offer.

Such an incredibly generous man.

She tipped her face up. "Will you kiss me while I do it?"

His expression hardened and his voice went low and rough. "My pleasure, baby."

This kiss felt different. Regina hadn't realized he'd been holding back, that there were so many nuances to kissing until that moment when she felt all his carnal intent in the way he devoured her mouth. It was an eating kiss, hot and hard and overwhelming. He would make love to her now—she understood that and reveled in the reality.

Again and again, his tongue sank past her parted lips and into her mouth, stroking seductively. She felt consumed. That was enough of a distraction that Riley had to nudge himself forward into her belly to remind her of what she wanted, of what *he* wanted.

Bringing her hands around, she first toyed with his navel. His abdomen had grown rigid, the muscles clearly defined, growing more so as she touched him until he felt like granite with no give to his flesh at all. The hair there was just as silky as she'd imagined.

Breathing hard, her awareness suspended, she encountered the waistband of his shorts, the ultrasoft cotton material and finally the long, solid length of his penis.

They both groaned.

Riley's fingers tightened and he lifted his mouth away to gulp for air. Keeping his forehead against hers,

he encouraged her by saying, "That's it. Damn, Red…"
And he groaned again, harsh and broken.

Regina could have spent an hour just exploring him.
On so many levels, he fascinated her, the freedom he
allowed, his open response. Her fingertips trailed up
his length, measuring him, then back down again—and
she felt the shuddering response of his body.

Driven by curiosity, she cupped beneath his shaft,
cradling his heavy testicles in her palm and heard him
hiss in a breath.

"Easy." His long fingers gripped her upper arms.

"Like this?"

"Yeah." His grip loosened, caressed, encouraged.

They spoke in muted whispers, hers awed, his raw
with arousal.

Suddenly he kissed her again, so ravenously that
she forgot what she was doing and her hands left him
to grasp his neck, holding tight. Strong arms enclosed
her, stealing her breath. Her lips were swollen, her head
spinning, when Riley again cupped her face to place
sweet little pecks on her chin, her cheeks, her forehead.

"You know what I think, Red?"

Overwhelmed, she whispered, "What?"

"That turnabout is fair play."

Her stomach jumped and her heart began a wild
race. When she got her eyes open, Riley was smiling at her.

"You'll love having me touch you, Red. I promise.
But for right now, we should take this indoors before
things get out of hand and neither one of us makes a
clearheaded decision."

Her head would never be clear again.

Riley nodded in the direction of the yard. "Butch fell asleep with his new lady friend."

A safer topic if ever there was one. Regina turned and saw that Blaze had stretched out on her side in the thick grass. Her golden fur looked beautiful with the sun glinting off it. Butch was curled up on her neck, his whole head practically in her ear. They made such an adorable picture, Regina's heart nearly melted and stupidly, tears filled her eyes.

"Tonight," Riley whispered to her, "I want to sleep with you curled that close." He didn't give her a chance to reply to that, not that she had a reply anyway. He picked her up and started into the house.

"Butch…"

"Will enjoy his freedom in the yard. I'll leave the window open. Don't fret, honey. We'll hear him if he needs us." Riley walked right past the room he'd given to her and into his own bedroom.

When he reached the bed, he went down with her in his arms. She'd known of his strength, but still he amazed her. He treated her weight as negligible, arranging her as easily as he would a pillow. Straightening away, balanced on one arm, he said, "You're wearing entirely too many clothes, Red. What'd you say we take them all off?" And before she could find her voice, he already had her sleeveless sweater up and over her head.

Riley knew if he gave her too much time to consider things, she'd decide it wasn't proper to be having sex with him in the middle of the afternoon with the window open. He was done giving her time. She now felt comfortable touching him sexually, and he knew, even if she didn't, that they had a future together.

The rest would fall into place.

The second her sweater cleared her head, he reached for the clasp to her bra. He heard her gasping breaths, felt the urgent bite of her nails in his upper arms.

The bra, bless her feminine little heart, was white lace and so damn sexy he could have spent an hour just appreciating the way it decorated her small breasts. Instead, he flicked the front clasp open, pulled the thin cups apart, and visually sated himself.

"Beautiful."

Regina made a sound of startled embarrassment and covered herself with her hands.

Riley forced his gaze from her white breasts to her face. "Harris was wrong. Pink and red go real nice together."

Her embarrassment faded behind confusion. "What are you talking about?"

A long curl of titian hair had come loose, and Riley used it like a feather to tease the side of her breast. "Red hair and pink nipples. It's a sexy combination."

"Oh." More color exploded in her cheeks. "But what does Harris have to do with—"

No way would Riley tell her about Harris picking up her pink panties. "And this pretty blush." He put his mouth to her cheek and felt the heat of her flush. "You're beautiful, Regina, and I don't want you to be embarrassed with me."

He gently caught her wrists, aware of the fragile bones, how small she felt in his big hands. Drawing her arms up, he pressed her hands firmly to the mattress at either side of her head. He released her and her breasts shivered with her nervous, jerky breaths.

"But I—"

Her protest died on a gasp when Riley leaned down and took one soft, plump nipple into his mouth. Regina's back arched and her fingers threaded through his hair.

Holding her shoulders down on the bed, he sucked gently, keeping the pressure light, using his tongue to tease her nipple into a stiff little point. When he lifted his head, Regina had her eyes squeezed shut, her bottom lip caught in her teeth and her body held tight.

"You like that, honey?"

Without opening her eyes, she bobbed her head.

Riley smiled, then looked at her body. Her upper torso was so slim, her rib cage narrow and her breasts pert. He skimmed his palm down her side, then inward to the clasp of her slacks. "I want you naked. I want to see all of you."

Her eyes flew open.

"Once you're naked, I can get naked and think how good that's going to feel."

Her lips parted. "Yes."

Gently, he pried her fingers from his hair and again raised her arms over her head. "I love seeing you like this, Red, stretched out on my bed." He studied her from top to toes, then kissed her belly. "Now don't move."

She agreed by curling her fingers into the bedding, holding on tight.

Her sandals slipped off easily enough, but Riley took the time to kiss each arch, then each ankle. There was one spot just behind the ankle bone that when pinched, could cause agonizing pain, maybe even paralyze the limb. In the same regard, a featherlight touch sent thousands of acute nerve endings on alert. Riley tickled with his tongue, soothed with soft kisses.

She had sexy legs, long and sleek. Her casual white slacks unbuttoned with ease, and building the anticipation, he slowly drew down the zipper. Her belly hollowed out with her sharply indrawn breath.

Riley spread his fingers wide over her hips and dragged the pants down to her knees. Her panties were the same lace as her bra, showing the springy auburn curls over her mound. He wanted her so badly he hurt, but he didn't want to rush her, he didn't want her to start searching for her damn books.

Using one fingertip, Riley traced the triangle of pubic hair. He couldn't wait to taste her, to have her completely naked and open....

"Riley?"

"Yeah?"

A long heavy silence filled the air before she said, "I don't think I can take all this waiting. My patience isn't as strong as yours."

Riley looked up at her face. Her hands were fisted, her pupils dilated, lips parted.

"Just a little longer."

Her pants tangled around her ankles with her trying to kick them off and Riley had to finish that chore for her. Her panties came off next, and then she was beautifully bare.

Her aroused scent filled his head. He kissed her belly, each hipbone, an inner thigh. Alternately, he made the kisses gentle, then rough, sometimes laving with his tongue, sometimes nipping with his teeth.

Regina squirmed and gasped, on edge, unsure what the next touch would bring. He could feel the urgency pounding through her.

Parting her legs, he licked the joint of her thigh and groin, where her skin was ultrasmooth and delicate.

"Riley, please…"

Regardless of what she said, she couldn't be ready yet. His mouth open and his kisses deliberately damp, Riley made his way back up her body. She grabbed him, kissing him hard, while his hands covered both her breasts. Her nipples were tight now, her breasts swollen. He caught her nipples and rolled, squeezed, tugged.

She pulled her mouth away. "Riley."

"Shh." He kissed her again, silencing her protests while continuing to torment her nipples. The more aroused she got, the more she'd enjoy his caresses. Her legs shifted restlessly, moving alongside his until he stilled them with one of his own. Caught under him, Regina could barely move, and that suited Riley just fine.

Keeping her legs trapped, he leaned up to look at her face. "I want you as ready as I am, Red."

"I am," she all but wailed.

"No." Smiling, he dragged his callused fingertips over her ribs, her belly and finally between her thighs. The crisp curls were damp, her lips puffy, sleek with moisture. His breath caught. "Well now, maybe you are." He pressed his middle finger inside, just past her swollen flesh, no deeper. She was most sensitive here, at her opening, so he used that knowledge to circle, dip, circle again. He relished her broken moan, the way her body tried to move with him.

"I should… I should be doing something."

"What is it you want to do?"

"Touch you."

His control nearly slipped. "No, not yet. I'm on the ragged edge as it is."

Her eyes opened and her head lifted off the pillow to shout into his face, "Then quit playing around!"

Riley almost laughed. Regina amused him so much, even at a time when laughter should have been eons away. "All right. Tell me how you like this."

Her head dropped back with a groan as he began moving his finger deeply in and out, making her wetter still. As he did so, he kissed his way down her body. The closer he got to her sex, the more she stiffened.

"Riley?"

"Hush." He nudged her thighs farther apart, took a moment to enjoy her scent, breathing deep, then with a groan, he covered her with his mouth.

She gave a small cry, arching hard.

At the first flick of his tongue, her body clamped down on his finger. He licked, stroked, and finally, catching her small clitoris carefully with his teeth, he suckled.

Her body strained away from him, but Riley held her hips, keeping her still. He loved the feel of her voluptuous bottom in his hands, the taste of her on his tongue, the hot, wild sounds she made. As her excitement peaked, he worked in another finger, stretching her, filling her. She lifted up to meet his mouth, grinding against him, so close.

When he knew she was ready to come, he sat up and snagged a condom from the nightstand. Regina cried out in protest at the delay, and the second he got the protection taken care of, she opened her arms to him.

Riley settled between her wide-open thighs. Wanting every possible connection, he held her face to kiss her and nudged his way inside. She was tight, but so wet he knew he wouldn't hurt her. With one hard thrust, he entered her completely and Regina lifted her legs to wrap around his waist. He found a rhythm that quickly had them both straining toward a climax.

Her mouth devoured his, biting his bottom lip, sucking on his tongue. He loved it.

He loved *her*. If only he could make her understand that.

Sweating, his heart thundering in his chest, he slid one hand under her behind to tilt her hips up so he could enter her more deeply. That was all it took. She started coming with broken groans and mewling cries and that pushed Riley right over the edge. He could feel the throbbing clench and release of her body on his cock, the frantic bite of her nails on his shoulders, the way she shuddered and writhed under him.

He pressed his face into her neck and growled out her name. Regina wasn't quite so restrained. She screamed.

Two seconds after Riley's body went utterly limp and he gave Regina his weight, Butch began barking hysterically.

He felt Regina stiffen, but he patted her hip and made the manly offering. "I'll go get him."

Her hands slid off his back to land limply on the bed. "Thanks."

Riley forced himself to his elbows to see her face. Her eyes were closed, her French braid ruined, her makeup smudged. She was sweaty, just as he'd predicted.

And, thank God, she was finally his.

Riley attempted to wake her with a kiss to her forehead. Regina moaned, rolled to the side and slept on.

They'd spent the night making love and apparently, Regina wasn't used to such excesses. Truthfully, neither was he.

It had surprised him how often he'd wanted her. Watching her eat a simple dinner in her robe, seeing her coddle the silly little dog, catching her secret smiles and sudden blushes, had all provoked him. He hadn't been able to keep his hands off her.

And she hadn't minded in the least.

It'd been tricky, getting Butch to leave the room without kicking up a fuss. Riley figured he'd need to stock up on toys and tasty chews to distract the dog.

After her fourth release, she'd conked out and hadn't really come to since. Once he'd realized she was done for, he'd worked her pajamas back onto her then let Butch in the room. She hadn't protested when the dog burrowed under the covers, or when Riley had pulled her close and held her all night long.

She hadn't even awakened.

It drove home to Riley just how exhausted she'd been, and the toll her worries must have taken on her.

He hoped his presence would ease those worries, because, from now on, she'd damn well be with him. Beyond that, he didn't know if his lauded control extended to sleeping chastely each night, even if they'd made love prior to going to bed.

He hated to disturb her now, but he didn't want

to leave for the day without saying goodbye. Butch seemed just as determined to keep him from doing so.

He and the dog had been up for an hour and more than once Butch had whined at her door, apparently wanting Regina to join them. Now that he was back in the bed with her, he dashed from Regina's feet to her head and back again, trying to protect all of her—from Riley.

Riley lifted the miniscule dog. "I may have gone overboard last night, bud, but I don't accost women in their sleep."

Regina's eyes fluttered open. "Riley?"

At the sound of her soft, sleepy voice, some insidious warmth expanded in his chest. "After last night, were you really expecting another man to wake you up?"

He saw confusion flit over her face, then realization. She snatched the sheet over her head. "What in the world are you doing in here?"

He sat on the bed beside her, causing a dip in the mattress. Her rump rolled into his hip. "I slept here. It's my bed, remember?"

She groaned.

"And because Butch wanted under the covers, I put your pajamas back on you, so you don't need to hide."

"It's not that," she mumbled from under the covers.

Ah, Riley thought, appearances again. Silly woman. "Do you have any idea how sexy you look all rumpled and warm?"

She went very still. "I do?"

"Yeah. Makes me want to strip naked and get back into bed with you." He gave a grievous sigh. "But unfortunately I have some stuff to do, so I only wanted to wake you so I could say goodbye."

One slender hand emerged from the blankets, shooing him away. "I'll be out in a second."

Smiling, Riley patted her hip and stood. As an enticement, he said, "I have coffee ready and waiting."

She made a rumbling sound of appreciation. "I'll be right there."

Ten minutes later she emerged with her hair brushed and pulled back in a ponytail, wearing a casual green sundress. Her eyes were still puffy and there was a crease in her cheek probably formed from a pillowcase.

Riley wanted to consume her. Again. Last night hadn't even taken the edge off his hunger. He didn't think a hundred years could do that.

As he watched, she made her way unsteadily toward the table. "Riley? I suppose I should admit that I'm not at my best in the morning." She ended that with an enormous and inelegant yawn, giving proof to her statement.

"Coffee will help. You sit and I'll pour it for you."

She plopped down in the chair. "Thank you."

The dog made a beeline for Regina. She roused herself enough to lift him into her lap and treat him to several kisses to his round head.

Riley could have used a few of those kisses. Not that he was jealous of the attention she gave Butch, and not that he didn't understand how sluggish she felt. But this was the proverbial morning after and she'd barely looked at him.

Then he decided *what the hell.*

He handed her a mug of coffee, but forestalled her from tasting it by leaning down and taking her mouth in a warm morning kiss. "Now that," Riley said as he straightened, "is the *proper* way to say hello after a night of satisfying debauchery."

Regina gave him a bemused look, snatched up her cup and swilled her coffee. There was no other word for it. In two long gulps, her mug was empty. Enjoying this side of her, Riley fixed her another cup then seated himself across from her.

"You do remember last night, don't you?"

Her eyes darted away from his. "Of course I do. No woman in her right mind would forget a night with you. Especially not a night like that."

"Thanks. I wanted verification, given the way you passed out on me."

She groaned and covered her face with one hand. "I'm sorry."

Riley reached across the table and took her slender wrist. Her skin was warm, smooth. "I'm not. You needed the sleep."

"That's no excuse for rudeness."

Riley nearly choked on his laugh. "You were not rude, I was excessive. And believe me, I have no complaints."

"But…"

"*None,* Red. Okay?"

Her expression softened. "I don't have any complaints either. In fact, I think I owe you a few compliments."

Riley grinned with her. "You can give them to me tonight."

"Why tonight?" She looked more awake now and somewhat interested. "I thought maybe we could…"

He groaned. "Don't tempt me, Red. Nothing would

please me more than hauling your sexy butt back to bed. But I'll be gone till this afternoon."

Her disappointment was plain to see, filling Riley with satisfaction. "I thought you were on vacation."

"I am, but I want to talk to your two swains, Carl and Luther, then stop by the station and see how things are going with our intruder."

Her brows pulled down. "I'm not at all sure I like this idea."

"Why?"

"Don't look so suspicious, Riley. I'm not hiding anything important."

That clarification *important* rang like a bell in his head. "So you're hiding unimportant stuff?"

"No! And don't twist my words. It's just that I'm sure neither Carl nor Luther has anything to do with my trouble."

"With this type of continued harassment, it's almost always someone you know, and more often than that, it's someone you've been romantically involved with." She quit her protests to groan instead. Riley laced his fingers in hers. "Now, don't take this the wrong way, but I'd like you to promise me you won't take off anywhere while I'm gone."

She rubbed her eyes tiredly. "I have nowhere to go. In fact," she said, giving him a direct look, "I thought I'd finish up my article on the talent show. Once that's done, I can start on your interview."

He didn't want to talk about the damn interview right now. While he intended to discover everything he could about Regina, he detested the thought of her prying into his past. He came to his feet and stepped around the table to reach her. Caging her in with one hand on the seat and the other on the back of her chair, Riley said, "We've got a lot to do today, sweetheart."

She stared at his mouth. "We do?"

He nodded. "We're going to start on your private lessons today, remember?"

"Oh."

Seeing her disappointment almost had him laughing out loud. Aware of Butch's low growls, he touched her nose. "I'll make sure you enjoy them, okay?"

Her eyes darkened. "Okay."

"Tonight is the ceremony at the Historical Society. They're honoring Senator Welling." He watched her face and added, "I thought maybe we could go."

Excitement brightened her eyes and added a smile. "You mean it?"

Now he was jealous. Welling represented her ideal man, and for most, his stature was as unattainable as the moon. "It won't be a social call, honey. I want a chance to talk to your senator, and this seems like it might be the best opportunity."

Her excitement remained plain to see. "He's not just my senator, and Riley, you'll like him a lot, I know it."

Riley would have liked the guy more if Regina weren't so infatuated with him. "If he cooperates with me, I'll have no complaints."

"I really don't think he'll have anything to share, but it'll be good to see him again."

Because he didn't want to hear her talk about Welling, Riley kissed her quick and hard. He felt Butch nipping at his chin, his ear, doing all he could to scare Riley off. Riley drew back to stare at the little dog. "Where's your toy?"

Butch's ears shot up. He maneuvered down Regina's leg to the floor and took off at a dead run for the hallway. He returned with the stuffed Chihuahua in his mouth and dropped it at Riley's feet.

Riley laughed. "Smart dog. All right, I can play for just a few minutes, but that's all." And to Regina he added, "Finish up your coffee. There's cereal in the cabinet, fruit in the fridge. Help yourself, okay?"

Her expression was tender when she nodded. "Thanks."

Ten minutes later, Riley was on the floor, the stuffed toy caught in his teeth while he and Butch indulged in a feigned tug of war. Butch gave it his all, jerking and growling in his attempt to tear the toy away from Riley. Riley growled back, a stuffed tail and leg caught in his mouth.

Regina laughed. "You're both nuts."

Riley straightened. "Now he knows how to grapple. Did you see his triceps? Or would they be triceps, considering dogs don't have arms?" Riley shook his head. "Either way, he's buff and built like a lean bulldog."

Butch took off in a flash, dragging the toy, but when Riley didn't pursue him he returned only to smack Riley's ankle with it. "No," he told Butch. "I gotta go. Get Regina to play."

Butch dutifully dragged the toy to Regina. She laughed. "Gee, thanks."

Riley tipped up her chin to give her a long, thorough kiss. "If you need anything while I'm gone, just call me on my cell phone."

He knew he had to leave before he decided not to go at all. Today he was going to get some answers. The sooner the better. Then he'd come home to Regina.

Soon he'd have everything worked out.

Chapter 8

The second Riley was out the door, Regina made plans. She called Rosie at work first to find out Ethan's and Harris's schedules. She didn't want to call either of their homes if there was a chance she'd wake them. As firefighters, their hours varied. Regina told her they were both on second shift that week, and that Ethan, at least, should be up and about.

She called him and made an appointment for him to visit her at Riley's house. Next, she called Buck and left him a message since he didn't pick up.

Finally she chanced a call to Harris. A woman answered, temporarily throwing Regina off. "Um, is Harris around?"

"Who is this?" the woman asked with heavy suspicion.

Regina was about to reply when she heard some

grumbling in the background, then Harris's voice on the phone. "Hello?"

"It's Regina. I'm so sorry I'm interrupting."

"No, you're not." That statement caused another ruckus in the background. Harris covered the phone, did some grousing, then came back to ask, "What's up? Everything okay?"

"Oh, yes. I just… I'm going to be doing an interview on Riley and since he's gone for most of the afternoon and he doesn't want me to leave his apartment, I figured I could start by talking to his closest friends. Ethan's coming over in a few minutes, and I hoped, if you weren't too busy, maybe you could come by after him."

She heard the amusement in Harris's voice when he asked, "Does Riley know you're inviting us over?"

"No, why?"

Now he laughed outright. "No reason. None at all. And yes, I'd love to come over. Hell, I wouldn't miss this for the world. Want me to pick up Buck and drag him along? You can kill two birds with one stone."

"I already called him. He's working."

"He's the boss. If he can't take off for a few hours, who can?"

Regina laughed. "No, that's okay. I'd rather talk to each of you one on one."

Harris snickered. "Really? All right then." He laughed again. "This is going to be fun." He hung up before Regina could ask him what he meant.

Riley made it to Cincinnati in a little less than an hour. It was easy enough to find the newspaper building. He thought about going in to talk to Carl first, but changed his mind and parked in the lot for the insurance company. At the lobby desk, he asked about seeing Luther, and was told to go to the fourth floor.

On the elevator ride up, Riley thought about what he'd say. He realized he wanted Regina's ex-beau to be guilty, just for the satisfaction of cleaning the guy out of her past. If she did have any residual feelings for him, finding out he was the one harassing her, with nothing but hurt feelings to motivate him, ought to take care of it.

There was no one at the receptionist's desk. Riley glanced at his wristwatch, saw it was lunchtime and waited only a moment before mentally saying, *To hell with it.* He strode to Luther's door, raised his hand to knock—and got a whiff of sickeningly sweet smoke. Pot.

What the hell?

He tried the door, but it was locked. After knocking sharply, he called out, "Luther Finley?"

There was a lot of shuffling movement behind the door before it finally opened. A man close to Riley's height, with straight black hair and shrewd blue eyes, stood there. His suit was immaculate, expensive and in good taste.

He made a great appearance. Shit. First the senator, and now this clown. If Regina was drawn to *GQ* men, Riley didn't stand a chance.

"Yeah? Who are you? What do you want?"

So this was the man Regina had bought sex books for? This was the man she'd hoped to please in bed?

Riley wanted to punch him in the nose. The urge to do so made it difficult to breathe. Ruthlessly, Riley brought himself under control. He would not behave like a Yeti. He would not prove himself to be a jealous fool.

Looking beyond Luther, Riley saw an open window, a desk drawer slightly ajar. Perfect. If he couldn't hit him, he could at least have the upper hand. There must be a fairy godmother sitting on his shoulder, to be given this advantage.

"Can I help you?" Luther said with strained impatience.

"You Luther Finley?" At the other man's nod, Riley flashed a badge. "I'm Riley Moore, with the Chester Police Department. I need a moment of your time."

Luther's eyes opened wide and he reeled back two steps. "The police? What the hell did I do?"

"I want to ask you about an acquaintance of yours. Understand, Mr. Finley, this is an informal visit and you're not in any trouble. Yet. I'd just like some information."

Riley saw the moment the man relaxed, wrongfully assuming he'd ignore the pot. "Yeah? About who?"

"Regina Foxworth. She seems to have gotten herself into a bit of trouble."

The look of curiosity faded beneath a smarmy smile. "Regina is in trouble?" He actually laughed. "Yeah, sure. Come on in and pull up a chair. I'm glad to help."

And Riley thought to himself, *I just bet you are.*

Regina handed Ethan a tall, icy glass of cola. "Now, tell me what you know about Riley."

Ethan looked more wary by the second. He glanced around the obviously empty apartment and said yet again, "I'm not sure this is a good idea, Regina."

"No, it's okay. Riley gave me permission to inter-

view him. And he didn't want me to leave the apartment, so this is a good compromise. He won't mind."

"Uh-huh." Ethan sipped his drink, still undecided.
"What exactly do you want to know?"

Regina studied Ethan while she considered what to
ask him first. He was a very attractive man with his
dark blond hair and deep, intelligent brown eyes. As a
firefighter he was, by necessity, built almost as hand-
somely as Riley. But she'd never had any interest in
Ethan. No, she'd seen Riley and been lost. She'd fought
her reaction to him, but fighting did her no good. Last
night had proven that.

She sighed. "Has Riley had any recent romantic involvement?"

Ethan choked, stared at her, and choked some more.
She got up to thwack him on the back, but Butch didn't
like that and started to howl. For some unknown reason, he'd taken a real dislike to Ethan.

Gasping and wheezing, Ethan waved her away. Regina resettled herself, allowing Butch to skulk back
into her lap with a surly look thrown toward Ethan.

"Well?"

"What does that have to do with your interview?"

In the primmest tone she could muster, Regina lied,
"His social habits will be of interest to everyone reading the article. They'll want to know about *him,* not
just his work."

Ethan didn't look convinced. He drew a deep breath,
cast her another suspicious look, and finally murmured,
"He dates. Not seriously, not often."

"Really?" Now that was interesting, considering the
amount of energy Buck and Harris apparently put into
tomcatting around. And from all accounts, Ethan had

been worse before Rosie brought him to his senses. "So he's selective?"

Ethan frowned over that. "I have no idea. It's just that Riley is…different. He's not like most guys I know. He thinks differently and he sees the world differently."

"He's dangerous."

Slowly, Ethan nodded. "I suppose you could say that, but only to someone on the wrong side of the law. To most people he's an advocate, a defender. Riley uses all his skill to help protect people." Ethan settled back in his seat, a little more at ease. "If you could have seen how he took that guy down—the one he found in your apartment—it was something else. Riley didn't look winded, didn't look like he'd used much effort, and he didn't look like he had a speck of emotion in him. Cold, swift and effective. One second the guy was running and the next he was completely immobilized by Riley. It was both awesome and a little unsettling." Then, more to himself than to Regina, Ethan murmured, "It still amazes me that he left the SWAT team to come here."

"Why did he? Do you have any idea?"

"Not a clue. Riley only lets people in so far. I'd trust him with my life and I know he's one of the best men around. But his past is off-limits. Not once in the five years I've known him has he given so much as a single clue."

Disappointed, Regina let out a long breath. Trying not to be too obvious, she asked, "Who has he been seeing most recently?"

Ethan rolled his eyes. "You."

"No, I mean before I moved in here."

"You."

"But we didn't…"

"Date? Doesn't matter." Ethan gave her a warm smile. "I remember we were all at Rosie's for dinner the day after we first met you. Riley talked about you—"

"Saying what?"

Ethan shrugged. "It wasn't what he said so much as how he said it. We all knew right then that he was interested. And the day of the fire…"

Ethan grew silent, stiff. He couldn't talk about that awful day without looking a little green. He closed his eyes, took two shallow breaths, and swallowed. "As distracted as I was that day with Rosie, I noticed how Riley staked a claim."

Regina pulled back. "He did *what?*"

Grinning, Ethan nodded. "He laid claim to you."

Flushing a little with umbrage—and with pleasure—Regina said, "But that's ridiculous."

"What did you think it meant when he picked you up and didn't put you down?"

"My head was bleeding. I was dazed."

"And unable to walk?" Ethan snorted. "He held you because he wanted to and because he decided you were his. Any guy within seeing distance knew it, and because Riley is who he is, they paid heed."

"But he hasn't asked me out or in any way acted interested." Ethan raised a brow and she quickly amended, "Until recently, I mean."

"Baloney. He's tried to teach you how to defend yourself and he's been following you around, keeping an eye on you, making your welfare his business. And he stares at you, Regina. Cracks Harris and Buck up, just to watch the way he watches you." Ethan smiled at that. So did Regina. "Riley's not one to spill his guts, but if I had to guess, I'd say you are a major distraction."

And then what? "You really think so?" She hated sounding so hopeful, but if Riley cared a little for her, if what he felt was more than just sexual…well, that would change everything.

"I know so." Ethan glanced at his watch, then stood. "Sorry to rush off, but Rosie has a few hours free." His grin told Regina all she needed to know. They loved each other so much. She wanted what they had, the closeness, the caring.

If she could have that with Riley, it'd be more than she'd ever dared to hope for.

Riley paced around the desk to the open window. "So you and Regina were engaged?"

Luther snorted. "Is that what she told you?"

Stiffening, Riley kept his back to the other man and asked softly, "Are you saying she lied?"

He snickered. "No. She *thought* we were engaged. But you know how it is. Regina's one of those women who has to have everything right and proper. She'd never have let me in her bed without a ring on her finger."

The clawing need to break the bastard's nose nearly choked Riley. "I see. So *you* lied?"

"I told her what she needed to hear. If you've met her, then you'll understand. She's so ladylike on the outside, I thought maybe she'd be a wildcat in bed. That made the deception worthwhile, or so I thought. But she was still stiff as a broom. No satisfaction at all. It was like sleeping with a damn board." He gave a hoarse laugh. "What the hell does this have to do with the trouble she's in?"

Riley turned to Luther with a cold smile. "Someone is bothering her. Damaging her property, scaring her. I'm trying to figure out who."

Luther shot to his feet. "You're accusing *me?*"

"Just gathering the facts—though it certainly sounds like you have a store of animosity for her."

"No. Hell no. You can stop gathering right now. When we split, I said good riddance to the little prude."

"No regrets, huh?"

Luther grunted. "Hardly." He took two incautious steps toward Riley. "You know what that twit had the nerve to do?"

Riley cocked a brow, but Luther didn't wait for him to reply. "She bought some goddamned books on sex, and she actually wanted to talk to me about them. She acted like I held part of the responsibility for her lack of enjoyment in the sack. I told her it was damned tough to satisfy a cold fish. She got pissed, and whenever she got that way, she got all stiff and righteous with her haughty little nose in the air."

Riley's smile hurt. "Yes, I know what you mean."

"You've seen it, haven't you?" Again, Luther didn't wait for a reply. He nodded, then chuckled. "Well, I was sick and tired of her acting superior so I told her it'd help if she'd try a little harder to get my interest. She's so damn skinny, I suggested a boob job." Here he laughed outright, even slapping his knee.

Riley churned with anger, but not by so much as the flicker of an eyelash did he let Luther know. "She's slight, but I haven't noticed her lacking at all."

"Then you haven't seen her naked. She's got a nice ass, but the upstairs leaves a lot to be desired."

Riley went mute with rage. It was bad enough

that Regina's childhood had instilled in her a need to make a good impression, but then to have this jerk tear her down and make her think her best wasn't good enough...

Luther's grin lingered. "Man, she hit the roof. She got all red-faced and told me she wouldn't marry a man who didn't want her as she is."

Satisfaction swelled inside Riley. *Bravo, sweetheart,* he silently congratulated her. Then through his teeth, he asked, "That ended the engagement?"

"Blew it to smithereens, which was more than fine by me. She tossed my ring back at me, walked away and I haven't seen her since. I haven't *wanted* to see her since." He leaned back on his desk and crossed his arms. "You know what? I bet she rubbed some other poor bastard the wrong way and he's retaliating. It'd serve the little witch right to get hassled a bit. Maybe it'll get her to loosen up and live a little."

Riley figured Regina would loosen up when the right man loved her, namely him. With trust would come complete comfort. But until then, he couldn't let Luther get away with insulting her.

He rubbed his chin thoughtfully, then moved forward half a step. Very calmly, giving Luther no warning, he said, "Let me explain something to you." Without haste, he reached for Luther's upper arm, clasped him in his right hand, easily found a pressure point, and applied the right grip to make the man's knees buckle and to force a short screech of pain from him.

Eyes wide with fear and teeth gritted in pain, Luther literally hung in Riley's one-handed grip.

Without compassion, Riley watched him writhe

in agony. In a voice more deadly because of its softness, he said, "Regina Foxworth is mine. Eventually
I'll marry her. Anyone who insults her insults me."

Luther let out a long broken groan. "You didn't tell
me that. Hey, I'm sorry!"

Riley shook his head. "No, not good enough. You
see, how do I know that you won't go spreading these
nasty rumors about her to other people? I think I should
impress on you exactly what I'll do if I ever hear of
you even mentioning her name again."

Luther gasped. "Please…"

Riley released him.

Slowly, holding his numb arm, Luther straightened.
His face was pale with lingering agony.

Legs braced apart, hands on his hips, Riley said,
"You have a lot more pressure points, Luther, places
that when manipulated just right, can cause pain you
can't even imagine. How many do I need to demon-
strate before you fully understand?"

"One's enough. I swear."

Riley said, "I don't know…"

Luther rushed behind his desk, which gave him a
false sense of safety. His arm hanging limp and useless,
he managed to stand more or less upright. "You better
get out of here," he groused in a shaky voice. "You're a
policeman. You can't do this to me. I'll report you—"

Riley pulled open his desk drawer. "Yeah? Well, I
can haul you in for smoking dope on the job." He lifted
out a joint, along with a small bag of marijuana. "What
do you think your supervisors will say to that?"

Luther's eyes went wide.

"I'll only say this once, Luther, so pay attention.
Stay away from Regina, keep your foul mouth shut,

and what you do on the job is your business. I really couldn't care less."

Luther slumped, but then another voice intruded from the doorway. "I care."

Riley looked up to see a slender woman in her midthirties, dressed much as Regina often did in business-casual wear, staring at Luther with hatred.

"You're the receptionist?" Riley asked.

Her chin went up another notch. "And I was his fiancée." She pulled off a miniscule diamond ring and pinged it off Luther's forehead. "Not anymore."

Luther groaned.

Riley went around the desk to the woman. "You overheard?"

"Yes. All of it. I came back to my desk a few minutes ago and I eavesdropped."

Riley felt a little uncomfortable. "I should apologize…"

"No. He's a pig and I'm sorry if he hurt your girlfriend at all."

"He hasn't. Regina is too smart to be hurt by him." At least, Riley hoped that was true. He'd find out for sure tonight—*after* he got her naked and let her know in no uncertain terms that he thought her utterly beautiful. Anything she didn't have, she didn't need.

The receptionist's shoulders went back. "What you did to him…the way you barely touched him yet he started whining in pain. How did that work?"

"Why?"

"I think it might be a useful thing to know."

Grinning, Riley fished a business card out of his wallet and handed it to her. "If you ever get over to Chester, stop into my gym and I'll teach you."

"Thank you."

As he left the insurance building, Riley admitted to himself that it probably wasn't Luther bothering Regina now. He'd watched the man's every expression and had seen only weakness, conceit and lewd innuendo. No real deception. Riley would keep an eye on him, but he doubted anything would turn up.

Once outside, he stopped on the sidewalk to stare at the newspaper building across the street.

One down, two to go.

Regina grinned at the determined way Buck tried to make friends with Butch. Buck looked like a felled titan in his black T-shirt and worn jeans, stretched out on the floor on his stomach, his chin on his crossed hands, meeting the dog at eye level.

Butch didn't cooperate.

No matter how softly Buck spoke to him or how he cajoled, the dog continued to give a low, vibrating growl of warning.

Buck glanced up at Regina, his green eyes alight with mischief. "You sure this damn dog isn't part badger?"

"I don't understand it. He's always so sweet to me."

Buck came to his feet, ruffled Regina's hair fondly and said, "Well now, honey, you're very easy to be sweet to."

Half-embarrassed by that odd praise, Regina gave an uncertain smile. "Um, thank you. If you'd like to take a seat, I can get you something to drink."

"No, thanks. Let's get right to it. You want the scoop on Riley, right?"

"Well, yes." But she rushed to explain, "I'm doing an interview on him."

"Uh-huh." Buck stretched out his massive arms along the back of the sofa and grinned. "He's hung up on you big-time. Never thought to see the mighty Riley with a weakness, but damn if he isn't acting smitten. It's downright fun to watch."

Regina blinked, then blinked some more. "Oh, but I didn't mean to—"

"What? Find out how he feels about you? 'Course you did." Buck continued to grin. "I don't mind. Riley's tough, no way around that. But any man who guards his past that closely has a few serious wounds. I'd like to see him happy and I happen to think you can accomplish that. So whatever I can do to nudge things along, count me in."

Such an awesome outpouring, from *Buck* no less, left Regina momentarily distracted and without a single coherent thought in her head. "Uh…"

"I think some woman did him wrong, don't you?"

Regina stared. "Well, I…"

"That'd make sense, huh? If it was a guy, Riley would have just kicked his ass, not quit his job and moved away. And now here you are, putting him into a possessive lather, helping him to focus on better things. I'm glad you moved in with him. Ought to keep him occupied." He winked.

Regina went hot to the roots of her red hair.

"So." Buck slapped enormous hands on his thick thighs. "Is that all you wanted?"

She cleared her throat twice and attempted to get control of the situation. "I, uh, had hoped to learn more about Riley's job, what he does, his training…"

Shaking his head, Buck came to his feet. "Sorry. I don't know anything about that. He used to be SWAT, but left the city to come here. Since Chester has no need of a SWAT team, Riley fell back on his old training of CSI. That's the beginning and end of what I know." Then he frowned. "Well, one other thing."

"Yes?"

He pushed up his T-shirt sleeve over a massive, bulging shoulder and flexed his arm to show off a seriously impressive biceps muscle. "See that?"

"Yes." Regina knew she wouldn't be able to circle that muscle even if she used both hands. "It'd be rather hard to miss."

Buck nodded. "I'm strong. I do a lot of physical work, day in and day out at the lumberyard. Men walk a wide path around me if I'm annoyed. But I don't have a single doubt in my mind that Riley, scrawny as he is, would make mincemeat out of me if he ever had a notion to."

He smiled as he made that claim, especially the ridiculous part about Riley being scrawny. Compared to Buck, he was certainly leaner, but scrawny? Nope, not by anyone's standards.

Buck tugged his sleeve back down and nodded. "That's some serious training that goes beyond what you're taught for a job, even if that job is SWAT. It's a lifestyle, a personality, an inherent part of the man. Riley's like a warrior born in the wrong century. He'd die to protect those people he cares about, and he'd expect loyalty in return."

Was this Buck's idea of a warning for his friend? Regina didn't know for sure, but she touched the arm he'd just bared and offered a smile. "I would never do anything to hurt him."

Buck patted her hand. "I know. That's why I think you're perfect for him."

He started for the door, and both Regina and Butch followed. "You know, Buck, I'm a little surprised. You're usually so quiet."

"Naw. It's just that with Harris around, who can get a word in edgewise?" He laughed, opened the door, and there stood Harris with his hand raised to knock. "Well, speak of the devil."

Riley eyed the tall, thin fellow with the wire-rimmed glasses and neatly combed blond hair. He wore a suit, complete with a tie and jacket. Everyone else in the room had removed their coats and rolled up their shirt-sleeves, loosened their ties. Not Carl Edmond.

The outward attention to detail had probably ap-pealed to Regina, even if the man hadn't.

Bent close to the keyboard, a slight frown on his brow, Carl typed industriously at the computer. Riley snagged a chair and pulled it up close. Carl was so ab-sorbed in his task, he didn't notice Riley until he sat down.

Shifting around, first startled, then polite, Carl asked, "May I help you?"

"Carl Edmond, right?"

"That's correct."

He didn't look alarmed, only curious. He didn't look like a predator, either, but Riley had learned long ago that even the most innocent expression could hide deceit. It was a lesson he'd never forgotten. After discreetly flashing his badge, Riley said, "I'm here informally, just to ask a few questions if you're willing."

Looking around the crowded room with a slight blush, Carl said, "Perhaps we should go someplace more private?"

"Sure."

Riley allowed himself to be led into an employee lounge. There was no one else present. Carl glanced at him. "Would you like some coffee?"

"Please." He was so courteous, Riley wondered that Regina hadn't been taken with him. He reminded Riley of a masculine version of Regina. Carl set a steaming cup of coffee in front of Riley, along with a small square napkin.

With those courtesies taken care of, Riley said, "You know Regina Foxworth."

Carl had just started to sip his coffee, but he stopped, face alight with pleasure. "Yes, yes I do." And then with sudden concern, he added, "She's all right, isn't she?"

"She's fine. But someone has made her a target." Riley explained the things that had happened, all the while watching Carl Edmond for the slightest flicker of guilt.

There was none.

"But this is terrible. Regina is… Well, she's a gentle, beautiful person. I don't mean her looks…well, her looks, too. But she's one of the kindest women I know. I owe her a lot. If there's any way I can help you to find this evil person…"

Riley leaned back in exasperation. Carl had a touch of melodrama. "Why do you say you owe her?"

The man actually blushed. "Well, it's a long story,

and I really hate to admit it, but I fancied myself in love with her. I'm afraid I made a real nuisance of myself, too, following her around like a lovesick pup." Here he shook his head and chuckled. "But Regina remained kind. She sat me down, explained that she only cared about me as a friend, and then she suggested that I wise up and pay more notice to the bagel girl."

"The bagel girl?"

"She delivers fresh bagels to this room twice a day. I didn't understand at first, but I did as Regina suggested." He held up a hand, showing off the gold wedding band. "Thanks to her, I'm now married to Carolyn. It was love at first sight, at least for me."

Riley ran a hand through his hair. "Great. Congratulations." And another dead end. If the new wedding hadn't been enough, Carl's obvious happiness would have swayed Riley. He pulled out a card and pushed it across the table toward Carl. "If you think of anyone who might want to hassle Regina, would you give me a call?"

"I'd be glad to." When Riley stood, Carl reached out and caught his arm. "Mr. Moore? Please. Take good care of her, okay? She's a very, very special person."

Riley nodded. "You have my word."

Chapter 9

He heard the raucous noise even before he finished
unlocking the door. Music, laughter, playful barking.

Brows drawn, Riley turned the knob and silently
pushed the door open. No one noticed him.

Regina sat cross-legged on the floor, her back to
the sofa where Harris lounged on his side, his head
propped up on a fist. Butch ran up Red's body, over
her shoulder, along Harris's length, then back down
over Regina.

Her shoulders were touching his stomach.

Harris's nose was practically in her ear.

Riley closed the door with a resounding click that
seemed more effective than a hard slam. Butch jerked
up. His small furry face went blank with surprise, then
lit up with blinding pleasure. Yapping with berserk
glee, he tumbled off Harris, rolled over Regina and

came charging toward Riley. Ears bouncing and little paws moving with lightning speed, he reached Riley and slid to a halt.

"Well, hello to you, too, squirt." Riley lifted him up and got his face thoroughly bathed with a warm doggy tongue. All the while he stared at Harris.

Slowly, his mouth twisted as if to hide a grin, Harris straightened. "Hey, Riley."

Riley continued to stare.

Regina scurried to the stereo and turned it off. Hands behind her back, she smiled shyly at Riley. *Shyly?* Now what was she up to?

She hesitated a second, then with only a bit less enthusiasm than Butch had shown, she came to him, went on tiptoe and kissed him. Not a polite welcome peck. Nope. She cupped his face and moved her soft sweet lips over his until Riley forgot that Harris was behind her. He snagged an arm around her waist, hauled her up against him, and pressed his tongue past her parted lips. When she went limp against him, Riley reluctantly ended the kiss.

"You're home," she said in a breathless whisper.

"Earlier than you expected?"

Harris chuckled. "Gee, Riley, is that a gun in your pocket or are you glad to see… Regina?"

Regina gasped, her thoughts plain on her face, but Riley relieved her mind by saying, "It's a chew toy for the dog."

Regina looked down at his lap and blinked at the ludicrously large bulge there. "Oh."

Harris cleared his throat. "I think I'll take this as my cue to get lost."

He had the nerve to stop at Regina's side, kiss her

cheek, and then wink at Riley. When Riley narrowed his eyes, Harris laughed and held up both hands. "Don't hurt me, Riley, okay?"

Riley rolled his eyes. "What are you doing here?"

"Ah, well, I'm just one in a long line of guys who've trooped through your door today."

Regina elbowed him hard. Riley took her arm and pulled her to his side so she wouldn't hurt herself poking at Harris. Regina was red in the face, Butch was squirming to be petted and Harris was trying to sidle out the door.

Riley opened it for him. "Later, Harris."

"Right." With a fast salute, Harris took off.

Riley closed and locked the door, then, ignoring Regina for the moment, headed to the couch with Butch. "So, my man, you missed me?" He seated himself and Butch immediately climbed up on his chest to sniff his face. He barked, bit Riley's chin and then tried to dig underneath his shirt.

Laughing, Riley set him aside. "Anxious for your gift, huh?"

Regina inched over to the couch. She smiled. "You're spoiling him, Riley."

"I thought it might keep him occupied while I carried you off to bed."

He heard her gasp, but didn't comment on it. He was so wired, so damned…*needy* after talking to the other men, he knew if he didn't have her soon, he'd explode. He pulled a large rawhide bone out of his pocket. Butch's eyes widened and his ears came forward in an alert pose.

Setting the bone on the floor, Riley asked, "Think you can handle that?"

The dog ran down Riley's leg and circled the bone, examining it from every angle, making both Regina and Riley laugh.

"It's bigger than he is."

Butch got one corner in his mouth and started backing up with the bone until he was completely hidden beneath a side table.

"That ought to keep him busy." Riley stood and turned toward Regina. "Now for you."

Regina chewed her lower lip. "Yes?"

"I missed you."

Her smile quivered the tiniest bit. "I missed you, too."

Riley slipped his arms around her waist. Staring down at her, he said, "I was going to go really slow, Red. I was going to start by teaching you a few self-defense moves, because that's important. Then I was going to carry you to bed."

"You've been teaching me self-defense moves for a while now," she reminded him.

"Not alone. Not in private where I can mix the lessons with kissing and touching."

"You've changed your mind about teaching me?"

"No, I just don't think I can wait. We'll work on your lessons afterward."

Her smile was sweet, sensual and teasing. "I'm glad. I've been thinking about you all day, too. I don't want to wait."

She caught her breath when Riley lifted her into his arms. He strode into his bedroom, pushed the door quietly shut with his foot, and sat on the edge of the mattress with her in his lap. "How could you have been thinking about me when you had Harris here entertaining you?"

She pushed his jacket off his shoulders. Riley helped, moving his arms until the coat fell to the bed. Next she began undoing his buttons. "We talked about you."

"You did?" He didn't like the sound of that, but with her small cool hands now on his chest, he found it hard to concentrate.

"Yes." She bent and kissed his throat. "I wanted to start your interview by talking to your friends."

Riley stiffened, but she caught his neck and quickly kissed him, scattering his thoughts.

"They respect you a lot, Riley."

"They?"

"Ethan, Buck and Harris."

His groan was due partly to dismay, partly to the way she removed his shirt and rained tiny kisses across his chest. "Hell, Red, you had all three of them here?"

"Mmm. They don't know any more about you than I do." She pushed him flat to the mattress, straddled his thighs and started on his belt buckle.

Riley settled his hands on her waist, charmed with her seduction, and so turned on he wanted her under him right this instant. "You know everything about me that you need to know."

She glanced up to give him a chastising smile. "No, I don't. But I can be patient. I've decided not to do the interview until you're comfortable talking to me about your past."

"Red…"

"Raise your hips." She had his slacks undone, so Riley did as ordered. She quickly skimmed them, along with his boxers, down his legs. She paused to tug off his shoes and socks, and then he was naked.

Regina let out a breath. "You are such a gorgeous man, Riley Moore."

"I'm glad you think so. Now come here."

"Just a second." She stood beside the bed and stared down at him. "You spoke with Luther?"

"Yeah. I spoke to him." *And I made him very sorry he ever hurt you.*

Regina nodded. She bent to pull off her sandals. "He, ah, told you about our breakup, didn't he?"

Rolling to his side so he could see her better, Riley propped himself up on one elbow. "He explained that he was an obnoxious, blind ass who doesn't deserve you."

Her lips curled in a disbelieving smile. "Never in a million years would Luther say something like that."

"No, but that's the gist of it." Riley watched her fidget with the straps of her sundress. Would she be daring enough to lose the dress? He hoped so. "Whether he realized it or not, whether you realize it or not, you're an incredibly sexy woman, Red." With a grin, he added, "I sure as hell realized it the second I saw you."

He heard her inhale deeply. "Thank you." She reached for the hem and tugged her dress up and over her head. After tossing it aside, she pushed her panties down and stepped out of them. She straightened and waited.

It was the oddest feeling, Riley thought, shaking with lust while choking with tenderness. He'd never experienced it before, but then, as he'd just told her, he'd known from the beginning that she'd be different.

He reached for her and toppled her across his chest. He rolled, putting her beneath him, and cupped one satiny breast. "You're perfect."

"I'm—"

"Perfect." He looked up into her eyes. "I understand about hurt, Regina. People say and do things that, if we let them, can hurt us deep inside and linger for too damn many days and nights."

Her expression froze. "Someone hurt you?"

Riley decided then and there that he'd tell her. He wanted her trust, so perhaps he had to give it first. He wasn't a polished man and he didn't have the persona of the senator, but he could be honest. "My wife."

She went rigid beneath him. "You were married?"

"Yeah." Her naked body distracted him and he said in a growl, "Luther is an idiot. I wouldn't change a single thing about you." He bent and took a nipple into his mouth.

"Riley, wait…" she said on a groan.

"Can't." He gently sucked while pressing his hand between her thighs. She was warm and soft, her springy curls already damp.

Regina waylaid him by catching his wrist. "Riley? There's something I always wanted to try."

Breathing hard, Riley forced himself to stop. It wasn't easy when he ached with the need for release. "What?"

"This." He let her push him to his back. Her breasts were against his chest, one of her legs between his. Her hair hung loose, silky soft and tousled. "Don't move."

He considered that a tall order considering the gorgeous view of her backside that she presented while twisting around to rummage in his nightstand for a condom.

Riley said, "In a hurry?"

"Yes. Tell me if I put this on you wrong." She opened the small packet and bent close to his groin, intent on her task. He could feel her breath and it made him moan. She blinked at him in surprise. "I haven't even touched you yet."

"I know." It was a miracle he could string those two words together. Her hair tickled across his abdomen, his thighs.

She looked down at his cock and smiled. In the next instant, she had him in her small, soft hand, gently squeezing. "Is this what you want?"

His groan mixed with a laugh. "I want you any way I can have you."

"Would you like me to kiss you?"

His vision narrowed; every muscle in his body clenched. He said, "Yes," although he doubted she meant what he wanted her to mean. His body arched in delicious pleasure. "Oh God."

Her mouth was warm, damp, her tongue curious. Riley caught her head in his big hands and guided her, urging her to swallow more of him, raising his hips to help her with that.

Her small sound of wonder vibrated along his shaft, and his fingers clenched. He'd dreamed about this, about the prim Regina Foxworth giving him head— and enjoying it. The reality beat the fantasy all to hell and back.

For several minutes she drove him crazy, tasting, teasing, humming again. Finally, she lifted away and Riley's heart swelled at the evidence of her excitement.

Her green eyes glowed with heat, her cheeks were flushed. "You taste good, Riley," she said in wonder.

Riley curled a hand around her thigh. He needed to come. He needed to be inside her. "So do you."

They stared at each other for a long moment before Regina bent to press one last innocent kiss to the head of his erection. Riley watched her straddle his thighs, saw her frown as she carefully rolled the condom on.

He checked it with her fascinated gaze never wavering, then pulled her over him. "Now what, babe?"

"Now I want to do it like this, with me on top."

"Yeah?" He gave her a crooked smile that almost hurt, he was so turned on. "I like that idea. That means I can see and touch all of you."

Her eyes darkened. "Yes." She lifted up, guided his cock to her opening, and slowly began sinking onto him. Riley held her thighs. She braced her hands on his chest.

It was incredible…seeing her face, watching her expressive eyes and the telling way her lips parted and her breasts rose with each deepened breath. "A little more," he urged, and her eyes closed as she wiggled, seating herself fully upon him.

Neither of them moved. Riley gasped for air, Regina's body clenched and relaxed around him.

"I can feel you throbbing."

He groaned and couldn't stop the lifting of his hips. Through his teeth, he growled, "I'm a nanosecond away from coming."

"Really?" She smiled down at him, then lifted.

"Really." She dropped and he said, "Regina…"

"I like this. Do you?"

Groaning again, he cupped her breasts, brushed her

nipples with his thumbs, then caught them both in his fingers, lightly pinching, tugging. Her back arched, driving him even deeper.

He knew he wouldn't last so he moved one hand between her legs, gliding his middle finger along her swollen lips, taut around him, then up to her turgid clitoris. "Move, honey. Ride me."

Her fingers splayed over his chest and she began to rise and fall, faster and faster. He loved the small sounds she made, the way her face contorted with her concentration, her pleasure. Riley kept his fingers just where she needed them, treating her to a constant friction that worked with her own movements. Soon she was in the same shape as him, shaking, on the verge of exploding.

He brought his knees up to support her back and returned her thrusts, lifting her knees from the bed as he drove into her. With a startled cry, she collapsed against him. Her mouth opened on his shoulder, her teeth coming down in a tantalizing love bite.

The small pain pushed him over the edge. Riley lost control. He gripped her ass and pounded into her, groaning harshly with his own unending climax, the crushing waves of pleasure going on and on...

He wasn't sure how much time passed when he became aware of Butch jumping beside the bed, demanding attention. Regina was a soft sweaty weight over his heart.

"Hey?" He moved fistfuls of her hair aside, kissed her ear. "You okay?"

"Mmmrrmf."

Riley managed a grin. "What's that?"

"I'm fine," she said against his neck, wiggling lazily. "Better than fine. I feel extraordinary."

He stroked her behind. "Yes, you do."

Her giggle was one of the sweetest sounds he'd ever heard. She was totally relaxed with him. Soon, she'd love him—as much as he loved her.

"We have three problems. We're both sweaty and sticking together. The condom's going to become useless in about two seconds if we don't separate. And Butch is none too pleased to be ignored."

Regina pressed her face into his chest. "You smell good sweaty." Lifting up to see him, she asked, "Do I?"

Damn, but she wrenched at his heart. "Good enough to eat."

She smiled and blushed, then turned her attention to Butch. "You have to wait, sweetie. Give me a second to regain feeling in my legs, and I'll get up and play."

"That dog is worse than an infant."

"How would you know? Ever had an infant?" It was just an offhand remark, not really serious.

"No." Riley rolled her to his side, filling his hand with her hair so he could see her face. "I wanted a baby though."

That bald admission, especially after lovemaking, got her attention. "You did?"

"Yeah." He kissed her, then sat up in the bed. "Stay put. I'll be right back." He headed to the bathroom to dispose of the condom. It also gave him a moment to gather his thoughts and figure out how to say what he wanted her to know, to understand.

When he returned, she was sitting up against the headboard, wearing his shirt and holding Butch. The dog took one look at Riley and tried to keep him out of the bed with his pseudo-attacks.

"You mangy little mutt, I'm the one who brought you the bone, remember?"

At the mention of the enormous chew, Butch's ears perked up and he went to the edge of the bed, whining to be let down. With a sigh, Regina lowered him to the floor. He ran out the bedroom door in a flash.

Riley found his boxers, pulled them on, and sat on the bed at her side. "You look good in my shirt."

She laughed, making a halfhearted effort to smooth her wild hair. "You know what I think? I think you just like giving compliments."

"Only to people who deserve them." He fingered the collar of the shirt, then undid the button between her breasts. He didn't know if he'd ever get enough of her—

Something solid and damp landed on his foot. Butch had dragged the colossal chew bone over to him, and was now jumping at the side of the bed again.

"Oh no. I don't want that thing in my bed."

A barked argument ensued. When Riley held firm, Butch got hold of the very edge of the bone and tried to stand up against the bed. He couldn't. He looked ridiculous with his mouth full and he made an odd snorting noise during his struggle. Riley couldn't help but laugh. "All right, you pathetic little beggar. You win. But keep it down at the foot of the bed."

He lifted both dog and bone, then laughed again when Butch did his best to hide the gigantic thing under the covers. Riley helped by lifting the blankets for him, then caught Regina's sweet indulgent expression. "What?"

She reached out and touched his jaw. "When I first

met you, I knew you were very capable and strong. That's as noticeable as your blue eyes, and I told myself that I needed to get closer to you to learn some self-defense."

"Which you've yet to do."

She ignored that. "Then after a while I decided you were a terrific friend, too. You're so at ease with the guys and with Rosie. I wanted so badly to be a part of that."

"And you are."

"Yes." She touched his mouth, tracing his lower lip with her fingertips. "After I brought Butch home, I got to see how gentle you are. That was such a turn-on, Riley." Her smile trembled. "Now, seeing your patience and generosity, it occurs to me that you'd also make a wonderful father." She laughed. "Although you'd probably spoil your kids rotten."

Riley turned his head and kissed her palm. She was getting into some pretty deep stuff here. So far, she'd admitted to liking and admiring him. He wanted more. He wanted her love.

"I think we can spend a few minutes talking before we need to get dressed for the ceremony."

"I'd like to talk about…things."

"Yeah?" He moved into bed beside her, put his arm around her and tugged her into his side. "I haven't wanted to really talk to a woman in a long time."

"You prefer to just rush her into bed?"

He shrugged. "I haven't been a saint, but I haven't been sexually attracted to that many women either. Now here you are, and I want to talk to you and be inside you at the same time. It's damn strange."

"Gee, thanks."

Riley hugged her. "You go first then."

He felt her nod before she said, "I always knew it wasn't me."

Riley just held her, waiting.

"I've never been ashamed of my build or thought I was lacking. I'm just me and I try really hard to be the best that I can. But even though I realized Luther is a creep, I was still…worried."

"Without reason. You're incredible, a beautiful person inside and out."

"Thank you."

Riley smiled at her continued good manners. "Any problems in the sack were his, Red. It was never about you."

"Yes, I know." She stroked his abdomen and sighed. "Especially now. After today, after being with you, I won't worry anymore." Then she turned into his side, wrapped her arms tight around him as if to protect him, and whispered, "But you didn't know, did you? The woman who hurt you—you blame yourself."

Riley tensed. "It's not the same thing, honey."

"Will you tell me what happened? Not for an interview and not for nosiness, but because I care about you, Riley. And I know from experience that it helps to talk."

A good start, Riley thought, then wondered if she'd feel the same when he finished his tale. "I've never told anyone before." He wanted her to know that, to understand the level of his trust. He shuddered at the small kiss she pressed to his chest, right over his heart. "She died, Red."

A strange stillness settled over her. "Your wife?"

"Yes." He was glad Regina kept her face tucked

against him, rather than looking at him. He wasn't a coward, but he couldn't remember those awful days of lies and deceit—his and hers—without feeling raw. "She was having an affair with Phil, one of my friends from the SWAT team." With disgust he added, "A man I respected."

The silence felt heavy, almost suffocating Riley before she asked, "How do you know?"

Riley shook his head, once again wishing he could somehow change things. "I caught them in bed together. I came home from work early and found them in my bedroom, in my bed."

"I'm so sorry."

"I always have control, Regina. Always. But when I saw them, I didn't bother using it. I can't claim temporary insanity or a blinding jealous rage. That would be a lie. I was pissed off, completely furious, and I wanted to beat the hell out of Phil, so I did. I coldly, methodically, hurt him. Not permanently, but I did a lot of superficial damage."

"But listen to what you're saying. You could have killed him, Riley. You're more than capable. But you didn't. Instead you just hurt him, as he deserved."

Riley shook his head. "No one got what they deserved that awful day." He had to draw three breaths before he could continue. "My wife flew around me, screaming and crying. Phil… He was good, but he didn't stand a chance against me."

Regina fisted a hand on his chest. "He was in bed with your wife, Riley. Most men would react the way you did."

"Most men aren't me."

"Meaning you fight better than they could?"

He laughed. "There was no fight to it."

"And don't you see? Another man without your control might have killed him, even if he hadn't meant to."

He couldn't deny that. As a cop, he'd seen more than a few crimes of passion. "You know, it was strange, but a good part of my anger was for Phil's wife. She was seven months pregnant at the time."

Regina curled closer, both arms around him, one leg over his. Absently, Riley stroked her shoulder.

"God, Regina, when Phil finally left my house, my wife went with him and…" He hesitated, but she had a right to know. "They both died in a car wreck."

"They made their own decisions, Riley."

"They were both upset. Physically, Phil was in no condition to drive. I should have stopped them. I should have at least stopped her from going along. But I didn't." His throat hurt, but he said it all. "I wanted her out of my sight. I wanted her gone."

"But you didn't want her dead."

She sounded so sure of that. Many times, Riley had remembered that awful day and wondered. He'd been so detached through it all, as if his heart had been anesthetized. "No, I didn't want her dead." Saying it out loud made him finally believe it. He'd reacted, but without the intent of such dire consequences. "Hell, I didn't even want *him* dead. But when I got the call, I dunno, most of my concern was for Phil's wife. I kept seeing her in my mind, how happy she'd been, all the plans she'd been making for them as a family." He glanced down at Regina. "She was cute as hell pregnant and whenever we got together she'd show us the new baby clothes she'd bought or a bassinet or a toy."

"Oh God, how did she take the news about Phil and your wife…"

He shook his head. "I never told her, Red. Not about the cheating. I've never told anyone." He glanced down at her. "Except you."

Regina's eyes were big and soft, filled with understanding. "How did you explain them being in the car together?"

He laughed, but the sound wasn't humorous. "I was CSI—I knew how to cover my tracks. I made sure no one would know I'd been home when he and my wife left together, then I said my wife must have been helping him with a gift for the baby. I told everyone that they'd discussed it, made plans to buy something wonderful because Phil wanted to surprise his wife. No one doubted it. No one questioned me. Hell, no one even noticed my bloody knuckles." He swallowed down his own disgust. "They didn't see the bruises on Phil, either. The wreck was pretty bad and the car caught on fire." His voice went so quiet, it was barely audible. "Neither of them was all that recognizable."

Riley could feel Regina shivering. "Was anyone else hurt in the wreck?"

"No, thank God. They went off the side of the road, down into a gully. The car flipped and hit a tree. There were no other cars involved."

His stomach started churning; absently he rubbed it, trying to fight off the familiar sickness. Butch appeared, his little furry face so expressive, so concerned. He whined as if he'd sensed Riley's upset, then crawled up onto his chest and curled up under Riley's chin.

Stupidly enough, it helped.

Emotion clogged Riley's throat, but he hugged Regina with one arm, patted Butch with his other hand, and wished the damn story didn't still hurt so much.

Regina was frozen and silent for a long time before asking, "What ever became of Phil's wife?"

"I stuck around until after the birth, trying to help her out. She had a baby boy she named Phil, after his daddy. Phil had a life insurance policy so she's not too bad off financially. After that, I left. I quit my job and moved here. I heard she got remarried about a year ago. Her kid would be… I dunno, almost five now." He stroked his fingers through Regina's hair, taking comfort in her warmth and softness. "I hope she and the kid are happy."

Suddenly Regina sobbed.

Startled, Riley tried to see her face but she pressed herself so close, it felt like she wanted to crawl inside him. Butch panicked, whining at Riley, poking his nose into Regina's cheek.

"Hey. Honey, what's the matter?"

She hiccuped and in a strangled voice said, "I want to give you something, Riley, okay?"

As she spoke, she turned her face up to his and Riley grimaced. She didn't cry well. Already her eyes were watery and red, matching her nose. Her cheeks were blotchy. He smiled. "Yeah, sure. But please, don't cry, baby. I can't stand it."

That made her start sobbing again. She crawled out of the bed, still sniffling, and headed out of the room.

"Regina?"

"I'll be right back," she wailed.

Riley watched her go, enjoying the way his shirttails barely covered her tush. He looked at Butch. "Women." Then he added, "But damn, she looks good in my shirt, doesn't she?" And he murmured, "Even better out of it, though."

She came back into the bedroom, the framed photo in her hand. She plopped into bed, burrowed into Riley's side, and dropped the photo on his lap. "Here, you can have it."

Lip curled in distaste, Riley lifted the smug, smiling face of Senator Welling away from his body and dropped it on the nightstand. "Gee, thanks. Just what I always wanted."

Regina gave a choked laugh, lightly punched him, and then hugged him in a strangle hold. "You asked me earlier why I brought the stupid thing along."

Stupid thing? "Uh, yeah."

"I see the photo and I remember his commitment to his family and how he stands for all the things, I value. It gives me hope that someday I'll have those things, too."

Riley rolled his eyes. "Regina…"

"It gave me hope that some day I'd meet a man like him. But I don't need him for inspiration anymore." She smiled up at Riley and even with the blotchy cheeks, she looked beautiful. "You're the finest man I know, Riley. No one else could ever measure up to you."

Oh hell. It was bad enough when he thought she used Welling as a masculine measuring tape. But if he became the damn tape, she was bound for disappointment. "No, Regina, I'm just a man."

"A good man. A real man. And that's better than a public persona any day."

Riley's heart about stopped. Was it possible she loved him, too? Had he finally gotten through to her? He started to tell her so when his phone rang. Riley reached for the nightstand and snatched up the receiver. "Hello?" And then with foreboding, "Yeah, Dermot. What's up?"

Just as he suspected, Earl had been released. The judge returned not more than a few hours ago, but Earl had made his call and somehow gotten things expedited.

"Thanks for the heads-up. I guess all we can do now is hope he doesn't jump bail." He hung up and rubbed his face. "Looks like we're back to square one unless Senator Welling can remember something vital."

Regina gasped as if someone had pinched her. "Oh no. Senator Welling and the ceremony. We're going to be late."

Riley glanced at the clock and cursed. "We'll make it if we hurry." He threw the covers aside and stood.

Regina remained in bed, her bottom lip caught between her teeth. "Riley? Are you sure we can't just skip it? Somehow, I'm not as excited about seeing him as I had been."

He smiled, caught her under the arms and lifted her from the bed. "No, we can't skip it. I don't want to miss this chance. If we get there early, we can talk to the senator before the ceremony begins and get it out of the way."

"Then come back here and make love some more?"

Riley feigned a scandalized gasp. "Why, Ms. Fox-worth, you surprise me."

She grinned. "When we get home, I'll surprise you even more."

Home. He liked the sound of that. "It's a deal."

Chapter 10

Butch put on an awful, melodramatic fit about being left alone. He was a smart little dog who understood *everything* whenever the mood suited him, and right now he understood that two dressed humans heading for the door meant he'd be alone.

He didn't like it, and he didn't hold back in letting them know his deepest feelings. Not only did he howl pitifully, but he laid flat on his belly and did an army crawl, as if his little legs wouldn't work.

They tried stepping out and waiting to see if he'd calm down. He didn't. He made such a racket that he sounded like a pack of wolves. Riley feared complaints from his neighbors if they left Butch carrying on so enthusiastically.

In the end, since the ceremony would mostly be outdoors, Regina gave in and tucked him away in her satchel. She hooked his leash to his collar as a precaution in case he attempted to escape. She kept the leash wrapped around her hand and the strap of the big bag over her shoulder with Butch close to her side.

He seemed to like that just fine. He curled up and went to sleep like a baby in a knapsack.

"And you said *I'd* spoil him?"

Regina scowled at that accusation. "He's still getting used to us. There's been no stability in his life yet, what with me bringing him home, then bringing him here…"

Riley drew her close without mussing her hair, and pressed a warm kiss to her forehead. "I do understand. Even cantankerous little dogs need reassuring." Then he grinned. "Just remember that us old dogs need it, too."

Regina intended to reassure him in a big way as soon as they returned. She was going to tell him how she felt. Love was love and it should never be denied. To get it, you had to give it. That was the argument she'd used when choosing Butch, and now she'd apply it to Riley. She'd give him her heart and hope he gave his in return.

It had worked with Butch.

Riley drove his truck to the ceremony. Regina felt the difference now in just being with him. There was a new comfort, a new ease that existed between them. She thought of everything he'd told her, everything he'd gone through. No wonder he hadn't wanted to get involved again. He had not only the emotional turmoil of an unfaithful spouse, but he also had a battle with his professional conscience for being untruthful.

Regina considered his thoughtfulness for Phil's wife one of the most commendable things she'd ever heard.

Riley had put his own hurt aside to protect someone else—and that, more than anything, defined the type of man he was.

Milling crowds filled the lawn in front of the museum center where the Historical Society had planned the ceremony. Keeping Regina tucked close to his side with a precautionary, proprietary air, Riley repeatedly flashed his badge to dispatch a path to the quiet chambers inside the museum where Senator Welling passed the time until his introduction. In the end though, it was Regina who got them beyond the final barrier of guards.

She gave her name and politely asked them to inform Senator Welling that she would greatly appreciate a moment of his time. One unconvinced guard did as she asked, then returned with a smile, saying Senator Welling would love to see her again.

The guards wouldn't let Riley in, though, and Riley wouldn't let Regina in without him. He was most firm on that issue, so Regina stuck her head in the heavy carved wooden door of the museum's inner sanctum and requested that her escort be given entrance as well.

Senator Welling, smiling and as jovial as the last time she'd seen him, rose from behind a large desk and bid them both inside. "Ms. Foxworth—Regina—how wonderful to see you again."

It was enough of a surprise that he remembered her, but he also sounded sincerely happy to see her. Regina smiled with true pleasure. By rights, the senator should have looked exhausted from his recent travels. The commendation from the Historical Society came at the tail end of a two-week tour. Instead, he looked vital and energetic. "Senator Welling. I hope we're not imposing."

"Of course not. And please, no formality here. Call me Xavier. After all, we're old friends now."

"Why, thank you. I'd be honored."

Another guard came forward to frisk both her and Riley.

"I'm sorry," Xavier said with a wry, philosophical shrug. "They're quite insistent on doing their jobs."

"Oh, I understand. You're a very important man. Of course they have to protect you." Regina held her arms out to her sides and submitted to being patted down. Butch didn't take it well, snapping at the guard and startling him when he peeked inside the bag. The senator, a lover of animals, was merely amused when Butch peeked out at him and growled.

Unlike the others who'd called her dog a rat and worse, Xavier said, "Such distinctive coloring. A pure-bred Chihuahua?"

"Yes, thank you. I think he's beautiful, too." Regina beamed at Xavier for his exquisite taste in animals.

Riley didn't take the invasion of privacy much better than Butch had, but at least he didn't try to bite anyone. He introduced himself, showed his badge, and still got roughly checked for hidden weapons. Regina watched him warily, unsure what he might do.

When the security check had been completed, he merely nodded. "Senator Welling—"

"Xavier, please," he reminded Riley.

Riley conceded with a nod. "Xavier. Thank you for seeing us."

"It's my pleasure." After sharing a hearty handshake with Riley, he took Regina's hand and winked at her.

"We have plenty of time to spare before the ceremony and I've only been sitting here hoping I won't trip over my words."

His charming, self-deprecating grin could win over the worst skeptics, Regina decided. "I'm sure you'll keep them all enthralled."

Laughing, still holding her hand, Xavier turned to Riley. "My biggest fan, or so she tells me."

Riley's mouth flattened. "Yeah, she tells me that, too."

Regina frowned at Riley's tone—and noticed he was staring at Xavier's hand clasping hers. Could he be jealous? He'd made that comment about old dogs needing reassurance, too. Trying to be inconspicuous, she pulled away from Xavier. "Senator, how is your intern? That lovely young lady I met at the park with you."

His gray brows rose in confusion. "My intern?"

Regina forged on. "I recall she was very quiet, but you told me she worked hard and was very dedicated to you."

Xavier cleared his throat. "Yes, a hard worker. I'm sorry, but you know, I can't keep up with all the interns. They come and go, and…" Suddenly he stopped. He turned to his guards and said, "Wait outside."

The guards shared a look, hesitant to obey.

Xavier frowned and rounded his desk to shoo them away. "Really, I'm quite safe here with the young lady and her friend. Go. I'd like some privacy."

Regina was stunned at the sudden turn of events. Both men were forced out a door at the back of the office, behind where Xavier had been sitting. In a heartbeat, Riley was there, standing mostly in front of her, blocking her with his body. She tried to nudge him aside, but he wouldn't move.

"Riley, really," she whispered.

Glancing over his shoulder, he gave her one brief, hard look that stopped all other protests in her throat.

When Xavier turned back to them, his expression had become strained. "There. Much better, don't you think?" His smile didn't reach his eyes. "Please, take a seat and tell me what you've been up to." Xavier returned to his chair.

Regina started to take the nearest chair opposite the desk, but Riley stopped her by backing further into her.

"With your permission, Senator, I'd like to ask you a few questions about that day in the park."

Xavier's complexion paled. He looked down at his desk a moment, then faced Riley squarely. "Is there a problem?"

Regina could feel the tension in Riley, but she didn't understand it. He seemed braced for an attack, ready to charge. But why?

"Since that day, Regina has been repeatedly threatened by someone. I believe it started with the car that ran her off the road."

Xavier swallowed, and in a murmur said, "Thank God she wasn't injured that day. Terrible, terrible thing to happen to a young woman. She could have been killed."

Riley's arms hung loose at his sides. It was a negligent pose, but Regina had taken enough lessons from him to know he was readying himself, keeping limber, poised.

"Yes, she could have. And that wasn't the only incident. She's been accosted several times. The worst, however, was the fire."

Xavier's head shot up. "A fire?"

"Yes. A deliberate fire, in my opinion. It burned a building to the ground and almost took Regina and her friend with it."

Xavier squeezed his eyes shut and shook his head. "This is dreadful. Just dreadful."

By small degrees, Riley started backing up, forcing Regina toward the door where they'd entered.

The sense of foreboding was so thick in the air, Regina thought she might choke on it. "Senator?"

He shook his head. "I'm only a man, flawed, damn it."

"What the hell does that mean?" Riley demanded.

The senator looked up, then beyond Riley. His face went ashen.

Someone had stepped in the room behind them.

Startled, more than a little frightened, Regina jerked around—and let out a relieved breath. Mrs. Welling stood there, elegantly dressed in a turquoise suit with pearl jewelry.

Riley started to move Regina to his side, but Mrs. Welling reached out and took her hand. "Hello. I heard Xavier had guests."

Flustered, Regina all but gushed. "Mrs. Welling! It's so wonderful to finally meet you. I didn't know you were here, too, but then you always accompany Xavier, don't you?"

"'Xavier'?" She slanted a sardonic look at her husband. "I see you're a close friend, to call him by his first name."

"Oh." Regina felt the heat pulsing in her face. "No, not at all. He just—"

"It's all right. My husband has mentioned you, Ms. Foxworth." Mrs. Welling was tall, softened with age, but still striking in appearance. Her brown hair was stylishly laced with gray, her eyes a stunning, clear blue. She held Regina's hand overlong.

Regina was aware of Xavier slowly standing behind his desk, of Riley stepping aside so that he stood between husband and wife. Regina prayed Riley wouldn't lose his temper and do something outlandish.

She was trying to send him a warning look to behave when the door behind Xavier opened. Regina's view was blocked by Riley, but she heard him curse. With Mrs. Welling still clasping her hand, she stepped to the side to better see.

A tall man, probably a guard, stood there. He wasn't smiling, and he kept his narrowed, alert gaze on Riley. Slowly he lifted his right arm and pointed a gun.

Regina gasped. Instinctively, she tried to move toward Riley, but Mrs. Welling kept her immobile. "Meet Earl Rochelle, Ms. Foxworth. I believe he's made himself something of a nuisance to you."

Confusion warred with fear. "You…you're the one who broke into my apartment?" Regina had a hard time taking it in. Mrs. Welling seemed so cold, Xavier was rocking back and forth on his heels, muttering to himself and shaking his head. Riley just stood there, as sturdy and unshakable as a stone wall.

Earl nodded at Riley. "Your lover boy roughed me up. But now it's time for payback."

Riley shifted the tiniest bit. "You son of a bitch." His

voice was calm, without inflection. "So you're working for the senator?"

Xavier violently shook his head. "No. No, I'd never hurt anyone…"

Mrs. Welling laughed. "Xavier, be truthful. You hurt me all the time." Her lovely face contorted—with pain, with anger. "Every single time you crawl into bed with another woman. But no more, you bloated, pompous ass. I've stuck with you this long, and I'll be damned if I let you ruin our family now."

Regina turned to face her, her brain blank with shock, with disbelief. "Mrs. Welling… I'm sorry. I didn't know."

"Of course you didn't. Along with a good portion of the constituents, you think Xavier is an honorable man, a *family* man. In truth, my dear, he's a lying, cheating pig."

Xavier shook his head, his face now bright pink, his eyes pleading. "No, dear. It was only those few times…"

"I'm not a fool, Xavier. I've known of every single affair. Your intern—who by the way, Ms. Foxworth, is no more than a well-paid prostitute—was only one in a long line of young women. You preach family values, all the while you're paying for sex with a common whore."

Her voice had risen with her ire, and Earl moved closer. "Mrs. Welling, please. Discretion is necessary."

She released Regina to wave away his concerns. "I dismissed the guards for now. I told them to return when it's time for Xavier's introduction. We've at least fifteen more minutes."

Regina suddenly understood. "The photograph." She

stared at Mrs. Welling. "It has the intern... I mean, the prostitute, in the picture with the senator. They were..." Aghast, she turned to stare at Xavier. "They were having an affair *in the park?*"

"You begin to understand. The stupid park wasn't due to be open. Xavier knew I was watching him, and he thought he could lose my spies in the woods. But Earl kept a tail on him." She glanced at her husband with loathing. "Earl saw everything, including the damn picture you took. Xavier, the idiot, didn't think it was anything to worry about. He didn't think anyone would put two and two together. I know better. If that picture got out, the whole family would be ruined. I had Earl run you off the road, but you kept the camera around your neck and Xavier came to your aid."

Sadly, his shoulders slumped, Xavier said, "I couldn't let you hurt her."

"The way you hurt me?" Mrs. Welling turned away from him. "At the fire we finally got the camera, but it was filled with new film. Since then, we've been unable to find either the undeveloped film or the photograph."

Riley laughed. "She has it framed and keeps it in her bedside drawer."

Regina gaped at him even as she felt herself enveloped in mortified heat. *"Riley."*

Riley ignored her, moving closer to the desk, casually leaning a hip on the edge. Earl stiffened, but kept quiet.

The senator stared at her in astonishment.

Mrs. Welling's face contorted. "So you've slept with him, too?" she wrongly concluded. Outraged, she shook her head and addressed Riley. "Thank you for letting us know." Her lip curled, destroying her image of a respected and elegant politician's wife. "Retrieving the vile thing will be so much easier now, especially with you two out of the picture."

"And how exactly do you plan to accomplish that?"

At Riley's question, she pulled another gun out of her purse, but this one was odd-shaped, unlike any gun Regina had ever seen. "Why don't you let me worry about that, Mr. Moore?"

Riley shifted again. Regina felt sure he planned to do something, but what, she couldn't guess. She only wished he'd hurry up. She was starting to sweat nervously. Things did not look good. She realized that she should have been worried about him, but she somehow knew he'd handle things.

Then Mrs. Welling made the bad decision to grab Regina by the hair. She had the odd gun raised when suddenly Butch exploded from the bag with such a feral, wild snarl it sounded like a pack of demon dogs had been unleashed.

He bit Mrs. Welling's hand, her arm, and ran right up to her face where he sank his small sharp teeth into her nose. The woman screamed in reaction and swatted at the dog.

Regina saw red. She hadn't realized she'd learned anything substantial from Riley, but without any real thought she caught her small dog in one arm, grabbed the arm holding the gun in the other and deftly tripped Mrs. Welling to her back. The woman hit her head on the hardwood floor and stayed there, dazed.

Regina jerked the gun from her hand.

Almost at the same time, Riley moved with blinding speed. His leg came up and over the desk, landing his foot squarely in the senator's face. He went down with a grunt. Earl moved, but Riley already had the advantage. He grabbed Earl's gun arm, pulled him forward and delivered his elbow into his throat.

Gagging and gasping, Earl collapsed to his knees. The gun fell from his hand and Riley kicked it aside. Hesitating only a moment to make certain Earl was sufficiently incapacitated, Riley turned and reached for the fallen gun. Both doors exploded open as guards filed in. Riley groaned, his hands lifted in a nonthreatening pose. He started to explain, and finally saw that Dermot and Lanny headed up the cavalry. He actually laughed.

Dermot grinned. "We followed him. You seemed so sure he was up to something more than a break-in."

Lanny nodded. "And you being sure made us sure, so when the judge returned and we had to release him, we decided it might be smart to keep a close watch."

"Good job," Riley told them and they both puffed up like proud peacocks.

"Explaining to these guys wasn't easy though." Dermot nodded to the hired guards with a scowl.

They ignored him.

One stepped forward and picked up the strange gun by Mrs. Welling. "A tranquilizer gun?"

Regina's knees felt suddenly weak. She trembled from her head to her toes. "She was going to use it on us." Her voice was little more than a breathy squeak. "Then he—" she pointed to Earl "—was going to kill us."

The guards looked at her like she was nuts. Earl shouted denials. Senator Welling stirred just in time for a small bespectacled woman in a black suit to duck her head into the room and say, "Senator, it's time for… your…introduction." Her eyes rounded, looking huge behind her glasses.

One of the guards caught her arm and pulled her completely into the room, then shut and locked the door.

The senator moaned. Mrs. Welling, now sitting on the floor holding her head, said, "Forget it. There'll be no more honors for him."

Regina looked around at the chaos and wanted to cry. It was more than just the scandal that was sure to ensue, the political ramifications, the threat to her and Riley. Something she'd cherished, something she'd believed was real, had just been defiled in the worst possible way.

Her stomach actually cramped. She'd been such an utter fool.

Then Riley was there, his hand closing gently on her upper arm. "Babe, you're crushing Butch. Loosen up."

Regina glanced at Butch, at his bulgy little eyes, and saw it was true. She relinquished her hold on him.

"That's it. Here, let me hold him." Riley balanced the dog in one arm, up close to his chest because Butch seemed more than a little rattled by all that had happened. He was curled in on himself, his eyes still wild, and low growls continually emitted from deep in his throat as he watched everyone and everything. Once Riley held him, he looked less threatened.

With his other arm, Riley gathered Regina protectively into his side. Regina knew everyone was looking at her with varying degrees of expression—virulence from Mrs. Welling, disgrace from Xavier, concern from Lanny and Dermot.

She felt like a spectacle, something she detested, a feeling left over from her childhood. Ashamed, she turned into Riley to hide. "You told them where I kept the picture."

At her agonized whisper, he tightened his hold and his voice became hard. "Only to distract them, to keep them talking until I could best situate myself to react."

"Oh." She supposed that made sense. She'd put them into a situation and he'd had to rescue them because of it.

"Damn it, Red, I would never deliberately do anything to hurt you."

He sounded so outraged, Regina tried to soothe him. "Okay, Riley." The last thing she wanted was another spectacle.

To her surprise, Riley murmured near her ear, "Red, you've made me so proud."

"Proud?" She wasn't expecting that and her laugh was bitter and hurt. "I was a gullible idiot."

"No. You handled yourself well, disarming Mrs. Welling, protecting Butch, helping me."

Had she done all that? She had struck out at the crazy woman, but… "I got us in this situation in the first place by being an idiot."

"No." He turned her to face him, his expression volatile. "You're you, sweet and trusting and sincere, and I happen to love you an awful lot."

She jerked back. The suffocating crowd and her own embarrassment seemed to fade away. Her entire focus was on Riley and those awesome words he'd just uttered. "You what?"

With exasperation, he took her arm and towed her into the farthest corner of the room. It wasn't really far enough, merely a few feet away. The guards were watching them while another phoned a supervisor on his cell phone. The situation was sticky and could explode into an ugly scandal if it wasn't handled quickly and efficiently.

Riley cupped the back of her neck and put his forehead to hers. "Listen to me, Regina. I know the human garbage that exists in our world. Hell, I've dealt with them more times than I care to remember. Rapists, murderers, sadists... They're out there and we all have to be careful. But there are a lot of good people in the world, too, the kind of people you believe in."

"Like you."

"Like *you*." He looked pained. "I'm not perfect, Red. I'm as flawed as your senator. But I would never cheat on you or deliberately hurt you and I'll always try to make you happy. You have my word on that."

She stared at him.

"I love you for who you are. I don't want you to change, to be jaded by this. I *like* the things you believe in. Hell, I believe in them, too." He bent to see her face. "You still do, don't you? You won't let one creep distort things for you?"

Her smile came slowly, along with sudden insight. The senator wasn't the man she'd believed him to be—but Riley was. True, he wasn't perfect, so he'd likely make mistakes in his life, just as she would. But he was steadfast, solid, a man you could rely on.

A man she could trust with her love.

"No, I won't let him disillusion me." She touched Riley's chest. She knew Riley, so she knew how incredible a person could be. No one could ever change that. "I love you, too, Riley. I fought it, but I knew last night that I'd lost the battle."

He didn't smile, but new warmth darkened his blue eyes. "I've known how I feel for a long while now."

"Buck and Harris and Ethan knew how you felt, too."

"They *what?*"

Nodding, Regina said, "They told me, but I didn't really believe them." Then in a barely there whisper, she confessed, "I thought you only wanted sex."

He rolled his eyes. "Of course I want sex," he answered in the same low whisper, and then added with gentle awe, "Look at you."

At his very private words, she glanced around the room. She knew no one could hear him, but when Lanny winked at her, she blushed. They really should have found some privacy for this chat.

"I was giving you time, Red, and trying to get this mess sorted out so we wouldn't be distracted." He looked up at the sound of the door opening and two more men—very official in appearance—stepped in. "I think the mess just got messier, but at least you're out of it now. I can concentrate on you."

"On us?" she specified.

He pressed a firm kiss to her mouth. "Yes."

"I do love you, Riley, but now that this is over, I have no reason to stay with you. I'm not the type of woman who shacks up."

He went stiff as a board, and Regina said, "Will you marry me?"

He slumped against her, half in relief, half in amusement. Butch complained until he could squirrel up between their bodies and poke his face out.

"Riley?" Regina prayed he'd said yes.

"Yeah, I'll marry you." He grinned. "It's nice having a very proper woman around. Takes the guesswork out of things."

With that settled, Regina turned back to face the room. "What do you think will happen now?"

"I dunno. I don't really care as long as none of them can ever again threaten you."

A sort of wistful melancholy crept up on her. "It's strange, but I still think he's a good senator—he's just not a good husband."

"Maybe. I promise I'll be a good husband." When she smiled in agreement, Riley hugged her tight. "One thing, Red."

"What?"

"You remember what I said about babies?"

Regina softened all the way to her toes. Her knees felt like butter, her heart full and ripe. "Yes."

"I'm a homebody at heart. I want a house—"

"I have the house," she rushed to remind him, just in case he was getting cold feet.

"—and a dog."

"Got the dog, too. A perfect dog. A dog others will envy." She rubbed Butch's oversize ears.

Laughing, Riley hefted Butch up closer to his face and the dog playfully nipped his chin, appearing very pleased with the situation. "I'd really like a few kids *without* tails if you think we can manage that sometime in the misty future."

Tears filled her eyes. All around them was chaos, but the government could work itself out. This was important. "Since we love each other and we're getting married, and we intend to stay married forever, I'd say it would only be right and proper."

Riley stepped through the door, took one look at Regina, and backed out. With the music she had playing on the stereo, she hadn't heard him. He turned to his friends and said, "Wait out here a second."

Buck crossed his arms over his massive chest. "If you're going to leave me hanging in the street just so you can grab a nooner, forget it."

Harris laughed. "Men in love are so predictable."

Rosie shoved him for that inelegant remark. "You'll get yours someday, Harris. Just wait and see."

His horrified expression had both Riley and Ethan chuckling.

Shaking his head, Riley said, "No, it's not that. She's just not ready for you. Two minutes, I swear. That's all I need."

"Two minutes? Talk about a quickie," Harris muttered, then ducked behind Buck before Rosie could reach him.

Riley slipped through the door and locked it behind him. He loved the house that Regina had chosen. It wasn't all that large but it had a real family feel to it, a coziness that she enhanced by her mere presence.

Since she'd already taken care of a sizeable down payment, he'd splurged on most of the furnishings. Between their combined efforts, things were really coming together.

The music continued to play, and Regina still had her delectable rump in the air as she rummaged beneath the couch for Butch's bone. The dog sat beside her, his expression anxious and watchful.

"Can I help?"

She screeched, whipped around to sit on her butt, and stared at him. "You're home early!"

"It ended quicker than I thought." He'd had to testify in court on a burglary, then had stopped by to see his friends. They'd invited themselves over, but obviously Regina wasn't ready for company.

Before he could explain that he had them all with him, she was on her feet and racing Butch to the door to greet him. Both woman and dog appeared thrilled with his arrival.

Dressed in one of his shirts—something she knew he loved seeing—and with her rich hair wound into enormous curlers around her head, Regina launched herself into his arms. Since that day at the Historical Society, she'd grown completely at ease with him. Around others, she remained immeasurably polite and proper, but with Riley she shared every facet of herself, including her less polished moments. Like now.

When the delicious kiss ended, Butch demanded his attention with a yodeling bark. He stretched up to stand on his hind legs, dancing around in what Riley called his circus dog impersonation.

Riley picked him up and treated him to a full body rub before saying to Regina, "Sorry to break it to you, but everyone is with me."

Her hands went to her cheeks and her green eyes widened. "Everyone?"

He nodded toward the door. "Harris and Buck, Rosie and Ethan. They invited themselves over. They're waiting on the porch."

The words no sooner left his mouth than she whipped around and dashed down the hallway to their bedroom. Riley enjoyed the back view of her, watching her long legs and the way his shirttails bounced over her bottom. "I'll keep them entertained while you finish getting ready."

The slamming of the door was her only reply.

Fifteen minutes later Regina emerged dressed in pressed slacks, a beige cotton sweater and a huge smile. "Sorry I kept you all waiting. Usually I'm dressed and ready by this time of the day, but I got behind this morning after Barbara Walters's people called."

Rosie's mouth fell open. Ethan jerked around to face her. Buck, who'd been on the floor playing with Butch, froze. Harris snorted in disbelief.

Riley, the only one with his wits still about him, raised a brow. "Barbara Walters?" He wasn't all that surprised. It seemed everyone in the media wanted the scoop on Senator Welling's sudden withdrawal. With his influence, the senator had put a gag order on the entire event. The guards present that day would never speak a word. Lanny and Dermot had been warned that they could lose their jobs if they released any information to the press.

Riley had assured the senator's people up front that they couldn't use his job to threaten him. All he cared about was that Regina be kept safe. Beyond that stipulation, they could handle the situation as quietly and secretively as they wished. But they *would* have to handle it because he wouldn't tolerate any more threats to Regina. So far, they had things in hand.

Regina was the only one left that could talk—and she wasn't about to.

"What did she want?" Buck asked.

"The same thing the others wanted."

Agog with fascination, Rosie asked, "To hear first-hand what happened with the senator?"

"Right." Regina sat down on Riley's lap, which was the only seat available in the small living room. She leaned back against his chest and smiled. "I told them that they'd just have to find out the nitty-gritty details like everyone else, after the federal investigation ended."

Rosie flopped back against her husband's arm. "Wow. Barbara Walters and you turned her down."

Buck rolled to his back and propped up on his elbows. "I can't believe you don't want revenge after the hell Welling's wife put you through."

Regina shrugged. "What good would revenge do? The senator has lost a lot of credibility with his constituents. They apparently don't like secrets, but with his wife under indictment and his own blame in the whole thing, what else can he do but keep quiet?"

"He could have not cheated in the first place," Harris grouched with feeling, then looked blank when everyone stared at him. "What? I have morals, too, ya know."

Regina sighed. "They have two children, and I think the kids have been through enough. Even with his wife blaming everything on Earl, her involvement is bound to make headlines eventually. The whole family is going to suffer. I won't take part in that."

Harris nodded, giving her a look full of admiration. "You're something else, Regina, you know that?"

Riley scowled at his tender tone, but Harris blew it by saying, "And here I thought you were a nosy reporter."

"I am." Regina gave them all an evil grin. "But I still like the more personal and upbeat human-interest stories." She hesitated just long enough to add impact, then announced, "That's why I told Walters's retinue that if they wanted a real scoop they should bring their TV crew to Chester and check out the local heroes."

Riley choked on his own breath.

Ethan groaned as if in mortal pain.

"You'd never get them here for something like that," Rosie said. "They like stories of worldwide appeal."

"Oh, I dunno. What could be more appealing to the world than the local heroes who keep us safe?" She slanted Rosie a look. "I specifically mentioned Harris and Buck."

Buck bolted upright. "I'm no hero! Hell, I just own a lumberyard."

"You were right there by Riley the day he caught Earl. You may not have a hero's occupation, but you have the soul of a hero."

"I don't!"

"Yes, you do," she insisted. "Think of the interview as free advertising for your business."

Harris said, *"Oh gawd,"* with great disgust. "That's weak, Regina. Very weak."

She didn't seem the least upset by the criticism. "When I told them two of the men were still single, they sounded pretty interested. They told me they're doing this whole segment on singles in America, and heroes would naturally be prime fodder for the piece. They want me to call them back with more information."

Buck and Harris stared at each other, their Adam's apples bopping in panic.

"You wouldn't."

"You didn't."

Riley started to laugh. "I can tell you unequivocally that she would. For some insane reason, she thinks the two of you epitomize all that is good in mankind."

"They're your and Ethan's friends," Regina said with prim regard. "And you two are definitely heroic."

"Hear, hear," Rosie agreed.

"So of course they're good men. And since they won't let me interview them…" She left the sentence dangling with loaded suggestion.

"Hey, I put up with it," Ethan pointed out.

"Me, too," Riley added. His own interview had been carefully edited by Regina. Anything that might have been too personal or hurtful had been omitted.

It was still embarrassing, especially because the love she felt for him had shone through and Harris and Buck had harassed him for days afterward, pretending to swoon, blowing him kisses and asking for his autograph. But the public had gobbled it up, his chief was thrilled with the positive P.R. for the department and Regina had thanked him oh so sweetly, so he was glad he'd given in.

Buck finally said, "Regina, be reasonable. You have to call off Walters."

Her nose lifted. "I could do that—*if* you agree to give me a story." Her gaze slanted to Harris. "Both of you."

With hardy groans and a lot of grumbling, they surrendered to the inevitable. "Deal."

Regina relaxed. "I'll return their call after dinner. But I need the interviews before our wedding next week."

"Why the rush?" Harris asked, looking somewhat stricken by the whole idea of being in the limelight.

"After the wedding, I plan to be busy for a while—with my own personal hero."

Riley hugged her close. He knew the truth: Regina was the heroic one. With her big heart and unwavering faith in human nature, she had filled his soul. He intended to keep her safe for the rest of their lives. If that made him a hero, too, at least in her eyes, then he'd gladly live with the label.

* * * * *

A former job-hopper, **Jessica Lemmon** resides in Ohio with her husband and rescue dog. She holds a degree in graphic design, which is currently gathering dust in an impressive frame. When she's not writing supersexy heroes, she can be found cooking, drawing, drinking coffee (okay, wine) and eating potato chips. She firmly believes God gifts us with talents for a purpose, and with His help, you can create the life you want.

Jessica is a social media junkie who loves to hear from readers. You can learn more at jessicalemmon.com.

Books by Jessica Lemmon

Harlequin Desire

Dallas Billionaires Club

Lone Star Lovers
A Snowbound Scandal
A Christmas Proposition

Kiss and Tell

His Forbidden Kiss
One Wild Kiss
One Last Kiss

Visit the Author Profile page at Harlequin.com for more titles.

LONE STAR LOVERS

Jessica Lemmon

For Grandma Edie.
Thank you for putting that first Harlequin book in my hands. I wish you were here so I could put this one in yours.

Chapter 1

Texas in the springtime was a sight to behold. The Dallas sunshine warmed the patio of Hip Stir, where Penelope Brand sat across from her most recent client. Blue cloudless skies stretched over the glass-and-steel city buildings, practically begging the city-dwellers to take a deep breath. Given that nearly every table was full, it appeared that most of downtown had obeyed.

Pen adjusted her sunglasses before carefully lifting her filled-to-the-brim café au lait. The mug's contents wobbled but she made that first sip to her lips rather than to her lap. Which was a relief since Pen always wore white. Today she'd chosen her favorite white jacket with black silk piping over a vibrant pink cami. Her pants were white to match, slim-fitting and ended in a pair of black five-inch stilettos.

White was her power color. Pen's clients came to her

for crisis control—sometimes for a completely fresh start. As their public relations maven, a crisp, clean do-over had become Pen's specialty.

She'd started her business in the Midwest. Until last year, the Chicago elite had trusted her with their bank accounts, their marriages and their hard-won reputations. When her own reputation took a header, Pen was forced to regroup. That unfortunate circumstance was rapidly gaining ground as her "past." The woman sitting across from her now had laid the foundation for Penelope's future.

"I can't thank you enough." Stefanie Ferguson shook her head, tossing her dark blond ponytail to the side. "Though I suppose I should thank my stupid brother for the introduction." She lifted her espresso and rolled her eyes.

Pen smothered a smile. Stefanie's *stupid brother* was none other than the well-loved mayor of Dallas, and he'd called on Penelope's services to help his younger sister out of a mess that could mar his reputation.

Stef didn't share her brother's reverent love for politics and being careful in the public eye. She flew by the seat of her skinny jeans, the most recent flight landing her in the arms of one of the mayor's most critical opponents, Blake Eastwood.

Blake's development company wanted to break ground for a new civic center that Mayor Ferguson opposed. Critics argued that the mayor was biased, given the civic center was to be built near his family's oil wells, but the mayor's supporters argued the unneeded new-build would be a waste of city funds.

Either way, the photograph of Stefanie exiting a hotel, her arm wrapped around Blake's while they both wore wrinkled clothing and sexually satisfied smiles, had caused some unwanted media attention.

The mayor had hired Brand Consulting to smooth out the wrinkles of what could have turned into a PR nightmare. Penelope had done her job and done it well. One week after the snafu, and the media had already moved on to gossiping about someone else.

All in a day's work.

"You're coming to the party tonight, right?" Stef asked. "I'm looking forward to you being there so I have a girl to talk to."

Stef was younger than Pen by four years, but Pen could easily become close friends with her. Stef was smart, savvy and, while she was a tad too honest for her brother's taste, Pen welcomed that sort of frankness. Too bad a friendship with Stefanie broke Pen's most recently adopted rule: never become personally involved with a client.

That included an intimate friendship with the blonde across from her.

A pang of regret faded and faded fast as Pen remembered why she'd had to ink the rule in the first place. Her ex in Chicago had tanked her reputation, cashed her checks and forced her to journey to her own fresh start.

"I wouldn't miss it," Pen answered with a smile. Because yes, she wasn't going to become besties with Stefanie Ferguson, but neither would she turn down a coveted invitation to the mayor's birthday party.

Those who gained entry to the mayor's annual soiree, held at his private gated mansion, were the envy of the city. Pen had worked with billionaires, local celebrities and sports stars in her professional past, but she'd never worked directly with a civil servant. Attending the most sought-after party of the year was as good as a gold star on her résumé.

Pen picked up the tab for her client and said her goodbyes to Stefanie before walking two blocks back to her office.

Thank God for the mayor's troublemaking sister.

Stepping in at the pleasure of Mayor Chase Ferguson might have been the best decision Pen had made since moving to Dallas. Her heart thudded heavily against her breastbone as she thought about what this could mean for her growing PR firm—and for her future as an entrepreneur. There were going to be many, *many* people at this party who would eventually require her services. The world of politics teemed with scandal.

After finishing her work for the day, she locked the glass door on her tenth-floor suite and drew the blinds. In her private bathroom, Pen spritzed on a dash of floral perfume and brushed her teeth, swapping out her suit for the white dress she'd chosen to wear to the mayor's party. She'd brought it with her to work since her apartment was on the other side of town and the mayor's mansion was closer to her office.

She smoothed her palms down the skirt and checked the back view in the full-length mirror on the door. *Not bad at all.* After way too much vacillating this morning, she'd opted for hair down versus hair up. Soft waves fell around her shoulders and the color of her pale blue eyes popped beneath a veil of black-mascaraed lashes and smoky, silver-blue shadow.

The dress was doing her several favors, hugging her hips and her derriere in a way that wasn't inappropriate, but showcased her daily efforts at the gym.

I couldn't let you leave without pointing out how well you wear that dress.

Shivers tracked down her arms and she rubbed away the gooseflesh as the silken voice from two weeks ago wound around her brain.

Pen had moved to Dallas thinking she'd sworn off men forever, but after nearly a year of working nonstop to rebuild her business, she'd admitted she was lonely. She'd been at a swanky jazz club enjoying her martini when yet another man had approached to try his luck.

This one had been a tall, muscled, delicious male specimen with a confident walk and a paralyzing green stare that held her fastened in place. He'd introduced himself as "Just Zach," and then asked to sit. She'd surprised herself by saying yes.

Over a drink, she learned they'd crossed paths once before—at a party in Chicago. They knew the same billionaire family who owned Crane Hotels, though she'd never imagined running into Zach again anywhere other than Chicago.

She also never imagined she'd ask him to come home with her…but she did. When one drink led to another, Penelope let him lead her out of the club.

What a night it'd been.

His kisses had seared, branding her his for those stolen few hours. Hotter than his mouth were the acres of golden muscles, and she'd reveled in smoothing her palms over his bulging pecs and the bumps of his abs. Zach had a great ass, a better smile, and when he left in the morning, he'd even kissed her goodbye.

Stay in bed and recover, Penelope Brand.

A dimple had punctuated one of his cheeks, and her laugh had eased into a soft hum as she'd watched

Zach's silhouetted masculine form dress in the sunlight pressing through her white bedroom curtains.

Sigh.

It had been the perfect night, curing her of her loneliness and adding a much-needed spring in her step. Pen had felt like she could take over the damn world. Amazing what a few earth-shattering orgasms could do for a girl's morale.

She was still smiling at that memory of "Just Zach" from Chicago when she climbed behind the wheel of her Audi and started toward her destination. One night with Zach had been fun, but Pen wasn't foolish enough to believe it could have been more. As the daughter of entrepreneurs, success had been ingrained in Pen's mind from an early age. She'd taken her eye off the prize in Chicago and look what'd happened.

Never again.

At the gates of the mayor's mansion, Pen presented the shiny black invitation, personalized with her name in an elegant silver script, and smiled down at the slender silver bangle on her left wrist. It had been included with her invitation. Dangling from the bracelet was a letter *F*, and she'd bet her new shoes that the diamond set in the charm was a real one. Every first-time attendee received a gift from the mayor.

The security guard waved her through and she smiled in triumph. She was *in*. The world of politics was ripe with men and women who might need to hire her firm in the future, and she would make sure every guest knew her name by the end of the evening.

Pen passed her car keys to the valet and walked the cobblestone path to the mayor's mansion. The grounds were elegant, lined with tall, slender shrubberies and short, boxed hedges. Fragrant, colorful flowers were in full bloom thanks to an early spring. Looming oaks that'd been there since the Ferguson family earned their first dollar in Dallas, ushered her in.

Inside, she checked her wrap and tucked her clutch under her arm. When her turn came, an attendant walked her to the mayor for a proper introduction.

Standing before the mayor, was it any wonder the man had earned the hearts of the majority of Dallas's female voters? Chase Ferguson was tall, his dark hair pushed this way and that as if it couldn't be tamed, but the angle of his clean-shaven jaw and the lines on his dark suit showed control where it counted.

"Ms. Brand." Hazel eyes lowered to a respectable survey of her person before Chase offered a hand. She shook it and he released her to signal to a nearby waiter. "Stefanie is around here somewhere," he said of his younger sister. He leaned in. "And thanks to you, on her best behavior."

The mayor straightened as a waiter approached with a tray of champagne.

"Drink?" Chase's Texas accent had all but vanished beneath a perfected veneer, but Pen could hear the slightest drawl when he lowered his voice. "You'll get to meet my brother tonight."

She was embarrassed she didn't know a thing about another Ferguson sibling. She'd only been in Texas for a year, and between juggling her new business, moving into her apartment and handling crises for the Dallas elite, she hadn't climbed the Ferguson family tree any higher than Chase and Stefanie.

"Perfect timing," Chase said, his eyes going over her shoulder to welcome a new arrival.

"Hey, hey, big brother."

Now *that* was a drawl.

The back of her neck prickled. She recognized the voice instantly. It sent warmth pooling in her belly and lower. It stood her nipples on end. The Texas accent over her shoulder was a tad thicker than Chase's, but not as lazy as it'd been two weeks ago. Not like it was when she'd invited him home and he'd leaned close, his lips brushing the shell of her ear.

Lead the way, gorgeous.

Squaring her shoulders, Pen prayed Zach had the shortest memory ever, and turned to make his acquaintance.

Correction: re-acquaintance.

She was floored by broad shoulders outlined by a sharp black tux, longish dark blond hair smoothed away from his handsome face and the greenest eyes she'd ever seen. Zach had been gorgeous the first time she'd laid eyes on him, but his current look suited the air of control and power swirling around him.

A primal, hidden part of her wanted to lean into his solid form and rest in his capable, strong arms again. As tempting as reaching out to him was, she wouldn't. She'd had her night with him. She was in the process of assembling a solid bedrock for her fragile, rebuilt business and she refused to let her world fall apart because of a sexy man with a dimple.

A dimple that was notably missing since he was gaping at her with shock. His poker face needed work.

"I'll be damned," Zach muttered. "I didn't expect to see you here."

"That makes two of us," Pen said, and then she polished off half her champagne in one long drink.

Chapter 2

Zach schooled his expression—albeit a bit late.

Penelope Brand wore a curve-hugging white dress like the night he'd seen her at the club. He'd been there with a friend who had long since left with a woman. Zach hadn't been looking to hook up until he spotted Pen's upswept blond hair and the elegant line from her neck to her bare shoulders.

Seeing her hair down tonight dropkicked him two weeks into the past. Her apartment. The moment he'd tugged on the clip holding her hair back and let those luscious locks down. The way he'd speared his fingers into those silken strands, before kicking her door closed and carrying her to her bedroom.

He'd sampled her mouth before depositing her onto her bed and sampling every other part of her.

And he did mean *every* part.

They hadn't discussed rules, but each had known the score—he wouldn't call and she wouldn't want him to—so they'd made the most of that night. She'd tasted like every debased teenage fantasy he'd ever had, and she'd delivered. He'd left that morning with a smile on his face that matched hers.

When he'd stepped into the shower at home that morning, he'd experienced a brief pinch of regret that he wouldn't see her again.

Though, hell, maybe he *would* see her again given lightning had already stricken them twice. He hadn't wanted to let her get away that night at the bar—not without testing the attraction between them.

He felt a similar pull now.

"If you'll excuse me." His brother Chase moved off, arm extended to shake the palm of a round-bellied man who ruled half of Texas. As one-third owner of Ferguson Oil, it was Zach's job to know the powerful players in his brother's life—in the entire state—but this man was unfamiliar.

"Just Zach," Pen snapped, drawing his attention. Her blue eyes ignited. "I thought you were a contractor in Chicago."

"I used to be."

"And now you're the mayor's brother?"

"I've always been the mayor's brother," he told her with a sideways smile.

He'd also always been an oil tycoon. A brief stint of going out on his own in Chicago hadn't changed his parentage or his inheritance. When Zach had received a call from his mother letting him know his father, Rand Ferguson, had suffered a heart attack, Zach had left Chicago and never looked back.

He wasn't the black sheep—had never resented working for the family business. He'd simply wanted to do his own thing for a while. He had, and now he was back, and yeah, he was pretty damn good at being the head honcho of Ferguson Oil. It also let his mother breathe a sigh of relief to have Zach in charge.

Penelope's face pinched. "Are you adopted or something?"

He chuckled. Not the first time he'd heard that. "Actually, Chase and I are twins."

"Really?" Her nose scrunched. It was cute.

"No."

She pursed her lips and damn if he didn't want to experience their sweetness all over again. He hadn't dated much over the past year, but the way Penelope smiled at him had towed him in. He hadn't recognized her at first—the briefest of meetings at a Crane Hotel function three years ago hadn't cemented her in his mind—but there was a pull there he couldn't deny.

Pen finished her champagne and rested the flute on a passing waiter's tray. With straight shoulders and the lift of one fair eyebrow, she faced Zach again. "You didn't divulge your family status when I met you on Saturday."

"You didn't divulge yours."

Her eyes coasted over his tuxedo, obviously trying to square the man before her with the slacks and button-down he'd worn to the club.

"It's still me." He gave her a grin, one that popped his dimple. He pointed at it while she frowned. "You liked this a few weeks ago." He gestured to himself generally as he leaned in to murmur, "You liked a lot of this a few weeks ago."

Miffed wasn't a good enough word for the expression that crossed her pretty face. The attraction was still there, the lure that had existed as they came together that night in her bed twice—no, wait, *three times.*

Zach decided he'd end tonight with her in his bed. They'd been good together, and while he wasn't one to make a habit of two-night stands, he'd make an exception for Penelope Brand.

Because *damn.*

"I'll escort you to the dining room. You can sit with me." He offered his arm.

Pen sighed, the action lifting her breasts and softening her features. Zach's grin widened.

So close.

She qualified with, "Fine. But only because there are a lot of people here I would like to meet. This is a business function for me, so I'd appreciate—"

The words died on Penelope's lips when a female shriek rose on the air. "Where is he? Where is that son of a bitch who owes me money?"

The crowd gasped and Pen's hand tightened on his forearm.

Zach turned in the direction of the outburst to find a rail-thin redhead in a long black dress waving a rolled-slash-wadded stack of paper in her hand. Her brown eyes snapped around the room, and her upper lip curled in a way that made him wonder how he'd ever found her attractive.

Granted she wasn't foaming at the mouth when they'd exchanged their vows.

"You." Her eyes landed on him as the security guards positioned around the house rushed toward her. Zach held up a hand to stop them. He'd try and talk

Yvonne down from whatever crazy idea she'd birthed before they caused a bigger scene.

"V," he said, hoping to gain ground with the nickname he'd coined the night they met. A night soaked in tequila. "You're at my brother's birthday party. You have my attention. Is there something I can help you with?"

A big, bald security guy with an ugly scar down one cheek stepped closer to Yvonne, his mitts poised to drag her out the second Zach gave the signal.

"Write me a check for a million dollars and I'll be on my way." Yvonne cocked her head and waved the crumpled stack of papers in front of her. "Or else I'll tear up our annulment."

Tearing it up wouldn't make it go away. What was her angle?

"Marrying you entitled me to at least half your fortune, Zachary Ferguson."

It was laughable that she thought a million was *half*.

Penelope's hand slipped from his forearm and Zach reached over and put it back.

"Ex-wife," he corrected for Penelope's—hell, for everyone's—benefit. "And no, it doesn't."

"I'm going to make your life miserable, Zachary Ferguson. You just wait."

"Too late." He gave a subtle nod to the beefcake guard who circled Yvonne's upper arm in his firm grip as he warned her against fighting him.

To her credit, she didn't struggle. But neither did she go willingly. Yvonne's eyes sliced over to Penelope. "Who is this? Are you *cheating* on me?"

Here they went again. Yvonne had asked that question so many times in the two days they were married, Zach would swear she'd gone to bed sane and woken crazy.

He'd had the good sense to get out of the marriage, which was more than he could say for the sense he'd had going in. The details were fuzzy: Vegas, Elvis, the Chapel of Love, etcetera, etcetera... Getting married had seemed fun at the time, but spontaneity had its downfalls. Within twenty-four hours Yvonne had grown horns and a forked tongue.

"Make it two million dollars," Yvonne hissed, illustrating his point. The guard tugged her back a step, looking inconvenienced when she fought him.

Zach had money—plenty of it—but relinquishing it to the crazed redhead wasn't going to make her go away. If anything, she'd be back for more later.

"Get her out of here," Zach said smoothly, putting his hand over Pen's. "She's upsetting my fiancée."

"Your what?" Yvonne asked at the same time Penelope stiffened at his side.

"Penelope Brand, my fiancée. Yvonne, uh..." What was her maiden name? "Yvonne, my ex-wife." Yvonne's eyes burned with anger—flames Zach was only too happy to fan. "Penelope and I are engaged to be married. It's real, unlike what you and I had. You can contact my lawyers with any further questions."

Yvonne shrieked like the eels from *The Princess Bride* as security dragged her away.

Another security detail, this one slimmer but no less mean-looking, stepped in front of Zach.

"How the hell did she get in here?"

His eyes dipped to his shoes in chagrin before meeting Zach's angry expression again. "We'll call the police department, sir."

"No, don't. She's exuberant, but harmless." He took a breath. Who wanted to deal with the paperwork?

"Very well." Security Guy Number Two followed in the path of the beefy guy.

Chase took his place, using his extra two inches of height to scowl down at Zach. "Let me get this straight," his brother said in that exaggerated calm way he had about him. "You're engaged...and married?"

"*Was* married."

"You didn't tell me you were married."

"Well, it only lasted forty-four hours."

"And you—" Chase's hawk-like gaze snapped away from Zach to lock on Penelope "—didn't tell me you were engaged to my brother."

"I—" Pen started.

"It's not true." Zach couldn't bullshit a bullshitter, and his brother was in politics, so he was overqualified. "I wanted to refocus Yvonne's attention."

He would come clean with Chase, even though he'd been left out of the loop where Stefanie was concerned. Zach had known Stef was having some issues but he didn't realize his brother had called in the cavalry in the form of Penelope's PR services.

"You succeeded," Chase said. He smiled amiably at Penelope. "Looks like you've secured your next client, Ms. Brand. I trust you can clean up my brother's mess."

A few truncated sounds that might have been Pen struggling for breath came from her throat, but she reined in her simmering argument to say, "Yes. Of course."

"Excellent." Chase lifted his voice to address the guests milling around the bar. "If everyone would find your seats in the dining room, dinner will be served shortly." He turned his attention back to Zach and Penelope. "I assume you two would prefer to sit together."

Zach simply smiled as he looked down at a wide-eyed Penelope. This evening had fun written all over it. "I wouldn't allow my fiancée to sit with anyone else."

Chapter 3

Penelope strolled into the oversize ballroom on Zach's arm. The mansion boasted enough round tables and slipcovered chairs to seat the mayor's one-hundred-plus guests. Similar to a wedding, there was a head table for the guests of honor. In this case those guests were Mayor Chase Ferguson, Stefanie Ferguson, Zach and the recent addition of Penelope.

The rectangular table was set apart from the others and dotted with votive candles and low vases with flower arrangements.

A few staff members from the mayor's office were also seated at the head table. A plucky, talkative woman named Barb, Roger, who looked and acted the part of secret service, and a scowling, large-framed man named Emmett Keaton.

Emmett, who had been introduced as the mayor's

"friend and confidant," had short, cropped hair, a healthy dash of stubble on his face and eyed Stefanie with disdain the entire time he ate his pear and Gorgonzola salad. Stefanie had glared at him from her spot across the table before rolling her eyes and drinking down her white wine.

Clearly there was no love lost between those two.

Penelope wasn't surprised. Stefanie's recent scrape had drawn attention to the Ferguson family—and not the good kind. It would make sense that she wasn't favored among the mayor's staff.

Speaking of scrapes, Pen now had another to deal with in the form of Zach's ex-wife. Pen didn't know what shocked her more—that Zach had married the unhinged woman, or that he'd been married at all. It might be a tie.

Zach wasn't the marrying type. He was the one-night-stand type. Or so Pen had thought.

Slicing into the sun-dried-tomato-crusted rack of lamb on her plate, she kept her voice low and asked Zach the million-dollar question.

"Were you married when we slept together two weeks ago?"

His jaw paused midchew before he continued, smiling with his mouth shut, and then swallowed down the bite. He swept his tongue over his teeth and took a drink of water before responding. Pen didn't mind the delay. The lamb was spectacular. She sliced off another petite bite, this time plunging it into the ramekin of balsamic dipping sauce first.

"No," he finally said.

She patted her lips with her napkin. "When did it happen?"

"Last New Year's Eve." He glanced around the table, but no one was paying them any attention. Barb was chattering to Stefanie, and Emmett and Chase were having a low conversation of their own. Roger wasn't at the table any longer. When had he left? He was sneaky, but then—secret service, so it made sense.

"In Vegas," Zach finished.

Pen laughed, drawing Emmett's and Chase's attention before they returned to their conversation. "Cliché, Zach."

"Yeah, as was the annulment."

"And the need for our betrothal?"

Zach shrugged muscular, tux-covered shoulders. "You helped Stef. You're a good ally to have."

"You could have introduced me as an adviser. As anyone."

He stabbed a bite of meat with his fork and waved it as he said, "Fiancée had a nice ring to it."

"Very funny." Fiancée. Ring. At least his personality was the same as the night she'd invited him home with her. He'd been cheeky then, too.

She smiled, glued her eyes to his and enjoyed the sizzling heat in the scant space between them for the next three heartbeats. Then she focused on her food again.

Once the dinner dishes were cleared, dessert appeared in the form of a dark chocolate tart, a single, perfect raspberry interrupting a decadent white-chocolate drizzle.

"Speech time," Zach prompted his brother.

"Go get 'em, Tiger," Stefanie said, clearly teasing him.

Chase stood and buttoned his suit jacket, then glided

to the podium. From her side of the table, Pen wouldn't have to so much as turn her head to watch. Unlike everyone else who had swiveled in their chairs.

Chase had great presence. Elegant. Regal. He talked and the world quieted to listen. She remembered the first time she'd seen him on television and thought—

A gasp stole her throat when warm fingers landed on her knee.

Zach.

Barb looked over her shoulder and offered a wide smile. Pen gave the other woman a tight nod as she reached beneath the table and removed Zach's wandering hand.

Pen cleared her throat and refocused on Chase's speech when Zach's fingers returned. This time she managed to stifle the surprised bleat in her throat. She slanted a glare to her right where he lounged, elbow resting on the arm of his chair, his fingers pressed to his lips and his eyes narrowed as if hanging on to every word his brother said.

With the fingers of Zach's other hand swirling circles on the inside of her knee, Pen couldn't concentrate on a single word of the speech. A quick glance around confirmed that no one could see what was happening beneath the tablecloth.

She shifted in her seat, but before she could crush his fingers between her kneecaps, he gripped her leg with a tight hold. She swallowed down a ball of thick lust as he pushed her legs apart.

Pen flattened her hands on the tablecloth as Zach's hand traveled from her knee and climbed the inside of her thigh. She closed her eyes, visions of the night they'd spent together flashing on the screen of her mind.

His firm, insistent kisses on her jaw, her neck and lower.

The deep timbre of his laugh when she'd struggled with his belt.

He'd ended up stripping for her while she sat on her bed and watched every tantalizing second.

She was snapped to the present when Zach's fingertips dug into the soft skin of her thigh, and without warning, brushed her silk panties. Pen fisted one hand on the tablecloth, dragging her dessert plate to the edge of the table. Her glass of red gave a dangerous wobble.

She held her breath when he touched her intimately again, the scrap of silk going damp against his pressing fingers. When he pulled her panties aside and brushed bare skin, Pen bit down on her bottom lip to contain a whimper.

Then the mayor's voice crashed into her psyche.

"To Penelope and my brother, Zach. Many congratulations on your engagement."

She jerked ramrod straight to find every set of eyes in the room on her and glasses raised.

"Cheers," Chase said into the microphone.

Stiff as a cadaver, Pen managed a frozen smile. Conversely, Zach moved like a sunbathing cat, lazily tossing his napkin on the table before taking Pen's napkin from her lap and standing.

He offered his hand and a smirk, and Pen prayed that the flush of her cheeks would be taken for embarrassment at the attention.

Placing her palm in his, she surreptitiously tugged her skirt down and stood with him to accept the room's applause.

Smooth as butter, Zach pushed her dessert plate

from its perch at the edge of the table, handed Pen her wineglass and lifted his own.

Then, they drank to their engagement.

"I like this." Zach touched the *F* dangling from Pen's bracelet with his thumb. "Makes me feel possessive."

Her hand in his, Pen swayed to the music.

He liked her hand in his. He liked her laugh and the sweet scent of her perfume tickling his senses. He liked the way she smoothly handled Barb's question about a missing engagement ring.

Where is your diamond ring, darling?

Oh, we didn't want to upstage the mayor on his big day.

Pen was the right partner to choose for this particular snafu. She was a woman at the top of her game. Touching her under the table and listening as her breaths shortened and tightened was a bonus.

"What are you grinning about?" she asked him now.

"I think you know."

She hummed, not confirming or denying. Like he said, top of her game.

He turned her to the beat of the music, pressing his palm flat on her back and drawing her closer. She came rather than resist him, which he liked a whole hell of a lot.

"It's kind of your brother to give first-time guests such decadent gifts," she commented, redirecting his attention back to the bracelet. She waggled their joined hands so the pendant moved against her pale skin.

"You think *that's* what this is for?" Zach joked as he clucked his tongue. "You don't know the underground Chase Ferguson birthday secret."

Her eyes widened slightly and he didn't say more. Finally, she broke. "Are you going to tell me or not?"

"Depends." He leaned in, his whisper conspiratorial. "Are you into multiple sex partners?"

"Zach!" she quietly scolded. A second later her lips parted in a laugh that warmed the very center of his chest. She took her hand from his shoulder to playfully shove his chest. If he wasn't mistaken, she lingered a bit over his pectoral before resting her hand on his shoulder once again. "You're impossible."

He hovered just over her lips, testing her. "You're wearing the first letter of my last name, Pen. That means you're mine."

Blue eyes turned up to his and for a second he thought she might give him the gift of saying, *Show me to your room.* She hadn't been the least bit shy the night she'd invited him home with her.

Instead those blues rolled skyward and she hedged with, "Caveman."

But she'd given him an inch not arguing that she was his.

"What *really* happens next?" she asked. The crowd was thinning. Only a few couples danced, while others ringed the bar or sat with their coffees at the cleared tables.

"Things wind down. Cigars are smoked. Bourbon poured. Stef and I have rooms here so we usually stay the night."

"Well, make sure you tell me when it's the proper time to leave. I don't want to overstay my welcome on my maiden voyage to the mayor's birthday party."

"How about you don't leave?"

She'd been looking around the room, but now snapped her attention back to him. "What?"

"You heard me. Don't leave. Stay in my room. With me." He pulled her closer, resting his cheek on hers as he spoke into the delicate shell of her ear. "Spend the night in my bed, Penelope. You won't regret it."

Her hand tightened in his. "I—I can't. It's…inappropriate."

He pulled his face away from hers to find she looked as flustered as she sounded. Her eyes bounced from his face to his chest. Her steps faltered.

Zach dropped the pretense of dancing, and cradled her gorgeous face in both hands. "It's not only appropriate. It's expected. To this room of people, you're my future wife. I would never let my fiancée drive home alone this late."

A small smile found her face. "My God. You really are a caveman."

"Aw, honey," he said with a wink as he laced his fingers with hers. "But I'm your caveman."

Her silken laughter as he led them to the bar was a good sign she'd join him upstairs when the night wound to a close. Zach wasn't ready to draw the curtain on their evening yet, but he was anticipating getting her alone again. He'd give her the best night of her life.

Well, assuming the last night they'd spent together could be topped.

It was a challenge he embraced.

Chapter 4

"We're turning in. Happy birthday." Zach offered his brother a hand and Chase shook it, which Penelope found charming though formal. She wondered if those two had ever wrestled or punched each other in the face when growing up, and then figured they probably had. It wasn't hard to imagine rough and tumble boys beneath their polished exteriors.

"Penelope, make yourself at home," Chase told her. "My staff will get you whatever you need."

"*I'll* get her what she needs," Zach said, taking her hand in his. "She's my fiancée."

At his offered wink, Pen let herself smile. Zach was a lot of things—more than she knew before she learned he was Chase Ferguson's brother—but among his top qualities, Zach was *fun*. Now that Pen had taken him on, she was breaking her cardinal rule of not sleeping with a client. She'd break it this time—if only for him. He made rule-breaking downright delicious. He focused her attention on the present. Which was the exact reason she'd invited him home that night at the club.

An inkling of warning that her ex had cost her everything vibrated at the back of her skull, but the champagne bubbles swimming in her tummy drowned it out.

Her situation with Zach was totally different. The fake fiancée act was a ruse, true, but she couldn't see a reason not to take advantage of another night with him. He'd been working that angle since he touched her under the table tonight.

Hand in hand they passed by Stefanie, who pushed her lip into an exaggerated pout. "I can't believe you didn't tell me you were engaged to this idiot." Stef shot a thumb toward Zach.

"Your secret-keeping skills are dubious," he grumbled.

They'd opted not to share the truth with Stefanie— Chase's idea. He thought it was better if she was in the dark like everyone else.

"You have a lot of secrets lately." Stef eyed Zach, her mouth pulling at the corners.

"So do you," he said. "I had no idea you were working with my beautiful fiancée on a cover-up."

"It wasn't a cover-up," Pen interjected before these two sniped away her good mood. "We simply rerouted the public's attention."

"Thank you for that." Stefanie gripped Pen's arm and squeezed. "In all seriousness, I'm happy for you two."

"Thanks, sis," Zach said as a wave of guilt crashed

over Penelope. She didn't mind contorting public opinion but lying to Zach's sister felt…wrong.

"I'm not staying here tonight," Stef told them. "I have a date with another of my brother's mortal enemies."

Zach's shoulders went rigid, a wave of heat emanating from his form.

"Just kidding!" Stef's grin was wide. She bid them good-night and Pen stroked her hand up Zach's tuxedo jacket to soothe him.

"Down, boy."

His eyes snapped over to her, the heat there transforming from anger to lust—which was even more sinister.

"Boy?" Zach startled Pen by bending at the knees to lift her into his arms. The few guests left milling about reacted with gasps or soft laughs. Pen, eyes wide, held on to him, her fingers entwining in the thick blond hair at the back of his neck.

"Sounds like you need a reminder from the *man* who shared your bed a few weeks back."

His confident smile, strong arms and twinkling green eyes consumed her. She bit down on her lip and remembered all too well the details of that night. Nevertheless, she said, "I could, now that you mention it."

A smile spread his full lips.

Fake fiancée or not, for her, the attraction part of their relationship was very real. Penelope was going to take advantage of every exciting, promising part of it.

She barely had a moment to take in her surroundings when Zach's muscular chest was flush with her back. He swept her hair off her neck and put his lips over her pounding pulse.

"I don't have an overnight bag," she breathed, tilting her head to give him better access.

His tongue covered her earlobe before he tugged with his teeth. Goose bumps rose on her skin and she reached up to palm the back of his head.

His mouth was as intoxicating as any liquor, but a thousand times more potent.

"I'll at least need—" a gasp stole her words as his hand coasted from her waist to the sides of her breasts, teasing her "—a toothbrush," she finished.

He replied to her complaint by sliding warm fingers over her bare back, then snicking the zipper of her dress down over her backside.

"Gorgeous. Damn, Pen. I love your ass."

"Likewise." She managed a breathy laugh and turned in his arms. The way he looked at her made her feel gorgeous. Like she was the only one he wanted in this world.

His fingers pushed into her hair and he cupped the back of her neck, pegging her with a serious green stare. "Tell me the truth."

"About?" She raised her eyebrows in curiosity.

"Have you thought of me in the past few weeks?"

"Yes."

Zach's palm warmed her neck and shifted upward until he cradled the back of her skull. He dipped his head but didn't kiss her, continuing his interrogation.

"Tell me what you thought about, Penelope Brand." His dimple dented one cheek when he offered a lopsided smile. "In graphic detail."

It was a smile she couldn't help returning. Her hands

fisting the material of his shirt, she yanked it from his pants and stroked her hands along his hot, golden skin.

"You first," she whispered a hairsbreadth away from his lips.

She'd meant to be cute, but Zach's smile vanished. His other hand went to her back and, pressing her until her breasts flattened against his chest, he answered her.

"Every morning since I walked out of your apartment, I wake up hard and ready. The woman in my head missing her clothes has blond hair, pale blue eyes and your name."

His pupils dilated, the black darkening his surrounding green irises. "Your turn."

She remembered lots of things. The way he moved over her, the way he filled her, consumed her, during their lovemaking. But mostly the way he laughed and made her life fun for that slice of time.

He made her forget her obligations or the fact that she'd once let a man trample over her business and her good sense. Zach made her feel beautiful and cherished and hot. Really freaking hot.

"I remember," she started, tugging at his black leather belt, "your face when you came." She unfastened his pants and slipped her hand inside, gliding her palm along the thick ridge of his erection.

Zach's nostrils flared, his hands rerouting to her hips and digging in for purchase.

"You looked a lot like you do right now." She massaged his manhood, tipping her chin to swipe her tongue along his bottom lip. That lip tasted like she remembered—warm and firm and laced with desire. "In control but in danger of losing it."

She'd meant to spur him on. He didn't disappoint.

He reached for the skirt of her dress and peeled it past her hips and stomach and over her head. He tossed it inside out to the floor.

"I'm in no danger of losing control, Ms. Brand," Zach informed her, his lazy Texas drawl intensifying. "But you are."

Her white lace bra was the next article of clothing to get the heave-ho. He disarmed the strap so quickly that in a blink both her breasts were bare, her nipples standing up, begging for his attention.

Attention they got.

Zach's arms looped her back and Pen had to move both hands to his shoulders when he dropped his mouth to sample a breast. His tongue swirled and suckled and she let her head fall back, losing herself in the moment. That was what he did to her—made her live in the right now and not beyond.

Who could resist?

He backed her across the room and she went, turning to take in the bed they were about to make very good use of. The regal four-poster frame reached for the ceiling above a pile of gold-and-maroon bedding and pillows fit for royalty.

Thighs against hers, Zach walked her two steps until her butt collided with the mattress. She sat, eyes tipped to his. He stood looking down at her, shirt untucked, pants open, eyes aflame.

"Damn, I don't know what to do first."

"I do." Pen reached for his cock again but Zach snatched her hand.

"Not that." His smirk was confident when he hooked his fingers into her panties and swept them off her legs. At her ankles, he paused, watching her as he tossed one of her tall shoes over his shoulder, then the other. The scrap of silk went next. With a tip of his chin, he said, "Scoot."

She did, naked and so excited she wondered if he could see the shake in her arms as she settled herself on the middle of the bed.

He unbuttoned his tuxedo shirt, his eyes taking inventory of her like she was his next meal. Shirt discarded, he pushed his pants and briefs to his ankles, kicking off his shoes and socks in the process.

Penelope had to struggle not to drool.

Zach's lean, muscular chest was as mouthwatering as in her memory, the scant bit of chest hair whirling around two flat brown nipples. His erection jutted proudly between slim hips, which gave way to thick thighs. She realized she'd become lost staring at his body and quickly jerked her attention to his face.

Didn't help.

His body was to die for, but the real panty-melter was the dimple indenting one cheek when he smiled. His jaw was firm and strong, at odds with the playful twinkle in his eyes. Some might say his hair was in need of a trim, but Pen preferred the longish style. Especially when he braced himself over her and a thick lock fell rakishly over his forehead.

One knee depressed the mattress, then another. Her mouth dropped open when he lowered his head to her stomach and swiped her belly button with the tip of his tongue.

Flames licked her core. This was the treat she'd enjoyed most with him, and when he dragged his tongue an inch lower on her tummy, a high-pitched gasp betrayed her.

"That's what I like to hear." He hoisted a brow as he pulled her knees apart and settled between her thighs. "Be as loud as you want. No one stays in this part of the house, but if they do, I want them to know exactly why you agreed to marry me."

"Your money?" Pen teased to break the thick band of sexual tension strangling her.

"Oh, you'll pay for that." He didn't offer another teasing lick, but buried his face between her thighs and doled out the promised punishment.

She took every lash she was owed, her fists mangling the duvet, her head thrashing on the pillows that one by one met their final resting places on the floor.

He wrung an orgasm from her without trying, and two more when he stepped up his game.

Panting, delirious with pleasure, Pen lazily opened her eyelids when he began climbing her body. Zach's lips coasted over her ribs, breasts and to her neck where he bit her earlobe.

"Still on the pill?" His heated breath coated her ear.

"Yes." She gripped his biceps, anticipation wriggling within. She wanted him. Now. Hell, five minutes ago.

He positioned his hips over hers, his erection pressing into her pelvis and so very close to home.

"Have you been with anyone since our night together?"

The question pulled her out of the moment and she frowned ever so briefly.

"I haven't, Pen," he told her, sincerity on his face. "Unless you count my hand and a few showers where I tried to erase the memory of you."

He'd...thought about her. He was telling the truth.

Firm lips coasted over hers and a whisper of breath coated her mouth when he asked for her answer again.

"Have you?"

"No," she answered.

She was rewarded with the roll of Zach's hips and the feel of him sliding deep, overtaking her, filling her like she remembered.

His low groan reverberated against her breasts as she clung to his back, their bodies sealed by a thin layer of sweat.

He uttered a harsh curse that sounded a lot like a compliment before pushing his fingers into her hair and focusing his eyes on hers.

"You're mine, Pen."

Her eyes went to the bracelet sliding up her wrist when she looped her arms at his neck. The letter *F* dangling there like a brand.

"Say it," he demanded, claiming her with another deep thrust.

"I'm yours."

Another thrust had her pulse thrumming anew between her legs.

"Whose?" he growled, picking up the pace. All of her overheated. She knew what he was asking. Knew what he wanted. Pen threw her head back and gave him the answer he'd earned.

"Yours."

"Say my name, beautiful."

She did, on a shout. "Zach!"

The slide of his body against hers, the feel of his breath in her ear, the heat of his mouth on hers took her to new heights.

On another cry, she came again, and one more thrust

brought forth his release. Sobering from her own tumble down Mount Orgasm, Pen watched Zach's face contort into pleats of pleasure. The way his eyes squeezed closed, his lips peeled back from his teeth while his powerful body shook.

The almost surprised expression and awestruck wonder in his eyes.

He watched her for the space of a few heartbeats and then a familiar smile crested his handsome face.

She returned it, equally awestruck. Equally pleased.

Chapter 5

The morning after the party, Zach woke in the guest bedroom next to Pen, in the bed they'd all but destroyed the previous night. The comforter and blankets were on the floor, the remaining sheets twisted and pulled from three corners, revealing the naked mattress.

He was also naked and sporting the morning wood he'd bragged to Penelope about, but this time instead of him taking the problem in hand, she was willing to alleviate it for him.

She slid down his body and he watched her pretty blond head bob over his thighs, eliciting so much pleasure, he thought he might never recover.

He did, though.

Enough to make love to her again and talk her into a shared shower en suite. Soaping Pen's body could become his new favorite pastime.

Dressed in the white, albeit wrinkled, dress from last night, she looked like a woman who'd been claimed. Zach liked that look on her a hell of a lot. He liked learning she hadn't been with anyone since him more. Not only because he hadn't moved on from her yet, but also because that meant they could have sex without a condom, which was his other favorite pastime with her.

He took her hand and walked with her down the staircase. His brother was dressed in a suit, and it wouldn't surprise Zach to learn that he was working—even on a Saturday. Zach had pulled on a pair of pressed trousers and a button-down, but Chase had gone full-on jacket and tie.

His brother took in Zach and Pen as they entered the foyer, pausing with his cell phone in hand to smirk knowingly.

"Good morning, Zach. Penelope."

"Mayor," she said, chin held high.

Zach admired the hell out of her for that. In last night's clothes, her hair sexily rumpled and cheeks pink from their steamy shower this morning, Pen didn't care what Chase thought about her sleeping with his only brother.

"I have a meeting in thirty minutes," Chase informed Zach, his gaze returning to his phone. "Legislature for…"

He trailed off as he ran his thumb along the screen. His expression blanked, accentuating his pallor.

"Chase?" Zach asked, alarm rising within. "Is there a problem?"

Chase blinked and offered a tight smile. "An old friend." He gestured with the phone. "Haven't thought of her in a long time."

Her? Chase had a few *hers* in his past, but there was one more noteworthy than the others. But it couldn't be...

Zach wasn't going to find out anytime soon. Chase exited his house and climbed into the back seat of a town car idling out front.

"Sounds mysterious," Pen commented at Zach's side, curiosity outlining her pursed lips. Without digging deeper, she leaned in for a kiss and he gladly obliged. "I'm going to go. Thanks for...everything."

"Don't tell me you work today, too?"

She paused at the door and looked over her shoulder. "Your ex-wife situation isn't going to go away on its own."

Zach looped her arm in his. "I'll walk you out."

The valet had moved Pen's car next to his in the cobblestone drive. Her white Audi sat gleaming next to his black Porsche. He opened her car door but before he closed her inside, stole another kiss for the road.

"You'll be hearing from me, Mr. Ferguson."

"I'll be expecting a full report, Ms. Brand."

She looked sleepy and adorable, as well she should after he'd kept her up all night. He opened his mouth to add that he was in no hurry for her to wrap things up with Yvonne, but instead he backed away and watched as she drove off.

A week later Zach was sitting in his office, Penelope on the other side of his desk. She'd come to Ferguson Oil to discuss the details of the Yvonne Tsunami, which was swallowing up way too much of his time.

The arrangement was far from the way he wanted to spend time with Pen. For starters, she was way too clothed for his taste, and secondly, his brother was brooding in the corner, arms folded over his suit.

Zach stood in frustration the moment Pen stopped talking.

"I won't do it," he said, his words clipped.

"Hear her out," Chase advised from his position near the window. Dallas's cityscape shone outside in the sunny day, several buildings dwarfed from Zach's top-floor vantage.

"I heard her out," Zach told his meddling brother. He softened his voice with Pen, but kept a position of strength when he leaned over his desk to address her where she sat in his guest chair. "I'm not giving Yvonne any money."

"Zach…" Her pink mouth parted to argue and he cut her off.

"No." His desk phone chirped and he pushed a button. "Yes, Sam?"

His male assistant rattled off the name of an investor who was waiting on the line.

"Zach will call him back," Chase called loud enough to be heard.

"Yes, sir." Sam clicked off.

Zach sent his brother a death glare. Chase was unperturbed. He was in one of the highest ranks of government. A wilting glare from his younger brother wasn't going to rankle him anytime soon.

"Listen." Penelope stood, eye level with Zach since he was still looming over the desk. Her pale blue eyes locked with his and she softened her voice. "Yvonne has threatened to make more noise about your marriage. This could not only harm your newly minted position as Ferguson Oil's CEO, but also put a dent in the mayor's approval rating."

Zach fought a growl. Chase's mayoral reputation had been overshadowing everything for the past decade. God, how Zach hated politics. Unfortunately, he loved his brother, so he had a feeling this wouldn't be the last time he did something he didn't want to do for Chase's career.

"It's a relatively small amount of money to ensure her silence," Pen continued. "The world knows you were married, but I wouldn't put it past her to make up a few unbecoming stories and share them on social media. I've seen exes go public with false facts before." Her eyebrows lifted in determination.

"And if she goes against the agreement?" Chase asked, stepping into their tight circle.

"She'll have to pay Zach ten times the amount we're paying for her silence."

Chase and Zach exchanged glances.

"Short of that," Pen said, folding her arms to mirror Chase. "Zach could get ahold of a time machine and steer clear of the Chapel of Love last New Year's Eve."

"I don't like it," Zach told both of them.

"You don't have to like it. You just have to do it." Pen's voice was tender, reminding him of the gentle way she moaned when he was in bed with her three days ago. When he'd struck the pretend fiancée agreement with her, he'd hoped they'd share a bed more often than once a week. She'd been doing a good job of avoiding him on that front.

"Zach." Chase's voice crashed into Zach's fantasy about the blonde in front of him.

"Fine," he said between his teeth. "Now get out."

Chase let the command roll off him. "I have a lunch with important people, Penelope. Thank you."

"Anytime, Mr. Mayor." When he was gone, the door shut behind him, Zach breached the few inches separating him and Pen, tugged her by the nape of the neck and kissed her mouth. She hummed, her eyelids drooping in satisfaction.

"Where have you been hiding?" He thumbed her bottom lip when she pulled back too soon.

"I've been working. On your problems and a few others."

"None are my sister's I take it?"

"No." She shouldered her purse and tucked away her cell phone. "None are Stefanie's. She's been on her best behavior."

"Have dinner with me," he said as she pivoted on one high, high heel.

Pen peeked over her shoulder and Zach allowed his gaze to trickle down her fitted white jacket and short white skirt. Her platinum-blond hair was in a ponytail at the back of her head, the smooth length of it brushing her shoulder when she turned her head.

"I'm… I have to check my schedule."

"You have to make an appearance with me. Especially if we're going to approach Yvonne with a deal." Yvonne believed Zach and Pen were engaged. Everyone who'd attended his brother's party believed they were engaged.

"Okay. Dinner."

He pulled his shoulders back, proud to get a yes out of the evasive woman in front of him. His eyes dipped to the cleavage dividing the neckline of a sapphire blue shirt.

"And after dinner, you can come home with me."

She opened her mouth, maybe to protest, but smiled in spite of herself. He tucked two fingers into her shirt and pulled her closer, brushing her perky breasts.

"I'll make you breakfast in the morning," he told her. "And afterward, I'll make you something to eat."

She rolled her eyes but a soft chuckle escaped her. It was a yes if he'd ever heard one.

"I'll pick you up at your place at seven."

"I have to work late."

Zach was already back at his desk. "No. You don't. Seven o'clock."

He punched a button and summoned Sam. "Make reservations at One Eighty for myself and Ms. Brand for seven this evening."

"One Eighty?" Pen's brow rose. Was she impressed? He hoped so.

"Have you been?"

"Once. With a client who shall remain nameless."

"A male client?" he asked before he could stop himself.

Her Cheshire cat smile held. "Wouldn't you like to know?"

"Seven," he reiterated.

"Seven." She walked out of his office and Zach watched her go, looking forward to viewing her over candlelight the next time they saw each other. His phone beeped and Sam announced that the investor had called back.

Zach picked up the phone, but by the time he lifted his head, Pen was gone, his office door whispering shut.

Chapter 6

One Eighty was named for its half-circle shape. The restaurant hovered over Dallas, on the eighty-eighth floor of one of the city's most shimmering skyscrapers.

Outside the smudgeless windows, deep blue skies were losing their light and the moon was making its nightly appearance.

Pen had stopped working at five, unusual for her, but then so were billionaire dinner dates that were personal rather than solely business.

"How are your prawns?" Zach, fork and knife in hand, leaned over his steak dinner to ask.

"Delightful. How is your strip?"

"Fantastic."

They shared a grin over the low candlelight, and a ping of awareness that started in Pen's stomach radiated out until it created a bubble around her and Zach.

Along with that ping of awareness came a lower, subtler thrum of warning.

She liked him. A lot.

Their chemistry was off the charts in bed, but also out of it.

She could've easily dismissed him as a playboy—a charmer who knew what to say to get a woman out of her clothes. Admittedly, Zach had done just that. But along with getting her out of her clothes, he'd also made a point to keep her in his life.

After what went down with her ex-boyfriend, Cliff, in Chicago—where she'd quite literally been bamboozled by a smooth-talking charmer—she should be wary of Zach.

But she wasn't wary.

Maybe it was because she'd gotten to know his brother, the mayor, and Stefanie, his sister. Maybe it was because of the way Zach had asked her to dinner when he full well could have invited her to his place.

She'd have said yes either way.

Did he know that?

She sliced into her shrimp dinner—buttery, garlicky, lemony heaven. "I contacted Yvonne today and let her know you were willing to talk about—"

"Penelope."

Fork hovering over her plate, she hazarded a glance at her date. Zach didn't look perturbed as much as patient.

"Sorry," she said. "I want to get this over with."

His eyes narrowed, eyelashes a shade darker than his hair obliterating his gorgeous green stare. "With Yvonne, yes. You and I? Not so much."

When she'd called him a caveman at the mayor's

party, she hadn't been far off the mark. But she saw no reason to argue the point. The fact was she would wrap up the issue with Zach's ex-wife and then they'd have no reason to see each other. She'd make her services available for Chase or for their party-loving sister, but Pen and Zach had an expiration date.

So why are you here?

Excellent question.

"Did you pack a bag like I asked?" Zach lifted his wineglass, which was as foreign as the black shirt and black suit combo. She'd been so sure at that jazz club that she'd run into a blue-collar guy moonlighting in slacks. Now that she'd seen him in tuxes and suits, her brain scrambled to make sense of it.

He'd seemed safer when he was a contractor. Before she learned of his bank account or his heritage.

Nevertheless…

"I packed a change of clothes, yes." She took a dainty sip from her own wineglass. While she wasn't sure how to define what she and Zach had or to know how long they had access to it, she wasn't going to miss the opportunity to fill her head and heart full of sexy, vivid memories that would last if not a lifetime, at least a few years.

"Good. I want to show you my place. I think you'll like it." He took another bite of his steak, but not before dragging it through his mashed potatoes. A steak and potatoes guy. She shook her head as she tried to merge the two versions of Zach she thought she knew.

"Why did you leave Chicago? You seemed…at home there."

"I like the city. I liked the work more," he said. "But my family needed me, so I came home."

"Do you mean Stefanie?" She could imagine the youngest Ferguson sibling asking for his help.

"No. She leans on Chase." His smile took on a slightly sad quality. In a firmer voice, he added, "My father's heart attack required surgery and a long recovery. He was under strict orders not to return as acting CEO of Ferguson Oil."

"Doctors," Pen said with a roll of her eyes.

"Worse. My mother." Half of Zach's mouth pulled to one side in good humor, his dimple shadowing his stubbled cheek. She liked him a touch unkempt. "Once Dad was benched, that left me to work for the family business. Chase is obviously busy and Stef is obviously uninterested. She'll grow out of it."

Pen couldn't imagine Stef giving up her life as a socialite heiress to go into the oil business, but she kept that thought to herself.

"What about you?" Zach asked, turning the tables on her. She'd seen that possibility coming and had already decided she wouldn't deflect. She'd been eager to leave her life behind in Chicago, but face it—the internet was alive and well. If Zach typed her name into Google, he'd learn about her association with Cliff.

Still, she inhaled deeply before telling him the sordid, slightly embarrassing tale.

"Ever heard of the phrase 'the plumber's pipes are always leaking'?"

"The cobbler's children have no shoes?"

"Same idea." She laughed, already feeling better about confessing. She sobered quickly. "I had a PR problem I couldn't spin."

Zach's eyebrows lowered. He didn't know.

"Cliff Goodman started out as a client. He hired

me to repair his business's reputation when he was accused of dishonest practices." She'd believed him at the time—the research she'd done on him pointed to his upstanding reputation. "Once the issue was handled, he and I started dating and then—" she lifted her wine and ripped off the Band-Aid "—he became involved in my public relations business."

Her date's face darkened. Pen looked away from his intense stare. Diners quietly chatted at their tables, points of candlelight dotting the dimly lit room, mimicking the city lights outside the windows. The blue sky had gone black.

"Long story short, he went from involved to over-involved. I found out he'd been meeting with my clients in my place, cashing their checks and never following through. He left the city with a lot of my money after destroying my hard-won reputation. I didn't want to leave Chicago, but I didn't want to stay, either."

"Why Dallas?"

"A college friend of mine started an organic cosmetic company. She lives here and needed help maintaining her pure reputation in the face of a nasty divorce. So she hired me."

"And you stayed."

"I did."

They shared a silent moment. Pen wondered if he was thinking what she was thinking—that had it not been for her friend Miranda's phone call, Pen and Zach may never have seen each other again.

"It's a beautiful city." Pen swallowed some more wine, smoothly changing the subject.

"You're beautiful in it."

See? When he said things like that, she forgot all about her past and her rules and her personal struggles.

She forgot everything—including her promise to herself about not letting a client get too close. Especially a male client.

The waiter approached after they'd finished their plates.

"Madame, sir," the older man greeted, hands clasped in front of him. "Might I interest you in our fine dessert selections, or perhaps a glass of port wine or coffee?"

"No," Zach answered for them. "We'll pay and be on our way. My compliments to the chef."

"Such a gentleman," Pen teased.

"I grew up right." He leaned over the table and then, tossing the idea of his humble upbringing on its ear, took her hand and murmured, "I'm making you my dessert, tonight."

"Your post-dessert dessert." Zach's hand appeared from behind Pen, a glass of port wine in his grip. "It's a tawny, which I prefer. That bit of vanilla goes a long way."

She accepted the miniature wineglass and a kiss to her cheek. Zach rounded the enormous brown leather couch wearing nothing at all, another miniature glass dwarfed in his large hand.

Pen wasn't wearing anything, either, but had curled up in a blanket she'd found tossed over his ottoman. A blanket she now opened to include Zach. He accepted, cradling one of her breasts and delivering a tender kiss to the side of her mouth.

They'd stepped foot in his expansive apartment and stripped off each other's clothes in record time. She hadn't so much as seen the bedroom yet, though she did make a quick stop to the bathroom. Zach's apartment was a manly array of exposed brick, lights suspended from long, metal rods, his furniture deep browns and grays. The overall vibe was more industrial than rustic, yet had warmth that mirrored the owner himself.

She sipped the super-sweet wine, savoring the vanilla notes that Zach mentioned and quirking her lips at the way her dress had been haphazardly tossed over a chair along with Zach's discarded suit. Their shoes made a line from the foyer to the living room, the first articles of clothing they'd kicked off.

"You have a really nice apartment."

"Thanks."

"No billionaire mansion for you?"

"Nah, that's Chase's style."

"What about Stef? Does she tend toward high-rise apartment or sprawling mansion with horses and twenty-two bathrooms?"

"See, you think you're being cute, but my parents' house has twenty-two bathrooms."

"I know." She sipped her wine and peered over the tiny rim at Zach. "I looked them up and their house was in *Architectural Digest*. It's incredible."

"It's ridiculous. But my mother likes to redecorate. With thirty-seven thousand square feet, she's never at a loss for a room to have painted or altered to her ever-changing preferences."

Zach leaned back on the sofa, his arm draped around Pen. She snuggled closer and he adjusted the blanket to cover them both.

"Do you get along with them? Or are you the classically overlooked middle child?"

A low laugh that might have been confirmation bobbed his throat. "I get along with them. I joke about my mother's frivolity, but she's a great mother. My dad became sick and her world stopped on a dime."

"How is he now?"

"Good. Misses his bacon and sausage."

"And strip steaks?" she teased.

"It's Dallas, sweetheart. Men eat steak."

"Right. Heaven forbid you do something as effeminate as not eat a cow." She grinned, liking the way she could volley back at him. He was one of the easiest people she'd ever been around.

He moved in on her again and the kiss lasted a little longer than either of them intended. "Glad you packed a bag, Penelope Brand."

Her heart kicked into overdrive when Zach set aside his wine and took her wineglass from her hand. His insistent kisses peppered down her throat and collarbone. When he reached her stomach, his hand flattened on the space between her breasts and he pushed her to her back.

Then he lifted one of her legs onto his shoulder and made her dessert.

Again.

Chapter 7

"Tell me everything," Miranda's bubbly voice, on speakerphone, filled Pen's office.

Pen had called her friend to thank her for the generous basket she was now digging through. She pulled out a tube of lipstick and spun it to examine the lush red color.

"I love this lipstick. 'Red Rum,'" she read off the bottom of the tube with a laugh. Sassy. That was Miranda.

"It's long-wearing, not tested on animals and one hundred percent organic. Now, if you don't tell me everything about the man you've been having sex with for the last month, I'm going to come to your office with torture implements."

She laughed at her friend's colorful description. Pen had casually mentioned Zach and that she'd been seeing him.

"It was supposed to be one night, and then we had a two-week gap." She lifted the basket from her desk and put it on the couch. She was *so* giving herself a makeover later. "But when I saw him again at the mayor's party, well… I couldn't help starting up with him again."

"And you ended up engaged! It's a fairy tale. It's a fantasy!"

It was a load of crap, but Pen had to keep up the facade with everyone.

"Yes, I was very surprised." That, at least, was the truth.

"I'll bet. Zachary Ferguson is one yummy prospect if you don't mind my saying. And he must be a real catch for you to have leaped in with both feet so soon."

"Yes," Pen said, unable to trot out any more false explanations.

"Listen, doll, I have to go. We're working on the spring line and I have an appointment."

"Thank you again for the gift."

"You bet. I expect a wedding invitation."

Pen opened her mouth to make an empty promise, but Miranda clicked off. With a sigh, she cleaned a few pieces of crinkled pink paper that had been used as packing in her gift basket from her planner pages.

May's schedule wasn't as full as she'd like it to be, but she had a few phone calls to return. She turned to her weekly page and checked off the line item that read "call Miranda," eyes skimming past the list of messages she'd written down to return on Monday but hadn't gotten the chance. And here it was Friday already.

Halfway to dialing a number for Maude Braxton,

Pen's eyes landed on a tiny red heart beneath Monday's date, and she frowned.

She'd been on birth control pills since she was a teenager because of erratic periods, and since she'd been on birth control pills, her cycle was correct down to the minute.

She hastily flipped back to April, located the red heart, and counted the days to today.

She was five days late.

Five. Days.

"Oh, my God." Her stomach tightened, her mind racing. Could she be…? No. No way. She was on the pill. And even if her trusted form of birth control failed her, she was in her early thirties. At her age it was normal for things to go haywire. There could be a perfectly good explanation. Stress. It could totally be stress. But when she flipped back to April and saw the name of a jazz club scheduled for eight p.m., another *perfectly good explanation* came to mind.

This one an even better explanation for a missed period.

Numbly, she stood from her desk and pulled her purse out from behind the basket overflowing with tubes of lipsticks, moisturizers and eye shadow palettes. So much for giving herself a makeover.

Pen was off to buy a pregnancy test.

Penelope's wine sat untouched in front of her, but she couldn't bring herself to say no and raise Zach's suspicions. Even though telling him he was going to be the father of their unborn child was the very reason she was sitting here with him. She'd successfully avoided him all weekend, which wasn't easy. It took a lot of circumventing on her part, but she had to wrap her head around the unfathomable truth.

Despite being on the pill the entire time she and Zach were together, that night after the jazz club, one of his swimmers had reached its goal.

"I have a charity dinner on Friday. Come with me." He sat on one corner of the wrap couch rather than in the middle next to her, and for once she was grateful for the space. "Chase and several of the Dallas brass who attended his party will be there. Good networking opportunity. Plus, now that we've wrapped up everything with Yvonne, it's best that we're seen together."

"Right." Pen somehow managed the one-word response despite her heart being lodged in her esophagus. He was right. It made sense to continue seeing him. If they mysteriously ended their engagement right when Yvonne had agreed to keep her trap shut, no one would believe it was real. Which might not matter except that Chase had announced to one and all that his brother was going to be married. She didn't want to be responsible for making Dallas's trustworthy mayor into a liar. If that wasn't enough public attention, there was the business world wagging their tongues about Ferguson Oil's youngest CEO taking a wife. Soon they'd have to amend their announcement to add that Zach had impregnated his bride-to-be...who the public would later learn wasn't going to be his wife at all.

God. This was a nightmare.

Maybe she didn't have to tell him today. Hope sparked fresh in her chest. She had a good four weeks before her baby bump made itself known. Why not avoid him until then? And the paparazzi and public functions... She could become a hermit.

If she folded up the shingle on her PR business.

Sigh. That wasn't a realistic plan at all.

The only certainty was that she was keeping the baby. Her pregnancy was unexpected, yes, but Penelope believed deep in her soul that life unfolded in the order it did for a reason. If fate decided she was to be a mother, then she'd accept. It was as simple, and terrifying, as that.

Zach drank from his beer glass and eyed Pen's untouched wine. There was no way to avoid him for an extended period of time. He was a force—he was in her life. She had to do the mature thing and tell him the damn truth.

She filtered through her muddy mind until she located the speech she'd practiced in her office's bathroom mirror five times before she came here tonight. It was short, sweet and to the point.

"I'm pregnant."

Zach's limbs were stiff and unmoving, the blood sloshing against his eardrums making Pen's voice sound a mile away.

"I found out Friday night and I couldn't tell you over the weekend until I decided what to do. So here I am." Pen fastened her gaze on the wineglass. The wine she couldn't drink because she was *pregnant with his child.*

He focused on the beer glass in his hand for an exaggerated beat before managing, "What do you mean?"

His tone was as flat as the firm line of his pretend fiancée's unsmiling mouth. Pale blue eyes rested on his as if she was as shell-shocked as him. Only she couldn't be, because she'd been processing for three days and he'd had three seconds.

"I mean I'm having the baby—*your* baby. Keeping this a secret from you was never an option."

Hell, no, it's not, came the immediate thought.

He hadn't sat around and contemplated fatherhood, but now that he knew it was a reality, the surety of being involved rang tuning-fork true in the pit of his gut.

"The due date is December, right before Christmas." She shared it like she was talking about some other couple who was suddenly expecting a bundle of joy. For as distant as he felt from this announcement, she might as well be talking about someone else.

He set his beer aside and stood, unable to sit any longer. His measured steps were more of a stalk, but he reined in his energy to face the woman on his couch. Penelope had radically changed his future—his entire family's future—in a few short weeks.

Wait. Weeks? He did some quick math.

"It's been a little over two weeks since my brother's party. How the hell could you know you're pregnant already?"

Her porcelain skin went pink. "It's been *four* weeks, Zach, since you and I had sex the first time."

The first time?

Ah, hell.

He nodded to himself as reality reared its head. That was the clincher about math—the answer wasn't up for debate.

The jazz club. The night he'd explored her up and down and up again. The night he thought would be the last he saw of her.

He pulled a hand down his face, pausing with it over his mouth for a moment. His shock was a palpable entity swirling the room, his thoughts ranging from excitement to horror to wanting to accuse her of attempting to take his money like his ex-wife.

But this was Penelope he was talking about. Even if he didn't trust her—and he did—there was the significant matter of her not knowing he had that many zeroes in his bank account the night he took her back to her place.

"I have a plan," she said.

"A plan." Mind racing, his vision blurred as his thoughts circled the track again.

"I'm a public relations superhero, Zach. I have a plan." She patted the cushion next to her. He sat, but not next to her, and lifted his beer to take a hearty gulp. Hell, he might drink Pen's wine, too.

"It's simple. Over the next two weeks, you and I will be seen together less and less until we aren't seen together at all. We'll share a press release that you and I will not be raising the child together. We could even go with a story that we were friends and I wanted a child and you didn't and—"

"No." Zach's voice was thunderous, bouncing off the high ceilings and echoing around the room.

Pen's mouth was frozen midspeech for a second before she said, "I don't expect you to take on a baby. You're a CEO with a budding career. What we had—"

"Have."

Her slim eyebrows rose. "Pardon?"

"What we *have*. Present tense."

"What we *have* is a month-long, on-and-off sexual relationship."

"Until five minutes ago, that was true." She might have alarmed him with unexpected news, but his brain was now sliding into operation mode.

"I didn't mean for this to happen."

"That makes two of us."

"I came here to reassure you that I'm not coming after your money." She stood suddenly. He stood with her. She thrust her chin out, pride gleaming in her slitted eyes. "Plenty of working mothers manage to raise a child alone. I certainly don't need your wealth to do it."

"This isn't a challenge," Zach said, his voice firm. "I don't doubt you're capable of doing whatever you damn well set your mind to, but know this." With his thumb and forefinger, he tipped her chin up. "My child growing in your belly isn't insignificant to me. I'm not walking away."

From you or our baby.

None of the determination slipped from her gaze but tenderness joined it. "I'd never deny you the right to see or support your child, Zach. I was suggesting that I get out of the way."

"Whose way are you in, Penelope?"

She didn't say it but he could feel the word *yours* in the tense air between them.

He dipped his face and captured her lips, sliding his tongue into her mouth and claiming her as his yet again. She wouldn't be eschewing herself from his presence anytime soon.

In fact...

He bent and scooped her into his arms never breaking their lip-lock as he made a path for the bedroom. He was going to see to it that she didn't get any farther away than his apartment.

Baby or no, he'd staked a claim on the blonde in his arms long before her surprise announcement.

And now she'd given him another reason to convince her to stay.

Chapter 8

Penelope wasn't aware the charity dinner Zach invited her to would be at his parents' home. Until they pulled into the long driveway, fountains flanking either side, the grass mowed into an artistic crisscross pattern.

The house was gargantuan. She hadn't been joking about seeing it online, but one couldn't fathom thirty-seven thousand square feet until looking right at it. The place was like its own city.

"Wow," she murmured, gripping her wrap and clutch. "This is impressive."

From beside her in the back of the limo, Zach emitted a noncommittal grunt.

"Did you grow up in this house?"

"No. They bought this place about seven or eight years ago. We grew up in a big house, but not this big."

The driver pulled to a stop and an attendant in a fine

tuxedo opened the limo door for her. She accepted his offered hand, stepped out and transferred that hand to Zach.

"You've done this before," he commented. His tux was like the one he'd worn to Chase's birthday party, but he'd chosen an all-black ensemble: shirt and bowtie included. The darkness made his golden skin, bright green eyes and hair in need of a trim stand out in tantalizing contrast.

"Keep looking at me like that," he murmured into her hair, "and I'll have to show you to one of the many private bedrooms."

She should scold him but couldn't. Finding a bedroom sounded, well…lovely.

The charity function was being held in the house's ballroom on the far east side—or as Pen liked to think of it, "left." They joined the well-dressed throngs clicking through the marble hallways and stopping to admire what had to be million-dollar-plus paintings and sculptures dotting the long corridor.

"Pretentious, right?" Zach muttered, earning a gasp from an older woman whose gray curls were piled on top of her head.

Pen swallowed the laugh pushing against her throat. If that older woman knew who Zach was would she be more or less offended?

It wasn't until they entered the ballroom where the silent auction was underway that the butterflies in Pen's tummy took flight. Right at the same moment her date said…

"There's my mom."

His mom. As in *a mom*. As in what Penelope would

soon be—or was now, depending on when one started counting. She might start hyperventilating.

"Before I forget…" Zach stepped in her line of vision, taking it up with his fine attire and gorgeous self. "This is for you."

He reached into his pocket and light winked off a small metal object—okay, *now* she was going to hyperventilate.

He slid the band onto the third finger of Pen's left hand, a massive square-cut diamond in the center of an army of smaller diamonds. She…gaped. The ring was stunningly beautiful, and would likely require stronger biceps in order to hold her arm up while wearing it.

"Zach." Her gasp was muted, and then vanished altogether, when he lifted her knuckles and placed a kiss on them and the ring.

"Can't look engaged without the ring, now, can you?" His dimple made a brief appearance.

"I suppose not."

"Let's say hello." He offered his right arm and Pen looped her left hand around his elbow, trying hard not to stare at the blinding facets winking up at her.

"Eleanor Ferguson," he said when he reached his mother. "I have someone I'd like you to meet."

Eleanor turned, her martini balanced between manicured pink nails and a few stunning rings of her own, all diamond-encrusted and throwing off nearly as much light as Penelope's. Her blond hair was coiffed and stylish with warm honey highlights.

"Penelope, I presume."

Pen nodded.

"Please, call me Elle. It's wonderful to meet the woman who stole Zach's heart." There was nothing disingenuous about her smile, but Pen still felt as if the woman's reaction was a touch insincere.

"Heavens, Zach. Renaldo did well." Elle lifted Pen's left hand and examined the engagement ring. "Renaldo is our family jeweler. He's the best." She slid the pad of her thumb over the diamonds. "Perfect fit, too. A little wiggle room is always nice in case you eat too much salt."

Or if I'm pregnant with your grandchild.

"Where's Dad?"

"Hors d'oeuvres." Elle rolled eyes that were a muted shade of Zach's envious greens. "Since his heart attack, I make him eat healthy, but the very moment he's out of my sight, he's elbow deep in sausage canapés."

Elle waved over an extremely tall, white-haired man who was patting his lips with a napkin. Zach's father didn't look like a man who'd suffered a heart attack. He walked with a lazy swagger, his tuxedo fitted over his lean body. His hair tickled his collar, in need of a trim like his son's. His gray eyes narrowed on Penelope as he approached.

"Hey, son."

"Penelope Brand, this is my father, Rand, but everyone calls him Rider."

"Pretty girls like you can call me whatever you please," Rider said in a deep baritone before he kissed her hand. Then he held her hand out at arm's length. "Congratulations on your engagement to Zach. Looks like he chose better the second time around."

"Rand! Honestly," Elle scolded, clucking her tongue. "It's lovely to meet you, Penelope. Zach, your brother was looking for you earlier. If you see him, do ask him to bring his date by to say hello. He's being quite rude."

Zach's parents linked arms and walked away and Penelope let out the breath going stale in her lungs.

"They're intense," she said.

"Are they?" Zach looked after them and then turned to face Penelope. "My mother's favorite phrase is *quite rude* by the way, so don't let that alarm you."

Still, the woman made Pen's shoulders crawl under her ears.

"What can I get you to drink?"

"Anything clear and sparkling." Sadly. She could use a glass of champagne.

"Club soda?"

"With a lime." What the hell. Might as well go crazy.

"Perfect timing. Stef!" Zach lifted his voice to be heard and a few heads turned in their direction. It was clear that he was comfortable in the stuffy crowd. Pen already wanted to slip outside for some fresh air.

"Hey, kids." Stefanie approached in a fuchsia dress, her dark blond hair wound into a fancy twist. She smiled over her martini. "Penelope, you have to try these. The gin is the best I've ever had."

"Pen's not drinking this evening. Hang out here for a moment with her while I get her a club soda."

"Club soda?" Stef asked, but her words bounced off Zach's retreating back.

"I haven't been feeling well today." It was the truth. Pen woke with morning sickness that kept her in bed an extra hour. She nibbled on saltine crackers while checking her email on her phone. She'd yet to throw up as a result of morning sickness, but she'd become increasingly grateful that her private office had an attached bathroom.

"You don't look the least bit pale, so that's a plus." Stefanie's assessing gaze trickled over her, and Pen worried for a moment the younger woman might see right through her facade.

"I hear your oldest brother has a date," Pen said, successfully rerouting Stef's gaze.

Stef's eyes swept the room. "He does. I met her. She's a stiff like he is."

Pen saw them then, a slight woman with dark hair whose arm was linked with Chase's. He was talking to his parents now, so there was no need to pass on Elle's observation that he was being *quite rude*.

"Did you bid on anything?" Pen asked Stef.

"The spa package." She pointed to one corner and then to a painting to the right. "And that horrible artwork."

A chuckle erupted out of Pen before she could help it.

"I like you, Penelope." Stef's sincerity was obvious. The woman didn't say things she didn't mean. Pen knew that much. "If anyone is going to enter this family, I'm glad it's you. Zach hasn't always had the best taste."

"Oh?" Pen stepped closer, curious about Zach's dating habits. "Let me guess. Complete playboy."

"He has a good heart, but most women never access it. As for Yvonne and that Vegas wedding thing... What the hell?"

"It is curious that he tied the knot with her." The thin redhead seemed better suited for anyone other than Zach Ferguson.

"He said getting married sounded fun," Stef said. "But that's pretty much his prescription for life, isn't it? If it sounds like a good time, why not attempt?"

Penelope's stomach sank. This time she did palm her torso as a bout of queasiness overtook her.

What Stef said was true—and Pen had seen it in

action. Zach introduced her as his fiancée the evening of Chase's birthday party because it sounded fun. They slept together that first night—and several nights thereafter because it was fun. Pen fell in line with that thinking because being around Zach made her embrace the fun. His world was shimmering and enticing, and she'd wanted some of that for herself.

Only that *fun* had turned into a baby due at the end of this year. That *fun* had become a human being, half Zach, half Pen. A baby wasn't something you "attempted" because it sounded fun. There'd be no walking away if their son or daughter suddenly lost his or her luster. At least not for her. While she was definitely ill-equipped for motherhood, she was willing to live and learn. Her own mother had set a stellar example and, like her, Pen planned on rocking the business world as well as a breast pump. It'd take some practice and she was sure there would be moments where she had no idea what she was doing, but she'd manage.

What about Zach, though? Would her fake fiancé turn his back on their child if he or she suddenly didn't fit into his *fun* lifestyle? Did Pen make a mistake letting him talk her into staying?

"Pen? You don't look so good." Stef's hand rested on Penelope's shoulder as the world swam in and out.

Pen's cheeks heated, her head spun and she rocked on her high heels. She swept her blurring vision over to Zach, who approached with a drink in each hand.

The last thing she remembered was him dropping both glasses to rush over as her world was swallowed in black.

Chapter 9

Zach's concerned expression was the first sight Pen saw when she opened her eyes.

She reached for her forehead, where a damp weight sat, and pulled away a black washcloth.

He took it from her. "Stef, rewet this for me?"

His sister jumped to help, returning in a few seconds with a much cooler cloth. Zach pressed it to Pen's forehead again.

"No more high heels," he told her, a muscle flinching in his cheek.

"Leave her alone." Stef entered her range of vision again, this time with a water bottle. "Sip this, Pen."

Zach helped her sit up some and then Pen drank from the water bottle, her head much clearer than before. She'd been relocated to an enormous sitting room with settees and low coffee tables and several groupings of chairs. She looked down to find she was resting on a dove-gray chaise longue.

"You passed out. Did you eat today?" That was Zach, his voice low and angry, but his innate tenderness outlined every word.

"I ate a little," Pen mumbled, sitting up and putting her feet on the floor—her bare feet. "Where are my shoes?"

"I'll carry you to the limo. You're not putting those things on again." His mouth pulled down at the corners.

"Yes, I am. I can wear high heels as well as I can flats. Better, in fact."

"It's second nature after a while," Stef concurred. Then to Pen, she added, "He's being overly concerned."

"We need to check with the doctor." He stood from his kneeling position on the floor in front of her and sat on the edge of the lounger. "To make sure nothing's wrong."

"She's light-headed! There's nothing wrong." Stef rolled her eyes and took a bite out of what appeared to be a ham sandwich.

Pen's mouth watered. She literally licked her lips.

"Want half?" Stefanie offered a plate with the other half of her sandwich. "There was too much fancy food out there so I went to the kitchen and made a ham and cheese on white bread like a real American."

"I can get you anything you like from the caterer, Pen. You don't have to—" Zach started to argue.

"If you don't mind." She reached past him for the plate and Stef handed it over. Pen took one bite, then another, and in no time the half sandwich was demolished. "Thank you so much."

Zach took the plate. "Better?"

Pen slugged back the rest of the water and let out a satisfied *Mmm.* "Much better."

"Guess we forgot the eating for two part, didn't we?" He pushed a lock of hair away from her face before his eyes went wide at his faux pas.

"Oh my God! You guys are *pregnant*?" Stef stood from her seat on top of the coffee table, the remainder of her sandwich still in one hand. "I'm so excited! I'm going to be an aunt!"

"Stef," Zach growled. "We haven't told anyone yet."

His sister promptly returned her derrière to the coffee table and pressed her lips closed. She mimed zipping her lips but when she looked back to Pen, she air clapped.

"I'm going to take you home." Zach stood. "*My* home, where you'll be staying." He leveled Pen with an impatient glare before leaving the sitting room.

"Bossy." Stef polished off her sandwich and dusted her hands on her skirt like she was wearing jeans instead of Carolina Herrera.

"What does he mean 'where I'll be staying?'" she asked herself, but Stef answered.

"While you were unconscious, Zach said he was going to ask you to move in with him." Stef turned to study the doorway he'd disappeared through. "I guess that was his way of asking."

"You're overreacting," Penelope told Zach as he moved from the couch to the kitchen on Monday morning. She'd spent Saturday night at his house, and Sunday, too, but this was ridiculous. She was itching to go home. Despite him having stopped by her apartment to gather a few changes of clothes—and shoes—she was ready to sleep in her own bed. And, as of Monday morning, ready to work in her own office.

He returned to the living room with a steaming mug, a string and tag dangling from the edge.

"The doctor said plenty of fluids and that peppermint tea would help as long as you don't drink it too often." He placed the mug in front of her on the couch where he'd arranged a remote, a few paperback novels, magazines and a plate of cheese and crackers.

A doctor made a house call Saturday afternoon and told her everything seemed fine, though he'd like her to come in soon for an ultrasound. He did take her blood for a workup, so she was glad to have that unpleasantness over with.

Zach threw a blanket over her legs and Pen tossed it off with a laugh.

"It's nearly June, Zach. I don't need a blanket. I don't have the flu. I have morning sickness. I'm not going to sit here when I have work to do."

"Yes, you are."

"No. I'm not."

She stood and he took a step toward her. The room canted to one side and she gripped his biceps, willing her feet to keep her upright. Strong hands wrapped around her arms and when she looked sheepishly up at her caretaker, his eyes were filled with concern.

"Pen."

"Fine. I'll rest. But only for today. And I'm going to return emails, then maybe a few phone calls."

Sensing he'd lost the battle, Zach didn't argue. But then Penelope did make a show of sipping her tea and eating a cracker—no cheese yet; her stomach couldn't handle it.

"The doctor also said the nausea will subside. You won't feel like this every day." Zach, her new nurse-maid, delivered a paper napkin to her next. She knew everything the doctor had said. She'd been there. But Zach was making her his top priority, and that was really...nice.

"Thank you." In all sincerity, she should be thanking him. He was overbearing and a worrywart, but he was also looking out for her. For a woman who'd been on her own since she started staying home alone at age eleven, Pen wasn't accustomed to someone taking care of her.

"I had lunch and dinner delivered. The meals are prepared and in the fridge. All you have to do is take the lid off and eat them."

When Zach started listing ingredients like "chicken salad on rye" Pen's stomach did a cannonball.

She held out a hand. "Don't say the word chicken or rye." She swallowed thickly. "Or salad."

He lowered to sit next to her on the sofa, cradling her face in his hands. "You're going to be okay here while I go to work?"

"Yes. Go." She gave him a halfhearted shove and he stole a kiss before standing. One more wave good-bye and he left.

She sat back on the couch and flipped on the TV, using the remote. She sipped her tea, kept down the crackers and yes, a few pieces of the mild Swiss cheese, and decided that maybe she could rest for a little while.

With her body being uncooperative, she could use the break.

* * *

Zach's mind was a million miles from work and the man currently droning on in front of him at the board meeting. He slid his gaze to his right where Armand jotted notes on his steno pad, and then to his left where Celia pecked notes into her iPad.

His mind was on Penelope and the scare she'd given him the night of the charity function at his parents' house.

He was able to play it off as her not feeling well to everyone except for Stefanie, thanks to his gaffe when he mentioned Penelope eating for two.

Since then, he'd been in productive mode. He'd taken Pen home, called the doctor and scheduled a house visit and made sure she had everything she needed at his place.

His cell phone buzzed and he grabbed on to the interruption like a lifeline. The entire meeting halted as he stood and checked the screen. Stefanie. Good enough for him.

"Continue without me. Celia, if you could email me your notes." With that, he was out the door, lifting his cell phone to his ear. "Zachary Ferguson."

"Oh, so formal. I like it."

"I have to keep up appearances for the suits."

"Aren't you one of them now?" He could hear her smile.

"Never say die, Stef. What's up with you?"

"I'm going to plan a bridal shower for your future wife," she answered, bringing him to a halt a few yards from his office door. "And I didn't know, if by the time I threw it, we'd also include the baby shower part. Thoughts?"

Woodenly, he moved to the sanctuary of his office and shut the door behind him. "No showers. We're doing this low-key."

"No low-key. You're a Ferguson and we do things very high-key. Or off-key, if we're talking about Dad's singing. I'm en route to the florist for a consultation for a fund-raiser dinner Mom is throwing, but I thought I'd ask about bridal arrangements while I was there. By the way, when is the wedding date?"

"We don't have a wedding date. No showers."

"Well, you'd better set one because that baby has a due date and I have a feeling he or she will stick to it whether you're married or not."

His face went cold as the blood drained from his cheeks. When he'd become "engaged" to Pen, no part of him believed they'd actually get married. Now that there was a baby on the way, well…he still hadn't planned on marrying her, but he also hadn't considered that everyone would expect them to make things official. Especially with a child who would carry on the Ferguson name.

"Have to run. Ciao!" Stefanie hung up on him and Zach set the cell phone on his calendar and stared dumbly at the month of May.

His sister had a point. Their baby was coming whether or not he set a wedding date. If he and Pen didn't get married, in a few short weeks they'd have to announce a pregnancy and the decision not to wed.

It was archaic to believe they had to marry because they were expecting, but his parents would expect it. Especially now that they'd learned he'd married Yvonne on a whim.

Except no one knew the real reason for his marriage to Yvonne. It was a challenge in a way—to see if he could do it. Could he get over the past in one fell swoop without years of therapy or repression?

He could, as it turned out. He'd had to drink half the liquor in Nevada, but he'd walked down the aisle, had a spontaneous Vegas honeymoon and then wrapped things up in a matter of days.

All because once upon a time he'd been in love— for real. Yes, he'd been twenty-six, but he knew in his bones that Lonna was the one for him. She was four years older than him and had absolutely consumed every corner of his world.

They dated for a year and on that one-year anniversary when they sat across from each other at a rooftop bar, Zach proposed.

He recited a speech including how much he loved her, how there was no one else for him and how the rest of his life would be spent by her side.

Lonna had an announcement that evening, too. She'd come to break up with him. She'd had a speech prepared—it was about how she couldn't see herself with him past that year, and how she couldn't bring herself to lie to him because she didn't love him.

She'd said she never had.

It was a blow he was sure he'd never recover from. Thank God he'd kept the relationship quiet, only telling his parents and friends that they were "dating." After the breakup, he kept things quieter. He dodged questions, confided in no one and cried in private.

Then he decided he'd been humiliated for the last time, packed up his life and started a new one away from Dallas.

Now he had a decision to make. About a marriage. About a future with Penelope in his life.

No matter what those future plans entailed, one thing was certain: Pen and he might get married, they would have a baby, but Zach refused to allow himself to fall in love.

Not now.

Not ever again.

Chapter 10

She wasn't sure what happened, but after a few hours of sipping tea and watching mindless daytime television, Penelope abandoned the vicinity of *craptastic* and exited the off-ramp of *amazing*.

She showered at Zach's house, dressed in her favorite pantsuit—white, of course—and slipped her feet into five-inch heels. She arrived at her office building via a town car—the number she'd pilfered from Zach's refrigerator—thanked the driver and stepped onto the downtown sidewalk.

It wasn't officially summer yet, but the Texas sun was hot. Judging by the passing professionals, summer was already here. Men had gone without their jackets, the women wore shorter hemlines and everyone, Pen included, had sunglasses perched on their noses.

She'd returned as many emails and phone calls as

she could from her cell phone. She told herself that she was going to the office simply to retrieve her laptop, but now that she was here, she decided to stay. The idea of settling into her cushy desk chair, hands on the keyboard, was too tempting to resist.

Bonus, the embryo incubating in her uterus decided to allow her to keep the contents of her stomach. She'd be smart to take advantage of the reprieve.

Two hours into her routine, her planner boasted several checked-off boxes and lined-through tasks, and Pen's fingers were practically flying over the keys as she crafted an email to a reporter. Reporters and paparazzi were good friends to have when in PR. Even if they were less friends and more acquaintances with benefits.

She sent the email by punching the enter key with a flourish before standing to refill her water bottle. She'd pulled open her office door only a few inches when Zach rounded the corner, paper takeout bag in hand, a scowl on his face.

"Zach, hi!" Rather than fetch herself a much-needed drink, she pulled the door open the rest of the way and ushered him in. "How'd you know where to find me?"

"Tony told me."

The town car driver.

"Right. Well. Welcome to my humble office."

Zach didn't survey her digs, though. He set the paper bag on her desk and glowered down at her. "You're not at my house."

"Correct." She smiled.

"You didn't eat the food I left for you in the refrigerator."

At the mention of food, her stomach roared rather than wilted. That was a good sign—her appetite was back.

"I was going to order from the sandwich cart in the lobby." She'd been so wrapped up in work, she'd forgotten all about eating.

"Now you don't have to."

"Are you under the impression that I'm incapable of feeding myself?" She smiled sweetly.

"Don't be cute." His voice was thick with warning. "It's my responsibility to keep you in good health since this situation is at least half my doing."

"Ha! I'm not a prize pig, Zach. I'm responsible for myself. And I hope you're not suggesting that you need to ensure I eat for two because I'm neglecting our baby."

His brows slammed over his nose. "I'm not suggesting anything. I'm *telling* you that parenting, for me, starts here."

Her eyes went to the paper sack. That...was actually kind of sweet. Barbaric and completely chauvinist, but sweet. She hooked a finger on the edge of the bag and peeked inside. "You brought enough for both of us. Are you staying?"

Pen scraped the bottom of her salad bowl with the plastic fork to catch the last bit of honey mustard dressing and cranberry. She hummed while chewing, then opened her beautiful blue eyes and laid them right on Zach. He was glad to see that the color had returned to her face.

"Thank you," she said. "This was delicious."

He raised the plastic container containing the remaining half of his Reuben sandwich, dripping with

Thousand Island dressing and tart sauerkraut. "Want the rest of mine?"

Her eyes brightened. "Really?"

"Yes, really."

She eagerly accepted the container and wolfed down the rest of his sandwich. As she swiped her mouth with a napkin, he gathered the plastic containers and stuffed them into the paper sack so he could take them to the trash on the way out.

"Nice to have an appetite." She swallowed a few guzzles of water from the bottle he'd refilled for her. "It must kick in late afternoon."

The *bing* of her email inbox sounded again. That had to be the sixth or seventh time since they'd sat down to eat. She rose to check it and he rose with her, curling a hand around her slender wrist.

"It's after five, Pen. Time to clock off."

"Just let me check." She tilted her head, sending her blond hair sliding over breasts that were pushed against the low V-cut of her silky shirt.

Keeping her wrist captive, he lowered his lips to hers.

"No," he whispered, lifting his head to find her wearing a disdainful frown. "Gather your things and I'll drive you home."

"Oh, all right." She shut down her desktop computer and slid her laptop into a bag along with a few other files and her planner. "If you could send my things back to my place, I'd appreciate it. There are a few outfits I'd like to have on hand for this week."

"Home is my place, Penelope." He lifted the sack and her water bottle, holding the door open for her.

"No. I'm going to my house."

"Guess again. Let's go."

"Zach!" She straightened her back and squared her jaw, ready for a fight. He slid a lingering gaze down her body—over the fitted jacket and pants to the shoes he should have thrown out rather than hid in his closet.

He took a step closer to her and she adjusted the bag on her shoulder. "You're wearing the shoes I told you not to." His voice dipped to communicate his displeasure.

"It's a free country." She arched one fair eyebrow.

"You're coming to my house," he reiterated. He couldn't risk her slipping in the shoes or forgetting to eat or no one being there if she felt sick in the morning. He wanted her safe. He wanted her with him. "No more discussion."

"You can't keep me prisoner, you know." She propped a fist on one hip.

Stubborn thing…

Zach dropped the bag and scooped Pen against him, his arm locked at her lower back. He kissed her, his tongue plunging past her lips, pleased when her free hand went from pushing him away to fisting in his shirt and tugging him forward. A thrill pulsed through him when her lips went pliant and her tongue began sparring with his.

When she finally surfaced, he kissed her lips softly once, twice more, and made sure she was steady on her spindly shoes before letting her go.

He then bent and lifted the bag and smirked down at her. Her hair was rumpled, her jacket askance and her lips pink and swollen from his five o'clock shadow. *His.* Through and through.

"Your place." She said it with an eye roll, and offered a droll, "But only because there's no one at my house who kisses me like that," over her shoulder while they walked to the elevator.

Yeah, he thought she'd see things his way.

"Engaged?" Penelope's mother squawked into the phone.

Penelope'd had a feeling the news would be a surprise. Her mother knew Pen had all but sworn off men since one ran her out of Chicago.

Paula Brand had always been a busy woman. When Penelope was growing up, one indelible fact stood out about her mother: she worked.

Part of Pen's work ethic had come directly from her mother. Yes, her father worked on their co-owned real estate business, but it was Paula whom Penelope had always wanted to grow up and be like.

"I'm getting you the news a little late," Pen said. "There was a bit of a kerfuffle here in Dallas about my being engaged to the mayor's brother." Not that the news would have traveled to Chicago.

"Well, what's he like? Other than being the mayor's brother," her mother said, rustling papers. Paula was most likely sitting at the kitchen table of her latest project. Pen could imagine a paper-strewn surface surrounded by refinished cabinet drawers leaning against every wall, stacks of to-be-installed tile dotting worn linoleum. Paula was usually busy with one house project or the next, but she always made time for her only daughter.

"Well, I actually met him in Chicago in passing a few years back." Hopefully this would foster the notion that she hadn't rushed into anything. "He relocated to

Dallas, and when I did, too, I ran into him at…a concert." Concert seemed better than a club. No way was Pen sharing what transpired that evening. Namely: the conception of their son or daughter.

"What does the mayor's brother *do*?" Possibly the most important question her mother could've asked. Vocation in the Brand family was paramount. The answer would please her, Pen was sure.

"He's the CEO of Ferguson Oil."

A drawn out silence, and then, "Impressive." Her mother took a breath and then issued a warning of sorts. "I hope this man has more to him than money. I raised you to support yourself."

Paula, though in a strong marriage with Pen's father, had always encouraged her to be independent. She knew her mother was looking out for her rather than accusing her of chasing a man because of the size of his wallet.

"Funny story. I didn't even know about his monetary status until we became serious. He used to be a contractor. A very good one. He came home to run the family business."

"Even when you try to go blue-collar, you end up with a suit." Paula's tone was filled with mild humor, yet approving. "That sounds like you."

Zach looked as delicious in worn jeans as he did in suits, if memory served. Pen hadn't had much of an opportunity to see him in jeans—though he had worn a pair of low-slung sweats the other night that nearly made her eyes tumble from their sockets. This morning he'd kissed her while she slept, and walked out of the bedroom wearing his running gear. She regretted now not waking up completely to take in the view.

"If you are happy, darling, I'm happy," her mother said. "That's all I want."

"Thanks, Mom." Her support would make the baby bombshell easier to drop in the future.

"As long as this man is ten times the man Cliff was."

Unfortunately, Pen hadn't been able to hide the circumstance that drove her out of Chicago and away from her parents. When she'd decided to relocate to Dallas, she'd told them the truth.

"Zach is one hundred times the man Cliff was." She'd been pacing the living room as she talked on her cell phone, so when she turned on her heel to pace back, she was surprised to find the subject of her conversation already in the room. She bid her mother farewell, and with a promise to check in soon, ended the call.

"I can get used to coming home to high compliments." Zach's words were puffed out between a few labored breaths. "You're up."

"Did you take the stairs?" Not what she wanted to say, but she had to fill the gap of silence that had mostly involved her staring. Zach's black T-shirt was damp with sweat, his biceps pressing the edges of the sleeves, and his strong legs poking out from beneath a pair of gray shorts. Had she ever known a man with a body this incredible? She didn't have to think long to come up with that answer.

No. No was the answer.

"I confessed to my mother about the engagement. I figured if she was comfortable with the idea of us getting married, she'll embrace the idea of being a grandmother."

He nodded, taking the information in stride. "Guess

we should make that announcement eventually. I'm not sure how long we can hide it."

She dragged her palm over her flat stomach. She wasn't showing yet, but she would be soon enough.

"We could always tell everyone we were waiting until we were positive nothing would go wrong."

"It's our news to share whenever we want, for whatever reasons we decide."

She liked Zach's confidence. She liked sharing this with him. Though unexpected, the baby was their little secret—well, theirs and Stef's.

"I'm going to grab a shower. Join me?" His crooked smile went a long way to convincing her to do just that. Unfortunately…

"I already took one. And I have another phone call to make. Rain check?"

Even sweaty, he was sexy. He strolled over, water bottle in hand, and grinned down at her. The earthy outdoor scent wafting off him didn't deter her in the least—only made her want him more.

"In your case, Penelope, it's always raining."

The delicious lilt of his drawl was enough to bring her to her tiptoes. She placed a kiss on his lips and when he pulled back he dragged his top teeth along his full bottom lip. That move almost made her change her mind.

Almost.

Her mother's words echoed in her mind. Penelope had been raised to support herself.

Sexy baby daddy or no, her workday called.

Chapter 11

Serena Fern and Ashton Weaver sat at a round table by the swimming pool, Pen across from them in a matching cushioned wicker chair. She'd met them at Ashton's mansion, per his request, and was as grateful for the peppermint candy he offered as much as the warmth of the summer sun.

These two were currently interviewing for a public relations specialist to handle an incident that happened during a particularly wild party where Serena, who was engaged to Michael Guff, her manager, was photographed sliding lips with her fellow actor, Ashton.

And who could blame her? Serena and Ashton were in their early twenties and Michael was pushing forty.

In their matching aviator sunglasses, Serena and Ashton looked very much like a couple. Especially since they held hands on the tabletop next to three sweating glasses of lemonade.

"We want to go public," Ashton declared. "She doesn't love Michael."

Serena's smile was sweet—hopeful. She liked that Ashton claimed her; Pen could tell that much.

"You *are* public," Pen informed them. "You're public in a big way." TMZ had plastered those photos all over the internet. There was nothing demure about Serena in her string bikini in this very pool and Ashton's tongue visible as she clung to his neck. The engagement was off, but Serena said Michael hadn't dropped her as a client yet. Because he was smart. He knew Serena was at the top of her game, and wasn't about to let his cash cow go. So to speak.

"I don't want to be the bad guy here. I look like I cheated." Serena's full pout appeared. She was gorgeous, if not a petite little thing.

"You *did* cheat," Pen reminded her. Her clients came to her for the truth and she wasn't holding back. "The good news is, most of the public will see this as predatory. Michael knows what he's doing. He wooed you with his professionalism and expertise. We'll perpetuate the story that he was marrying you for a cut of your money. A few timely interviews and tweets, and then you and Ashton can go public. For now, you can be seen together, but no kissing. No hand-holding. Go out and have coffee—better yet, with your scripts like you're rehearsing. In a few weeks you can snog in public all you like."

Serena grinned. Ashton didn't.

"What about Michael?"

Pen smiled. And here came the part where the young actors hired her.

"I'd recommend Serena firing him."

Ashton grinned. Serena gasped.

"Can I...do that?" she asked.

"Not only can you do that, you should. I know a couple of wonderful agents who could recommend someone reputable for your career."

"And then we could stop sneaking around and pretending it was an accident." Serena grasped Ashton's hands with both of hers and then, the two most adorable people ever embraced and kissed in a way that made Pen uncomfortable.

Job acquired, Pen left Ashton's mansion and those two to their inevitable lovemaking. Serena's words wound around her brain as Pen climbed into her car. *Sneaking around.*

While Pen and Zach weren't exactly sneaking, it irked her that she didn't have a blueprint for their situation. This was what she did for a living—she should be able to draw up a concise plan.

Which would be...what?

She thought back to Chicago, to Reese and Merina Crane's marriage of convenience, and how it turned into love despite starting as a farce.

Is that what Pen was hoping would happen with her and Zach? Because that was...silly.

What they had was an engagement that had started out as a distraction for Zach's PR issue. What they currently had was an entanglement that couldn't be resolved by a few tweets and sound bites.

What they had was a budding family and Pen needed to decide how, exactly, to move forward while preserving the Ferguson family's good name.

She drove to her apartment, deep in thought about what that plan would look like. How she and Zach would maintain a friendship throughout raising their child. When the best time would be to announce the dissolving of their engagement.

Probably the wisest move was to announce the baby on the heels of them not being engaged—that way everyone would be too excited about the baby to focus on the breakup.

Sigh.

Maybe she should hire a PR person to handle her case.

From where she sat, everything looked muddy.

At her apartment, she pulled into the lot. Without a private garage like Zach had, she didn't have much choice but to park her car in the elements. As luxurious as his apartment and amenities were, she couldn't stay there forever. She had to start thinking about where to put the baby—and considering that her apartment was a compact one-bedroom, one-bath, that meant she would have to consider moving.

Perhaps that was the first order of business.

She stepped from her car and turned for the property manager's office directly across from her building. As luck would have it, Jenny was heading her way.

"Ms. Brand." Her cropped blond hair blew in the summer breeze. She wore a fitted pencil skirt and a button-down shirt over a pair of sensible pumps. "Great timing. I was coming to give you this."

"Oh?" Pen pushed her hair behind her ear and accepted the paper Jenny offered. "What is it?"

"Your lease has been terminated. Congratulations on your engagement!" Jenny squeezed Pen's upper arm. "I hate to see you go, but I'm thrilled you've found love. Zach told me it was a surprise—his wedding gift to you. *Ohmygoshisthatthering?*" She snatched Pen's left hand and admired the diamond resting there, before rerouting her hand to her chest. Pen swore the other woman was tearing up. "You have until the end of the month to clear your things. No hurry, but honestly, I wouldn't hesitate moving in with a man who gives you a rock like this one!"

Before she could respond to…well, any of it, Jenny waved and said something about returning to her desk. Pen watched her go, the paper in her hand blowing and folding in half. She straightened it and read over the words Paid In Full as her temper skyrocketed.

Yes, she'd been contemplating moving from her one-bedroom into a larger place, but she wasn't planning on moving in with Zach.

She lifted her cell phone and punched in his number. When he answered in his office-y voice, she let him have it.

"I'm homeless." She wrestled her keys from her bag and marched inside her building.

"You're far from homeless," came his easy response.

"I'm not moving into your apartment, Zach."

"No. You're not."

She blinked as she pushed the button on the elevator for her floor. "Pardon?"

"I'm looking at a house right now. There's not enough room for a baby at my place." His voice sounded distant when he spoke to someone other than her. "I'll take it."

"Zach?"

"Gotta go, gorgeous. I have paperwork to deal with."

"Zach."

But one glance at her cell phone and she could see he'd already ended the call.

Zach tried Pen's phone number again only to be greeted by voice mail. He tapped the screen on the dashboard to end the call and pulled off the highway, changing direction to drive to her apartment. If she wasn't there, he'd try her office, and if she wasn't *there*, he'd see her at his apartment tonight.

When he'd gone to her place of residence to pick up a few things for her a week ago, he'd nearly had an aneurysm. The apartment building was in need of more than paint and TLC, and the area wasn't the safest. He'd decided then and there to keep her close by. Safe. Now that she was having his baby, there was no need for her to struggle.

He didn't want their child growing up worried about his or her safety.

From what he could tell, Pen dumped all her money into her office. He understood why. With a job like hers, working with business and celebrity elite, she needed to look the part.

He drove through the parking lot but there was no sign of Pen's car. He'd try her office next. He hit the screen on his dashboard to call her cell again, knowing it was futile.

But then her voice surprised him.

"I'm trying to be mad at you."

He couldn't help smiling. Not because she was mad at him but because hearing her voice lined with anger meant she was safe. She was okay.

"Where are you?"

"Why? Planning on coming by and buying me out of whatever building I'm in? What if I'm shopping?"

"A shopping center is well within my pay grade."

Her silence let him know his joke didn't fly.

"I want to know where you are so I can show you our new house."

"Zach."

"We also need to talk about our plans and what we're sharing when. I'm not going to dodge questions when they start rolling in, regardless of my brother's political career or Ferguson Oil's reputation. I'm not going to hide you or what we're doing."

"I agree. We need a plan." Her voice was wooden, but he'd take the agreement. "I don't want that, either."

"All right, then. Where are you? I'll take you to dinner."

"I'm at your apartment. Throwing your clothes out the window." Her voice was petulant, but he could guess she was kidding.

"I guess I have to buy that shopping center after all."

More silence.

"Pen."

"Come home. We'll talk then."

The way she said *home*, with ownership, and invited him to join her, snagged his chest.

"I was serious about dinner," he said as he sat back in his seat and accelerated.

"You bet your sweet ass you are," Pen snapped. "I'll see you soon."

Another grin. Damn, he liked her feisty.

He liked her, period.

At home he found Penelope dressed down in a tight

pair of form-fitting pants and a baggy tee. Her hair was in a ponytail and she was on the floor, eyes closed, hands resting on her knees.

"Yoga?" he guessed, setting his cell phone and brief-case on the kitchen counter.

"I'm meditating so I don't kill you," she said without opening her eyes. Then she did, and pegged him with a pair of pale blues that never failed to make him smile. She had a pull on him—a physical one, sure, but there was a deeper connection there. Because of the baby? Yes, that was definitely part of it, but that wasn't all. "How was your day, dear?"

"Hectic. I bought a house."

"I heard." Her mouth flattened. She reached behind her and lifted a sheet of paper, waving it in the air for him. "I lost mine."

"I wanted it to be a surprise."

She stood from her mat and slapped the paper against his chest. "I was surprised."

He palmed the paper and followed her into the kitchen. She swallowed a few drinks of water before gesturing to the paper he still held. "Flip it over."

Her handwriting took up the entire backside of the page.

"'PR Plan for Zachary Ferguson and Penelope Brand,'" he read.

"I drafted our plan."

Under their names were dates and bulletpoints for items like "announce end of engagement" and "be seen shopping for baby" and "press release."

"This is…interesting." He couldn't come up with another word for it.

"This is the way we're doing it."

"I don't see a line item for moving into my house."

"Sorry. I'm going to be living apart from you before that happens." She waggled her hand where the engagement ring sat. "The breakup and all."

"I don't see why we have to break up." He felt his brow furrow while hers lifted.

"Because this isn't real. I've orchestrated engagements before. I've even dealt with unplanned pregnancies. Couples don't usually argue with my sound and reliable suggestion to announce a split." She bit her lip. "Mostly."

Mostly.

He wondered if that meant some of the couples she'd walked through the valley of the shadow of matrimony fell in love for real and unraveled her precious plans. That wasn't their case, but he could see the discomfort in her expression.

He set the paper aside and walked toward her until she plastered her back against the fridge and lifted her chin to take him in. There wasn't anything quite like her delicate features contrasted with all that strength and sass. She was a drug.

His palm on her stomach, he crowded her until his body was pressed against hers. "*This*. Is real."

"I know," she said just above a whisper. "But the engagement isn't."

"There's no reason to dismantle it yet. We could say we're waiting to marry until after you have the baby."

She gave him a slow nod, her eyes averting. "Is that what you want?"

Yes. Because he knew what he didn't want. He didn't want her to leave. He didn't want to miss a single moment of the pregnancy. That was only one of the reasons he wanted her to move in. He wanted to watch over her, but he also wanted to be with her.

"How about this for a proposal?" he asked, pleased when she turned her head, and her lips were dangerously close to his. "Move into my house. Have my baby. Wear this ring."

"And then what?"

"We have time to decide the *what*, Penelope." He palmed her soft cheek and ran his thumb over her bottom lip. "In the meantime, I want you in my house. In my bed. In my world."

"You don't have to—"

"Let me. Allow yourself to let me. You don't have to have a rigid plan for your own life, Pen. Live on the edge." He gave her a lazy grin. "It's fun here."

She licked her lips and before she could argue, he covered them with a kiss. Deflecting? Possibly. Where they were concerned, there was one surefire way to get them back on track and that was in the bedroom.

"You promised me dinner," she breathed, but her fists clung to him.

He was aware of the time, more aware of her pending hunger than his hardening manhood. "Are you hungry?"

"Starving." Her eyebrows bent in the sincerest apology. "How about after dinner?"

"You have to ask?" He shook his head, still marveling over how off-kilter this woman could throw him. "Dinner. Get changed."

Her beaming smile made him almost as happy as having her underneath him. She bounced out of the kitchen and down the hallway and Zach took another look at the paper in front of him.

He grabbed a pen from a nearby drawer and drew a line through "announce end of engagement."

Chapter 12

Having billions of dollars made moving much easier.

When Pen moved, she'd hired movers and packed every one of her belongings, plus loaded many of the boxes into her own car, for the traverse to Dallas from Chicago.

When Zach moved, he made one phone call to an assistant to gather Penelope's belongings from her apartment, and another to an interior designer to decorate his new home.

Two weeks had passed since the move from her apartment. His buying her out of her lease was heavy-handed, but she could admit it made sense in the short-term. Everyone would assume it was the natural next step after hearing about the pregnancy. Plus, Zach would need more room for the baby whether Pen lived with him or not.

He'd purchased a beautiful home just outside the city, with six bedrooms and six bathrooms and a sprawling yard. A low stone wall ran the perimeter of the property, and the front featured a gate, not unlike Chase's mansion.

The house was far more approachable than a mansion, however, with a wide front porch and white columns, and, thanks to a savvy interior decorator, a pair of rockers on the porch overlooking the front yard and curved driveway.

That was where she and Zach sat tonight.

She'd finished up at work and he'd met her at home for dinner—a dinner cooked by a chef he'd hired to monitor her feedings, or so she'd joked. Now they sat, a mug of peppermint tea for her, and a cold beer for him, rocking back and forth on the porch.

"This is really beautiful, Zach."

He turned his head and smiled. Tonight he wore jeans and a T-shirt, looking the part of laid-back country boy. Even the recent trim of his hair couldn't dash the relaxed line of his long body. He pushed, one knee crooked, the other leg straight out, and rocked again, finishing his bottle of beer before setting it on the wooden porch.

"Glad you like it."

She tapped her mug with her fingernails and thought. The PR plan for them had been drawn up. She'd typed it neatly, presented it to him and he'd made changes—some she'd agreed to, others she hadn't.

Maintain engagement (to be revisited after the baby is born)

Shopping for the baby (covered by the press)

Press release confirming baby Ferguson

"We should talk," she said.

Zach's hands gripped the arms of the rocker and he slowly turned to face her. His eyebrows were down, his mouth flat.

"It's not bad!" she assured him with a soft laugh.

"Do me the favor of never saying those three words to me again?" He visibly relaxed some, sucking in a deep breath.

There had to be a story behind his request, but she wasn't going into that now.

"It's time to tell our families." She placed her hand over her tummy. She'd always had a slim waist, but the bump was showing enough that people would start talking. "I can't hide this much longer. And I'd like to tell them before we're seen at the store."

"That'd be best, yes." His ease returned, along with his smile.

"How about this weekend? We can stop by your parents' house before going to Love & Tumble." The upscale boutique selling children's clothing was bordering pretentious, but for the press release, they needed the attention. What better store to emerge from carrying several shiny sage-green bags in their hands while kissing? She'd already lined up a photographer and requested the shots.

"And your parents?"

"We can't very well fly to Chicago, now can we?"

"Why not?" He shrugged. "It's a two-hour flight."

"On your private jet?" She snorted. This amount of convenience was all so...hard to get used to.

"I don't own one, but I can charter a plane." He leaned on one arm, coming closer to her chair. "Your parents might want to meet me."

She nodded, her fantasy world ripping at the seams. Once her parents met him, once he was on her stomping grounds, would the fantasy bubble burst? She'd been sheltered, in a way. Living in this safe existence with work and Zach. Sequestered from reality while she juggled nausea, fatigue and doctor's appointments.

"I'll book it for Friday. We can grab a hotel."

A dry laugh chafed her throat. "My parents would die if we booked a hotel. They would insist we stay with them."

"We can stay with them."

She watched him for a solid beat, wondering who this man was, really. Was he the billionaire who moved them into a regal house with the snap of his fingers? Or the family guy kicked back on a rocking chair? Could he be both?

"Friday," she repeated, still unsure.

He grabbed his empty beer bottle, stood from the rocker and bent to kiss her. "But we're still having sex at your parents' house, whether they like it or not."

She pressed a hand to her cheek as he walked inside, waiting until he'd gone to react. Despite her worries about Friday—when reality met fantasy—Zach's comment made her laugh.

"How perfect that you both made it here for Fourth of July weekend!" Paula Brand grinned as she piled raw seasoned steaks and chicken breasts onto a platter.

Penelope's father, Louis, came in from the back and accepted the platter, slicing Zach in two with a curt nod.

Zach was accustomed to suspicious reactions from fathers of the women he'd dated—he'd met a few.

Mothers loved him but the dads were harder to win over. Zach took a healthy slug from his beer bottle. He just had to come up with the how.

He'd played down the "Dallas billionaire" bit, sliding into his clothing from his Chicago days. A comfortable and approachable pair of jeans paired with a gray T-shirt.

Penelope opted for a billowy summer dress, cut to disguise the roundness of her belly starting to make itself known. She was leaning against the counter, a carbon copy of her mother, with an hourglass figure and blond hair. Paula's blond was a paler shade, her stature shorter, but she was as womanly and beautiful as her daughter.

A vision of Pen at that age, standing over a sink while Zach flipped through the mail hit him square in the solar plexus. His next breath was a struggle, but he managed.

"Zach, honey?"

He blinked out of his fortune-seeing stupor to find Paula's brows lifted in question.

"Another beer?"

"Oh. Sure. Yeah. Thanks."

Pen raised an eyebrow in his direction but moved to the fridge on his behalf. When she handed over the bottle, she smiled up at him, her eyes sparkling and skin glowing.

It seemed no matter how he tried to cordon off this situation as one he could control, she continually kicked down barriers and knocked him off center.

The real kicker? He didn't mind it a bit.

"Pen tells me you were a contractor when you lived

here," Paula said as Zach took a swig of his fresh beer. "What do you think of this place?"

Paula and Louis bought and sold real estate for a living, so their current digs was a three-bed, two-bath fixer-upper north of Chicago.

"Good bones," he said, happy to turn his attention to the surrounding rooms. They'd obviously moved in here while they did the work. The house was clean, but there were various projects started in the kitchen, one of the bedrooms, and the half-bath downstairs had been gutted.

"We bought it for a steal." Paula washed the cutting board and her hands. "Foreclosure. We're hoping to double our profit. Louis insists on rebuilding the back deck, but I wanted to tear it down."

"The deck is a good feature." Zach walked to the back door. Louis manned the grill, his stout, muscular body stiff. The deck was worn and splintered, and a pile of fresh wood was lying under a tarp in the back-yard.

Maybe after they told Pen's parents about the baby, and Louis *didn't* murder him and bury his body in the backyard, Zach and Pen's father would have a topic in common.

Zach knew how to build a deck.

Pen didn't miss the wind in the windy city, that was for sure. She'd wrestled her hair into a ponytail and was forced to hold her paper plate down with one hand while she ate her chicken sandwich to keep it from blowing away.

Her parents' temporary deck, strewn with Crafts-man tools, made her feel right at home. She remembered many occasions where she'd sidestepped piles of wood or stacks of tile in whatever house they were currently working on. After she moved out, they'd started moving into the homes they were flipping. She was glad they'd waited because as much as the nomadic lifestyle appealed to her hardworking family, Pen liked to be in one place. It was what had made leaving Chicago so difficult.

Her mother peppered Zach with questions about his family and his job, which he handled with ease as he sawed into his second steak. Pen's father did a good job of shoving food in his mouth whenever her mom tried to include him in the conversation, so that all he had to do was nod or shake his head in response.

Pen pushed her sandwich aside, focusing on the potato salad on her plate. She waited for a lull in the conversation and when it came she reached under the picnic table and grabbed Zach's knee. He jerked his attention toward her, gave her a subtle nod and put down his cutlery.

"Mr. and Mrs. Brand," he started, and Pen's stomach flopped. She hoped her dinner stayed down.

Paula looked up, eyebrows aloft and Louis did his impersonation of Sam the Eagle from *The Muppets*. Seriously. If his eyebrows were any lower they'd be his mustache.

"Pen and I have an ulterior motive for visiting this weekend, other than showing off the engagement ring."

Miraculously, her father managed to lower his eyebrows farther.

"We're excited to tell you that—" Zach put an arm around Pen and hugged her close, looking down into her eyes when he made the announcement "—we're expecting a baby in December." He faced her parents first, then Pen followed suit, in time to witness their twin expressions of shock.

"I beg your pardon?" That was her mom, who, knife and fork in hand over her plate, sat statue-still while the wind whipped her hair.

"We're pregnant, Mom. You and Dad are going to be grandparents."

"Oh, my. I'm…" Her mouth froze open until finally, *finally*, that gape turned into a wide smile. "I'm so happy!" She was off her chair so fast to wrap her arms around Pen's neck that Louis had to slap his hand down on her plate to keep it from blowing off the table.

Paula returned to her seat, chattering about due dates and how she'd have to apply for a credit card that offered frequent flier miles so she could visit Dallas on a regular basis.

"No need, Mrs. Brand," Zach said smoothly. "We'll fly you down."

At the kind offer, Louis stood with his plate and climbed over the picnic bench's seat. He grunted once, then stormed into the house, letting the screen door bang behind him.

That went about like Pen had expected.

Chapter 13

"They're okay." Paula was peeking out of the kitchen window overlooking the deck.

"You mean Dad isn't strangling Zach or freezing him out completely?"

"Nope." Paula returned to the living room with two mugs of tea. "They're measuring."

"Measuring…do I want to ask what?"

"The deck, sweetheart." Paula handed over a mug.

"Oh, that."

Her mother sat on the dilapidated couch next to her, placing a comforting hand on Pen's knee. "This seems very sudden."

"Three months is one quarter of the year. It's not that sudden." Pen held her tea close to her lips. She hadn't meant to sound so defensive.

"Three months is how long you've been pregnant. When did you meet him?"

"I told you. When I lived here. That's been years ago." Pen lifted her thumbnail and nibbled. Her mother's serious expression remained. "Yes. Okay, it was sudden."

"But you're in love."

Thank goodness her mother didn't put a question mark at the end of that sentence. Pen didn't like to lie. She smiled instead. No, she and Zach weren't in love. What they had wasn't ever supposed to be about love. She couldn't deny she felt close to him—and that she liked him a whole lot.

When she thought of her baby, a worrisome thought niggled its way forward. Would her son or daughter grow up thinking love was a fairy tale?

No, she decided in an instant.

Pen would show her child love, and Zach would, too. Romantic love was avoidable. She thought back through her past boyfriends and wasn't sure she'd ever been in love herself. There'd always been an obstacle, an excuse she'd found to keep from getting in too deep.

Maybe because she'd arranged many false marriages and engagements for publicity and had become the ultimate skeptic. Or maybe the idea of giving in and being someone's all meant she'd be at risk to lose it all.

With a child on the way, she couldn't afford to be selfish.

A pair of low male laughs carried on the Chicago wind and into the living room and Penelope and Paula exchanged glances.

"Are they…?" Pen started.

Paula blinked, then smiled. "I think they are."

Zach and Pen's baby would know love—so much of it, he or she would never want for more.

But as she made that empty assurance to herself Pen wondered if she could settle for the same.

Louis not only liked to talk about houses and building, he was also a Dallas Cowboys fan.

Go fucking figure.

Zach ended up at the picnic table drinking beers and yapping with Pen's father until well after midnight.

"I should go up," Louis said. He cast a glance at an upstairs window. "Paula waits for me."

How…nice. Zach's parents got along fine, but he didn't remember his mother ever waiting on his dad, or his dad cutting anything short to go to her.

Louis stood and Zach stood with him. "Thanks for letting us stay."

"Paula insisted on always having a guest room for Pen since she moved to Dallas. We lost her to Texas a year before we're losing her to you." Louis's words held no venom, and actually sounded kind of sad. "You'll see when that baby is born. Just how much you'll do for it. Just how protective you'll become."

Zach could imagine. He'd already been that way with Penelope. He met Louis's eyes and confessed just that.

"I'm like that about your daughter. She'll never want for anything. Our child wasn't the reason we became engaged." His ex-wife was, but Zach sure as hell wasn't sharing that. "But the baby definitely gave us a good reason to stay that way."

Louis nodded slowly, obviously trying to accept the fact that his baby girl had gotten engaged and impregnated by some billionaire cowboy. Damn if Zach could understand Pen's father's position when he imagined having a daughter of his own.

With a slap to Zach's shoulder, Louis echoed his fear. "God help you if you have a girl."

Zach shut the door to the guest bedroom after brushing his teeth, stepping lightly across the real wood floors that were scarred and in need of a good wax. Paula had mentioned as much when she'd shown them to their room before looking to Zach to check if he'd be appalled by staying in such squalor. Her words, said on a tight laugh.

He'd assured her he could sleep anywhere, and though he'd kept it to himself, he'd also considered that he *would* sleep anywhere as long as Penelope was by his side.

He climbed into the double bed, a tight fit, the mattress sagging in the center. Pen let out a soft hum and wiggled under the blankets. Wrapping his arm around her middle, he tugged her close and buried his nose in her hair.

When he'd met her years ago in Chicago at a party, he'd been in full-on playboy mode. He'd set his Dallas drawl to full-tilt and laid on the charm, promising not to get into any trouble lest Pen's PR firm would have to step in and straighten him out. He hadn't seen her after that, so running into her at a swanky club in Texas had taken him by surprise.

He wasn't a man who believed in fate, kismet or meant-to-be, but as he allowed his fingers to drape over his fiancée's abdomen, he wondered if he wasn't seeing this for what it was.

A second chance.

But as the thought hit him, so did the palpable fear of screwing it up. Of being in a position to lose not only the woman beside him but also access to their child.

Zach hadn't thought about fatherhood. Hadn't thought about it even when he'd asked Lonna to marry him. But the moment Pen announced her pregnancy an overwhelming feeling of right swept over him.

It wasn't just the baby. It wasn't just that he was in his thirties and it was past time for him to consider starting a family. It wasn't that he'd crafted a fake engagement to distract from the real issue at hand.

The game-changer was Penelope Brand.

She murmured in her sleep—or her half sleep, as it were—and he kissed her shoulder. He'd promised to claim her in this very bed, parents' house or no, believing their sexual chemistry would rival the need for sleep and trump the need to be quiet with her parents down the hall.

Now, though...

She rolled in his direction, her eyes opening briefly then shutting again. The moonlight streamed through the window, highlighting her fair hair and kissing her curved cheekbone.

He'd claim her in a different way tonight.

He scooted in the springy bed to give her room. Her body was going through the rigorous toils of crafting a baby—their baby—and she needed all the sleep she could get.

He couldn't give her everything, but that, he could.

The flight home from Chicago was quick, and soon enough Zach and Pen were changing from their comfy flight clothes into slightly more formalwear for visiting the Ferguson house.

One set of parents down, one to go.

She'd let Zach choose the nature of the venue, which he'd scheduled for cocktail hour. She'd argued about building their visit around alcohol since she wouldn't be having any but he'd assured her she didn't have to worry.

At a little after seven Saturday evening, Pen settled onto the settee across from the chaise longue in the sitting room at the Ferguson mansion.

Elle was perched formally on the edge of a high-backed chair, Rider settled into the one next to it. A female member of the house staff walked in with a tray holding four martinis with speared olives in each elegant glass.

Zach accepted his glass, but held up a hand when the younger woman bent to give Penelope her drink. "My fiancée is expecting, so she'll need something nonalcoholic. Club soda with a lime, okay?" He pegged Pen with a playful look while she struggled not to swallow her tongue.

Evidently, breaking the news to his parents wasn't going to be a slow build.

Rider accepted his drink, Elle hers, and Pen offered a shaky smile in response. Elle's right eyebrow was curved so high on her forehead, it'd been lost in her hair.

No one said a word until Pen had a club soda in hand. Elle went first.

"And here we thought you'd come to tell us that your engagement was a sham to distract from your ex-wife."

"Eleanor, for the love of—" Rider let out an exasperated huff and swallowed a mouthful of his martini.

"You're only allowed one of those, don't forget. Savor it."

Pen stiffened, but the comforting weight of Zach's arm was around her back in an instant.

"We're due in December. We wanted to tell you in person before you found out from someone else."

Elle pursed her already pursed lips, her cool green stare assessing and, from Pen's vantage point, not all that approving.

"I think it's great," Rider said with a huge smile. Pen latched on to the man's sentiment like a lifeline. "We already wrote you a check." He reached into the pocket of his slacks and came out with a folded paper. "It's for the wedding, but now I suppose you can include it with preparing for our first grandchild."

He let out a hearty laugh and embraced Elle's hand. "Better than croaking of a heart attack before I get to meet my grandkids, eh, Elle?"

"I suppose that's true." She narrowed her eyes again and Pen shifted in her seat. "What interested you most in my son, Ms. Brand? His money or his DNA?"

Next to her, Zach went on alert, but Pen stayed his retort by touching his arm.

"I can understand how this information comes as a shock to you, but there's no need to be rude, Mrs. Ferguson. I'm neither a gold digger nor a woman who expected to get pregnant. Trust me when I tell you that you don't want to know the part of your son that most interests me. I simply saw someone I liked." She paused to take in Zach, whose mouth flinched like he might be fighting a proud smile. "And had to have him."

She snapped her attention back to Elle, who'd dropped her jaw. Likely no one dared speak to the Oil Queen of Dallas the way Pen had, but the older woman had started it.

"Mom."

Elle turned her stunned reaction to Zach.

"We're not asking your permission, or for your approval. But I expect you to be much more gracious when the baby is here. He or she will be the first-born grandchild in the family."

Elle drank down her martini in hearty gulps, then retrieved the spare martini left behind when Pen refused it and gulped that one, too.

Rider, his good humor intact, let out a crack of laughter. "Guess she'll be having my second one, then."

Chapter 14

"Pen, hang on."

The moment they'd exited Zach's parents' house, Pen marched down the driveway, fists at her sides.

"Wait." Zach caught her easily, snagging her biceps with a gentle hand and spinning her to face him. He was grinning and she glared at the dimple rather than admire it. Nothing about this evening had been funny.

"They hate me."

"No, they don't."

"Your mother hates me."

"No, she doesn't. She's just…in shock. Not everyone is going to take this news as well as we did."

"I didn't take it well. I avoided you for three days and drafted nine PR plans before I decided I couldn't make one until I told the father of my child I was having his baby!"

Zach's emerald eyes darkened when he tugged her closer, his grip tight but tender. She'd been battling fatigue, nausea and dizziness for weeks, but now it seemed the worst was behind her. The sexual tension that existed between them returned.

"You handling Eleanor Ferguson was quite possibly the sexiest moment I've ever witnessed."

Some of the fire went out of her. "Ever?"

His grin widened. "No. Not ever. Why don't I take you home and we can try for a new sexiest moment ever?"

"It's been a while."

"I know."

"You haven't complained." He'd been damn near angelic.

"I know."

She took a few steps closer in heels he hadn't bitched about tonight. Her shoes were a battle he'd allowed her to win. She fingered his collar and slipped her other hand down his buttoned shirt and over his black slacks.

A low grunt came from his throat when she pressed her lips to his, continuing her intimate massage down below. A few firm strokes and soon that part of him was much bigger than before.

He deepened their kiss, hands coming around to cup her ass. Every firm inch of him was flush against her and her hormones perked up.

"Zach." The breathy lilt of her voice was one she'd forgotten she'd possessed. "How about we take the car out in the yard and see if I can't break the sexiest moment record here."

"In the car?" His voice took on a husky quality and she laughed.

"Don't tell me you've never had a girl go down on you in a car."

"Not a girl as classy as you are," he all but growled.

"Good." She put a teasing kiss on the center of his mouth. "I love being first."

He wasn't wearing a tie, so she settled for dragging him to his car by the shirtsleeve. Zach followed, wide steps allowing for the part of him currently cheering the most for Pen's bold offer.

She liked that she had the power to affect him. It made her feel as if she could do anything. It made her feel like the woman she'd been before Cliff strangled her business into submission.

Zach put the car in gear and drove them behind the house and to the back of the grounds where trimmed trees and perfectly clipped grass met elegantly arranged flowers and shrubberies that were works of art.

"Your mom's going to freak about the landscaping when she sees the tire treads."

"First." Zach turned off the car and rolled the windows down. "That's the last time you mention my mom tonight. Second. I can't think of a second because my brains have relocated to my crotch."

"Hmm." Pen stifled her laughter to take advantage of the very sexy scene this created. Bucket leather seats, windows down, a warm Texas breeze heating the interior of the car and covering her neck in a light sheet of sweat where her hair fell. "I'm going to have to get a closer look to confirm."

Nothing felt better than turning him on. He wore lust so baldly—the flare of his nostrils, the widening of his pupils.

She undid his belt and released the clasp on his

slacks. He was hard and ready, and when she slipped the waistband of his boxers past his erection, she licked her lips.

"You're doing that on purpose."

"Well. Yes." She rolled her eyes and he crushed another kiss onto her lips before she pulled away and lowered her head. She took him on her tongue, guiding his length deep into her mouth. His legs went rigid, knees locking as she continued working him over. His utterances were a mixture of swear words, reverent callouts to the Almighty, and incoherent groans. Just when she was starting to enjoy herself, he tugged her up and pressed another kiss onto her lips.

"Don't you dare move."

He jerked his pants over his hips and came around to her side of the car, pulling the door open and offering his hand like a prince helping her from a carriage. Except his pants were sagging open, his erection outlined by the tails of his untucked, wrinkled white shirt.

"No laughing," he warned.

She didn't laugh, and when the heels of her shoes sank into the soft earth, she kicked them off. Zach maneuvered them to a particularly soft patch of grass surrounded by bushes.

He hoisted her dress over her head, tossed her bra aside and gently lowered her to the ground. He kissed her nipples, leaving them to pucker in the breeze while he unbuttoned his shirt and whipped it off his shoulders. Pants around his thighs, he didn't bother taking them off, and she couldn't think of a single reason he should.

She peeled her thong down her legs, ready for him and grateful to avoid another delay.

He slipped inside her, dropping his forehead to hers and letting out what might be a shudder. She tilted her hips and closed her eyes, head tossed back to appreciate the way she felt whenever he was inside her.

Full.

No.

Whole.

Her eyes flew open to meet his and he started moving again. Slowly, fluidly. Pumping in and out at a rhythm he set and she easily matched. Never had sex felt this intimate before Zach—before now. She reminded herself that her rounding belly and raging hormones were responsible for a plethora of emotions she hadn't experienced before.

Until he said, "You've never been more beautiful than you are now."

She pressed her fingertips to his mouth and he gave them a playful nip.

"You're saying that," she breathed as she braced for another sensual slide, "because you have to."

"I'm saying that—" another harsh breath from him blew her hair from her forehead "—because it's the truth."

She pushed on his chest. "On your back, cowboy."

His pause was momentary, but a second later he cupped her head and hip and, keeping them joined, shifted so that he was on his back instead.

"Impressive move with your pants around your knees." She smiled down at him.

"Thank ya, ma'am."

She rolled her eyes as he tipped a pretend cowboy hat, but his good humor erased when she pushed his chest to leverage herself up, and sank down on him again.

A hiss of air came from between his teeth, but he didn't close his eyes. No, he kept them right on her as she moved. His hands covered her breasts, his hips rising to meet hers.

And when her orgasm all but shattered her, Zach caught her against him, holding her hair from her face as he kissed her. He tilted his hips while she held on to the moving earth and then he came inside her.

The only sounds in the garden were crickets humming, the distant bark of a dog and Zach's father's shout on the air.

"Seriously?" The Zen of Penelope's orgasm washed away as her eyes went wide, her hands covering her breasts.

He let out a laugh. She speared him with a murderous glare before looking over her shoulder. He'd driven them deep into the gardens at the side of the house, so all his old man had seen—or could currently see—was the black blob of Zach's car.

And he and Pen were safely hidden on one side of it.

He sat up, keeping their connection as a tremor ran down his spine. Damn, he could have used a few more minutes to Zen out with her. Cradling her face, he gave her a swift kiss. Unfortunately, timing was of the essence before Rider called the cops.

"Get dressed," Zach told Pen. "I'll handle this."

Not since he was sixteen had he been caught with his pants around his ankles, and he wasn't starting today. He yanked them up, buckling his belt and pushing a hand through his hair.

He snatched his shirt off the ground and turned to find Pen, grass in her hair, roll her tiny scrap of a pair of panties up those long, golden legs.

He lifted her dress off the ground and handed it to her, noticing the grass stain a microsecond before she did. She merely shook her head and pulled it on, tugging it down and wadding the bra in her hand while Zach stepped into his shoes.

He spared one last glance the second his dad turned on the floodlight, enough to see her grow a little more irked, and in the process, a whole lot more beautiful.

Who knew that could happen?

"Zach?" his dad bellowed.

"It's me!" he called back. "Don't shoot!" He was only half kidding. From what he could see, Rider wasn't carrying a shotgun, but one could never be too careful.

So much for his parents never using this part of the house. He'd been sure this side was left to the staff or only opened up for parties.

His father strolled into the yard. Zach approached while he finished buttoning his white collared shirt.

"What in Sam hell are you doing?" Rider asked, his voice filled with mirth. "Trying to give me another heart attack? Because if your mother knew you were out here having sex in the petunias, she'd make sure I had one."

Rider turned to look over his shoulder but only briefly. They both knew Eleanor was in her bath by now with the TV on and a magazine in hand.

"I don't think those were petunias," Zach said in response.

"You two have your own place and you're carrying

on like teenagers." His father sent a look over to the car where Pen sat in the front seat, elbow on the window, one hand hiding her face. "She knows I know that's her, right?"

"Yeah. She does." His own gaze lingered there a moment before he bid his dad adieu. "I'll pay to repair the lawn."

"You know I don't give a shit about that." Rider chuckled. "Get your girl home. Continue what you started indoors."

Zach's back straightened on his walk to the car, his swagger taking over. He was proud that this woman was with him. And that she'd offered to do dastardly things outside with him. Pen embodied the motto "work hard, play hard." He liked that a hell of a lot.

Zach reached the car and Rider called out, "'Night, Penny!" His loud boom of a guffaw heard as clear as day.

When Zach sank into his leather seat, Pen watched him for a solid thirty seconds. Fine by him. It gave him a moment to rebutton his shirt since he'd done it wrong on the walk over to his dad. He adjusted his seat belt and started the car, aware of her watching him the entire time.

"What?"

"Now your mom definitely hates me."

"She has no idea. Dad won't tell her." He reversed the car and drove through the grass.

Pen went stone silent.

Zach grasped her chin and turned her to face him, his car idling at the gate of his parents' gargantuan home. "I would never let her hate you. Give her time."

Pen's blue eyes softened with worry.

"I mean it. Give her a little time and she'll love you as much as my dad does."

He pulled out of the driveway and onto the street, the words he'd said wending around his brain. He'd meant them. Everyone loved Penelope—her clients, his siblings, his dad.

Do you? came the unplanned thought.

But that kind of love was different—he'd learned long ago that loving with his full heart wasn't rewarded. He wouldn't make that mistake again.

He drove home, arm leaning on his open window and the summer air blowing his hair.

Some thoughts were best left unexplored.

Chapter 15

"Have your assistant return everything but this." Pen held up a tiny pair of shoes. "I can't part with these even though they're hysterically overpriced. The rest of it I can shop for online." She stood over the boutique baby clothes spread on Zach's king-size bed, her hands on her hips. There was a line in the center of her brows communicating her worry.

"Why?" He slid out of his suit jacket and hung it in his closet.

"Because a growing baby doesn't need extravagant—" she gestured to the stacks of gender-neutral clothing "—everything."

She'd set up the visit to the baby boutique for Saturday afternoon, and then they did something he'd never pictured himself doing. They shopped for their future son or daughter.

He'd purchased the clothing, shoes and toys that he and Pen carried out in the boutique's signature shiny bags, but he didn't stop there. He'd also snapped several pictures of furniture with his iPhone and sent them to his interior designer. Like right now, Pen had loved it but protested the inflated price tag.

"No one *needs* extravagant everything," Zach commented, unbuttoning his shirt. Pen paused, a yellow stuffed elephant rattle in her hand, and watched. He liked the way she looked at him—like he was her next meal. "Come take your clothes off."

"There's an invitation," she said with a laugh.

She tossed the elephant aside and came to him in the closet. Her eyes were sleepy despite it being hours before bedtime. After a shopping excursion and a late lunch, she looked beat. Not that it hindered her beauty at all.

Holding herself steady on the closet's interior wall, she slipped off one high-heeled shoe and then the other.

"Ah, so much better."

He'd lectured her nonstop about the damn shoes. It hadn't done any good.

"Just so we're clear," he said, shrugging off his shirt and tossing it into a hamper, "our child is entitled to have as many extravagant things as we see fit."

Her eyes roamed over his bare chest and he sucked in a breath to expand it farther. She smiled and gave him a playful shove.

"That's what I'd like to avoid. An *entitled* child." She turned and lifted her hair and he pulled down the delicate zipper holding her dress closed. "I want our son or daughter to be loved and know that 'stuff' doesn't matter."

Zach ran his fingers down her exposed back, pausing at her bra strap. "This, too?"

She eyed him over her shoulder, a spark of want in her eyes mingling with the fatigue. As tempting as it was to seduce her, he'd digress.

"I'm going to work at home for a bit. Why not grab a nap?"

She slipped out of her dress, revealing smooth skin and a softly rounding belly. His chest flooded with possessiveness.

She covered her stomach and her brows bent.

He moved her hand and gave her a smile. "I like watching the changes in your body."

She cocked her head as if to challenge him. "You mean my growing girth?"

"You're making a human being. That takes up some real estate." It was a miracle in every sense of the word. "It's okay to take a break."

"I'll relax, but I want to keep my eye on the internet for our inevitable online debut."

The photographer had shown up like Pen arranged, snapping pictures of them inside the store through the windows as well as from across the street when they left the baby boutique.

"Right. The blogger."

"Not just any blogger." She hung her white dress and pulled on a pair of stretchy pale-pink pants.

He wanted to dispute the long white shirt covering her, until he realized he could see the shape of her nipples and the swell of her heavy breasts outlined by the thin fabric.

"The Dallas Duchess," Pen stated with a gesture that sent her breasts jiggling.

He pulled on a T-shirt and jeans and slipped into a pair of tennis shoes. "And she's important, I gather."

"Mmm-hmm. She keeps an eye on the Dallas movers and shakers. She'll have our photo up by this afternoon or tomorrow morning. I made sure of it."

That rogue twinkle in Pen's eye lit whenever she talked about her work. Whether she was digging a pair of canoodling actors out of a steaming pile of drama or arranging Zach's internet debut. He couldn't resist capturing some of that fire for himself. Not while she stood this close to him.

He wrapped an arm around her back and lowered his lips to hers, pressing her breasts to his chest as he made out with her long and slow. She tracked her fingers along his abs, and his belly clenched. He let out a low growl as she dropped from her toes and smiled up at him. He wanted her. Badly.

"You don't have to work right away, do you?" she asked with the quirk of one eyebrow.

"Hell, no," he answered, and then hoisted her in his arms and carried her the short distance to the bed.

She and Zach had played their roles while shopping earlier today. They'd kissed and hugged and smiled. She'd coached him this morning en route to the store, and he'd grumbled about the preparation, arguing that he wasn't that good of an actor.

Yet this afternoon, there he was, heat in his eyes and firmness in his kiss. But that wasn't all acting, now, was it? He'd been looking at her with heated eyes and owning her with his kisses since they'd re-met. And their going to bed together when they returned home was definitely par for course.

Mercy. She wondered how much of the sex she could blame on the hormones.

She finished packing the baby clothes and toys into the shopping bags for returning later. She was serious about not wanting an entitled child.

What she hadn't told him was that she'd also started thinking about the massive income gap between hers and Zach's annual earnings. Obviously, that'd always been a factor, but today especially, as she thought about providing for her son or daughter, she realized that half the child's time would be spent at Zach's house where everything would be provided in abundance. The other half? Spent with her where she'd earn a decent living, yes, and her child would never do without the necessities, but a two hundred dollar jumper wouldn't be hanging in the closet.

She shoved thoughts of the future aside and focused on the task in front of her. An email from the Dallas Duchess herself. The duchess confirmed that the blog would go live tomorrow.

So that was that.

Penelope and Zach would be making their announcement publicly soon after, confirming that yes, they were expecting. Being that Zach was both CEO of Ferguson Oil and the mayor's brother, the story was news to anyone looking for gossip. The Fergusons weren't royal family status, but neither were they ignored. Their staggering good looks paired with their billionaire incomes made the two brothers and sister popular in this city.

"Way to pick a baby daddy," Pen joked aloud. But she didn't feel an ounce of regret for going to bed with

Zach—or moving in with him. Like Cinderella, her fairy tale would soon come to an end.

She glanced around the living room—masculine browns and earth tones like his apartment with a touch of hominess in shades of blue—and admitted she liked nesting here, even if it wasn't permanent. There would be time to ready her apartment—to *acquire* an apartment. In the meantime, she would be treated like a queen.

She scraped her bottom lip with her teeth as she turned over the shallow thoughts. Pen wasn't accustomed to being dependent on anyone but herself. Her mother had raised her to be her own godmother, not the princess flailing about wearing only one glass slipper.

Once upon a time Pen had been involved with a client who had offered to "take care of everything" and look how that'd ended up. She'd vowed never to let her guard down again—yet here she was, breaking her rules for Zach.

Had she traded her pluck for comfort? Was she shallow? Or, was Zach different? Was what they had something she'd never truly experienced—the beginning of a trusting relationship that might lead to that elusive beast: love?

Surely not.

Pen had looked forward to the day she'd moved away from home. She'd excelled at running her own life. So well, in fact, she'd begun advising others how to run theirs and charging them for it.

Right now she was simply being practical. Her affinity for Zach—the doting as well as the sex—was temporary. Soon, she'd have a child to raise. A baby to nurse. And still have her business to run. She wouldn't have time for frivolous relationships any more than she'd have time for a mani-pedi on a Sunday afternoon.

They were sacrifices she was willing to make. And with Zach in the picture, it wasn't as if she'd be doing it alone. She'd have help. Albeit not living under this same roof, because that was impractical. But they'd have shared custody…

The sentence trailed to a muted end and her head spun.

Zach *would* share custody, wouldn't he? He wouldn't try and take her child from her? Of course he wouldn't. Unless…he dated someone else in the future. Maybe things would get serious and the woman would want to play a bigger role in their child's life.

Pen's eyebrows snapped together. She didn't want their child raised by another woman. And what if that other woman ended up like Yvonne, with no scruples and a money-grubbing attitude? Zach hadn't only dated Yvonne, he'd *married* her.

"Whoa. You okay?" Zach stepped into the living room, casual attire doing nothing to dash the air of power surrounding him. Power and money. "You look…not okay."

She could imagine. If her face revealed any of her thoughts about a future custody battle, she must resemble a gladiator readying for a fight. Pen launched into a conversation without any preempting whatsoever.

"I wanted to talk to you about custody of our baby." The words were as thick as wet sand, but she got them out.

He frowned as he came deeper into the living room and sat next to her on the couch. She set aside her phone.

"We'll share it. Obviously," she stated.

"When the time comes." His eyelids narrowed. "Your home is here, Pen. I'm in no hurry to have you gone."

"But eventually, I'll leave."

"Maybe. Maybe not."

"Zach." He'd been saying that a lot and she'd gone along, but what happened when her carriage turned into a pumpkin? "Eventually. I'll leave. I hope you won't fight me for full custody of our child."

"I'm not going to fight you for anything involving our child." He tipped his head toward the bags of clothing she'd set by the front door. "Except you keeping the purchases we made at the boutique."

"It's too much."

"Penelope." He placed his hand on her neck, his thumb sliding along her jaw as he met her eyes with his potent green stare. "I'm having a child, too. Buying for our baby, taking care of you, are the only ways I know how to participate. Let me."

His eyebrows lifted into an earnest expression and she closed her eyes. Maybe she was too emotional about…well, everything. Shaking her head, she said, "I'm sorry. I'm worrying about everything."

"Worry about one thing. What you want for dinner. And then tell me and I'll either make it or have it delivered." He stood from the couch, bending and placing a kiss on her forehead. She watched him walk out of the room, his sure, strong steps and presence making every hectic thought in her tired brain calmer.

She might not be in love with the father of her baby, but she could admit that the biggest part she'd miss about the princess treatment was going to be Zach himself.

Chapter 16

Zach had adapted to his role as CEO of Ferguson Oil easily, sliding into the slot left for him by his father like he was meant to be there all along. Kind of made him wonder if he'd been avoiding his destiny when he left for Chicago.

Which kind of made him wonder if no matter what direction he ran, he would've still ended up right back here in this very position: father-to-be of a baby boy or girl.

The night he took Penelope home from the jazz club, he'd never considered that they might someday share a child. Shortsighted? A bit. Sex equaled babies for lots of couples. But he'd been in the habit of chasing his physical desires rather than worrying about outcomes.

He rubbed eyes that were crossing to center. When he reopened them, the spreadsheet on his computer screen blurred. He redirected his gaze to the wall clock to see it was past five; another day had gotten away from him.

His assistant patched through a call. "Mr. Ferguson, it's the mayor on line three."

"It's Zach, and my brother's name is Chase," he reminded Sam, who insisted on the formality.

"Yes, sir," Sam replied. "Will you be taking the mayor's call?"

Zach shook his head at the futility and answered the line.

"Chase," he said into the phone. "What's up?"

"Were you planning on telling me about my niece or nephew?" came his brother's terse question.

Zach's eyes sank closed as he pressed his fingers into his eyelids. "Shit, Chase. I meant to tell you."

What an oversight.

"You mean before my press conference where a reporter asked if *I* was expecting a baby because you and Penelope were spotted baby shopping over the weekend? Yeah. You should've told me."

There was a twist neither Zach nor Pen had seen coming.

"The press assumed it was you who was having a baby?"

"Me and the woman on my arm at the charity event at our parents' house. She's a financial adviser and I offered to show her around." Zach could tell by his brother's grumbling that he was serious about the woman being an acquaintance. The mayor wasn't into spur of the moment or temporary relationships. For Chase, every woman on his arm had a purpose, a reason for being there.

"That photo of us was supposed to pad our public announcement of the pregnancy, not start a rumor mill about you."

He grunted at the irony. Chase was the star of the Ferguson show no matter what happened to any of them.

"Stefanie already knew." Chase's tone was clipped.

"Not on purpose. I let it slip and swore her to secrecy."

"Mom and Dad. They know. *She* had to tell me." Before Zach could make an excuse about how it'd been a busy week, his brother added, "What the hell are you doing?"

Zach straightened his back, on alert. "What's that supposed to mean?"

"Your engagement with Penelope Brand is fake. Or *was* anyway. Has that changed?" His brother believed that relationships had beginnings and endings that were mapped out ahead of time. But Zach didn't have to think that way. He wasn't the one who'd put his balls in the public sling.

"Not that I have to explain anything to you," Zach told his brother, "but Pen was pregnant the night of your birthday party. We just didn't know it at the time."

Chase uttered a curse under his breath. "Are you planning on making it a real engagement to go along with your real future child?"

"What if I do?"

"Then I suggest you consider how long you want to keep this up."

Off his chair, Zach felt his blood pressure rise. "Come again?"

"You're not the only one involved, Zach. You'll have

a child soon and you can't marry Pen because it sounds *fun*. The stakes are sky-high."

"I know that." Zach's words gritted from between his clenched teeth. "I can handle my own life. You're just worried how my actions will affect your precious career."

"Wrong. I'm reminding you because I've seen the two of you together. You're behaving like a couple. A *real* one. Has that sunk in for you yet?"

He thought it had. Until Chase pointed out he'd noticed a difference. Zach dated casually, sure, but he felt like his brother was referring to a relationship in Zach's past—way in his past. One in particular that hadn't ended well.

"I'm handling it," Zach repeated rather than broach the topic of Lonna.

"Let's start over." Chase blew out a heavy breath. "What I should've said, rather than dispense a big brother lecture, was that I'm excited for you. For our family. The first baby is a big deal."

"You're jealous you didn't get there first." Zach allowed a sideways smile when his brother chuckled.

"Yeah, you win."

But Chase's words settled in the center of Zach's chest. A baby *was* a big deal. So was an engagement. And Penelope living in his house.

"I'm taking this seriously." Zach felt the urge to clarify. After a pause, Chase spoke.

"How is she?"

"Healthy. Gorgeous. Stubborn." *Impossible*, he mentally added. "Returned every bit of the baby clothes we purchased because they were too expensive."

"You call that stubborn? I call it practical."

"Stubborn," Zach reiterated.

"Almost as stubborn as you." Chase wasn't wrong. "Way to pick 'em, brother. How about you?"

"How about me what?" He closed the spreadsheet and powered down the computer.

"How are you?"

"I'm good. I'm fine."

Chase waited, not buying the blow-off.

Zach sat back down and rested his forehead on his hand. Then he confessed something to Chase he hadn't told anyone. "I'm trying not to screw everything up for my child."

"You'll figure it out. You're not a screw-up, Zach. You try everything once, and that's not a bad thing. I'm the careful planner, and knowing what I know of Penelope, I'm guessing she's a careful planner, too."

"The *carefulest*."

"You'll find your way. You don't know how to fail. You stay on the balls of your feet and roll with the punches better than anyone I've ever known."

The vote of confidence from the man he admired most, second to Dad, meant the world to Zach. His throat thick with emotion, he couldn't even manage a muttered "Thanks." Zach wasn't the get-choked-up kind, but *damn*.

"When do you find out if I'm having a niece or a nephew?"

He smiled at his brother's use of the monikers again—if he wasn't mistaken, Chase was looking forward to being an uncle.

"Next week." Zach swept his eyes to his desk calendar to confirm.

"Tell me *first* this time."

"We'll see. Stefanie has already mentioned some gender reveal something-or-another."

Chase's reaction was a mumbled curse followed by, "Of course she did."

Zach ended the call with his brother as a quick knock came from Sam who ushered in Mara, his bubbly and completely kick-ass CFO.

"Zach." Her eyes sparkled with interest. Not in him personally—he'd never before met someone so happily married—but like she knew something he didn't. "Here are the reports you asked for."

She handed them over and then stood smiling at him. He studied her with a frown for a moment, then decided to give it up. She knew. It was evident in every jittering line of her body.

"We can't officially announce it yet, so I appreciate your discretion."

Mara clapped her hands and let out a discreet "Yay!" To his shock, she rounded the desk and gave him a quick side hug.

"I'm so thrilled for you both! When Vic and I had our baby it was exciting and scary and amazing. You're going to do great. And Penelope is so gorgeous—you'll have the prettiest baby in the world! Second to mine, of course."

Okay, that made him smile.

Mara skipped away. As she pulled the door shut, she gave him a wink in the diminishing gap and said in a stage whisper, "I won't breathe a word to anyone."

"Thanks, Mara."

She shut the door behind her and he glanced at his desk calendar where he'd jotted Pen's ultrasound with the shorthand *ult* in case of wandering eyes.

Chase was right. Zach would slide seamlessly into the role of father as well as he'd slid into CEO at Ferguson Oil. And if he had a hiccup or two along the way, Pen would be there to bail him out—planner that she was.

Smile on his face, he relaxed in his chair.

They had this.

A blur of elegance from outside the wall of her glass office windows caught Penelope's eye. She blinked once, then twice to make sure what she was seeing wasn't a mirage.

Nope.

It was Zach's mother, all right.

Pen beckoned her in and rounded her desk. "Elle. This is a surprise."

Especially since she didn't know how Elle knew where she worked. Pen's mind went to their last interaction. Elle reacted poorly to the news of the pregnancy and then Pen and Zach had sex in the woman's flower beds.

Real classy, Pen.

Elle clutched a large camel-colored handbag and gestured to the white leather couch. "May I sit?"

"Yes, please. I was just wrapping up." Pen sat with her, pretty sure the fluttering in her stomach wasn't her baby but nerves instead. Maybe a bit of both.

"How are you feeling?"

"Lately, much better than before."

"I'm so glad for you! When I was pregnant with Stefanie, I remember the worst morning sickness and bloating." Elle waved a hand dismissively. "If I had that with Chase and Zach, I've blocked it because all I remember is how painful the birth was." Elle let out a soft laugh and then a look of chagrin colored her features. "I didn't mean to alarm you. What a thing to say."

"It's fine, really." Pen meant it. "Believe it or not, I've heard a thing or two about childbirth being painful."

A gap in the conversation settled in the room like a third party. Pen filtered through her brain for a topic to fill the dead air. Luckily, Elle filled it for her.

"I came by to apologize for my poor reaction when you came to tell us about your bundle of joy."

"Thank you. We sprung it on you, so it's understandable."

"No. It's not. Rider's mother wanted to throttle us when she found out I was pregnant with Chase before the wedding." Elle rolled her eyes, and it wasn't hard to imagine what she'd looked like as a much younger woman railing against her future in-laws. "I've made a few mistakes with my children when it comes to their relationships. Being a matriarch is a tough business."

Pen's eyebrows climbed her forehead.

"Oh, you think the men are in charge in our family?" Elle picked at an invisible piece of lint on her skirt and smoothed her hand over the material. "We let them think that. You're a strong woman. You're an amazing addition to this family."

Guiltily, Pen looked at her lap. She felt like she was lying by letting Elle believe Pen and Zach were really together, but there was no way to unravel the lie without causing damage to everyone.

"I'm about to overstep my boundaries," Elle said next.

Pen lifted her head to meet eyes with the older woman.

"Do you know about Lonna?"

The name didn't bring forth the barest whisper of familiarity. "I don't think so."

"I don't know that Zach knows *I* know how in-deep he was with her. But I'm his mother. I knew."

Pen was dancing in dangerous territory. Part of her wanted to ask Elle about the woman from Zach's past, and another part of her felt loyalty to her fake fiancé. In the end, her curiosity won.

"Who was she?"

"They dated when Zach was in his midtwenties. She was a few years older than him and there was always something I didn't like about her. Her strength wasn't so much strength as fierce independence. Independence she cherished over our son's heart.

"Zach would sooner die than admit to us that she broke his heart, but I could tell. He was different after her. After they split, he withdrew. Then he moved to Chicago and we swore we'd never see him again."

That was why he moved to Chicago? *Away* from a woman? Rather than chasing a dream? Did that make a difference?

Yes, Pen realized.

She'd run from Chicago because of a business endeavor—because she'd needed to reform her reputation. Not because she couldn't bear to be in the same state as an ex.

"My point of telling you this isn't to worry you, Penelope." Elle placed her hand gently over Pen's, making Pen wonder if the worry showed on her brow. "My point is to let you know that I'd started believing he'd never commit to another woman. Not seriously." Elle sneered, but still managed to look elegant doing it.

"We all know that Yvonne debacle was a blip of rash stupidity."

"Let's hope," Pen blurted.

"I know my son. I'm right. But here you are, and Penelope, believe me when I tell you that Zach has finally given his heart to someone. To you. He wouldn't get engaged again so soon unless he meant it."

Pen's smile was as brittle as burned paper. *Or unless he wanted to get out of hot water with his raving lunatic of an ex-wife.*

"You're going to be an amazing mother, Penelope, and you'll have a dedicated husband and father at your side. Trust me when I tell you that."

Pen blinked her eyes against forming tears and when her vision cleared, Elle was reaching into her handbag and bringing out a blue-and-white crocheted blanket.

"This was Zach's when he was a baby. His great-grandmother Edna made it for him." She handed over the soft pile of yarn, a few frayed ends tied into knots. "He'll kill me if I tell you this, but what the hell." Elle cupped her mouth with one hand and stage-whispered, "He slept with it until he was eleven."

Pen laughed and lost the battle with a few tears that streaked down her cheeks. She swiped at them quickly, and then held the blanket in both hands.

Her baby would someday be a grown man or woman and have a history—a history with two parents who pretended to be in love. A history that had to be history.

The more distance she put between this baby's birth and her living with and pretending with Zach, the better. She wasn't being fair to anyone. Not Zach's siblings or parents, or her own parents, or especially her child.

Lying was going to have a ripple effect on her baby's

life and she couldn't allow that. As kind as it was for Elle to stop by and apologize and declare her son's love for Pen, there was one fact that remained unchallenged.

Zach and Pen, while they liked each other just fine, weren't in love. They didn't share their plans for a long future, or discuss grandmothers or past heartbreaks.

They shared plans and a schedule. They shared a bed.

And those things did not a love story make.

Chapter 17

Pen blew out a breath, lying on a table in the doctor's office and not feeling the least little bit relaxed. Today she and Zach would learn if they were having a son or a daughter and the anticipation was almost too much to handle.

She hadn't told Zach that his mother had stopped by to chat. Reason being, she wasn't sure how to broach the topic. The Lonna Story was his story to tell, and frankly, that he hadn't told her was...well, *telling*. Pen and Zach were in deep together. They were engaged—kinda—expecting a baby and he'd pretty much decreed that she wasn't moving out.

Yet when it came to divulging his personal past, he was silent. Which could only mean one thing. Zach had been hurt and quite possibly wasn't over the mysterious Lonna.

"How are you doing, Ms. Brand?" The doctor stepped into the room. Dr. Cho was young and beautiful, her silken black hair tied back at the base of her neck. Her kind, almond-shaped eyes swept to Zach and she nodded in greeting.

Zach promised Pen that Dr. Cho was the best in Dallas. He'd insisted on the very best care and Pen hadn't argued. She might not relish the idea of piles of outrageous baby clothing, but she agreed that the best care for their child was the *only* care.

"I'm nervous," Pen admitted.

"Nothing to be nervous about." Dr. Cho squirted clear goo onto a flat plastic ultrasound paddle and warned it'd be cold. "How about you, Dad?"

Pen's eyes clashed with Zach's and he held her gaze while he said, "Doing just fine."

"Good."

Cold, definitely, but the shock of the chill faded as Pen searched the image on screen for her baby. And there it was. A whooshing sound of the heartbeat and what actually resembled a human being.

Incredible.

Tears pricked the corners of her eyes but accompanied a resilient smile. Zach breathed a "Wow" next to her, his gaze glued to the screen, his mouth ajar.

It was a miracle.

An unexpected, unrelenting miracle.

After a few minutes and measurements, Dr. Cho asked if they'd like to know the sex.

"Yes," Pen and Zach answered eagerly—both on the same page. This little gem had given them enough surprises.

Pen held her breath and wondered if Zach did the same. Then Dr. Cho told them the sex of their baby.

"It's incredible, isn't it?" Zach said on the ride home from the doctor's office. Hearing the heartbeat had been one thing, but seeing their child on the screen and knowing a little Ferguson would soon be entering their lives was unbelievable.

Pen was lying back against the headrest, the A/C cranked up so high her hair blew in the air coming from the vent. August in Texas was hell. But Zach didn't mind the heat or the fact that he had to lift his voice to talk over the vent forcing out cool air. He was on cloud nine.

In spite of today's announcement ruining a particular surprise.

He pulled into the garage of his new house and rounded the car to open Pen's door for her. She wore a long white dress and heels, but her shoes were lower heeled than her normal nine-to-five wear. His favorite part of the dress was the wispy material that slitted up both sides showing peeks of her smooth calves when she walked as well as the off-the-shoulder straps that showcased not only a gorgeous collarbone but also cleavage that was going for the World's Record for holding Zach's undivided attention.

Inside he gave her the bad news. "I had a surprise planned, and now it's not as good of a surprise unless you want to leave the house for a day or two so I can fix it."

She slanted her head and narrowed one eye, her smile playful. "What'd you do?"

He shook his head in chagrin, but found his smile wasn't going anywhere, either. "You're gonna laugh."

"Now I have to know."

Here went nothing. Time to own it.

He led her through the house and upstairs to the baby's room. His designer had come in and furnished the room with a crib and dresser and changing table—the same furniture that Pen had pointed out at Love & Tumble. The style was what he preferred: clean, simple, warm. No pastels or frilly anything. His designer had insisted on beige with white crown molding running along the center of the wall, which he at first protested. She'd argued it was "the perfect blank palette ready for a splash of color" for when they found out the sex. When he'd first showed Pen, she loved it. Zach turned the knob, gave Pen one last lift of his eyebrows and pushed the door wide.

He was right about the laughing.

His surprise? Decking their child's room floor to ceiling in Dallas Cowboys paraphernalia.

"You were awfully certain we were having a boy," Pen said with a giggle as she stepped into the room.

"I was." And then the ultrasound proved him wrong. He shook his head but he didn't have a single ounce of regret about the outcome.

A daughter with Pen's gorgeous blue eyes? He'd take it. He'd have to scare off testosterone-infused boys once she was a teen, but he'd worry about that later. This was Texas. He had a shotgun.

"Zach." Pen searched the room, her eyes landing on framed posters of the players, a mobile featuring footballs and cowboy hats, and on the shelf, a signed football in a case. He'd gone all out. The mother of his child faced him.

Fingers shoved in his front pockets, he explained with a shrug. "Maybe she's a Cowboys fan."

"Clearly you're one."

"Honey, I'm in Dallas. I'm a Cowboys fan." He took a look around for himself. He was pretty damn proud of the cool stuff he'd picked out. "We can tone it down a little."

"A little?" She lifted a blanket thrown over the crib that resembled a football field—green with the yardage marked in white. "Really?"

"I wanted to surprise you. You're surprised. Mission accomplished."

"Yeah. I'm surprised, all right." She rested her hand on the crib and palmed her belly, not yet as big as it would be. He felt a firm tug in his chest. "I'm grateful that it's a girl after your mother told me how big you two boys were."

"When did she tell you that?" She hadn't mentioned talking with his mother.

"Last week. She stopped by my office."

A pair of chairs flanked a side table with a lamp and, yes, a Cowboys lampshade, and Pen sat in one and beckoned for him to sit in the other one.

She opened the side table drawer as he sat, coming out with his crocheted baby blanket he hadn't seen in decades.

"She dropped this off for our daughter."

"It's blue." He took it, then gestured around the room. "Matches the theme."

"She apologized for her reaction. I know she wanted

to smooth things over. She wasn't proud of herself. I didn't hold it against her, though."

"No, you wouldn't," he said. "You take issues on. You don't push them off on others." And just so Pen didn't think he meant it any other way, he amended, "That's a compliment."

"I know it is." She inhaled and held her breath for a few seconds and that tug in his chest turned uncomfortable. What else did his mother say when she stopped by?

"Is there more?"

Pen released the breath she'd been holding. "Elle said… Well, she brought up a woman named Lonna. Then she told me she never thought you'd fall in love again."

His shoulders stiffened. He kneaded the super-soft blanket in his hands, avoiding looking at Pen. His mother knew about Lonna, of course, but what gave her the right to barge in on his fiancée and offer her opinion on his heart, for God's sake?

"I bring it up because your mom thinks we're in love."

That lifted his head. He watched her carefully. "She doesn't know anything about Lonna." The edge in his voice forced him from his seated position. He dropped the baby blanket on the chair and paced to the door.

"Did you love her? For real?"

Anger stopped him in his tracks. As if he was only capable of "unreal" relationships? His eyes went to the stairs leading to the front door, but he didn't run away from problems any longer. He ran toward them. He ran back to Texas, ran headfirst into a Vegas wedding to prove to himself he was "fine" and ran straight to Pen when she delivered news most men would've run *from*.

He faced Pen, leaned on the jamb and shoved his fingers back into his pockets. She lifted her hand to push a lock of hair from her face, and the diamond ring he'd slipped onto her finger glinted in the sunlight streaming in through the Cowboys-blue curtains.

Zach was a lot of things but he wasn't a liar. So, he told Pen the truth. "Yes."

She took the news well, simply nodding. But she wasn't done.

"Did you go to Chicago because she broke up with you?"

In part, but he saw no reason to explain himself. "Yes."

Pen took that news well, too, but had one final question for him. "Are you over her?"

That question required no hesitation. "Yes."

If he wasn't mistaken, that was a relieved breath Pen just blew out. "Your mother believes we're in love, Zach. She thinks this is our happily-ever-after and I couldn't correct her."

"You and my mother had quite the conversation."

"I didn't know she was going to go into all of that. And I honestly wouldn't ask you to clarify any of this if it wasn't for what lies before us."

That statement settled into the room like an elephant.

"Which is what?" She kept making decisions and telling him last. He didn't like it.

"When we announce the sex of the baby at our surprise shower, we should also announce that we won't be getting married. Hear me out." She held a hand in front of her as if to silence him, probably because he'd filled his chest full of air to protest how they didn't have to do anything. Before she said more, he managed to blow out one question in an infuriated tone.

"What surprise shower?"

"I'm guessing that's why your sister asked me to clear a spot on my calendar in two weeks for a 'cake-tasting appointment.'" Pen used air quotes. "It sounded very…suspicious. Plus, she asked that we tell no one the sex of the baby—not even her."

"The gender reveal," he mumbled. "She'd mentioned she wanted to host one and then never said another word." He'd hoped she would forget about it. He should've known better.

Zach swiped a hand over his forehead, frustrated. Why the hell was everyone arranging parties around him, talking about him like he was a backdrop? Like he was a store mannequin. He was the one who arranged his life. It was *his* life, dammit.

"Before you blow up, let me finish."

He gave her the most patient glare he could manage, aware of the heat warming his face.

"We thank everyone for the gifts. And we hold hands—I'll take this off first—" she waggled her ring finger "—and then we'll let everyone know that while we'll be living separate lives we are very much going to raise our daughter together. Everyone will be so overjoyed to learn that we're having a girl that I'm betting they won't even focus on the fact that we're announcing a breakup."

"We're not breaking up."

"Zach." She stood, her hand protectively over her middle. "We're not in love. You can't believe our sex-soaked relationship isn't going to fall apart. There's nothing holding us together except our attraction for each other. What about when that fades?"

"What if it doesn't?" He saw no reason to put a headstone on what they had. Not yet. They had time.

"Come on. We've both been in relationships. Did the infatuation stage last forever?"

He ground his back teeth together. "We're not breaking up. Wear the ring on Sunday. We're not doing this."

"You can't run from this forever."

"I'm not running from anything." To illustrate his point, he stepped deeper into the room and stood in front of her. "I'm here, right in front of you. And that's where I'm staying until I decide. Not you. Not my mother. Not my family. Not the duchess of fucking Dallas. *Me*."

Chapter 18

Pen smoothed cocoa butter over her stomach, determined to avoid stretch marks at any cost. She'd read that moisturizing helped, and she'd started her nightly routine almost right after she found out she was pregnant.

As she ran her hand over her rounding belly, she considered the warring feelings inside her.

Frustration with Zach. Frustration with herself. Amusement for how he'd decorated the room for a son. Admiration at the way he was determined to be a good father. And the biggest: so much love for her unborn baby, she was ready to burst with it.

If she was being honest with herself, that love was inching closer and closer to Zach himself. Encircling him and swallowing him up in it. But she couldn't confuse her love for their daughter for romantic love with him. They weren't the same.

When she'd asked him about Lonna, he'd confirmed one of Pen's biggest fears. Falling in love meant you could lose it all. And for all of Zachary Ferguson's bliss-chasing, he'd drawn a very distinct boundary around true love.

Romantic love had no place in his plans. Not any longer. Not since Lonna.

It was unfair.

Unfair because for the first time in her life, Pen feared she was starting to fall in love…with a man incapable of loving her back.

"Hey," came a soft rumble from the doorway.

Pen spun the lid on the lotion and set it on her nightstand. "Hey."

Zach's hooded eyes and sideways smile had replaced his flattened mouth and ruddy complexion. After their conversation in the baby's room, he'd mumbled something about working and shut himself in his office. She hadn't seen him since.

They weren't fighting. Not really. They just had very different views of the way things were.

For Penelope, she needed to leave before she fell for him and couldn't pull away as easily. For Zach, there was no hurry because falling for her wasn't a remote possibility.

Perhaps acknowledging that was what hurt most.

"I overreacted," he said, walking into the room. "Did you eat?"

"All I do is eat." She gave him a tired smile. "Did you?"

"Just ate a sandwich."

"Dinner at nine-thirty."

"Bachelor," he explained.

Her heart squeezed at the word. That was the problem. Even with his pregnant fiancée in the house, Zach still considered himself single.

His eyes searched the room before landing on her again. "I don't want you to move out. I don't want to miss anything."

She had to close herself off from the sincerity in his voice. There was a bigger picture—the baby girl residing in her growing belly.

"You won't miss anything," she promised. "My stomach is going to get larger, my ankles more swollen, my temper more out of control. It might even get as bad as yours."

He shook his head in agreement. "I'm sorry about that."

He sat on the bed and lifted the delicate edge of her short cotton nightie, skimming the lace hemline up to expose her thighs. When one large, warm hand landed on her skin, she found it suddenly hard to breathe.

This was such a bad idea. Sealing her tumultuous feelings with sex wouldn't bring her closer to a resolution but take her further from it.

"How tired are you?" His green eyes sought hers.

Who was she fooling? Could she really convince herself she wasn't in love with him? Not when he looked at her the way he looked at her now. Not when he was watching the monitor at Dr. Cho's office with rapt attention and pride. And not when he touched her—especially when he touched her.

Zach claimed her as his that night in the mayor's mansion. She thought then it'd been about sex and physical love, but now she realized that claim was staked deep in her heart and soul. And the proof of it was incubating in her womb.

"Not too tired," she whispered, her eyes glazing over with staunch acceptance. She'd rather have him than not—even if it drove another stake into her lovesick heart.

He leaned forward to place a kiss on her bared shoulder. His tongue flicked under the strap, then dragged up her neck, giving her all of his attention like no other woman in his past or present who'd commanded it.

Warmth flooded her tummy, the flutter between her legs having everything to do with a million jettisoning hormones. She buried her lovelorn emotions into a deep, dark corner of her being and focused on the present. Focused on giving in to her physical needs—and riding Zach like the cowboy she once thought he was.

Her nightie was gone in a whisper as he lifted it over her head and tossed it to the floor. He smoothed his hand along her swollen belly, moving to her breasts next.

Lying back, she closed her eyes as his amazing mouth skated over one nipple then the other. The sensations assaulting her brought an end to the warring emotions in her chest and the thoughts littering her brain. And when his hands moved between her thighs and stroked, every ounce of her attention went there. Nothing felt as natural, as all-consuming, as making love with Zachary Ferguson.

His lips were at home on her body—*anywhere* on her body. Every inch of her belonged to him.

She reached for his T-shirt, tugging at it weakly. "Off."

"Yes, ma'am." There was the drawl she loved so much. He whipped off his shirt to reveal his chest and once again, breathing became difficult. Was it any wonder she let herself indulge in what she thought would only be one night with him? Was it any wonder she indulged now?

She took a page from Zach's book and released her worries of responsibility and the future, letting go like dandelion fluff on a thick summer's breeze. She focused on his physicality instead.

His broad shoulders, round like he spent the day hauling hay bales instead of sliding a mouse across his desk. His biceps, straining as he shoved his jeans to his knees. Thick thighs, covered in coarse, dark-blond hair and leading down to sturdy feet. All of him was gorgeous. And for the moment, hers.

"You keep looking at me like that, Penelope Brand, and I'm not going to last a minute." His green eyes sparked in challenge. His dimple dented his cheek as he shucked his boxers.

She embraced the idea of behaving like an out-of-control teenager. Pen had always been drawn to stability…until she'd moved to Dallas. Until she'd laid eyes on Zach. He made her embrace the moment. Made her live in right now.

His hot skin came in contact with hers and she could've sworn she felt sparks dance on her skin. He stripped her panties down her legs and once she was naked, pressed every part of himself against her.

She moaned. He was perfect.

He was hers. In a superficial, temporary sense, but nonetheless *hers*.

"Remember to pretend to be surprised," Penelope told Zach as they stepped up to the entryway of the hotel. At the top floor stood the Regal Room, their destination. A popular choice for parties of the upscale variety. She'd never been, but knew about it, and had recommended it for some of her more elite clients in Dallas.

"Should I add clutching my heart for effect?" Zach leaned over to ask, his voice low. Then pressed the button for the elevator.

"That might be poor form since Rider will be there."

"Oh, right." But his smirk hinted that he'd already figured that out.

This was the way things had been in the two weeks since their argument that ended in bed. They'd ended up in bed several times since and each interaction was like the last. Penelope fell deeper in love with him, and Zach maintained his position as kind, caring father of her child.

It should be enough. She wanted to be the woman for whom it would be enough. Where his loyalty and limited offerings would be substantial for as long as they lasted.

But they weren't.

It was the wrong time to broach the topic, but she'd been unable to summon the bravery to do it before. Now or never, as the saying went. So while the elevator zipped them to their destination, she blurted, "I'm going to announce that the wedding is on hold when I announce that we're having a daughter."

His steely glare matched the hardness of his jaw. "Penelope."

"I'm not asking permission." She lifted her chin. It was past time she pulled the plug on the relationship that was rapidly eating away at her heart.

"This isn't—" he started, but the elevator doors swished open at that moment.

They stepped out of the elevator and were greeted by a sea of smiling faces, very few of which she recognized.

Collectively, a shout rose in the room. "Congratulations!"

The "surprise" baby shower wasn't pink and blue or even green and yellow. The palette was a sophisticated blend of white and gold, right down to the confetti now littering the floor. Balloons tied with gold-and-black ribbon were suspended from the main table, which boasted flutes of champagne and an array of tapas displayed on elegant platters.

The banner draping the back of the room was white with gold metallic cursive lettering reading, "It's a baby!"

A few flashes from cameras snapped as Stefanie broke off from the crowd and enveloped Pen into a warm hug. Pen held on a beat longer than she expected. Ending the engagement with Zach also would mean distancing herself from his family, and she was going to miss Stef when she left.

"We're very surprised," Pen said, including Zach, who stood at her side like a wall. She quirked an eyebrow at him and his mouth pulled into a tight smile for the benefit of their guests. Yes, probably her timing wasn't the best on telling him her plans.

Stef hugged her brother next. "I know you hate surprises, Zach, but try to lighten up."

"I'll try," came his gruff response.

"So, I lied about this being a cake-tasting," Stefanie

said, gesturing to a round table off to the side, "but we do have cake."

Chase, Elle and Rider emerged from the crowd next to deliver hugs and welcomes. Elle, in particular, was notably excited.

"Granddaughter or grandson?" she asked Pen conspiratorially. "One blink for a girl, two for a boy."

"No! Absolutely not." Stefanie positioned herself between her mother and Penelope. "Nine o'clock is the announcement, and not a moment before."

"Nine o'clock," Pen said, her own smile faltering. A quick glance to Zach confirmed that his was gone completely. "Uh, Stefanie, this room is amazing. The party, the food. Everything looks incredible."

She had to focus on her appreciation for what Stef had done, and pray that she could somehow dismantle the engagement and announce that she was expecting a girl without ruining the vibe of the party, or undoing Stef's hard work. She hoped Stef would understand and forgive her.

Stefanie put a hand on her hip and gestured like a model on *The Price is Right*. "I did it myself. I mean, yeah, okay, I had a team helping, but the ideas came out of my brain."

"Well, it's incredible," Pen said, meaning it. "If I need a party of any kind in the future, I'm coming to you."

"Sparkling grape juice." Stef plucked a flute from a waiter's tray. "I put little purple ribbons on the nonalcoholic drinks for you." Pen accepted her bubbly drink, a lump settling in her throat. She forced it down and called up her party smile again.

"Come see what else I have planned." Stef wrapped

her arm around Pen's and led her away. Pen gladly took the reprieve—anything to keep Zach from bringing up the conversation she'd railroaded him with in the elevator.

He was easy to avoid over the next two hours given that Stef had filled the evening with games—albeit sophisticated ones.

"We're adults," Stef had said with committed seriousness. "I'm not melting chocolate bars in diapers, or asking guests to guess your belly width with lengths of toilet paper."

"Thank you for that." As sisters went, Zach hit the jackpot. Pen ignored the feeling of melancholy that swept over her. No matter where Pen and Zach ended up, Stef would always be their daughter's aunt. Pen would hold on to that.

Dessert was a selection of miniature cakes or cupcakes, and cake pops on sticks, all decorated in white fondant with edible gold sprinkles. Pen sampled the sweets, and drank down another sparkling grape juice as she played coy about her baby's sex. She'd lost count of how many times she'd told someone "Sorry. The announcement is at nine."

About twenty minutes before the evening's most anticipated hour, she found an opening and slipped away from the crowd. Zach and Chase were speaking to their grandparents' friends and since Pen had already spoken with Rudy and Ana, she knew their conversation could last well past the time Pen and Zach were to take the mic.

August in Illinois was hot, but nothing like Texas hot. There wasn't much fresh air to be had on the balcony, but it was private, and she desperately needed a break from the fake smiles. Her cheeks were starting to ache.

Sweltering heat, even this late in the day, blanketed her bare shoulders. Hot, yes, but quiet. She rested her hands on the railing and looked out at the city beyond. Of all the goals for a fresh start she'd made when she left Chicago, none of them had involved a giant engagement ring on her finger, a billionaire fiancé and a baby due by Christmas.

The phrase "Man plans and God laughs" flitted through her brain, but she could admit she was laughing with Him. True, she hadn't planned any of this, but she was also so incredibly grateful to be pregnant— something she likely never would've planned.

Her eyes tracked to the windows and she spotted Zach, dark slacks accentuating his height, button-down pale blue shirt unable to hide his muscular build.

Her heart did what it'd been doing for a few weeks now, and gave an almost painful squeeze. She'd fallen for him. Head over heels. Ass over teakettle. Hook, line and sinker.

No matter how hard she tried to compartmentalize her feelings from the relationship, they managed to glob together into one four-letter word.

Love.

Whenever he walked into a room, she lit up. She sank into him whenever he pulled her close for a kiss, like she could fuse her very being with his. But all of this oneness and overwhelming feeling of rightness wasn't shared by her betrothed.

Zach offered support, loyalty and means but not love. Love for his daughter? Most definitely. But for Pen, his caring stopped at friendship, and some days before that. Since she'd learned about his ex, Lonna, it was like she could visibly spot each and every boundary line he drew. Those boundaries were intentional—whether he was aware he was doing it or not.

He took care of her, provided for her every need and was adamant about not missing a moment of his daughter's life. Zach made love to Penelope with a single-minded focus on her pleasure, and if she were a fresh-faced twentysomething, she might mistake his actions for love.

But as a thirtysomething who'd been around the proverbial block a few times, she knew better.

He gave and gave and gave…everything but his heart. That part of his anatomy was walled off so solidly, she hadn't managed to breach the outer layer. And if she noticed the distance between them—her besotted, and him casually comfortable—so would his family, eventually. And so would their daughter.

Pen had made a lot of decisions recently—big, sweeping life decisions—and the number-one decision she'd made was to put her daughter first.

She would sacrifice anything—her job, her home, her very lifestyle—to give her daughter what she needed. She'd even sacrifice what she had with Zach. And that was saying something as it was the first time she'd truly been in love.

In the quiet, dark corners of her mind lay a flickering hope that Zach might come around. That he might open up and learn to love her. The optimist in her thought he might, but the realist in her couldn't risk what it meant if he never did.

She wasn't waiting around for him to decide to love her. Not with their daughter watching. And that was why she also couldn't let the engagement continue. Sure, there'd be a stir of interest and a touch of gossip, but she could spin their interest toward their daughter. She was the reason for the relationship anyway. Most of it.

Some of it, Pen sadly corrected.

Regardless, percentages didn't matter. Penelope didn't want her love for Zach to grow bitter and stale after years of not being returned. More important, she didn't want her daughter to witness her mother's feelings for her father crumbling into dust.

Their daughter would have a mother and a father who cared about one another, who respected one another. Who loved her with all their hearts. And that was going to have to be enough. For all of them.

Zach must've escaped the clutches of his grandparents' friends, because he now stood at the balcony door with Chase. They were talking, looking very much like brothers with the same strong lines of their backs and hands buried in pants pockets.

Zach chose that moment to look over and catch her eye. He didn't smile, but held her gaze with a smoldering one of his own. His longish hair was tickling the collar of his shirt, his full mouth flinching in displeasure.

As magnanimous as she'd sounded in her own ears moments ago, Pen's heart throbbed with the need to satisfy her own desires rather than her daughter's.

She only wished loving Zach satisfied both.

Chapter 19

Zach took in Pen on the balcony, observing her as he had when he'd first laid eyes on her. A white lace dress hugged every inch of her, from exquisite breasts to shapely hips. The graceful line of her neck led to pale blue eyes that could stop a man dead in his tracks—and full lips that had stopped his heart for at least one beat on several occasions.

Now, knowing her the way he did, he still appreciated her physical attributes, but what he mostly saw was beauty. Beauty in a dress that showed off what women at the party kept referring to as her "baby bump." Beauty, decadently outlined in white lace, snatching away first place from the breathtaking sunset behind her.

Beauty that was all woman.

That was all his.

Was. That word punched him in the solar plexus so hard, the room around him seemed to cant. He'd been possessive over her since the beginning, not wanting to let her go.

And now she was going.

Pen played with a few strands of her hair that had come down from an elegant twist at the back of her neck, her other hand resting on the railing. Her red shoes had tall, spindly heels, in spite of how many times he'd asked her not to wear them.

Throughout the evening, his flared temper had died down. His thoughts, while meeting guests who were his parents' friends more than his, kept returning to Penelope and his unborn child. His future.

Not only his future.

Theirs.

He envisioned his daughter's birthdays. Holidays. Family vacations.

As he'd glimpsed each fractured bit, he realized it was an impermanent, if not impossible, future.

Because Penelope was backing away from him.

There was no escaping how much she'd infiltrated his life in a short period of time. Zach barely recognized himself from the man who'd smoothly followed her back to her apartment for what was supposed to be a hell of a one-night stand.

And tonight it was ending.

Pen turned and caught his gaze, only to face the city lights once again. Over his shoulder, Chase spoke, and Zach wrenched his attention away from her.

"You've done it, haven't you?" Chase asked, expression serious.

Zach threw back his champagne and wished it was

beer. He had a good idea of what his brother was referring to, but damned if he was about to guess.

"The pretending has become real."

"The pretending," Zach said, relinquishing his
empty glass to a nearby table, "is about to come to an
end." At Chase's frown, Zach explained in a low voice
so no one could overhear. "The engagement is over."

"Why?"

"Why?" Zach practically spat the word. "Weren't
you the one advising me not to get in too deep because
I thought this would be 'fun'?"

"Yes."

Their silent standoff ended with Chase explaining.

"It's become clear to me that she means a lot more
than a good time to you. So again, I ask, why?"

Zach blinked, his brother's stern visage blurring as
Stef's voice crackled over the speakers in the room.

"Five minutes until we learn whether I have a niece
or a nephew!"

The crowd clapped, and there were a few titters of
excitement.

"If you don't know, you'd better figure it out in
five minutes," Chase recommended. Zach followed
his brother's gaze to Penelope and the world wasn't
just canting but *swimming*.

"If you were going to succumb to a woman—"
Chase nodded his head in greeting when Pen turned
to look at them "—that'd be the one to lie down for."

"I've tried," Zach mumbled through numb lips. She
was the one ending it. He was the one who wanted to
keep her close.

"Try harder." One more cocky tilt of his lips and
Chase was gone.

Rather than make another excuse that he had tried, Zach considered that maybe he hadn't. That maybe a fake engagement wasn't enough for the woman who spelled out future with a capital *F.*

Like the F *dangling from the bracelet on her wrist.*

His. Pen was still his. She needed to know that the engagement he'd thrown out as a distraction had become real for him. That was what Chase had meant when he'd told Zach to try harder.

Decisively, and damn that felt better than uncertainty, Zach slid the balcony door aside and stepped out into the heated air with his fiancée.

"Is it time?" Her tone was neutral, her body held in check. She was ready to unravel everything at that microphone, and Zach had about two minutes to stop her from doing it.

"We have to talk."

Her fair eyebrows lifted. "Didn't I get in trouble for saying something similar to you before?"

He didn't break stride, reaching her in a few steps and cradling her elbow. The deep hues of a purple-and-pink sky had given way to ink-blue.

"We have to talk about the announcement," he said, throat tight, sweat beading on his forehead, and *not* from the summer temperatures. He wasn't at the mercy of his nerves—not ever. Not when he proposed to Lonna years ago, or when he proposed to his ex-wife in Vegas, but now that he was faced with proposing to Penelope, there was no other word for it.

He was nervous.

Not only did he have no idea if she'd say yes, but he was almost positive she'd say no.

He needed her not to say no.

Not just for him. For herself—for their daughter. For all of them.

"Penelope Brand." He cleared his throat, the seriousness in his tone causing her lips to softly part. He lifted her left hand and thumbed the engagement ring he'd placed there on a whim. Or some kind of mental dare. Now that he knew her inside and out, and knowing she'd bear his first child, he knew better.

It might have started out as a whim, but now? He meant it.

"I know what we have started out as fake, but over the past several months, having you at my side, being with you day in and day out… The announcement that you were pregnant, learning we're expecting a daughter…" He trailed off, the magnitude of what they'd shared stealing his breath. "The reality is, Penelope—" he locked his gaze on her startled one "—this isn't fake. Not anymore."

"Zach…"

"Let me finish."

His eyebrows closed over his nose in concentration as the second hand rapidly ticked away precious minutes. Quickly, he reordered his thoughts. Now to deliver them in the most genuine, efficient way possible.

"We're good together," he told her. "Not only in the bedroom. As a unit. We're learning our way, and I probably have further to go than you do, but we're committed to the same important goal. Raising our child surrounded by so much love she'll never want for anything."

Pen's eyes filled and she blinked. In her expression, Zach saw hope—hope that gave him the courage to continue.

"I love our daughter with a fierceness I didn't know was possible. I care about you, Penelope. I don't want to end what we have because your PR timeline says we should."

Her expression blanked. He couldn't tell if she was shocked or in agreement, or if she felt equal measures of both.

He thumbed her diamond engagement ring so that it was centered on her finger. Then he looked her dead in the eye and forced past his constricting throat, "Will you marry me? For real this time."

In the space of one heartbeat, then two, Pen only stared. Then her lips firmed, tears streaked down her cheeks and she tugged her hand away from his.

Pen swiped her tears away almost angrily as the city melted in her watery vision. She sucked in a gulp of air, calling upon her very strong constitution for assistance. Her heart was cracked when she'd arrived.

Zach had just shattered it.

He moved to comfort her instantly, his wide, warm hands on her hips, strong chest flanking her back.

"Pen. I know how this sounds. I know you think it's too late…"

But that wasn't it. This wasn't about timing.

I love our daughter. I care about you.

He couldn't have been any clearer about the division of his feelings—about the clearly marked boundary lines—during his proposal.

She'd believed when he'd started his speech that miraculously, she'd broken through. That during the course of this party, Zach had seen the light.

I love our daughter. I care about you.

His was a marriage proposal of convenience the first time, and now it was one of merged interests. It hadn't come from his heart and soul. A long time ago she'd convinced herself she didn't need romantic love. But now that she was looking at Zach, her heart twisting like a wrung-out cloth, she was certain about two things.

One, she loved him, and two, she refused to enter a marriage where Zach was only half in.

He might never leave her, cheat on her, or abandon her, but he also wouldn't ever love her the way she deserved to be loved.

And she *deserved* love.

He stood behind her, his breath on her ear when he bent forward. "I know I'm springing this on you, but this is the best plan. We can have each other, have our daughter, have our lives together."

She closed her eyes against the surge of longing in her chest. There was a part of her, and it wasn't small, that wanted to turn in the circle of his arms and say *yes*. Give in to the idea that Zach might someday love her the way she loved him.

But that was a fairy tale. Her life wasn't glass slippers and godmothers. It was pumpkins and practicality.

She turned and faced him, shoulders back, chin tipped to take in his handsome face, and spoke in her most practical voice. "We can't be this selfish because we like to have sex, Zach."

His head jerked on his neck like she'd slapped him instead of spoken.

"What the hell's that supposed to mean?" he bit out.

"It means exactly what I said. We have a child to think about."

"A child who needs both of her parents around," he said, his voice escalating, "not one at a time at prearranged intervals."

"Our child needs parents who love her and love each other. If we can't fulfill both of those bare minimums, then we have nothing more to talk about."

"Marriage isn't good enough for you?" Zach's cheeks reddened. "Marriage *and* sex isn't good enough for you?" His voice was measured and low, but anger outlined every word.

"Is it good enough for you?"

"Marriage and sex and you? Damn straight it's good enough. What more do you want from me, Penelope?"

She parted her lips to tell him there was so, *so* much more to want. So much more to marriage apart from sex and sharing a house. She and Zach could be so much more than parents. What about when their daughter was raised and out of the house? What about Penelope's *own* life beyond being a mother? What about that deep, committed love she'd seen in her parents' lives? Didn't he want that?

"The original agreement was to untangle these knots *before* our baby was born. And that's what we're doing." She started for the balcony door, but Zach caught her upper arm and tugged her back.

In his face, she saw a plethora of emotion. Pain. Fear. Anger. Hope.

As per his usual, he went with his standby: demanding.

"I can't let you do that. I'm far from done exploring what we have. Sharing what we've built."

She shook out of his grip. "What we *have* is built on a lie and an accident!"

The moment she lifted her voice to shout the accusation, his eyes slid over her shoulder and the sound of low, casual chatter filtered out onto the balcony.

Reason being, Stefanie Ferguson stood at the threshold to the balcony, door open wide. Her eyes welled with unshed tears, betrayal radiating off her strong, petite form.

"Stefanie," Pen started, but Stef steeled her spine and looked, not to Penelope, but to Zach for answers.

"Is that true?" Stef asked him.

Behind her, onlookers peered out, eyebrows raised, mouths forming *O*s of curiosity. Stef shut the door behind her and stepped onto the patio, crossing her arms over her midsection.

"What lie?" she asked.

"Stef," Pen tried again, but the younger woman stood in front of her brother. Zach, who'd released Pen the moment Stefanie appeared, shoved his hands into his pockets.

"Penelope and I are discussing something very important. Go inside and we'll be in soon."

"Tell me what lie and I'll leave you to it," Stef said.

"I said—"

"The engagement isn't real," Pen blurted. Zach's jaw clenched and he shot Pen a look showcasing both his outrage and feelings of betrayal. Well, too bad. She felt betrayed, too.

Pen took her eyes off him to comfort her almost-future-sister-in-law, who looked thoroughly heartbroken.

"Zach made up the engagement when Yvonne interrupted Chase's birthday party," Pen said softly. "He needed a distraction."

"And you agreed." Stef's voice was steel, similar to the tone her brother had used many times before.

"I agreed to help him, yes." Pen thrust her chin forward. She hadn't done anything wrong.

"And the pregnancy?" Mortification colored Stef's features as she swept her eyes to Pen's belly. "Is it real?"

"Yes." Pen let out a gusty sigh. "God. Yes, Stefanie. I'd never lie about that. I was pregnant the night of Chase's birthday party, but didn't know it."

Stef's sigh of relief was short-lived. "You lied to me." She swung her gaze from Pen to include Zach. "Both of you."

"It started out as a lie to distract from Yvonne, yes," Zach said. "But things between Pen and me have developed since then." He fastened his eyes on Penelope, but spoke to his sister. "I proposed to Pen right before you walked out here."

The warm breeze lifted Stefanie's bangs from her forehead. She tightened her arms around her middle and shook her head.

"I don't think your proposal went over well." Stef backed to the door. "I came out here to tell you we're ready for the announcement about the baby…" Inside a sea of curious faces studied the scene beyond the wide windows. Pen and Zach and Stef must look like a dramatic silent movie from their guests' vantage point. "Now it seems you owe your guests an explanation.

"Tell them the truth, Zach," Stef said. "It's the least you could've done for me." She pulled open the door but before she went inside, skewered Pen with, "I expected it from him. Not from you."

Once she was inside, Chase pushed out the door next and angled his head at his brother.

"Excuse me." Penelope bumped past Chase's suited arm and darted through the crowd. Zach called her name, but when she peeked over her shoulder, Chase was blocking the door and giving advice she knew Zach didn't want to hear.

"Let her go."

Chapter 20

Zach muscled past his brother. Or tried anyway. Chase, despite his suit and community standing, pushed *back*.

He banded an arm around Zach, which might look like he was consoling his younger brother, but felt more like he was attempting to crush Zach's ribs until they audibly snapped.

Through his teeth, Chase said, "Hold it together," as he shut the door to the balcony behind them. "We're outside having a brotherly chat."

Chase released him and pulled his shoulders back and Zach mirrored his stance. Inside family and friends dashed concerned looks to the balcony and then in the direction Penelope had left.

"You have thirty seconds. I'm not going to stand out here when I should be going after her."

"Stefanie went after her. Didn't you see?" Chase replied calmly. Years of experience in the public eye had made him adept at handling a crisis situation with ease. "If Pen wanted to talk to you, she'd still be standing on this balcony. Everyone inside is waiting for an announcement. Granted, they got one, but it wasn't the one they were expecting."

Zach thrust his hand into his hair. Of course it hadn't been what they were expecting. Pen's reaction to his proposal hadn't been what *he* was expecting.

"Your options," Chase continued, "are to either leave and let the gossip begin. Or stay and offer a generic explanation."

"Like what?"

"If it were me? I'd apologize with no more explanation than a 'my fault.'" Chase demonstrated with his hands in surrender pose.

"*My* fault," Zach growled. "*My fault?* It's my fault for asking Penelope to marry me? For asking the woman carrying my baby to stay with me the rest of our lives?"

"Lower your voice."

"You're as bad as the rest of them, Chase. I don't give a fuck about public opinion or what anyone in that room needs."

"Yes, that's clear." Chase reprimanded in an irritatingly calm tone. "You only care about one person. *You.*"

That was it. He'd had it. Had it with trying to do the right thing and being crucified for it.

"You know what?" Zach shouldered by Chase and gripped the handle to the door. "Tell them whatever the hell you want."

* * *

"Penelope! Wait."

Pen paused on the sidewalk, surprised that Stefanie had followed her down. Stef had been clear upstairs that she didn't appreciate being left in the dark.

"Where are you going?" the younger woman called as she clipped to a stop next to Pen.

"You were right in there. You deserved to know. I'm sorry I didn't tell you. I couldn't."

"You should be. I'm mad at you and my idiot brother for keeping a secret this huge from me. I kept your pregnancy to myself! I could've kept this quiet, too." Stefanie stepped closer, kindness in her eyes. "But no matter how mad I am, I'd still give you a ride home."

Pen folded her arms over her middle, the reality of her situation settling in. She didn't have a home… only the home she shared with Zach. "I don't want to go home."

Not tonight. Maybe never again. This was as good of a break as any. Her leaving had always been inevitable. From the first time she spotted Zach in Chicago, to the jazz club, to the morning he kissed her goodbye, some part of her knew that holding on to him would be like trying to hold on to the wind.

Maybe getting it over with would allow her to heal quickly.

She hoped.

"I won't ask you to choose between me and your brother," Pen told Stef, because she refused to be unfair.

"I'm not *choosing*." Stefanie dug through her clutch. "I'm helping out a friend. If that makes Zach mad, so be it."

Stefanie approached the valet with her ticket. "We're in a hurry."

"Yes, ma'am," the valet replied with a hat-tip. Then he ran—yes, *ran*—to get the car.

Sadly, not fast enough.

This time when Penelope heard her name, it was Zach. He slowed his jog when he was close, brow pinched and fists bunched.

"I'm taking her home with me," Stefanie stated.

"No, you're not."

Stef turned on him. "Yes. I am."

"Pen." In his eyes, Penelope saw the plea. A dab of pain that hadn't been there before. But she couldn't open up again, not after what it took to get to this point.

"I have nothing more to discuss, Zach," Pen announced sadly. "You offered me everything and nothing at the same time."

His mouth froze open for a moment before clacking shut. Baring his teeth, he said, "I offered you everything I could."

She swallowed past a thick throat as the valet pulled Stef's car to the curb. Through a watery, sad smile, she nodded. "I know. And it's not enough."

Zach, arms folded, watched one of the movers walk the last of Penelope's boxes downstairs before loading the box into a moving truck.

He wasn't one for admitting defeat, but with Penelope standing in the hallway, notebook in hand as she checked off a list, it was clear they were over.

"What about the baby stuff?" the other mover asked, pointing to the room behind Zach.

Pen turned, her white summer dress rounded at the front, her heeled sandals reasonably high for a change.

"Yes," Zach answered at the same time Penelope said, "No."

Their gazes clashed, and in her pale blue eyes, he saw both challenge and loss. Or maybe he felt it.

"Take it," he told her.

"You'll need it," she said with a head-shake.

"I can buy more." He could replace every single thing in this house with a phone call, save one. The blonde across from him on the landing.

He'd tried contacting her for the past few days, but after the one night she slept at Stef's, he hadn't been able to reach her. Even Pen's office had been dark when he stopped by.

Then, this morning she'd texted him to ask if he'd be home. Foolishly, he'd believed she was coming by to reconcile. Instead, she'd shown up driving ahead of a moving truck.

So this was it.

She'd made up her mind. She was leaving.

"I can buy more, too, Zach. I have time before she's born. And anyway, I'm not sure how much of the furniture I can fit in my apartment."

His chest tightened as his eyes dipped to Pen's stomach. He was losing…everything. And it flat-out pissed him off.

"Are we going to talk about this?" he all but shouted. A mover leaned on the wall outside the bedroom door to watch. Oh, hell no. Zach curled his lip when he addressed him. "Get the hell out of my house."

He went, ambling down the stairs, and bitching to

his friend who stood on the porch. But both men stayed outside.

Zach turned back to Pen. "Well?"

"Well, what? There's nothing to talk about." She gestured with her notebook. "I've decided. Luckily, my landlady loves me and ushered me into the first available two-bedroom she had."

"You had the space you needed here." He widened his arms to encompass the massive house he now lived in alone.

"I never asked for this," she replied. He wished she would've yelled. Her maintaining her composure made him wonder if she cared about him at all.

"There are arrangements to be made," he growled, hating the loss of control, the feeling of spinning out of it. "Decisions about our daughter."

"Yes." She flipped to the back of the notebook, tore out a sheet of paper and handed it to him. "They've been made. Consider this a proposal. We can define the particulars later."

Penelope the Planner had an answer for everything. He folded his arms rather than take the sheet of paper.

"Why are you doing this really?" he asked.

"Because." She sighed. "As much as you claim to know what you want—" she tucked the paper back into her notebook "—you deserve better than an arranged marriage with a child as the prize."

Her smile was sad when she finished with, "And so do I."

Stepping close to him, she placed her hand on his chest, went up on her toes and placed a brief kiss on the corner of his mouth. Too brief. When he moved to hold her, she backed away.

"We'll be okay," she promised. Her eyes went to the baby's room. "Keep the furniture. You'll need it for when she visits."

Pen walked downstairs, calling out to the movers, "We're done here, guys. I'll follow in my car."

Zach's screen door shut with a bang behind her as car and truck engines turned over and pulled out of the driveway. He lowered to the top step upstairs, elbows on his knees and listened to the quiet of the house.

There was defeat in the silence.

Zachary Ferguson didn't do defeat.

He stood, in that instant deciding he'd do whatever it took to win Penelope back. To make her understand what she was walking away from. To make crystal clear that the best path for their future was a future with him in it.

He had a few billion in the bank.

Surely he could come up with something.

Chapter 21

Pen's mother sprayed the dusting cloth with Pledge and wiped the rungs of a wooden crib. Paula and Louis had driven to Texas, claiming the road trip would do them good. They'd arrived the day after the movers left everything behind and Pen had been so glad to see them, she could've cried.

In fact, she had.

"It was yours when you were a baby," her mother said as she polished the crib. "I honestly didn't remember that we had it. Your father cleaned out the storage unit and there it was."

"Thank you, Mom."

Paula Brand abandoned her work and scooped Pen into a hug with just the right amount of pressure. Pen would have cried more if there were any tears left.

"Are you going to tell me the real reason behind you

walking out on your billionaire fiancé?" Her mom held her at arm's length and waited.

Pen's lips compressed as she considered doing just that. She was willing to tell her mother a partial truth, but she couldn't bear confessing that the engagement was never real. Especially since, for Pen, her love for Zach was *very* real.

"When Zach proposed—" *both times* "—he did it out of obligation rather than love. I couldn't settle for less than his whole heart." Speaking of heart, hers gave a mournful wail. Walking out on him instead of accepting half measures was harder than she'd like to believe.

She'd been comfortable with him. She had a home, combined parenting, and yes, the money was a source of comfort, as well. But she wasn't the type of woman to let comfort and stability rule her world. If she were, she never would've left Chicago.

Hand resting on her swollen stomach, Pen thanked God that she had left Chicago. That she carried this baby in her belly and that, for all the heartache Zach had caused her, she'd finally experienced love.

"I'm sorry, sweetheart." Paula shook her head and let out an exasperated sigh. "I wish I could share a story so I could relate, but the truth is I was lucky to find your father when I was young."

Penelope's parents were high school sweethearts who married and built a business and had a baby because they were ready. Not because, in the midst of finding companionship, the birth control hadn't worked. But she didn't begrudge them their happiness.

"I'm glad you can't relate," she told her mother with a smile.

"Regardless, life is not without its struggles." Paula palmed her daughter's cheeks and returned her smile.

"I'll be fine. I've picked myself up and dusted myself off more times than I can count." Pen felt like bawling, but she was going to have to buck up. She wanted her daughter to be as proud of her as Pen was of her own mother.

Pen had done the unthinkable—she'd fallen for a guy who was unwilling to share his heart. His world, his money, yes. But not his heart. And in the end, that was all she'd wanted.

"I have something for you." Paula went to her purse and came out with an envelope. A very flat envelope. "We had an unexpected windfall after that last house flip—"

"Mom, no." Pen backed away like her mother held a live spider by the leg rather than an envelope by the corner.

"Your dad and I want you to have this. We're going to be grandparents. We want to start our spoiling early." She shook the envelope. "I mean it."

Pen accepted it with a murmured "Thank you."

Paula rubbed her hands together. "I can't wait to go shopping for this baby!"

Pen thought of the Love & Tumble boutique, of the photographer she'd hired and the Dallas Duchess blog. She'd avoided much of the handling of her own potential PR nightmare for the last week-plus. She didn't care about her reputation—none of it was career-altering—but there were elements to handle that affected the Fergusons.

The mayor.

Stefanie.

Zach.

Penelope resolved to handle them as soon as possible.

"I don't know what to say," Pen said, holding the envelope in both hands. Blank on the outside, and who knew how much money on the inside. It didn't matter. What mattered was that her parents were supportive of her decision to raise her child apart from Zach, and that they loved her no matter what.

Anything beyond that involved items on Pen's own to-do list. Items like shared custody and drop-offs. Announcing the sex of the baby as well as confirming the breakup for the public.

"I'm going to run to work, if that's okay?" She phrased it like a question but knew her mother's response before she gave it.

"That a girl." Paula smiled proudly.

In her downtown office, Pen sat at her desk and jotted a quick list of phone calls to make, pausing to mourn the space. She'd have to abandon her office to work at home. Start having meetings in coffee shops and her clients' offices again. She could no longer afford both Brand Consulting's shingle and her daughter.

Hand on her tummy, she closed her eyes and reminded herself of what was important.

Then she picked up her desk phone and called the mayor of Dallas.

Chase showed up in Zach's office five minutes before five o'clock, a shadow of the same hour decorating his jaw.

"You look like shit," Zach offered. "Rough day?"

Chase held his gaze but didn't cop to the status of his day, instead returning, "I'd talk. You look like your rough days had friends who came by to beat the hell out of you at night."

"Wonder why that is." Zach blinked tired eyes. He hadn't been sleeping well. Or eating well. Or thinking well, either. Suffering from a breakup would do that. And he did mean *suffering*.

"Penelope called me this afternoon," Chase said.

That snapped Zach awake. "You? Why?"

"She let me know she was announcing your amicable breakup via a blogger. Duchess something. Pen asked me to pass it on. In person."

"That was bold." No one told the mayor of Dallas what to do. "And you agreed."

"I came to tell you that and one more thing."

"Which is?" Zach asked as he typed in the URL for the Dallas Duchess. No news about himself was on the front page, but an ad for Love & Tumble caught his eye and snagged his heart.

"Penelope misses you."

Zach tore his eyes from the screen. "Did she say that?"

"She didn't have to. She sounded...sad." Chase's eyes skated over Zach's rumpled shirt. "I wonder if she looks as bad as you do. I doubt it. She's a helluva lot prettier."

No arguing that finer point.

"I can't go by your gut, Chase." But even as he said it, Zach's mind was turning. He'd been racking his brain all week for ways to win her back.

His eyes on the blog in front of him, he considered a new possibility. Maybe he could out-PR the PR maven.

"I'm not giving up," Zach told his brother.

"It's hard to know when to give up and when to dig in." Chase's tone was contemplative. He sucked in a breath and expelled such a personal comment, Zach stared at him in shock. "Like when Mimi and I unraveled. Mom and Dad were right. She wasn't a good fit for a political partner, but at the time, I struggled. I didn't know my future. I didn't know if I'd actually make it to mayor when she left. But I knew if I did, I'd be better off without her."

Despite Chase's assuredness as he recited the tale of the decay of his past relationship, Zach had been there when it happened. He remembered his older brother's state when he lost Mimi. He'd been devastated for months. Then again, devastation on Chase looked different than it did on other people. Chase had dug his heels in and honed his focus on world domination.

He'd fallen just short of the world, but he'd landed Dallas. Zach wasn't sure if his stiff-lipped older brother was a good template with which to map out his own future or not.

"The point is you need to figure out what you want your life to look like in five, ten, twenty years," Chase said. "What role does Penelope play? She's the mother of your child, but is marrying her really what's best for you? Or is the best thing for you to back away from her and let the future fall into place?"

As Chase spoke, Zach rose from his chair.

"Are you kidding me right now? This is the advice you're offering? You don't know what Pen and I were like together. When she was in my house. In my *life*."

When she was settled across from him in a restaurant, laughing over her wine. Or in the doctor's office, with tears of joy shining in her eyes. Or when she'd moved out of his house with such resolve, that Zach questioned whether or not he'd imagined her every reaction beforehand.

"Simple question," Chase said in his typical uber-calm state. "She misses you. Do you miss her?"

More than anyone knew.

"Yes."

"Do you love her?" Since the inflection and volume of Chase's voice hadn't changed even a little, Zach had to let that question settle into the pit of his gut.

His churning, uncertain, fear-filled gut.

"There's your answer," Chase said. "Let her go, Zach. Love, even when it's real and lasting, isn't a sure thing. But when it's not there, you're betting on a loss. The longer you let a loveless relationship go on, the bigger that loss is."

On that note, Chase gave him a curt nod and left the office.

Chapter 22

Pen stepped into her building and the woman positioned at the front desk waved her over. "This came for you, Ms. Brand."

Oh, no. Not again.

Penelope pasted a smile on her face and accepted a padded envelope…and then another one.

"One more," the woman said, handing over a small box. She eyed Pen's rounded tummy. "I can carry these up if it's too much for you."

"No, I have them." The packages were awkward, especially while juggling her purse and working the elevator, but they weren't heavy.

Upstairs she dropped everything on a chair in her living room and stared at the packages in contemplation.

The return address was Love & Tumble. She'd received packages from there every day—several of them. So far, they'd been the items she'd had Zach's assistant return to the store right after they'd purchased them. Zach had tried to talk her into keeping them but of course, she hadn't. Now, one by one, or in this case *three by three*, those same items they'd returned had been showing up on her doorstep.

She opened the envelopes. One held a onesie, the other a baby blanket. The smaller box required scissors to cut the tape, so Penelope took the box to the countertop and grabbed her kitchen shears.

Inside the box, wrapped in Love & Tumble's signature shimmer-green tissue paper, was a pair of shoes. But not just any pair of shoes. Blinged out, faux fur, rhinestone encrusted high-top tennies for a girl.

Pen batted her lashes, fighting tears. This wasn't something she'd purchased prior. She and Zach had looked at this pair in the store and she'd mentioned if she had a girl, she'd *never* buy her six-hundred-dollar shoes. He'd argued that if they learned they were having a girl, those would be the *first* pair he'd buy her.

And he had.

A tear streaked Pen's cheek as she thumbed the tiny soles. Zach had been trying to buy back her affection since she left with the movers. He was being very sweet. Very thoughtful.

As the father of her child, she couldn't have picked a better man to love her baby more.

But he still didn't love *her*.

She hated how right she'd been in saying no to his proposal. He'd proposed to keep their budding family together, which was honorable, and for some women might have been enough. Still, when she imagined

Zach or her marrying other people, Pen's heart ached
with loss.

A swift knock at the door jolted her out of her
thoughts. One glance at the clock reminded her what
she already knew. This morning Stefanie had texted
to ask if she could swing by tonight. Pen had texted
back yes, then phoned the front desk telling them to
send her up when she arrived.

She swiped the hollows of her eyes and shook off
her somber attitude, then rushed to open the door. Stef
stood at the entry, her bright smile fading as soon as
she got one look at Pen.

"Oh, my gosh. What happened now?" Zach's sister
pushed her way into the apartment, her hands wrapping around Pen's shoulders.

Rather than explain, Pen gestured around the apartment. At the pile of boxes she'd been meaning to break
down for recycling. At another pile of their contents:
baby clothes and toys and blankets, taking up the
length of the sofa. She lost her battle holding back
tears. "Your brother mails me gifts every day."

"That jerk," Stefanie said.

Pen let out a startled laugh, but Stef didn't laugh
with her.

"Has he come to see you?"

Pen shook her head. "No, but I wouldn't want him
to."

"Has he called you?"

Pen shook her head again.

"Texted?" Stef asked, her voice small.

Pen confirmed with another head shake.

Stef clucked her tongue and proffered an envelope.

"This came for you, and Zach handed it to me when I barged in on him at the office."

Pen took the envelope. Her name was on the front in fanciful calligraphy, addressed to the house Zach had purchased.

"How…is he?" Pen hated herself for asking, but she couldn't not ask.

"Stressed. He looks tired. Heartbroken. About like you do." At Pen's wan smile, Stef tapped the envelope. "Expensive card stock. What do you think it is?"

Pen flipped over the envelope where there was a return address in black block letters, but no name.

"Not sure." Pen tore open the back and pulled out a sturdy white square with a vellum overlay. In gold lettering, two names stood out. Ashton Weaver and Serena Fern. "It's a wedding invitation."

Stef snatched it back and read the invite. "The actors?"

"Yep."

"Wow. I don't get starstruck often, but *wow*."

"They'll probably make it." Pen, shoulders rounded in defeat, trudged to the couch, shoved the baby stuff aside and collapsed onto a cushion. "And then I'll have to go to their twenty-fifth anniversary party knowing that two unlikely souls made it at the same time my engagement ended."

She pulled a pillow onto her lap and squeezed. Stef made room for herself and joined Pen on the couch. Pen had decided not to wallow. She'd decided to move on and pick up the pieces and focus on being the best mom *ever*. Her wounded heart had delayed those plans.

"I didn't mean to," Pen admitted around a sob.

"You didn't mean to what?" Stef's voice softened.

She rubbed Pen's back and Pen realized abruptly how badly she'd needed a girlfriend to confide in. Stefanie was the exact wrong person to lean on. As Zach's sister, she shouldn't be forced to choose sides.

And yet, when Pen opened her mouth to say "Never mind," she said, "I fell in love with your stupid brother," instead.

"Chase?"

Pen let out a surprised bleat. Stef smirked.

"Chase is *stupid*. Zach is the *idiot*." But Stef's smile was one of concern when she continued rubbing Pen's back. "You love Zach. You're having my niece. He proposed. What's the problem?"

"Oh, you know. Just that he doesn't love me." Pen swiped her cheeks and sniffed. "He loves the idea of a family and us being together. We're super-compatible in bed." She sniffed. "Sorry if that's too much information," she mumbled when Stef wrinkled her nose in disgust.

"I'm trying to absorb it. I am." Stef sighed. "How can he not love you? *I* love you." After a brief pause, she added, "Do you want to marry me?"

Pen let out a watery laugh. "I'll be fine. No, I'll be great. It's hormones, you know? And there have been a lot of big changes lately. I'm sure it'll all shake out."

Pen gave Stef a reassuring nod, but when Zach's sister nodded back, it was obvious the youngest Ferguson was placating her. Pen could take the placation. What she couldn't take another second of were the tears of regret.

"Enough of that." Pen slapped her hands to her thighs. "Do you want to help me take the tags off my daughter's clothes and sort them for the laundry?"

Stef's face brightened. "That, I can gladly do." With a quick clap of her hands, she leaped off the couch, baby clothes in hand.

Laundry was a lot better than wallowing.

The baby clothes weren't working.

Zach sent package after package from Love & Tumble, and had yet to hear anything from Penelope. He'd have to move on to something else.

Something *bigger*.

He'd fill her apartment with flowers. Hire a skywriter. Buy an island…

He didn't own an island yet.

iPad on his lap, he typed *islands for sale* into the search engine as a red sports car growled to a stop at the front of his house. Yeah, *the house*. He'd sworn he'd move back into his bachelor-pad apartment, but after Pen put the final nail in the coffin of their *us* status, leaving felt like giving up.

He wasn't about to give up.

His sister stepped out of the car into morning sunshine and Zach met her at the door.

"You're up early."

A large pair of sunglasses suggested she was out late. She propped them on top of her head as she came into the house, but her eyes were clear and alert.

"I was up late," she confirmed, "but pregnant ladies don't drink, so Penelope and I indulged in cookies and tea instead." She shrugged her mouth. "Not a bad way to spend a Friday night, actually."

She was at Penelope's apartment?

"How is she?" he asked without hesitation.

"Funny, she asked the same question about you."

Stefanie offered a Ferguson-family smirk. "Do you have coffee?"

"I'm working my way through a pot now." He followed Stefanie into the kitchen where she poured herself a mug and offered him a refill. He set the iPad aside and retrieved his mug. When he walked back into the kitchen, Stef was frowning down at the tablet.

"You are not going to buy an island."

"Why not?" He refilled his mug.

"Are you moving there?"

"No." Although if Pen kept ignoring him, an island would be the ideal place to live. "Maybe. I don't know. I was going to buy it for Penelope."

Stefanie scowled. "Seriously, Zach."

"Seriously, Stef." He opened his mouth to argue until it belatedly occurred to him that his sister was a woman.

He didn't have a lot of women at his disposal. He had yet to poll a woman about how to move forward with *Mission: Get Pen Back*. And God knew Chase hadn't been a lot of help.

"Is skywriting a better idea?"

"Man. This is bad." Stef gave him a pitying shake of her head.

"I can buy out every flower shop downtown. Hell, I can *buy* every flower shop downtown. Is that…a better idea?" He palmed the back of his neck and leaned a hip on the counter. He was completely out of his element. "She didn't respond to the baby clothes."

"I'm not sure this is a situation you can buy yourself out of, Zach. If you didn't have billions in the bank, what would you do?"

He drank his coffee. Partially to buy time and partially because the caffeine might help him think.

"If you couldn't *name a planet* after her, what would you do?"

"A planet. Hand me that iPad."

Stef narrowed her eyes in warning.

"I'm kidding. I feel like you're dancing around a point."

"Why are you doing all of this?"

"I'm winning her back." *Duh*. Wasn't that obvious? "We're good together and as soon as I can get her to stop ignoring the truth…"

"Which is?"

He blinked at his sister. What the hell was that supposed to mean?

"Why are you good together, Zach?" she pressed.

He frowned. "What do you mean *why*?"

"How do you feel about her?"

He let out an uncomfortable laugh and pushed away from the counter. "How do I feel… That's obvious, isn't it? I want her around. I want to raise our daughter together."

Stefanie sat down at the breakfast bar and pilfered a cookie from an open bag. "Why?" she asked around a bite.

"Pen's fun. She gets me." And in the bedroom? Forget it. There wasn't a high enough rating for how explosive they were when they came together.

"What else?" Stef cocked her head.

"I…miss her." That hurt to admit.

"And?"

"And what?" He put down his mug before he sloshed

hot coffee on his arm. Flattening both hands on the bar, he bent to look his sister in the eyes. "Spell it out."

"Sorry." Stef polished off her cookie and dusted her hands together, not the least bit sorry. "Can't. This is heart stuff not head stuff, and Lord only knows what you're feeling in there. Do you have feelings?"

She pretended to study the ceiling as she contemplatively chewed.

"I have too many feelings. I'm drowning in feelings! Can't you see that? I'm willing to turn over my entire life. To get married!"

"You were married to a crazy person last year. Why is Pen different?"

"That was…" He swallowed thickly, on the verge of admitting the truth for the first time ever. "That was a test."

"A test *marriage*?"

"A test to make sure I could marry and it could mean nothing." Damn. He hadn't meant to be *that* honest.

"So marrying Pen would be nothing?" his sister asked gently.

"Marrying Pen would mean everything." That same jittery fear he felt when he spoke to Chase about her returned, spreading through his chest like wildfire.

Stef waited for him to say more. Could he? Could he admit what was quaking in his gut? What was making his head spin?

"She's…the mother of my child," he started. Lamely. "There's more."

Chin propped in hand, Stef waited.

"She's…" He closed his eyes and then reopened them. Screw it. The truth was obvious to Stef, so he might as well tell her what she already knew. "I'm in love with her."

Stef burst off the stool and thrust both arms into the air.

"Yessssss!" She strangled him with a hug.

He smiled against her hair, and embraced his sister. His chest filled to the brim with a feeling of *right*. That ball-zinging surety that had been eluding him—or maybe he'd been denying it for some time now.

He just as quickly deflated.

The sad reality was that he was in love with Penelope and she wanted nothing to do with him.

"She'll never come back to you if you keep showering her with gifts. You have to make a big statement," Stef said. "And trust me, I want her back almost as much as you do." Stef was on the move, her hand lashed around Zach's wrist. "There has to be some clue in this house as to how to go about getting her back."

"She took everything that was hers out of this house," he said as he allowed Stef to drag him room to room. He followed her up the stairs where she made the same sad assessment he had for days in a row.

There was no sign of Penelope here.

Other than the baby's room, it was like she hadn't been here at all.

Stef turned from the Dallas Cowboys decorations Zach hadn't bothered taking down. He'd meant to, but again, that felt like giving up.

He expected his sister to shrug and state that he was a lost cause, but instead a slow grin spread across her lips.

She grabbed his arm and gave him a shake. "I figured it out. I know how you can win her back."

Chapter 23

Now that the other bedroom in her apartment housed a crib and a changing table, and Pen had let her office go, she'd taken to working from the sofa. She spread her planner, cell phone and laptop on the coffee table: command central. It was perfect, really, since she was only a few yards away from the coffeepot she couldn't wait to utilize again, and the bathroom.

Okay, so it wasn't perfect.

She missed her office. She needed a designated space. Once her daughter was born, she'd be home fulltime—Pen had almost convinced herself that working from home was the best-case scenario.

Until she went mad from being housebound. Then she'd have to…she didn't know what.

At least she'd landed a new account on Monday. Bridget Baxter, a chirpy, adorable blonde had requested

Pen meet her for coffee. Bridget had been referred by Serena, and had a little PR problem of her own. Pen learned that Bridget, who co-managed the Dallas Cowboys, had had a one-night stand with one of the players. She was worried he'd ruin her reputation with the team, and she didn't want to lose her high-up position. Bridget explained she'd worked hard to prove she was qualified.

Pen could *so* relate to having her reputation ruined by a man. She could also understand how Bridget had blindly followed her heart and had wound up at a destination she hadn't foreseen. Pen didn't hesitate accepting the job.

A job that smacked of her recently annihilated relationship, but also gave her something better to focus on than attempting to heal her heart, which had a million tiny lacerations.

Or maybe she was being dramatic.

The reminder for Bridget's appointment popped up on the laptop screen. Pen needed to leave soon if she expected to arrive at the stadium on time.

She'd given a lot of thought to Bridget's situation. How to best utilize the media, if at all. The more she turned it over, the angrier she became. Why was it up to Bridget to save her job? The guy she slept with certainly wasn't in danger of being ousted from the team because he slept with an executive.

It was all so unfair.

Life was unfair.

The team was practicing today, which was why Bridget wanted to meet there. That was where her former beau would be, and she wanted to pull him in on the conversation if needed.

After winding around a bunch of corridors and walking into the wrong office, Pen stopped a coach-looking guy wearing a cap and holding a clipboard, and asked for her client.

"Bridget Baxter?" he repeated, regarding Pen like she'd sprouted a horn.

"We have an appointment."

"She's practicing on the field." He shook his head. "You can follow me if you want."

She followed, her head held high. If Bridget was getting this much disrespect from the coach, Pen could imagine the uphill climb she'd have if everyone found out Bridget had slept with a guy on the team.

Determination propelled her steps out into the sticky weather where teammates and cheerleaders dotted the field.

This kind of unfairness wouldn't stand. Pen would make sure Bridget saw justice. She scanned the crowd for the tiny blonde. Ho boy. There were a *sea* of blondes in cheerleader uniforms and not a single pencil skirt in the mix.

Then one of the blondes separated from the crowd and shot Pen a wide grin.

Bridget.

Wearing a cheerleader uniform.

What?

"She's here!" Bridget shouted. In a blur of blue and silver, the cheerleaders formed a line on the field. The guys didn't stop practice, but a few of them looked at her and smiled.

Bridget bopped over to stand in front of Pen. "Sorry for the subversion. It was his plan. But I did have fun playing a corporate mogul." With a wink and a buoyant giggle, Bridget ran back to her girls.

"Whose plan?" Pen asked, confused.

"Give me a *Z*!" Bridget called out, and the cheerleaders echoed with, "*Z*!" What followed was an *A*, a *C*, and an *H*.

With each letter, Pen felt her knees weaken.

"What's that spell?" Bridget called. In answer, the cheerleaders parted, pom-poms swishing, and a tall, blond man wearing a tuxedo emerged.

Zach's hair had been recently trimmed, and his sexy dimple was in full force. Talk about input overload. The sun, the cheering, the crash of football players in the background, and in the center of it all, the very man she'd been trying to put in her rearview mirror.

"Penelope Brand," he said, looking confident and cool, and…different from before. There was sureness in each step he took toward her. Certainty in the way he dismissed the cheerleaders with a "Thanks, ladies."

"What are you doing?" Her voice was cautious for a very good reason. If he'd gone through this trouble, it was because he was making a gesture of some sort. One that didn't involve sending the UPS truck to her building every single day.

And if he asked her again to share his life with him, she didn't trust herself to tell him no. If nothing had changed in his heart, then she couldn't allow anything to change in hers.

He lifted her hand, the hand where her engagement ring used to sit. She'd left it on Zach's dresser the day she went with the movers to the house. She couldn't bear to look at it on her hand when she knew the truth behind it.

That the love she felt for Zach had ultimately not been returned.

It'd all been a ruse.

"A long time ago," he said, "I made a rule to never get hurt again."

Oh, my God, he was doing this...right here. Right now.

"Zach, please."

"You asked about Lonna. Do you want to hear the rest or not?"

She swallowed around a lump forming in her throat, curiosity and hope—so much hope it made her head spin—at a peak.

She nodded. He dipped his chin and continued.

"After I proposed to Lonna and she told me in no uncertain terms that she couldn't take me seriously, I swore I'd never fall in love again. Avoiding love was the only pathway to happiness. The only path to a fulfilled life. Or so I thought. Then I met you."

She couldn't look away from his earnest green eyes—from the sincerity in them.

"I love our daughter, Penelope, but you have to understand something." He gave her fingers a gentle squeeze. "I love her because of how much I love you."

Pen froze, eyes wide, mouth slightly ajar. Did she hear him right? She shook her head, refusing to hope. Refusing to believe.

"You're...you're... That's not true," she finished on a whisper.

"I'm not attached physically to our baby girl the way you are, Pen," he stated. "The *only* way I could feel this much love and devotion for her is because I felt it for you first. I've been in denial about this for a long time.

Since the moment I proposed at my brother's birthday party."

She blinked.

"Even then, I knew." He tugged her close, locking an arm around her lower back. Between them, her swollen belly pressed against his torso.

"I love you, Penelope Brand. I'm sorry I bullied you into everything. Staying when you didn't want to stay. Moving in with me when you didn't want to give up your place. Proposing without confessing how I felt about you. It was a childish way to get what I wanted— you—without putting my heart on the line. I take it all back. I don't want you to marry me."

He didn't? She blinked, confused. That wasn't where she saw this speech headed.

"Unless," he added with a cocky smile, "you love me, too." He lifted one thick eyebrow and when she didn't respond right away, some of that certainty bled from his expression.

He wasn't sure how she felt.

Because she'd never told him.

She'd been as guilty as he was about not sharing. She'd never given him the chance to know how she felt about him. So she'd tell him now.

"I love you so much I can't imagine my life without you." She curled her hand around one of his. "And believe me, I've been trying."

His grin was cunning, wicked with intent and promises to come. "In that case…"

He rested his teeth on his bottom lip and let out a sharp whistle. Behind him, in a flurry of movement, the cheerleaders reformed a line and held up giant white cards with letters that spelled *Marry Me?*

Zach made a circling motion with his finger and a cute redheaded cheerleader at the end flipped her card—a question mark—so that it was an exclamation point instead.

Zach faced Pen, who dropped her purse on the ground at her feet, wrapped her arms around his neck and pushed to her toes.

He sealed her mouth with his.

Behind them, cheers and whistles, and low male hollers of approval, lifted on the air as Pen allowed herself to sink into Zach's embrace.

Into the promise of his words, especially the three that meant more than anything.

He loved her.

As much as she loved him.

Epilogue

"Penelope told me she hated me," Zach announced. "Over and over."

His father, sister and brother regarded him in shocked concern. His mother, on the other hand, stood from her seat in the waiting room and let out a loud chuckle.

"Women who give birth always say that. Remember, Rider?"

"Three times," his father confirmed, standing next to his wife. "Three times I went through the birthing process at her side and she hated me every time." He pointed at Chase. "Mostly with you, though. Since you were first."

Chase and Stefanie stood from their chairs, Stef ribbing him about how it was no surprise he was the cause of the most strife of the three of them.

Zach's smile emerged—so big, it hurt his face. It'd been a relatively fast labor, but a long night. "Ready to meet her?"

Stef and his mom shrieked happy sounds, and his father and brother didn't hold back their widest grins. Zach shook his head at their attire. "I hate that she is meeting you all dressed like this, though."

"Ugly sweaters are tradition!" Stef argued, her glowing-nose-reindeer sweater one for the books.

He led his family into the room, and a collective gasp lifted on the air when they spotted the pink-wrapped bundle resting on Penelope's chest.

Pen's eyes were drooped, her hair tangled. Her own ugly sweater tossed aside on a chair with the rest of her clothing in favor of the hospital gown she now wore. She was the most beautiful sight Zach had ever seen.

Well. Second to his daughter.

"What's her name?" Elle cooed as she scooped her granddaughter into her arms. "Can you finally tell us?"

"Olivia Edna," Penelope announced with a smile. "After my grandmother, and Zach's."

His father and siblings bent over Olivia in his mother's arms. Even when handed off, Zach's daughter slept soundly.

"Your mom and dad are on their way from the airport," Zach told Pen, swiping her hair from her forehead.

Her eyes drooped sleepily, but her smile was everlasting.

He bent and placed a kiss to her forehead. "You did it."

Her pale blue eyes opened and stabbed him in the heart. How had he ever denied loving her when she was his everything?

"*We* did it," she corrected, giving him credit he hadn't earned.

A gurgle came from Olivia and she fussed in Chase's arms. Those years of holding and kissing babies must have paid off, because the mayor of Dallas bounced and shushed her and a moment later, she cooed.

Chase shot his brother a cocky smile.

"I love you," Pen whispered to Zach, reaching for his arm with her hand—a hand that boasted both a wedding band and an engagement ring. They hadn't waited. They hadn't wanted to.

Zach kissed her lips, lingering a moment. "I love you."

She played with the longer hair at his nape, in need of a trim, and whispered two words that made Zach more grateful than he'd ever been in his life.

"Merry Christmas."

Olivia was the perfect gift. Better than every wrapped present they'd left piled in his parents' living room to rush Penelope to the hospital. Better than the moment Zach spotted Penelope in the jazz club and wondered if she'd let him sample her mouth.

Better, he mused, than the moment she vowed to be with him and he with her, until death do they part.

"Uh-oh, she's had it with us," Stef announced, placing Zach's daughter in his arms.

He adjusted her so that she sank comfortably in the crook of his elbow. Looking down at the faint sweep of blond hair, puckered rosebud lips and tiny fisted hands, Zach's heart filled to capacity—who knew there was more room in there?

"Hey, Livvie," he said, his voice choked with emotion. "Merry Christmas to you, too."

* * * * *

SPECIAL EXCERPT FROM

⟨H⟩ HARLEQUIN

DESIRE

*To oust his twin brother from the family company,
CEO Samuel Kane sets him up to break the company's
cardinal rule—no workplace relationships. But it's Samuel
who finds himself tempted when Arlie Banks reawakens
a passion that could cost him everything...*

Read on for a sneak peek at
Corner Office Confessions
by USA TODAY *bestselling author Cynthia St. Aubin.*

A sharp rap on her door startled Arlie out of her misery.

"Just a minute!" she called, twisting off the shower.

Opening the shower door, she slid into one of the complimentary plush robes, then gathered the long skein of her hair and squeezed the water out of it with a towel before draping it over her shoulder.

Good enough for food delivery. She exited the bathroom in a cloud of steam and pulled open the propped door.

Samuel Kane's face appeared in the gap.

Only he didn't look like Samuel Kane.

He looked like wrath in a Brooks Brothers suit. Jaw set, the muscles flexed, mouth a thin, grim line. Eyes blazing emerald against chiseled cheekbones.

"Oh," she said dumbly. "Hi."

A sinking feeling of self-consciousness further heated her already shower-warmed skin as he stared at her.

"Do you want to come in?" she added when he made no reply. She stepped aside to grant him entry, catching the subtle scent of him as he moved past her into the hallway.

"Why didn't you tell me?" he asked.

Arlie's heart sank into her guts. There were too many answers to this question. And too many questions he didn't even know to ask.

"Tell you what?" she asked, opting for the safest path.

Coward.

Samuel stepped closer, her glowing white robe reflected in icy arcs in his glacier-green eyes. "About my father. About what he said to you this morning."

The wave of relief was so complete and acute it actually weakened her knees.

"Our families have a lot of shared history," Arlie said. "Not all of it good."

"He had no right—"

"I'm sorry," she interrupted, knowing it was a weak and deliberate dodge. She didn't want to talk about this. Not with him. "It's absolutely mandatory that you surrender your tie and suit jacket for this conversation. I'm entirely underdressed and frankly feeling a little vulnerable about it."

Walking into the well-appointed sitting area, Samuel shrugged out of his suit jacket and laid it across the chaise longue. As he turned, they snagged gazes. He gripped the knot of his tie, loosening it with small deliberate strokes that inexplicably kindled heat between Arlie's thighs.

"Better?" he asked.

On a different night, in a different universe, it would have ended there.

But for reasons she could neither explain nor ignore, Arlie padded barefoot across the space between them.

"Almost." Lifting her hands to his neck, she undid the button closest to his collar. Then another. And another.

To her great surprise and delight, Samuel wore no T-shirt beneath.

Dizzy with desire, Arlie tilted her face up to his. The air was alive with electricity, crackling and sizzling with anticipation. The breathless inevitability of this thing between them made her feel loose-limbed and drunk.

"All my life, I could have anything I wanted." Cupping her jaw, he ran the pad of his thumb over her lower lip. "Except you."

Arlie's breath came in irregular bursts, something deep inside her tightening at his admission. "You want me?"

Samuel only looked at her, silent but saying all.

His wordlessness the purest part of what he had always given her.

The look that passed between them was both question and answer.

Yes?

Yes.

Don't miss what happens next in…
Corner Office Confessions
by USA TODAY *bestselling author Cynthia St. Aubin.*

Available May 2022 wherever
Harlequin Desire books and ebooks are sold.

Harlequin.com

IF YOU ENJOYED THIS BOOK
WE THINK YOU WILL ALSO LOVE

HARLEQUIN

PRESENTS

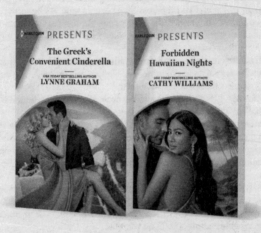

Escape to exotic locations where passion knows no bounds.

Welcome to the glamorous lives of royals and billionaires, where passion knows no bounds. Be swept into a world of luxury, wealth and exotic locations.

8 NEW BOOKS AVAILABLE EVERY MONTH!

"I don't understand this…sitting around in pretty rooms and *talking*," Delaney seethed at him, her blue eyes shooting sparks when they met his. "I like to be outside. I like dirt under my feet. I like a day that ends with me having to scrub soil out from beneath my fingernails."

She glared at the walls as if they had betrayed her.

Then at him, as if he was doing so even now.

For a moment he almost felt as if he had—but that was ridiculous.

"When you are recognized as the true crown princess of Ile d'Montagne, the whole island will be your garden," he told her. Trying to soothe her. He wanted to lift a hand to his own chest and massage the brand that wasn't there, but *soothing* was for others, not him. He ignored the too-hot sensation. "You can work in the dirt of your ancestors to your heart's content."

Delaney shot a look at him, pure blue fire. "Even if I did agree to do such a crazy thing, you still wouldn't get what you want. It doesn't matter what blood is in my veins. I am a farm girl, born and bred. I will never look the part of the princess you imagine. Never."

She sounded almost as final as he had, but Cayetano allowed himself a smile, because that wasn't a flat refusal. It sounded more like a *maybe* to him.

He could work with *maybe*.

In point of fact, he couldn't wait.

He rose then. And he made his way toward her, watching the way her eyes widened. The way her lips parted. There was an unmistakable flush on her cheeks as he drew near, and he could see her pulse beat at her neck.

Cayetano was the warlord of these mountains and would soon enough be the king of this island. And he had been prepared to ignore the fire in him, the fever. The ways he wanted her that had intruded into his work, his sleep. But here and now, he granted himself permission to want this woman. *His* woman. Because he could see that she wanted him.

With that and her *maybe*, he knew he'd already won.

"Let me worry about how you look," he said as he came to a stop before her, enjoying the way she had to look up to hold his gaze. It made her seem softer. He could see the hectic need all over her, matching his own. "There is something far more interesting for you to concentrate on."

Delaney made a noise of frustration. "The barbaric nature of ancient laws and customs?"

"Or this."

And then Cayetano followed the urge that had been with him since he'd seen her standing in a dirt-filled yard with a battered kerchief on her head and kissed her.

He expected her to be sweet. He expected to enjoy himself.

He expected to want her all the more, to tempt his own feverish need with a little taste of her.

But he was totally unprepared for the punch of it. Of a simple kiss—a kiss to show her there was more here than righting old wrongs and reclaiming lost thrones. A kiss to share a little bit of the fire that had been burning in him since he'd first laid eyes on her.

It was a blaze and it took him over.

It was a dark, drugging heat.

It was a mad blaze of passion.

It was a delirium—and he wanted more.

Don't miss
Crowning His Lost Princess,
available April 2022 wherever
Harlequin Presents books and ebooks are sold.

Harlequin.com

HPEXP0322